Rachel Dawson

Rachel Dawson is a lesbian, working-class Welsh writer. In 2020, she was awarded a bursary by Literature Wales, which enabled her to write her debut novel, *Neon Roses*. She was born in Swansea and has done a variety of jobs, including selling sausage rolls and vibrators (not at the same time), and volunteering for an MP. She now works in the third sector and lives with her wife in Cardiff.

NEON ROSES

RACHEL DAWSON

JOHN MURRAY

First published in Great Britain in 2023 by John Murray (Publishers)

This paperback edition published in 2024

4

A CIP catalogue record for this title is available from the British Library

Paperback ISBN 9781399801935
ebook ISBN 9781399801942

Typeset in Sabon MT by Hewer Text UK Ltd
Printed and bound in Great Britain by Clays Ltd, Elcograf S.p.A.

John Murray policy is to use papers that are natural, renewable and
recyclable products and made from wood grown in sustainable forests.
The logging and manufacturing processes are expected to conform
to the environmental regulations of the country of origin.

Carmelite House
50 Victoria Embankment
London EC4Y 0DZ

www.johnmurraypress.co.uk

John Murray Press, part of Hodder & Stoughton Limited
An Hachette UK company

I Doreen, hoffwn pe byddem wedi cael
mwy o amser i siarad am y pethau hyn

1

15 October 1984

Drive is off before Eluned can stuff her skinny paper ticket in her coat pocket. Luckily, she knows what's coming. She grips the side of his cab, bending her knees while the floor bucks underneath her. The terraces lining the street face off like a pair of cowboys with pistols drawn, so it takes some forceful steering from Drive to turn the bus in the space between them. The white pebbledash of the end terrace fills the bus window, like they're driving through a blizzard. Bit close today. The bus pitches forward as he guides them back down to the main road, brakes squealing as he controls their descent. Eluned grapples her way up the aisle using the rails on the back of each seat, Mabli following behind.

Mabs always prefers to sit at the back of the bus. These days there is never much competition for the seats. There are still a few girls off to work at the Tick Tock. But you used to see the Mamgus on their way into town, with their smart framed handbags and Portcullis patterned coats. Eluned hasn't seen the jeweller's shopgirl, Michelle the Gems, in ages. If Eluned is early for the bus home, she lingers outside the jeweller's window to admire the tricolour twisted hoops, the way Michelle must have angled the spotlight to perfectly set the diamonds aflame. Eluned knows she's kidding herself when she thinks that perhaps the other bus, the one east along the bottom of the Beacons and down the Neath valley, is busier. Everyone is skint, from Cynheidre to Blaenavon.

Eluned hangs on the grab rail to let Mabli scootch up next to the window. Mabli shifts along the seat, one leg neatly folded over the other, to give Eluned room to spread out. Eluned can't help the way her fat knees go. Mabli teases that they're like cousin Tirion's eyes, always trying to escape each other. The bus heads north at first, kissing the feet of the Beacons before racing the River Tawe down the valley. The Tawe gets rowdier as it gathers the Llech, the Geidd, the Haffes and the Twrch like a group of lads on the piss, roping in other stop-outs as they stumble from pub to pub. The bus leaves the Tawe, where the river puts its arm round the shoulder of the Clydach, before making its final stagger down to Swansea Bay.

This time of year, Eluned's favourite part of the journey is catching the sun creeping over the top of Varteg Hill and washing the exposed sandstone of Mynydd Allt-y-Grug in rose gold. Grug was Mamgu's middle name – heather. The sun must be a Welsh speaker because it's like she's purposefully lit the heather so that its delicate flowers glow in every shade from apricot to cerise. Even the grasses in the gaps between the heather look as if they've been individually tipped in gold, like tiny metal spears.

Dad used to call Mynydd Allt-y-Grug the moving mountain. When Eluned and Mabli were little he took them walking to see where the old road was buried, and to peep through the trees at rubble that was once a home. After that, Mabli used to hold her breath as they drove past, as if that would be enough to hold back a landslide.

Eluned takes the Binatone Mini and its headphones out of her handbag and flicks open the back with her thumbnail before rubbing the batteries from side to side. They're a precious commodity these days, and these cold mornings drain them faster.

The Binatone headphones have a metal headband and two round plastic speakers that lie flush against your ears. They haven't had enough money to buy the type you can separate and poke in your ears directly, so Mabli holds the headphones up between them, putting her ear against the outside of one speaker, while Eluned does the same on the other. Not ideal, but it does the job. Eluned would be lying if she said that the thought of other people overhearing their music didn't give her a bit of a thrill.

Mabli's recorded last night's Peter Powell's 'Five 45's at 5.45' onto a cassette, so that they can review the new releases together. Powell's picks are rarely avant-garde; Mabli says she heard that the record labels pay for the artists to be featured. But it's a much better feature than 'Select-A-Disc', where they are subjected to airheads crying about their boyfriends, requesting songs that have already had the arse kicked out of them. Eluned's had a grudge against that feature since she sent in a postcard for Mabli's sixteenth birthday and it never got played. Eluned had requested 'The Model' by Kraftwerk, the very week before it soared to number two.

Before March, they used to listen to 'Five 45's' as a family. Mam would be finishing tea, while Mabli and Eluned buttered bread and defrosted peas, and Dad laid the table. Now, the strike has disrupted all their routines. Dad won't budge from *Wales at Six*, there's rarely extra bread with their evening meal, and they're lucky if Mabli turns up at all.

Mabli is adept at cutting off the end of the 5.30 *Newsbeat* bulletin when she records off the radio. It's a good job too, as the news starts arguments these days. They've only got one blank tape left, so Mabli keeps rewinding back and recording over it. Eluned startles when the tape starts with a clash of different jingles. Her ears are sharp; in just a few seconds she picks out the different snippets. There's the knock-off Prince bassline, the electric guitar from Janice Long's rock show, and the toe-curling singing from the beginning of 'Best Sound in Britain'. Finally, Mabli's latest recording starts midway through Powell's exuberant, synth-heavy intro.

Powell's first pick is 'Freedom' by Wham! Mabli identifies it from the first blast of trumpet, digging her nails into Eluned's knee with a hissed, '*George!*'

It's tremendous, obviously. It will be their third number one this year. But it's hardly new; Wham! did the song on *Wogan* last weekend. The family had gathered around to watch, Mam inducing hilarity with her insistence that before Eluned came along, Dad had hair like Andrew Ridgeley.

The second song is Chaka Khan, 'I Feel For You'. Eluned always enjoyed this track on Prince's album, despite Dad trying to sing along in his ropey falsetto. This is faster, more frenetic. Lloyd told her that it's Stevie Wonder on the harmonica, but surely Stevie has got better things to do. The rapper is supposed to be big in the States, but the only word she can make out on this record is 'Chaka'. She'll have to give it another listen on the hi-fi at home. These tinny headphones, and the way they have to hold them, can't be doing it justice. Mabli likes it, shimmying her shoulders enough that they jostle Eluned, but subtly enough that no one else would notice. Most of the time, Mabli gives the impression that she would rather die than be seen enjoying herself in public.

Powell segues into another R&B track, 'In My House'. Eluned hasn't heard this one yet, and she mashes the speaker further into the shell of her ear to make sure that she's hearing as much as she can. The steady drumbeat is undeniable. Mabli taps her pointed work shoe, bought with Eluned's staff discount, against Eluned's shin. Eluned stares out of the window. Drive has done all the village pick-ups and now they're sailing down the A4067, eating up the scenery as the song struts to its final chorus.

'Calamity Crush', the penultimate track, is a bit of a change. This is new to her as well. It wasn't long ago that Eluned would have heard songs before Peter Powell, London-or-no-London. But since she's been helping Mam with the food parcels she hasn't had the time to listen to as much radio, and she hasn't had enough money for her magazines either.

Mabli pulls her ear away from the headphones. 'I've had enough of this. I can't afford a headache. It sounds like someone has leant on all the buttons at once.'

Can't afford a headache. Does that mean she might show her face at the picket line? Finally. Eluned has pestered her about it since March.

'Are you coming later then?' Eluned asks. 'Mair says I can go after lunch and have half pay for it. She reckons she'd come herself if she didn't have the shop.'

Mabli snorts. 'It sounds like the shop's been dead lately. It's a nice way for Mair to save a bit of money and look like a martyr.'

'Easy to be a cynic. So are you coming then?'

Mabli pushes the loose end of her watch strap until it forms the shape of a hot air balloon. She stares down at it, then pulls it taut again. 'No. I'm sorry,' she says. 'They can't spare me. I'm taking minutes for the senior partner.'

'Come on,' Eluned cajoles. 'Dad would love it if you came. I know you might not remember; but you got so into it in '72.'

Mabli turns her head to stare out the window.

Eluned persists. 'We made Dad potassium permanganate soaks in the washing-up bowl. You used to love swooshing the water around his feet while the crystals dissolved. They stained his skin a horrific plum colour, like he'd been beaten up. You loved the power cuts, you used to make us pretend that we were at the beginning of *The Railway Children*, eating bread and marmalade by candlelight and listening out for mice.'

Mabli finally smiles. 'I do remember missing Dad when he went up to Birmingham, and then he brought us back those white teddies. I loved mine. But that guy, Freddie Matthews, died not long after. The Union men love pretending that they're at the Battle of the Alamo, and now every time they walk out it has to be even more of a spectacle.'

'How do you remember the name of a man who died when you were six?'

Eluned knows the answer before she asks the question.

'Graham and I were talking about it the other night,' Mabli says. 'It was after he died that people started taking it out on the police.'

Ah, yes. Just one more conversational topic that she repeats verbatim from her pig boyfriend. Eluned asks, 'How old was he then? Knocking thirty?'

Mabli rolls her eyes. 'Graham has only just turned thirty. He was the same age that I am, just about to start police college.'

There's no point trying to persuade Mabli that Graham is too old for her. They first met on one of Eluned's minibus trips down to Talk of the Abbey, a nightclub in Neath. Mabli had been nagging for months to go with her older sister, and Eluned had finally interceded on Mabli's behalf. God, she shouldn't have bothered. Graham had been lurking in the shadows, apparently investigating local complaints about their monthly gay night. Eluned wasn't interested in his anecdotes about alleyway handjobs. Everyone needs somewhere to cop off. She'd left Mabli to it and joined her own boyfriend, Lloyd, on the dance floor with a pint of watered-down cider. Eluned danced with one eye over Lloyd's shoulder, watching Mabli apparently rapt as Graham gesticulated at her.

It wasn't long after Talk of the Abbey that Graham started picking up Mabli from the house in his Vauxhall Astra. Dad had asked Mabli and Eluned to excuse themselves upstairs for a moment and, according to Mam, gently reminded Graham of Mabli's age. For the few weeks after that, everywhere Dad went he was trailed by police cars. Eluned had called him paranoid, then he drove her to work on a morning when she'd missed her bus. As soon as they reached the Gurnos, one of those jam-butty police cars popped up in the rear-view. It never put its lights on but was up their arse all the way to Ponty. Dad tried changing lanes, speeding up, but it remained doggedly behind them. After that, they agreed to leave Mabli to it.

'Look. Earlier, Mam suggested, and I think it's a good idea, too, that it would be tremendous if you could do a question-and-answer session at the Welfare. We've been there a lot recently, and people have been asking about what they're entitled to, what they can claim, that sort of thing.'

'I'm not going to help people fiddle the system.'

Already, that stuck-up tone. Eluned clicks in the rewind button and holds it down while the tape whirs back to the beginning, the plastic casing vibrating slightly in her hand. No wonder Mam won't have this conversation with her.

'There's no fiddling. It's making sure that people are applying for everything they have the right to receive. Some people don't have any money coming in.'

'It's sad that people are skint. But I don't want you telling people that I'm a legal expert when I'm just a secretary. All I do is . . .' Mabli mimes typing, eyes frozen in the middle distance as she flicks her imaginary carriage and keeps going.

'Come off it, Mabli. You could impress them! You'd be showing that you've got initiative, you're a real go-getter.'

'Or, more likely, get told off for being a troublemaker.'

'Mam will get you the paperwork from the dole office and you can break it down. People would listen to you. You've always been so good at explaining things.'

French declensions, factorising algebraic equations, that speech from *Macbeth*. Mabli always lapped Eluned at school.

'I haven't even got my feet under the table yet, and you should hear what the partners say about Scargill. It starts with, "What sort of leader calls a strike at the end of winter?"

but it doesn't end as polite. With Graham in the police as well . . . it looks bad. I won't do myself any favours by making a holy show of myself.'

Eluned says, 'This is urgent. Thatcher is cutting benefits because she says that the NUM is handing out fifteen quid a week to members, but you know they've not been able to hand out that kind of money for months.'

'I don't know if you've noticed while you've been out playing with cans of soup, but children are dying in Ethiopia. Those IRA nutters are on the up. The Fed are punching themselves and asking the government, "Why are you hurting me?" There's more going on than this pissing contest between Comrade Scargill and whoever his enemies are this week.'

'It's nothing like that,' Eluned snaps. 'You know Dad hates taking money off us, but imagine how bad it would be if we weren't bringing something in.'

Mabli mutters, 'For a man who hates doing it, he certainly does it a lot.'

Silence festers. Eluned looks out at the double-fronted stone houses that she always admires on this stretch of road. There's a Coal Not Dole poster in almost every window. There are more people supporting the strike than not in this part of the world. Eluned winds the headphone lead round their Binatone.

Mabli usually gets off at the stop by the Dillwyn Arms, but today she starts gathering her stuff as soon as Brecon Road turns into High Street.

Eluned holds out their Binatone. It's Mabli's turn to have it.

Mabli's eyes flicker dismissively between the cassette player and Eluned's face. 'No thanks, I'll get a lift off Graham.'

'Well, I'll be on the minibus with Mam.'

'Take it anyway,' says Mabli. 'If the shop is quiet, you can listen in the stockroom. There's Janice Long's show on the end of the tape.'

Eluned gives a tight nod. 'Diolch. Have a good one.'

Eluned crushes herself back into the bus seat as Mabli slithers across and into the aisle. Mabli smooths the front of her skirt, and pushes her bag strap up her shoulder.

'I hope today goes well,' she says.

Eluned's christening shoes were from Blossoms; butter-soft white Mary Janes. When she was fifteen, she opened her first payslip there too. In all that time, Mair Bevan hasn't changed a bit. Mair's dark brown hair is lacquered until it's as smooth and stiff as a snail's shell. Emerald earrings swing from her earlobes; the holes have been pulled so long you could push a 2p through them. When Eluned gets close enough to kiss her cheek, stale alcohol lingers underneath L'Air du Temps.

Mair keeps a tub of Atrixo underneath the counter and slathers her hands in the unctuous lotion at least three times a day, buffing it into the raised veins and papery creases. Mair is convinced that the key to shifting stock is in her elegant hands; she must have spent hours teaching Eluned to hold a shoe with her hands positioned like an oyster shell.

Eluned barely opens the till, only ringing up a tin of boot polish and a pair of socks with loose-fit cuffs. Some women loiter for a chat, littering the shop with their worries like those balls of tissue paper that sneak out of their shoeboxes and get everywhere. They each poke a couple of coppers in the slot on the old Smash tin on the counter, liberally covered with yellow National Union of Mineworkers stickers. Mair and Eluned have been collecting for the last few months, although donations have dwindled since the summer. Eluned untwists a paperclip and digs for dirt under her nails until the skin turns a lurid pink. When that stings too much, she bashes the handle of the card-imprinting machine back and forth. Finally, she signs a couple of credit card receipts with her own large, looping signature, pretending it's an autograph.

Mair pulls back the lace curtain that separates the shop from the window display. She drags her finger along the shelf in the window and flicks a grey slug of dust onto the floor. 'Bach, can you dust these shelves for me before you go?'

Before the strike, Eluned had been so excited to build their window display. Mair had ordered in some new shoes from an Italian supplier. When they arrived, a pair of high heels immediately caught Eluned's eye. Vibrant teal suede, with metallic violet lightning bolts stretching down the sides. Shoes for dancing, for pleasure. They even smelt tremendous; Eluned often found herself in the stockroom, taking a huff of their velvety, earthy scent. When Mair wrote '£20' on the cardboard tags with her Sheaffer fountain pen, Eluned immediately calculated how many hours she would need to work to buy them.

Mair had wagered with Eluned that if she shifted four pairs of them by the end of the spring then she could have the last pair for herself. It was a bad bet. No one around here can afford them now. Mam never spent £20 on her own wedding shoes.

Eluned finds her dusting rag and wipes over the window display. One side of her dream shoes are faded to a drab blue. The only woman who's asked to try them on was a scab's wife. Eluned had taken the initiative to tell her that nothing at Blossoms would be available to purchase until her husband was back on the pickets. The shameless cow had stuffed her dirty money back in her handbag and walked rigidly out of the shop. As soon as this sabre-rattling is over, women will start coming back to shop. She'll soon get those shoes flying off the shelves, then she can get her own. When it's blown over, the boys will organise minibuses to Swansea again, and she'll wear her shoes on the dance floor of Barons nightclub. She's been repeating the same thing for the last seven months.

2

The minibus picks Eluned up at the war memorial at two. She's not the only one being picked up from Ponty. Eluned hasn't been to the pickets in weeks, but today she helps Rhiannon heft Dan in his pushchair onto the minibus and clambers up after her. Mam's already on the bus, sitting up front with her new committee friends. Rhiannon was always a decent girl, and they were in form together, but regarded each other with the wariness of two hefty girls each not wanting to be confused for the other. Rhiannon used to wear her hair in two long copper plaits. Now it's been cut into short, fine layers, and as her hair is buffeted by the wind it gives the impression of an untempered bonfire.

The minibus is already steamy with their body heat. Rhiannon slides in by the window and wipes a hole in the condensation with the bobble of Dan's discarded hat. It's a Mickey Mouse bus, seats so narrow that Eluned can still only fit half a bum-cheek on. Eluned holds the seatbelt round her body as far as it will go and braces her foot flat on the floor behind Dan's pushchair, ready to catch it if it starts rolling. Dan doesn't seem to mind; he just laughs as the bus judders and rocks its way over the uneven roads.

Rhiannon's burnished hair smells of lavender, so soothing that Eluned can forget that they're heading into a battle of sorts. Eluned looks out of Rhiannon's porthole as the minibus climbs. The space below them has filled with that peculiar Valleys phenomenon, dragon's breath. Thick grey wisps sneak up behind the bus, curling into the space between the steep sides of the hills.

From here, it's harder to guess which are organic slopes and which are just spoil, left over from centuries of industry. The minibus doesn't rise out of the fog until well past Seven Sisters. It still tickles Eluned to think of the Roman soldiers trekking up this same road to their vantage point just above the village where, in summer, the sun exposes a perfect fort-shaped square in the dry grass. She can't fault them. The towns further down the valley seem stifling compared to the weather-beaten moors and big skies. Maybe, before we fucked with it, the Romans found it beautiful. Some of the spoil tips have already been smoothed over, planted with tufty young conifers. Soon, like the crumbling ironworks and railway bridges leading nowhere, they will be forgotten. Eluned can barely remember the row of corrugated metal houses that were torn down when Mabli was still a baby. If Thatcher has her way, more of this landscape will disappear, leaving only relics.

The minibus pulls off just before the village, down the long gravel track to the colliery. The women park up at the main gate, where the pickets have been gathered for hours. On a good day Eluned could sketch a picture of the colliery, pieced together from geography lessons, Dad and Lloyd, and the dreary paintings hung up in the pub. There's the gigantic winding wheel, its silhouette as familiar as the long strips of terraced houses. Hoist. Chute. For all her familiarity with its mechanics, being this close has something of the strangeness of parents' evening, seeing Dad squashed on to the same plywood chairs she spent all day on.

Mam bustles off with the other ladies from the Committee. It's sweet that she's so involved these days. Dad is loafing at the back in his waxed flat cap with the other old codgers. Lloyd is easy to spot, at least a head taller than the rest of the pickets even though he slouches over his wooden placard, twisting it in the gravel. From this distance, it's easier to look at him as though he's a stranger. After a full summer on the pickets, he's caught colour in his face for the first time since he was a teenager. His T-shirt is no longer pulled taut between his broad shoulders. The sleeves don't cut into his upper arms in the way they used to. He could play a hunky boy next door in *Coronation Street*. He looks shrunken and unfamiliar.

Rhiannon's hubby is near Lloyd, so they push Dan over the gravel, swerving round the puddles gathered in the pits of the long drive. Eluned lays a quick kiss on Lloyd's cheek. The tip of his nose is a nub of ice. Lloyd stuffs his hand in her pocket and burrows his fingers deep enough that he roughly kneads at her mons, hard enough her knees buckle. Just because he can find it, he thinks he's so funny.

'Cut it out boyo,' Eluned says. She grips his placard, trying to wrestle it off him. Lloyd is stronger, but she doesn't let go, using her weight to force the wooden stake down to stab at his feet. Lloyd laughs, bumping his shoulder into hers before giving up and letting her do her worst. The lads are all in steel-capped work boots anyway. He feigns injury, then slips his hand in the back pocket of her jeans.

'Mabli didn't fancy this then?' Lloyd asks.

Eluned can't help sighing heavily. 'Nah. She had to go to some meeting.' It's not worth summarising the conversation. He's had the same shit off Mabli himself, and it will only demoralise him further. 'She wasn't interested in the legal advice session either.'

'She must be doing alright on that course then, no photocopying any more.'

Mabli still seems to spend a fair amount of time photocopying, but it's gratifying that Lloyd is proud too. Mabli might be going the long way round, learning on the job rather than in a university, but she's still on the path. Lloyd has seen Mabli go from a little girl making pictures on her Lite-Brite to a serious, aspiring solicitor.

'She needs to get her head out of her arse though,' says Eluned.

Lloyd shrugs. 'There's more than enough here, your mam played a blinder getting everyone on the minibus, and we don't want her passing anything back to that twat she's knocking around with.'

Dad might call Lloyd the Jolly Twp Giant but he can be insightful.

Rhys says, 'Can't trust a copper. My mate said that he's been hearing clicks on the phone line.'

Lloyd hums. 'Dad said there was a bloke with shiny shoes asking about my cousin Mike the other day. Dad said he hadn't spoken to Mike in years, but he was round for Sunday dinner last week.'

'Sensible,' Rhys says, twisting up his Mars wrapper and tucking it in his jacket pocket. 'Don't give them nothing.'

The fog has followed them, and it gives the unremarkable gravel drive the feeling of a Roman arena. Beyond the metal gates there is a phalanx of willowherb; tall, red-tipped spears standing up from the froth of their delicate fuchsia flowers. Two sets of gladiators face off. On one side, the miners in a muddle of green, grey, and brown with Coal Not Dole badges like daisies on their chests. On the other, the police stand in navy blue woollen jackets with their feet spread apart and hands clasped in front of their goolies. They stare through Eluned with glassy eyes. She'd like to ping one of their gold buttons off and into the mud.

This is her first picket as a miner's girlfriend. Most of her school year is here. Eluned is going to be stuck with this cohort for the rest of her life, whether at chapel, the rugby, or the pub. It's not that the men have always dreamt about mining. No one wants a bad back, or blackened lungs, or, God forbid, to get the call that the whole pit has sunk in on itself like a sugar cube dipped in warm water. In 1972 they pulled the country to a standstill, but it was only a brief reprieve. In some ways Mabli is right, this is a losing battle. Whether it ends with nuclear power or Polish coal, it will end. They're helping the men limp on for the sake of dignity. When she stops to imagine the future – washing machines full of neon orange overalls, Friday pints at the Welfare, a trike on its side on the grass – her stomach feels heavy and solid.

At first, Eluned can barely differentiate between the policemen. But the longer she looks, the more she notices the differences in their faces. One has a constellation of acne scars round his chin, another already has streaks of grey in his moustache. She's sure that one of them was in the year above her at school; she remembers him playing the trumpet at the Eisteddfod.

Eluned bobs from side to side, trying to get the greying officer to follow her with his eyes. He's good. His attention doesn't flicker. Lloyd parks himself in front of a shorter pig and skims his gaze over the top of his helmet. He tries to maintain the same slack-jawed humourless look. The expression is so alien on Lloyd, he's doing well to keep his face straight at all. Eluned squeezes his hand encouragingly. The policeman stretches his neck to give himself an extra inch or two. Lloyd does the same, peering down his nose at him.

For a split second, Eluned thinks they might get a quick smile back, but one of the pickets shouts, 'They're coming!'

The taxis dump the scabs near the picket line, scattering gravel in their haste to turn round and get back down the track. Eluned hefts her placard up in the air, as high as she can, a cardboard rectangle on a long wooden post. The scabs scurry past the picket line, stuffing their hands in their pockets and wrapping their scarves over their faces. Anything to avoid looking at their striking workmates. Good. They should be ashamed.

The picket line is louder than a rugby match, and more vicious. There is a chorus of political slogans and personal lamentations. Hard bodies press into her. The smell of sweat, Old Spice and wet wool is intense. Lloyd's warm breath puffs down the back of her neck. Women smaller than Eluned are shuffled to and fro. Eluned finds Mam in the crowd. She's such a dwt she probably can't even see the scabs, but she's still shouting fiercely.

Lloyd's body swells with air. He releases it in a bellow that shakes the moustache of the policeman opposite him. 'You've got a little girl. Carys! What does Carys think?'

The scab doesn't even look at Lloyd as he flips his collar up, and scurries past.

After the first lot of scabs disappear, the crowd disperses. It doesn't look like much, but the placard gets heavy after a while. Eluned's hands are stiff, slow to uncurl as she settles the sign against her leg. The wind whips up, pushing the fog further down the valley. Lloyd bends behind her shoulders to light a fag and gives her the first half.

The police break formation, too, going back to their cars. They return cradling parcels of tinfoil. The smoky, fatty smell hits Eluned before they're even unwrapped. God, even from the other side of the car park it smells fucking immense. She hasn't had a bacon bap in months. The visions are vivid: yellow butter soaking through the soft white bread, pulling at the stringy rind with her teeth, licking up a tart smear of brown sauce off her wrist. Her stomach gurgles. She breathes through her mouth, trying to suck in the taste through the air. Bacon will be the first thing she buys when this is over. She'll make sandwiches for the whole family, four rashers in each one.

'Ignore them. They do this every day.'

'Cannibals!' Lloyd shouts. He uses his finger to bend his nose up, oinking for good measure. They don't react. Instead, they bite down with visible relish, ostentatiously wiping grease from around their mouths.

Eluned refuses to look at the food. Instead, she stares at the policemen themselves, their smug lips, and unfeeling eyes. She smirks when one of them gets a dribble of red sauce down the middle of his tie.

After they finish their breakfast, the policemen have a quick fag. None of them smoke it all the way down. They get halfway through and flick them off down the car park. Lloyd's eyes trail jealously after the half-smoked cigarettes. He must be longing to scrabble after them, on hands and knees, dignity holding him back. She wouldn't blame him. Tobacco is a precious commodity – she's been smoking twos with her mum, puffing until they're right down to the filter. What she'd give to be grinding that policeman's face into the gravel.

The second group of scabs arrive on foot. These lot are brazen. They saunter slowly past the picketers, lobbing insults with ease.

'Hey, Mark!' the scab caws to the man next to Lloyd.

Mark peers through the gap between the policemen's heads. He's so close that his chest almost touches the gold buttons on their uniforms.

The scab hisses, 'Your wife wishes you'd go back to work so she can get back to shagging Dai the Meat in the afternoons.'

Mark roars, launching himself into the air. A policeman catches Mark round his middle. Mark flails, hands clawed as he tries to scramble up and over them. He falls back, bending his knees and squaring his shoulders to try to push through that way. The police knit closer together, and Mark is shut out.

One of the policemen unsheathes the wooden truncheon at his hip, and Lloyd yanks Mark back by the arm.

Lloyd lays his hand on Mark's shoulder. 'Come on. Don't be a twat.'

Mark hasn't got a chance. They won't hesitate to use those truncheons. And then where will he be? Crawling home with a face full of bruises or lying on a hard cot at the police station.

Mark twists to escape Lloyd's grip. His green cap falls off his head and before Eluned can swipe it up from the ground, he steps on it with his heavy, muddy boots. She picks it up anyway, trying to wipe off the mud as best as she can. He'll be wanting that later.

Lloyd pleads with the policeman. 'He's a good egg. He's never hurt a fly.'

Mark sneers and hawks noisily. He dredges up a wad of spit, but it doesn't fly far. Most of it never gets further than his own chin.

The officer nearest them shakes his head and makes his way back to the van. Eluned sees him reach for the radio on the dashboard. For fuck's sake, the last thing they need is more of these fuckers. Or, even worse, fuckers on horseback.

'Ignore him, Mark,' Lloyd placates. 'He's always been a nasty prick. Chill out man, or they'll get the horses in.'

What can she say to help him calm down? He's got to calm down. He can't carry on like this. You can't give the coppers any excuse. Once they bring in the horses, things kick off quick.

Eluned shouts, 'That prick is winding you up! You know Sharon would never do that.'

A barefaced lie. Everyone knows Sharon has been shagging Dai the Meat for years.

They are too late to avoid the horses. Her stomach churns as they trot down the track to the picket line. The crunch of hooves on gravel bounces around the car park.

Unlike Mabli, as a child Eluned had never been the sort of girl to beg for a horse. She had never tried to feed apples to the wild ponies at the top of the Roman road or stroke their long manes. These police horses are tall and chestnut brown, with shining muscular thighs and white diamonds down their long faces. Even Lloyd needs to crane his neck to look at them.

Two policemen on horseback approach Lloyd and Mark. Lloyd steps back immediately, holding his hands up in surrender. Without Lloyd holding him, Mark goes floppy and the police grab and cuff him, before bundling him off. He doesn't resist, lets them move his body like a ragdoll into the van. Dan the baby starts to cry.

'Any more trouble, my boy,' the policeman spits at Lloyd, 'and you'll be joining your mate in the back of my van.'

'He was trying to calm Mark down, you dickhead!'

It's out of her mouth before she can hold it back. Of everyone, Lloyd is the person least likely to try to cause any serious aggro. A little mischief, but no aggro.

A policeman brings his horse over to Eluned in a slow trot. He sits so far above her that his face is cast into shadow by his helmet. The horse's nostrils quiver, each nostril about the size of Eluned's palm. Flies buzz on its eyelashes and the tips of its ears. The horse reeks, thick and earthy. Eluned's knees turn to jelly. It's too close, much too close. Its whiskered lips are closed, but at any moment they could draw back. Her hand searches blindly for Lloyd's, fingers scrabbling round his wrist and squeezing in relief.

'Boys, we got some of Scargill's Slags here!'

She knows that voice.

'Graham!' she shouts. 'He was only trying to help.'

She's hardly proud of knowing Graham, but perhaps appealing to him will help call off the horses. They have met before, in the awkward shuffle of Lloyd picking up Eluned and Graham picking up Mabli. He must know that Lloyd, despite being built like a brick shithouse, is one of the gentlest men in Wales. All he ever wants is a warm meal and a bit of fuss and maldod.

Graham leans down. His eyes scrutinise Eluned's face and she scratches at her nose, brushing away dirt that isn't there.

'Go home, Eluned. This isn't the place for you. You need to find yourself a boyfriend with a proper job. Mabli doesn't need to worry about any of this shit; I'm taking her out for an Italian later.'

An Italian on a weeknight! Mabli never said. The last time she went to an Italian was for Mabli's sixteenth birthday. It makes her sick to think of Mabli's pearl earrings dangling as Graham handles the menu and the bill. She'd love some garlic bread, her fingers juicy with run-off butter.

But there's no job more proper than mining. Keeping the lights on and the ovens hot, what's more proper than that? She opens her mouth to shout back at Graham, then out of the corner of her eye she sees Dan throw his rattle out of the pram and onto the ground.

The wind catches the rattle, blowing it through the gate and bouncing down the path towards the colliery. Dan wails, flexing his chubby hand. Lloyd takes off after the rattle, hoicking up his jeans as he runs. He slips past the police and chases down the flimsy plastic toy. Rhiannon crouches down in front of Dan to suck in her cheeks and move her lips like a fish. Eluned could ralph at the thought of Lloyd catching the attention of the police, but Rhiannon is cool as a cucumber, gurning until Dan giggles.

As Lloyd jogs over the threshold to the colliery proper, three of the officers on horseback draw their truncheons.

'We'll have you for trespassing!' Graham yells, pulling on the reins of his horse.

Lloyd stops in his tracks, and slopes back to the picket line without a word. It's not just getting charged with trespass; it's that once a miner is over that line, they're liable to get the sack, instantly.

The wind blows the rattle further through the gates. It bounces over the gravel before landing in a puddle.

Some of the women up north have been having their own fun with the police. They can still be done for trespass, if the police can be bothered, but they can't get the sack. Perhaps she'll have a go herself.

'Mam, look after Dan a minute,' Eluned shouts.

Eluned grabs Rhiannon's hand firmly and runs until she's dragged Rhiannon over the line. Eluned swipes the rattle up from the puddle, wiping it over her jeans before passing it to Rhiannon. She doesn't dare to go much further. They could probably be through the gate and back at the picket in a few short strides.

Eluned sings something Tadcu used to holler after a few drinks. 'The people's flag is deepest red, er . . . something . . . something martyrs dead!'

'I only know the chorus!' shouts Rhiannon.

Eluned jumps ahead. 'Though cowards flinch and traitors sneer . . .'

Rhiannon finishes, '. . . We keep the red flag flying here!'

Rhiannon takes Eluned's hand and slots her palm underneath Eluned's. It's a nice change; usually Lloyd wraps his hand over hers.

'What next?' Rhiannon asks.

Graham stays by the picket, perched atop his horse and seemingly unsure what to do. She supposes that arresting two young women for singing might undermine his authority. But, on the other hand, the miners might be buoyed by seeing the girls get away with it. He glowers at the girls, resting his hands on his truncheon. Prick.

Eluned thinks of a song from the radio; they might as well enjoy themselves while they're still getting away with it. She moves her hips from side to side, clicking her fingers like she's seen George and Andrew do. 'Wake me up . . .!'

Rhiannon sings the next line as Eluned twirls her under her arm. The pickets cheer the girls on, voices blending as they spin.

'She needs a better bra, that one. Look at those udders swinging!'

Eluned's arms snap over her breasts, pressing them against her chest as hard as she can. Her feet stop moving immediately, rooting her to the spot.

Graham holds his hands midway down his chest and swings them back and forth with a grotesque grin. The fucker. The absolute low-down, hateful, class traitor, creepy pervert fucker. Her skin is on fire. The last few seconds run on a loop in her head. She can't look at her parents or Lloyd. All she can hope for is that they haven't heard.

'Ignore them,' Rhiannon says. 'They're only pigs! Come on!'

Eluned opens her mouth to sing, but no sound comes out. She's got to find a place to hide, needs to pull on the thickest, most enveloping jumper she can find and disappear. She tries to swallow the blistering anger, but it surges up her throat like sour vomit. She's not quick enough to contain it.

'Cunt!' she yells. 'You're a cunt, Graham!'

Graham forces his horse towards Eluned, reins in his left hand, his truncheon high in his right. It picks up speed quickly, whinnying as Graham urges it on. Its hooves pound the ground, spitting gravel behind them. It's already too big for Eluned's comfort and it's only getting bigger as Graham charges her. Its hooves thump louder than the pickets shouting and louder than the wild battering of Eluned's heart in her chest.

Eluned's frozen, hands clenched into useless fists at her sides as the horse towers over her. The whites of its eyes are threaded through with red veins. Its gums are repulsively shiny. Its hot breath gusts on her cheek, the stench of it weakens her knees. Its gnashing teeth are so long, so thick. They would break straight through her skin, like a hammer on an apple.

Graham's truncheon whistles as it slices the air. Holy fuck. He brings it down over her head. It's solid wood. It's 14 inches of solid wood, about to crack her straight on the head, and will she even survive it? People have died on the pickets and what if she's one of them? Bleeding out in front of her parents on a Thursday afternoon. Eluned lobs her weight to the side and the black truncheon cuts down in front of her face. She staggers backwards, knees finally giving out.

Eluned lands heavily in a brown puddle. Her hands burn from where she tried to break her fall, gravel embedded in her palms, cold water already seeping through her jeans and into her knickers.

The horse stamps, less than a yard from her. She folds her arms across her head, praying that Graham doesn't have a second go. Her legs shake. She doesn't have the strength to run. She'd have to lie down and take it.

Graham snarls down at her. 'Get back to your father before I do it again, bitch.'

Eluned scrambles to her feet. Her jeans are soggy, and the weight pulls them down until they slip under her belly. She pushes her index fingers through her belt loops and waddles back to the picket line.

Lloyd grabs her first. He wraps his arms round her, cupping her head against his chest. She squashes her eyes closed to keep the tears in.

Around her, the pickets push against the line of officers on foot. Her head spins with the noise of it.

'You should be ashamed of yourselves!'

'The girls did nothing wrong!'

'Fucking scum!'

If only she was at home. If only she was cwtched up with a tea and *Countdown* on the telly. If only the strikes were over, and Margaret Thatcher and Graham were both dead. Rhiannon has run back to Dan, handing him back his rattle.

Eluned stumbles home. The outer parts of her thighs are numb from the cold wind whipping through the wet denim, but her inner thighs burn from where the fabric has chapped her skin raw. On the doorstep Eluned toes off her work shoes and unbuttons her jeans, rolling the sodden fabric down her legs. She's throwing them over her arm when there's a bang upstairs. Maybe the cat from 63 has come in again. Another noise. This time, it sounds like a wooden drawer sliding. Eluned grabs a peach hand towel from the pile of clean washing at the bottom of the stairs and holds it in front of her hips like a miniskirt. Surely no one would be out burgling; there's nothing worth stealing for miles around. The only thing of value they have is the family record collection. Eluned is still tamping. She feels hopped enough that she could easily deck whoever is creeping around upstairs.

Eluned climbs the stairs quietly, indulging her lurid fantasies about bashing some spotty scrote over the head with Mam's heavy metal hairdryer. Pushing back the bedroom door, she holds her breath. Mabli. Everything on Mabli's side of the room is gone, from the bottle of Anaïs Anaïs on the windowsill, to the googly-eyed seashell tortoise that Mabli had once begged for in Tenby. Mabli is busy moving the notes she's made on her FILEX course from one of Dad's old box files to an enormous ringbinder, slipping each page into its own poly-pocket. The pages from the module she's already passed are unceremoniously dumped in the wastepaper bin. Their treasured record collection is split into two piles on the floor.

Mabli stares at her, taking in the too-small towel and Eluned's grazed knees, which look like a couple of smashed-up corned beef pasties. 'What happened to you?'

Mabli's gently aghast tone is at odds with the adrenaline still fizzing through Eluned's hands.

'What happened to me?' Eluned is incredulous. 'Your boyfriend happened to me!'

Mabli tosses *Touch* by Eurythmics on to one of the piles. 'Not this again,' she says, gracefully getting to her feet.

'"This again?" How dare you! And now you're moving in with him?' Eluned's bellow bounces off the walls of their small bedroom.

'Well, duh! We've wanted to take the next step for a while. I knew you would all freak, so I had no choice.' Mabli smooths down the front of her dress. It's ankle-length, olive green, and probably unbearably itchy.

'Did you invent your all-important meeting then?' Eluned demands.

Mabli nods. 'It was the only way I could get some peace to get on with it.'

That must be why the bastard looked so smug, up there on his fucking horse. He must have got a kick out of winding her up, knowing Mabli was at home packing her belongings. No wonder they're going to a pissing Italian on a weeknight. Eluned's head buzzes with static. On the bus, too, Mabli must have known that Graham was policing the picket line today. Why didn't she warn them? She might have tried to keep her hair on if she'd known Graham was going to be there, laughing at her.

'How can you do that after everything Mam and Dad have done for us?'

Mabli's look pins her to the floor as if she were a beetle in a glass cabinet. She asks, 'What have they done, exactly? Dad won't get off his arse and go back to work. Mum is too busy collecting cans of beans to give to other people . . .'

Eluned can't listen to this shit. It's the lying she can't take. Dad has been fighting for their way of life, their community since the beginning of March. Instead, Mabli has been conspiring to get away. If Mabli is ashamed of being a Hughes, then maybe she shouldn't be one any more. Eluned seizes the glass photo frame from Mabli's bedside cabinet and surges forward. She brings it sharply down towards Mabli's head, stopping centimetres from her scalp. Her hands shake.

Mabli cowers against her empty wardrobe.

'That's what your boyfriend did to me today,' Eluned spits. 'He called me a bitch and made fun of my tits.'

Shame sits on Eluned's shoulders like a wet coat. Mabli used to know her better than anyone. Mabli used to come shopping with Eluned in Swansea when it only used to cause a row with Mam. Mabli was there when her measurements grew big enough to drop off the edge of the list printed inside the paper tag. She'd caught her sewing extra fabric into her cups to hide the way her nipples stuck out like grapes in the cold. She should know why what Graham said was a low blow.

Mabli doesn't cower long. She straightens up and crosses her arms. Her voice is cool when she says, 'What did you do to provoke him, Eluned? I know you think they're sweet angels, but Graham says they act like animals.'

Eluned can't stand it when Mabli takes this hectoring tone.

Mabli's hand grabs Eluned's wrist. Her nails are painted with Revlon's Rose Cream. That's Eluned's bottle, she better not have packed it.

Softly, Mabli says, 'You know, I'll only be in Creunant.'

Creunant! Who would want to live there? Eluned wrenches her wrist away from Mabli and stomps to the bathroom and bolts the door behind her. She grabs the brown TCP bottle from the bathroom cabinet and soaks a cotton pad with the pungent liquid, then rests her foot on the shaggy toilet seat cover while she presses the pad to her knee. It burns. Eluned presses harder, squashing it into her minced flesh as she tries not to cry.

3

20 October 1984

Eluned heads straight from Blossoms to the Welfare Hall, the coin tin stretching out the straps of her peeling PVC bag. She saw someone slip a pound in yesterday, and it might finally have enough in it to make it worth presenting to the Committee.

The Welfare is austere from the outside; a plain cube of pebble-dashed brick and corrugated steel. Inside, it is a hive of activity. The women have set up a line of trestle tables in the middle of the hall, chairs stacked up and pushed to the sides. Looks massive now. Eluned finds a spot near Mam and tips the tin out onto a tea towel. She gets into a rhythm, click click click, as she stacks them in piles of ten. Two quid, four quid, a fiver, seven. Mam has her rhythm, loading cans of tomato soup into boxes for families in need.

Mam is talking to her friend Betsan. 'Emyr and me saw a couple of them holding hands outside Woolworths in Swansea. They were wearing shorts with shirts tucked in, and they had more hair on their legs than on their heads! I said to him, "Emyr, I think maybe they've got the right idea. I don't know how many hours of my life I've wasted shaving my legs!" Do you know what he said?'

'What did he say?'

'"Well that's one way of keeping the heating bills down in winter!"'

Mam and Betsan burst into peals of laughter.

Did the women hear? Did they cross to the other side of the street, or are they used to being a spectacle?

'What you talking about lesbians for?' Eluned asks.

'You missed it, bach! We've got some coming down here from London next month; we're going to have a party.'

She can't imagine it. Gays and lesbians in the village. She thinks of the pictures of London nightclubs in the magazines that she and Mabli have pored over. They love seeing that Caerphilly boy, Steve Strange, out with his latex gloves, glossy red lips, and military cap. Mabs cut those pictures out and tacked them up on the wall. Maybe that sort of scene is what the gays and lesbians will be used to, what they will be expecting.

'But why, Mam?'

Rhiannon shouts from the next table over. 'Because they've raised a shedload of money for us, that's why! They've started a group called Lesbians and Gays Support the Miners. Dai's already been up to see them in London, he took them up a copy of *The Fed*.'

'Bless him,' says Mam. 'What are they going to do with that?'

It's not unusual. They've had money sent to them from different groups across the UK, and further afield. The government, those bastards, will take whatever they can from the NUM, so it's safer for groups to send it direct. The NUM have asked Wales to fundraise in Ireland. No surprise, Scargill took the best areas for himself. Yorkshire's twinned with the whole of North America! The Irish have done what they can. Dad says there's old solidarity there, since before Tadcu's time, but between the IRA and the fact that there's even more poverty than here, they've needed some extra help. Dai's been travelling up to London every now and again, on the q-t, to find groups that are willing to raise money for them.

If they're coming from London, they might have some good magazines that even the big Smiths in Cardiff doesn't stock.

They might even have a copy of *The Face*. Surely the men, at least, will be fashionable. She will have to take apart one of her old dresses and make something new. Some fluted fabric might spruce up a neckline or a hem. If she can find something translucent, and some cord, she could make something with a bit of Jayne Torvill about it. Eluned hasn't spoken to her sister since last week, when Graham tried to brain her, but perhaps she could give Mabli a ring later and see if she wants to come. Mabli might even apologise, given the opportunity. Even if she does, the invite is strictly for her only. Mabli thinks the Committee is a talking shop for NUM dinosaurs, but this proves that they're making a difference. They must be if people from London have heard about what they're doing.

'We'll have to show them a good time, make sure we say thank you properly.'

Mam caws, 'Well I'll be telling Emyr and Lloyd to keep their backs to the wall; we don't need them having too good a time.'

Eluned looks down at her grey-stained hands. They stink of metal.

Eluned walks round the corner to Lloyd's house. He is parked by the postbox, leaning against his dad's knackered Ford Escort, throwing his keys in the air and catching them. He throws them higher. Higher. He teases himself like a dog, pitching the keys to the side. Quick off the mark, he darts and stoops to catch them before they hit the pavement. He hasn't spotted her yet. His fist curls triumphantly, and she can't help smiling.

'Where are we going tonight?'

She doesn't even know why she asks. It's not like they'll be going anywhere new. It's been so long since they had a drive up to Henrhyd Falls. In sixth form, you weren't anyone if you hadn't had a shag behind the waterfalls. They used to do it every time Lloyd was allowed the car. Lloyd would go take the torch and lead the way, while Eluned gripped his belt loops with one hand, and felt along the sandstone walls, wet and spongy as a tongue, with her other. Thinking about it brings back the smell of the damp, the sensation of silky moss on her back.

Maybe he'll have enough petrol to get them to their favourite layby. There is never anyone else parked up outside the hillside cemetery, where the graves, carved with Welsh and English, are slowly succumbing to gravity. In daylight, you can see the flat wedge of Fan Gyhirych. It has always looked like an invitation to make noise, like if you stood on the edge of its flat peak and screamed, the sound would reverberate down the valley.

Lloyd rubs his hand over the back of his neck. 'Nowhere. I'm sorry. I've run out of petrol. I'm such a knob. I haven't got enough money to fill the tank up again.'

'You're not a knob. Everyone's skint.'

He still opens the door for her first. The skin underneath his eyes is grey, and tiny red veins have sprung up around his nostrils. He pushes a cassette into the tape deck. Janice Long's show from last week. Tidy – she was helping Mam at the Welfare when it was on.

The streets are deserted. No money to be out these days. People their age used to hire a minibus to take them down to Swansea every few weekends. It was always carnage, the aisle running with sick on the way home. She still craves it. The burnt smell of the smoke machine, chugging back a sickly purple pint of snakebite, dancing across the lit-up floor. It feels like another world. When this is over, she'll book the minibus herself.

Lloyd stares into space, drumming his fingers against the black plastic dashboard. She checks the windows on both sides of the terrace. You've got to be wary of nosy old women.

'Lloydy, baby, look at this . . .'

Eluned plucks open the first two buttons of her blouse. She has repurposed a bra that she hasn't worn for years, lengthening the wings and sewing in another set of centre back eyes. It's still too small and it cuts into her skin, giving her two distinct rolls of fat. But she's not going to let Lloyd see that. She's chosen this bra for what it does for her at the front.

There we go. His ears pinken. She cups the back of his head and brings him to her, trusting that his dark head and wide shoulders will shield her from anyone peeping in. Eluned's hips slide forward on the seat. If they can fool around for an hour or two, her mind can slide somewhere else entirely.

Lloyd pulls back. The cold air rushes into the gap between them, bringing goosepimples up on her chest.

'I'm sorry. I can't. I'm knackered.' Lloyd carefully tucks her damp breast back into her bra.

This cannot be happening. Lloyd being up for it is one of life's few certainties.

'I never thought I'd see the day when you didn't want a shag.'

She rubs him lightly through his jeans, like she's trying to roll out a rope of dough, but he remains soft.

Lloyd grabs her wrist. 'No, 'Lun. I'm too tired.'

She whines, 'I'm tired, too. I was on my feet in the shop all day.'

There might not be many customers, but she still needs to sweep the floor, polish the mirrors, and tidy the stockroom.

'And what do you think I've been doing? Sat at home on my arse?' Lloyd growls.

'No, I never said that. I mean—'

'You don't know what it's like. You remember Owen Harries from the year above us at school? Earlier, he walked past me fanning himself with his payslip, the little cunt.'

Eluned flinches. Lloyd hardly ever says cunt.

'I'm sorry, I didn't mean . . .'

Lloyd clenches his jaw. He's a little boy again. Eluned scrambles over the gearstick, cradling him as his shoulders jerk. He's only cried in front of her a couple of times: his Hen Famgu's funeral, and the day he took a rugby ball to the bollocks. Lloyd keens, an awful, rending sound. Eluned meets her own eyes in the wing mirror. What the fuck is she meant to do now?

She presses their heads together. Her jawbone vibrates with the force of Lloyd's teeth grinding.

'I'm thinking of going back to work,' he says.

'You're going to say "psych", right?'

'I can't cope with this no more. I want to go down the pit with the boys, get my wages, put a little aside for the wedding, and then have a pint on a Friday.'

'You don't want to be a scab. Scabs get bricks thrown through their windows,' she implores.

There's nothing worse than a scab. Nothing more treacherous, nothing more shameful. If Lloyd wants to scab, then they might as well move to Dundee afterwards, for all the welcome they'll have from their families.

'I know.' He laughs mirthlessly. 'It's me and the boys that put 'em through windows.'

Eluned opens the door of his glove compartment. She reaches past the black leather pouch he hides his condoms in and takes out the playing cards behind them. They're well-used, with bashed-up corners and the plastic coating peeling back in strips. She deals two hands of six and balances the rest of the pack on the dashboard.

'Let's play and relax for a bit, then go home,' she suggests gently.

Lloyd swallows firmly and picks up the cards he has been dealt. He frowns as he concentrates on sorting his hand into order. Distract him. Cheer him up. Send him home. He'll have forgotten about scabbing by tomorrow. She'll ask Mam to check to see if his family have received any food parcels, and make sure they're on the list if they haven't. Maybe Dad should have a word. Lloyd always listens to Dad, even after the time Dad suggested Lloyd grew a moustache, which resulted in the whole village calling him Freddie Mercury for a month.

Lloyd wins cribbage. And if Eluned slips a pair of fives, or a seven and an eight, or two jacks, into his box, then who's checking? Eluned deals cards for whist and rummy, and he takes those from her, too. Clenching his fists above his head, he leans in for a snog.

Eluned grabs his chin as she eyeballs him, pressing her blunt thumbnail in as hard as she can. He always likes that. 'And you'll be on the pickets tomorrow?' she asks.

Lloyd nods, his eyes wide and dark like rich soil. 'I will.'

Eluned stomps back up the hill to Mam and Dad's house, wrapping the lining of her coat pockets round her hands to shield them from the wind. If this is what October is like, it's going to be awful by January or February. It was never meant to drag on past the summer. She can't have the boys shivering their bollocks off in the snow. They've got to win soon. There's no way they can let that miserable, pussy-bowed witch win.

4

26 October 1984

On the day the gays arrive, Eluned spends the afternoon in Blossoms. She passes most of the day doodling on the back of old shoeboxes; it feels gorgeous when the pen glides across the slightly spongy surface.

'If you want to titivate before the poofters arrive, you can leave,' Mair says, leaning over the counter to poke Eluned's forearm.

She can't lose an hour's wages. Every £3 that she clocks up is £3 towards the family shop. If they end up with more than they need, it can go towards the food parcels at the Welfare. The gays are bringing more food with them. Some from the CND, and some from the peace camp they're packing up at Greenham Common.

'No, it's fine. I can stay until you close. You never know, we might get someone in.'

They won't. Women are darning holes in their slippers and strapping outdoor shoes together with gaffer tape. This job is a face-saving farce. A penance, so that her parents have some money coming in.

'I'll pay you for the hour, but I can't stand you clock-watching.'

Eluned scrutinises Mair's face. Is she serious? Is it a test? Her earrings wink in the light. She smells of gin and lavender.

'You can go. Don't worry, it's my treat.'

Eluned has her bag over her shoulder and one hand on the door before Mair has blinked.

At home, Eluned stuffs a polka-dot blouse into a hastily shortened scarlet skirt, the offcuts cannibalised into a ruffle above her knees. She raids Mam's wardrobe for slim leather belts and straps a couple round her waist, buckling them a few holes wider than her mam ever has. How were people that small in the 1960s?

Mam lets her cut the fingers off Mamgu's chapel gloves to finish off the look. The tight lace itches her palms and her wrists, but she wedges on a bulky cocktail ring over the top. Mam and Dad have a full-length mirror in their room, and she sneaks in for a look. She pokes her pasty calves, pulls her scrunchie to get her ponytail in the right place. The other women better make an effort. So many of them won't be prised out of their jeans and jumper combo. If she was here, Mabli would give Eluned an honest assessment. Mabli would take the cocktail ring off. She would say it's gaudy and ridiculous. Fuck her, it's staying on.

It feels like the whole street walks down the long hill to the Welfare Hall together, like when they organise the bring-and-buy for Harvest, or the May Day party. By the time they arrive a country and western band is twanging away on the low stage. Fair play, the Committee have done a proper job of decorating the hall. It usually smells of beer, nicotine and stale piss. Tonight, the lemony tang of Flash cleaner is strong enough to clear anyone's sinuses. It's surreal; their rowdy social club isn't supposed to smell like a hospital. A thick layer of grey dust has been swept off the velvet curtains, so that they shine a deep, Valentine's red. The floorboards have been buffed and polished, and every single pint has a cardboard beer mat underneath it. Someone's even thought to change the time on the large white clock above the bulky wooden bar. For the first time in years, it's not twenty minutes late.

Mam and Dad are sat in their usual places on the upholstered bench that runs along the wall. Dad's sat with his heels together and knees apart, and Mam next to him with one knee crossed over the other. Eluned swings her bag onto the seat next to Dad and steals a gulp of his beer.

'We closed up early! Have they arrived yet?'

'The minibus is still shuttling back and forth from Neath,' Mam says. She circles her wrist gingerly, wincing every time she bends it back.

'You alright?'

'I'm aching! Everyone in the Committee has been flapping and there was no one around to take minutes, so I said I'd give it a go. Haven't written that much since my O levels!'

Eluned hides a laugh. 'You'll be staying away from those heavy beer glasses, will you?'

Dad says, 'Your mam's got magic healing powers where booze is concerned!'

Mam slaps his knee with one of the Committee's precious new beer mats. 'Alcohol's a painkiller, Emyr. They used to chop people's legs off after a gobful of rum!'

Eluned looks around for Lloyd. He's sitting with the boys tonight, at their usual table over by the wooden bar. He's such a show-off when he's with them. He likes to fling his arm round her and make her watch whatever childish game they've come up with, like competing to see who can throw a knotted-up crisp packet in the bin from far away. He wolf-whistles across to her as she walks a wide circle round their booth.

'Not now, Lloyd! I've got to get Mam and Dad a pint before the gays arrive.'

Carrying three pints of Felinfoel in one go takes skill and guts, but she manages with only a little beer soaking into her blouse. She'd usually plonk them down without a beer mat, but she'll be run out of town if she's caught leaving white rings on the tables today.

'Quick, Dad, quick! Get me a beer mat.'

Dad pushes the cardboard mats underneath the glasses as Eluned's hands start to shake.

Mam's breath catches. Eluned's head snaps to the door. Yes, the gays must finally be here! Someone from the committee told Mam that twenty-seven of them would be coming down. Twenty-seven! But they must still be lost somewhere in the hills because it's only Mabli standing in the doorway.

Mabli looks expensive. That's a perm, not rollers. The neckline of her dress is wide and elegant, showing off the tight curls brushing sweetly against her shoulders. Her collarbones stick out more than they used to. A golden locket trembles in the hollow of her throat.

Mabli doesn't cross the middle of the hall, but picks her way to them round the dance floor with neat, quick steps.

'Can I sit with you?'

Eluned didn't think she'd actually come. Eluned cwtches up to Mam so Mabli can squeeze in between her and Dad. Dad clears his throat, but no one speaks. Mabli keeps her handbag on her lap, and wraps and rewraps the strap round her hand.

'Can I get a round in?' Mabli asks, taking out her wallet. It's new. Jane Shilton. Who paid for that? As if she even needs to ask.

'I just did,' Eluned says curtly. She holds Mabli's gaze. Mabli is going to look away first.

But Mabli doesn't look away, she raises her eyebrow. 'I'll get the next one.'

Eluned keeps staring, jaw clenched. Look away first, you stuck-up cow. Eluned wins. Mabli turns to face the bar. This is the Miners' Welfare Hall. She's done fuck all for any miner lately.

'I'm going to ask if they've got any Chardonnay,' Mabli grinds out.

'I thought she'd like to come,' says Dad, once Mabli has gone.

When Eluned first heard about the gays coming to visit, she had wanted to invite Mabli as well. But after she'd rung Graham's house twice and not got an answer, she'd written her off.

Eventually, Dai and the rest of the committee arrive, the long-awaited gays tramping behind them. Eluned leans forward to suss them out. Only a couple of girls.

'Christ sake, 'Lun. Let them have a beer and a packet of crisps first,' Mam hisses, pushing Eluned back into the bench behind them.

She was only trying to show an interest, give them a welcome. Amongst the locals there are a couple of people with crossed arms, the same people you'd expect to be funny with anyone a bit different. Dai beckons them in after him, and as they shuffle in a few people start clapping. It's contagious, and Mam joins in, slapping her hand against the hard leather of her handbag. Eluned claps too; they've raised more money than she's even thought of.

Their leader is just a bit older than Eluned. His baggy grey jacket and black docker's cap is unassuming, but he carries himself with the confidence of a rock star. The other men look American, with tight jeans and boxy leather jackets. Not one of them looks a bit like Boy George.

Eluned should pay attention, but the speeches are the same as the ones she's listened to since she was young enough to get away with napping under the table. Solidarity. Common purpose. Instead, she studies their outfits: popped collars, a girl with long braids down her back, a tuft of pillar-box-red hair peeping out from beneath a flat cap. She's never seen hair that red outside of a magazine before.

After the speeches, the gays clump together on one of the long bench tables. It's underwhelming. Her parents finish their pints and swing their coats over their shoulders, heading home in time to watch the news. With them gone, she'll just have to make an effort to talk to Mabli.

'Why are you here? Does *he* know you're here?' Eluned asks Mabli. Everyone knows that Thatcher is using the police to crush the strikes, and the papers have been drumming up suspicion about how the miners are getting their money. She wouldn't put it past Mabli to be passing information back to Graham.

Mabli shrugs. 'I said I was going for a drink with my family. There's nothing wrong with that, is there?'

Eluned snorts.

'Besides,' Mabli continues, 'I can appreciate what this lot have done. They're not involved because they were born into it and it's what everyone expects of them. They've done their research and come to their own conclusions. I want the freedom to do the same without being strung up.'

Huh. There is a sort of Mabli-esque logic to that. It's been a good day. Eluned finished work early, she's a couple of pints in, and everyone is here to celebrate the hard work of their surprising, generous allies. Maybe she should just give Mabli a break.

Eluned itches her eye, their secret sisters' code, in the direction of the most feminine lesbian. She's wearing a Laura Ashley-style blouse tucked into an aubergine corduroy skirt.

'I could see you in that,' Eluned says.

'Hrm,' says Mabli. 'I like the colour, but I couldn't wear it. It's far too—'

'Corduroy is too hot for me as well,' Eluned finishes.

Mabli leans over and pokes Eluned's knee, then points at one of the LGSM lot, all alone at the bar. Mabli whispers, 'I know it's "Lesbians and Gays Support the Miners", right, but which one is that supposed to be?'

If truth be told, Eluned isn't sure either, from the back. The person is small and slight, with dandelion-blond hair cut into a Grace Jones-style flat-top. Eluned would guess they were a natural blonde; even the wispy baby hairs at their nape are white. Their ears stick out a little, exposing a large, dark mole behind their ear. Their jacket is massive, seams lagging halfway down their upper arms. It's too long as well as too wide, covering half of their back pockets. Eluned could alter it for them. Leather is hard to work with but not impossible. Maybe it's the London style. Still, everyone wants to show a bit of bum, even the boys.

The person bobs and weaves between the men at the bar, up on their toes. They're stuck between Frank Gwyn and Gav the Books. Gav the Books reaches past them to grab a new beer mat and they defer, neatly swivelling their body to the side. He leans in to talk to them, and Eluned gets a glimpse of a dainty jawbone, and a small, pointed nose as they turn their face towards him. Gav thinks of himself as a bit of a comedian, and he soon has them laughing. They laugh with their mouth open and their chin drawn back into their neck, snaggle-tooth just peeking out. Eluned wishes she was in on the joke.

'Have some respect, they've raised £400 for us, and there's more on the way,' Eluned says.

'Chill out. You can't tell either. Go and talk to it. Go on!'

'Shut up, Mabli. You might be small-minded but I'm not.'

She'll show Mabli. While she's shacked up with a copper, Eluned will be making friends with gays from London. She grabs her pint and strides across the hall.

'Hiya butt! You come all the way down from London then?' Eluned asks, clapping them on the shoulder as Dai and Gav take their leave.

Before Eluned can pull her hand back the poor dab jerks and spins, so they're backed up against the bar, practically on tiptoes. Their eyes are pale blue and black-ringed under a strong browbone. Their lips would be plush if they weren't also dry and splitting, with angry red streaks glistening under the bar lights.

Eluned shouts across over the bar to Carly, 'This one wants a pint, alright?'

Carly nods as she smoothly brings the tap down. 'I've got a couple more to do but I'm getting to it.'

'Thanks,' the lesbian says, flicking fag ash into the crystal ashtray. 'It's June.'

The pale slivers of her wrists poke out of her cuffs, and her cracked leather boots look older than June herself. The laces have been pulled out and replaced with thick black ribbon, safety pins threaded through the eyelets.

'I'm Eluned.'

June nods. You'd expect the gays to be chattier. June's steady silence makes her want to fill the space.

'It's tremendous, what you've done for us. We're not too bad off, because I'm earning. My sister was as well, but now she's moved out. Long story. You've been so tidy, sending jumpers. We couldn't have asked for more. Mam said some people are burning shoes to . . .'

June seems shocked into opening her mouth. Silver hoops jingle all the way up her ear as she shakes her head firmly. 'Starving our own people out. Disgusting.'

June's English, but not a Londoner. Her accent is hard to place; it has the same sing-song quality as Eluned's own. Eluned gets another glimpse of her snaggle-tooth before it's shuttered back behind her lips. They must be around the same age.

'Where to are you from?' Eluned asks.

'West Midlands, bab.'

'How come you got involved with LGSM?'

'I saw an advert in *City Limits* magazine. My da, my brothers and my uncles are miners. They might not give a shit about me, but I don't want them to starve.'

'Why wouldn't they give a shit?'

June stands up properly, taking her elbow off the bar for the first time since she started speaking. She's only a dwt. June gestures from her head to her toes. Oh. Yeah. Christ, June is braver than she thought.

Eluned watches the bubbles in her beer rise to the top. June frets at her fingernails, splitting the ends into flakes.

'What else do you do up London?'

June must have some stories. Gigs, clubs, that sort of thing.

'I'm an artist.'

'Tremendous! I love art!'

Eluned was hoping that there would be someone like-minded.

June widens her eyes. 'What sort of stuff do you do?'

Eluned hasn't done anything proper, with paints and cups of murky water, since she was at school. She and Mabs used to work for hours, foil tubes scattered over the kitchen table. All she ever does now is doodle models from the magazines to fill time when the shop is quiet.

'Clothes. People.'

'Good for you,' June says, resting her chin on her palm again. Her elbow splays out along the bar, dangerously close to someone else's pint.

'What about you?' Eluned asks.

'I print, mainly, but I'll give anything a go.' June thumbs at a small brooch on her lapel. 'I made this.'

The brooch is made of small red beads strung on wire, twisted into a lumpy shape like a wishbone with a ball-sack hanging inside of it. Eluned can't work it out. She bends towards June, squints while she tries to work out what she's looking at.

June smirks. 'It's a clit. That's what it looks like underneath. It's a scandal that women are taught that it's a tiny nub, instead of this big, powerful thing.'

'Big and powerful? It's hardly pissing *Knight Rider.*'

June throws back her head and laughs. Eluned gets a better look at her teeth now; her pointy canine juts proudly out from the gum and overlaps the next tooth along.

Mabli squints over at them, nursing a second glass of wine. Eluned hopes Mabli's getting a real eyeful of them chatting away. Drink it in. It's been so long since she's spoken to anyone other than her family, Mair, and Lloyd. June is a cold lemon squash on a hot afternoon.

Eluned touches June's wrist. June flinches and with her other hand she brushes down her sleeve until her fingers disappear into the leather bulk.

'Sorry,' Eluned says. 'It's nice to share a joke with a stranger.' It has been such a long time since she did that.

June takes a long chug of her pint and lights another fag, squashing her last in the crystal ashtray between them. June has got to stay here at the bar, with Eluned. She has got to think of something good to make her stay.

'I've been collecting for the strike as well. I made £95.'

'Good on you, bab. The most money I ever made was shaking buckets in the darkrooms.'

'In photography studios?'

Eluned has seen pictures of photographers in darkrooms, floating film in trays of chemicals and hanging them on washing lines. June seems smart enough to do that.

June swallows her cigarette smoke. She hacks violently, bent over the bar. Her fingers spasm, letting her cigarette fall, then bounce along the bar.

Eluned darts to rescue it. The committee will go apeshit if Eluned lets June scorch a mark in the wood.

'No,' June wheezes. She coughs again, a wet, phlegmy one, and takes a deep breath. 'A darkroom. Like, in a gay bar.'

Developing pictures in nightclubs? Surely they could use a Polaroid.

'Like, where people go to fuck.' June's eyes are sly and narrow.

'Where you can see?'

'Yes,' June says slowly. There's another flash of her snaggletooth. Eluned could probably sketch it out from memory now.

'And you saw it? Like, *it*?'

She can't get over this. Not men doing the actual act in public. She and Lloyd might take advantage of his car, but this is on another level.

'Yeah.' June shrugs. She fetches her cigarette back from between Eluned's fingers and takes another drag.

'How do they manage it?' Eluned's got to ask.

'Lube, a deep breath, and a prayer.'

'What, and you were shaking your bucket at them while they were going at it? No wonder you made a packet. They probably wanted you to fuck off so that they could finish up.'

June sniggers around her cigarette. Well, at least Eluned made her laugh as well as Gav the bloody Books.

'Is your dad out?' June asks.

'And my boyfriend,' Eluned answers. 'That's him, over there.'

Lloyd is still sat with his mates. His head is tipped back, mouth wide open, with one of the new cardboard beer mats balancing on his nose. Lewis is next to him, trying to flick it off while Lloyd ducks and weaves.

'He looks like a catch.'

'Sorry, ladies. June, I need you.' A man interrupts.

June turns to Eluned, proffers her half-smoked cigarette. 'Good chat. Want this?'

Eluned takes the fag from June. The cigarette filter has been squashed so it's no longer a cylinder, but some sort of oval shape. Does she always hold it so tightly between her fingers? Eluned finishes it at the bar. Anything to delay going back to Mabli's sour face.

Maybe she'll have a dance. As usual, some of the women have gathered at the other side of the room to dance while the men sit with their pints. 'Do You Really Want to Hurt Me?' is on the speaker, as it often is, and the women are moving lazily, shuffling their feet to the soft reggae.

Eluned makes eye contact with Rhiannon, and she beckons Eluned over to the dance floor. Boy George's mournful last note fades away and is replaced by a jaunty fiddle. Dexy's Midnight Runners. None of these songs are from after 1982. June will leave thinking they're all backwards. They should let Eluned pick the tunes; she's got better taste than most.

June and the man have disappeared into one of the rooms at the back. The Committee meet in a dusty old room where they keep all sorts, including a Victorian miner's lamp and a German bullet that was pulled out of someone's leg. The Committee have organised to give them a miniature miner's lamp; someone probably bought a job lot of them years ago. At home, Eluned has got a picture of Mamgu Fawr standing with Keir Hardie. Perhaps, if June does like that old stuff, she'd like to see it.

She should order June another drink from the bar for when she comes back. They must be knackered, after being on the road all day. They've been further than Eluned has been in her entire life. They're probably too tired to be forced to feign interest in dusty cloth banners and lumps of coal.

June reappears, alone. She paces in the doorway, craning her neck.

Back in a minute, Eluned mouths to Rhiannon, wiggling her way out of the circle of women.

'You lost, are you June?'

'Just looking for the toilet.'

It's easy to look past the door when you don't know the building. She tells June as much, unable to stop herself from prattling on.

When they get to the women's toilet, Eluned hovers by the

door. 'I'll wait outside, in case you can't find your way back to the main hall,' she says.

June nods. Eluned waits, picking loose threads off her gloves. They are already fraying where she's cut the fingers off roughly. Eventually, June emerges, winding a length of stiff blue tissue round her fingers.

'Sorry about that stuff,' says Eluned, 'It's so rough. It takes the skin off your fingers! We used to have a dryer, but we are trying to cut down on the elect—'

'It's fine,' June says.

June stops walking. Eluned stops with her. They're stood in front of the framed picture of the 1968 colliery rugby team. 'You don't have to worry. We weren't expecting hospitality. We only want to hand over the cash, and let you know that you're not alone in this struggle.'

Eluned has been puzzled, all evening, by why she's felt so drawn to June. It comes to her in the same way her camera bites down when she finally turns the focus wheel perfectly; like hearing a song on the radio after weeks of singing it wrong.

'What are you smiling about?' June takes a step closer to Eluned.

'I think I finally understand the word comrade, and why people say it's an international brotherhood – sisterhood. Whatever. That sense of being in the same fight.'

June's eyes widen, then she hoots with laughter, slapping her hand on the wall next to them. The team of 1968 jiggle in their frame.

'What?' Eluned asks.

'That wasn't what I expected you to say.'

'What did you think I was going to say?'

'Don't worry about it. Come on.' June splays her hand over Eluned's back. 'Let's get you back before you start singing "The Internationale", for Christ's sake.'

* * *

They come back to the main hall to the jagged synth of 'Sweet Dreams (Are Made of This)'. The electronic beat uncoils something wretched in the pit of Eluned's stomach. Rhiannon and her friends are prancing around the dance floor with some of June's boys.

'I love Eurythmics,' says Eluned.

'Fuck yeah,' spits June. 'I love Annie Lennox in that video. With the gloves and the cane. Do you know what I mean?'

June's smile is downright feral. Eluned drops her gaze to the polished wood floor.

'Will you dance with us?'

'Nah, you're alright bab. Not much of a dancer. Why don't you ask your boyfriend?'

Eluned says, 'He's not much of a dancer either.'

None of the men are. You can never get them to join in, it's pointless even trying.

'You dance then. I'll stand here and watch,' says June. She leans against the bar, lights up another fag. This time, she leaves the cigarette in her mouth between drags.

Eluned joins Rhiannon. Everyone loves this song. Eluned tries to snap her hips in time with the bass drum. She wants it sharp, staccato. She moves her hips fast enough to make her thighs jiggle. At first, she's too far behind the beat, then too far ahead. She bites her lip. Casting a look over her shoulder, she meets June's eyes.

Rhiannon cups Eluned's ear. 'Did you try and get her to dance with us?'

'The gays are already dancing, Rhi. Everyone is having a laugh.'

Rhiannon wrinkles her nose. She says, 'The boys look like they have a wash from time to time. Her, I dunno.'

'Not even! She's decent, I swear.'

'I think she's watching your arse.'

Doubt it. June's not here to find a girlfriend, she's here to do a job. They've come down to hand over the money they've raised, demonstrate their solidarity, and go back to London to do the same again.

Still, Eluned feels the warmth of June's gaze on her, as she draws her fingers through the ruffles on her dress. Abruptly, the warmth disappears. She turns to the bar, crestfallen when she sees June's empty glass next to the ashtray piled with fag ends.

By the time Eluned calls it a night, there's plenty of empties on the table where Lloyd and his mates sit. The lads are talking over each other, snickering like naughty schoolboys. Good, they deserve it. Lloyd loops his hand round her waist and sneaks it down to make a grab at her bum. No, he's not drunk enough to be getting away with that. Not here. She squirms away, swats him quickly around the head, and leans down to kiss his temple.

'I'm off now, babes,' Eluned says, tucking her bag under her armpit.

'Where's Mabs?'

'Dunno, she must have left already.'

Lloyd struggles to his feet. 'I'll walk you home, cariad. We can get some chips on the way.' He winks clumsily at Eluned. She rolls her eyes. It doesn't take a genius to realise what he's angling for.

Evan bangs the bottom of his pint glass on the table, chanting, 'Lloyd's getting a shag! Lloyd's getting a shag!'

To his credit, Lloyd puts his hand over the top of Evan's pint glass to stop the banging. He looks at Eluned sheepishly, as he should, with round red cheeks.

Eluned is tempted to accept. Maybe they'd go round the back of the chapel, for old times' sake. Fucking against the thick wall of the old chapel was a good laugh, chunks of white paint coming off under her fingernails. But more than that, she wants a Dairy Milk and a fag in bed. In an ideal world, there'd be a new magazine as well. She could get herself wet just thinking about the inky smell of a brand-new magazine.

'Don't worry about walking me home. You enjoy your drink. You've earned it.'

Lloyd's dark eyes crinkle. 'You're an angel.'

Eluned leaves the Welfare Hall and heads away from its bright lights. If she stays too long, she'll have to suffer 'Sailing' by Rod Stewart. She doesn't need streetlamps; she's been walking this route since she was little. The disco fades into the distance, until she can only hear her own footsteps.

The corner shop is open for another ten minutes. Eluned flicks through *Smash Hits* and *Blitz*. Why does Mrs Thomas even bother stocking magazines these days? No fucker has money for them. Eluned reads as fast as she can manage; Mrs Thomas isn't afraid to tell people off for freeloading. Janet Jackson and James DeBarge are on the rocks, Geldof's doing something for charity.

The bell clatters above the shop door, and June stumbles in after it. She lands on the doormat and sharply pulls her lapels together. Her boots are splayed out like the hands of a clock. Eluned tries to look away, but June catches her eyes too quick.

'Thank fuck it's still open. I thought I was out of fags for the night,' June says. 'I left the bar half an hour ago, but I swear I've been walking up and down the same fucking hill for at least twenty minutes. All the streets look the same. What kind of newsagent shuts at 10 p.m. on a Saturday?'

Eluned is glad that Mrs Thomas is out of earshot for that outburst. She's always taken a dim view of bad language.

'Well, I'm sorry we don't do things like in London. We don't need to stay open all night, keeping people from their families,' Eluned says. She's not even sure why she takes such offence.

June sways towards Eluned. 'That's a good point. Eight hours' rest, eight hours' recreation and eight hours' work, isn't it? One of the cornerstones of socialism.'

'Robert Owen. A Welshman,' she says.

Mamgu's history lessons continue to come in handy.

'Naturally.' June plucks a tin of peaches off the shelf behind Eluned. 'Midnight snack,' June explains.

'Enjoy. Nos da.'

Eluned leaves empty-handed. She lingers under the shop's awning to rummage in her handbag for a lighter. God knows where it is. There's her blusher compact, her lipstick, and a half-eaten Lion bar. Her lighter must have slipped into the lining somewhere. It does that, slippery little dickhead.

June lights her cigarette in one smooth movement as the door swings shut behind her; its orange tip illuminates the hollows under her cheekbones.

'Can I borrow your lighter?' Eluned asks.

June nods, but doesn't hand it to Eluned. Instead, she moves close enough that she can light Eluned's cigarette from the end of her own. It doesn't catch immediately, and June cups her hand round it to protect it from the wind. She's such a dwt, she needs to rock up on her toes.

When they were fifteen, Megan Jones went camping in France and came back saying that a local boy had done that for her. Apparently, he'd told her that, '*In France, that means we fuck.*' She'd repeated this to the girls in a bad French accent and they'd taunted her mercilessly about it until the day they left school.

June interrupts her thoughts. 'What's it like?'

'What?'

'Having that great big meatsack thrusting over you.'

'Excuse me?'

'Your boyfriend. Before I left, I saw him leering at the barmaid with the rest of his brainless chums.'

Eluned snorts. 'He would never. She's got about as much flesh on her as a turkey the day after Boxing Day.'

They lapse into silence until June jabs her finger through the air. 'Women's magazines are such a load of shit. Why were you even looking at them?'

Eluned's not fazed, she's been getting the same question off Dad for years. 'I read them for the music reviews and the fashion shoots. I need to know what's going on.'

'You work in fashion, do you?' June asks.

'Well, I work in a shoe shop, but you've got to think about the whole outfit.'

June laughs. 'Sometimes I make bootleg T-shirts and sell them outside the Electric Ballroom, so I guess we're in the same industry.'

Eluned knows of the Electric Ballroom, has heard all about it. It's in Camden, what seems to be the epicentre of music in London, perhaps the world. The Clash shot their first album cover on some side street next to the canal. Boy George is always photographed in the Camden Palace wearing outrageous make-up. Even Madonna played there last year. It's thrilling to hear June mention it so casually, even if she is laughing at Eluned.

LGSM are putting on a benefit concert at the Electric Ballroom next month. It's mostly Committee going, but there are a few spaces left on the bus. Eluned would love to go, kill to go, but Mam is putting her foot down. Eluned won't be going to London on her own. Lloyd says he hasn't got beer money, and Rhiannon hasn't got the time. Unless Mabli pulls that stick out from her arse, Eluned won't be going.

'That must be immense. I bet you get to see all the best bands.'

'I catch the odd one, yeah.' June tosses her butt into the gutter and stamps it out with her heavy black boots. 'You never answered my question about The Meatsack. What it's like to have . . .'

Eluned is still smarting about not knowing what a dark-room is, so she takes the opportunity for revenge.

'It's good; Mabli's boyfriend, Graham, is a twat and Mam says Dad has never lasted more than six minutes in their entire marriage.' Eluned pauses to take a drag on her cigarette. 'So, I think I'm doing the best of the three of us.'

June's eyes widen for a second, and then she howls. 'Well, I'm glad you're getting more than six minutes at least!'

'Who are you staying with?' Eluned asks. 'I can walk you to where you're staying, so you don't get lost again.'

June rummages in her jacket, producing a small square of paper. 'I'm staying with, er, Sian and Gary Davies.'

Sian and Gary are good people. It's good that June is staying with someone decent, or she would have had to take her home herself.

By the time they are halfway up the hill, June is wheezing. She doubles over, bracing her hands on her thighs, then straightens up and reaches into her jacket, pulling out two stubby lagers.

'Take one of these, while I get my breath back.'

Eluned leans the neck of the bottle at an angle against the top of a garden wall. She brings the heel of her hand down firmly on the top of the bottle. It hisses, and the metal top flies off, disappearing somewhere in the grass verge alongside the road. Eluned hands the bottle back to June and then does the same to the second one.

'Smooth,' June says, knocking back the first third in one gulp.

'Dad showed me.'

'How the fuck do you cope with these hills?' June asks, propping her foot up against the wall.

Eluned shrugs. 'I have to; they've been here longer than I have.' She leans down and slaps the back of her calf, where the muscle bulges out of the skin like a bowling ball. It doesn't move, even with the full impact of her hand.

'You'd fit right in at a dyke bar,' June says, peeling the label off her bottle in strips.

What on Earth is she meant to say to that? She tugs at her earring. It's a ridiculous thought. As if there are bars specifically for them. For *dykes.* Surely there aren't enough of them to be packing out more than one bar. Eluned's got to steer this conversation back to neutral ground. Find something innocuous to ask June about. Music. That'll do.

'What bands have you seen at the Electric Ballroom then?'

'I saw The Cure a few weeks ago.'

'I love The Cure!' Eluned enthuses. 'Lloyd wants "The Lovecats" as the first dance at our wedding.'

'Not bad. I thought most weddings had some dreary ballad playing out while they try not to cry about their ruined lives.'

Eluned's cheeks must be glowing as brightly as the streetlights. It's the booze. Booze always makes her go red. Silence stretches between them.

'When are you getting married then?' June asks.

'Uh,' Eluned stumbles. 'A couple of years.'

Here we go. It's not just people from the village who can't keep their thoughts to themselves. You'd think June would have better things to think about.

'Why not sooner? If Mr Six-Minutes-Or-More is keen? You're about the same age as me, right? Where I'm from, the normal girls are shacked up already.'

'I've got things I want to do.'

'What sort of things?'

To be fair, June looks earnest when she asks. But it's hard to make a list of the things she wants to do. They're not impressive things, like taking down apartheid or seeing Madonna in concert. Or maybe they could be. Eluned stares down at the rows of identical terraces and the orange lights in the window of the Welfare.

June's voice softens. She says, 'I shouldn't even have an opinion; I don't think I'd get married if I could. But it shouldn't be a dead end; it should be an open door. I'm sure even The Meatsack would appreciate that.'

Eluned can't turn her head. Her throat is thick. Breathe, Eluned, breathe.

'You can tell someone if you decide it's not what you want,' says June.

Who the fuck could she tell? Her mother? Mabli? Rhiannon? She stares at the lights of the Hall, tries to draw round the squares with her eyes. If she stares at them, she won't cry. If she stares harder, perhaps she will be able to block out June's voice altogether.

'The world is changing. Like, uh – the suffragettes. They weren't that long ago. For Christ's sake, there's an old dyke I know from the CND who remembers the suffragettes. But look what's changed since they were kicking around. It's still changing; women are changing things. It's us raising cash, making speeches, standing up to the police. It won't go back to how it was, not after this.'

'Did I tell you a pig almost sparked me out for singing Wham!? And it turned out to be my sister's cunt of a boyfriend?'

'I can't blame him!' June laughs. 'The only people that like Wham! are sprogs and housewives. They're wasting their time; everyone knows he's a bender.'

'George Michael is never a ben— He's not gay.' Eluned is incredulous.

'A friend of a friend said that they saw him on Hampstead Heath.' June says it like it solves the matter unequivocally.

Hampstead Heath is a new one on her, but she's not about to ask for an explanation.

'Are you coming to Pits and Perverts?' June asks.

'Don't think I can make it.'

There's no point getting disappointed about not going to the concert. The only way she'll get to go is to swallow her pride and beg Mabli, but there's no way that Mabli is going to go to something with perverts in the name, so she might as well give up. The headliner is Bronski Beat. Someone knows someone who knows Jimmy Somerville. Typical. She doesn't even like Bronski Beat, but she can't stomach that there's other people in the village who will see them up close. She knows more about music than most people round here. She should be going.

'That's a shame, let me know if that changes. I'd like to see you there,' says June. 'You're right. It has been good to share a joke with a stranger.'

June strokes her fingers over Eluned's wrist. Against her white lace gloves, they look yellow with nicotine and the skin around the nails is cracked and bleeding.

Eluned doesn't pull away. June feathers her thumb up the inside of her forearm. Sensation crackles. June drags her thumb back down Eluned's forearm more firmly than the first time. Someone walks over Eluned's grave.

June's leather sleeve is soft and creased from wear. Eluned tugs June lightly towards her. June's knees are locked, feet firmly planted on the ground. She sways but doesn't move. Their mouths are still so far apart.

Do it already, June, you're supposed to be the expert here. It would be easier to be blameless. June doesn't move. Fine then. Eluned brings both of her hands to June's shoulders. Her hands sink into the leather; underneath the bulk of her jacket, June's shoulders are birdlike. She smooths her hands along the line of June's shoulders, bringing them up to her neck.

June's eyes cloud with something that looks like apprehension. Fuck, does she think Eluned is going to choke her? She'd never want to hurt her, but she can't be gentle either. She seizes

June's lapels and yanks June against her own solid body, pulling so hard that June's feet may have left the ground.

If Eluned had considered what kissing a woman might be like, before tonight, then she might have guessed it would be soft or delicate. It's not. June's snaggle-tooth catches on Eluned's lips, and she gnashes back.

June's fingers yank their way through her hair, stiff with Elnett, while Eluned scrabbles dumbly at the zip of June's jacket. It's strange to bend her neck downwards while kissing. She usually needs to stretch up when she kisses Lloyd. Lloyd. Fuck.

'I'm sorry.' Eluned lurches back, wiping her mouth with the back of her hand. 'I don't know what I was doing.'

June squares her shoulders immediately. Her hands are like spades at her thighs.

'I might have known,' she snarls, 'that my role in this was helping a breeder sort out her shit.'

Breeder is a new one on her, but it's easy enough to work out.

June coughs deeply and leans past Eluned to spit into the gutter. Her mouth is ringed with Eluned's lipstick, and pink-stained spit dribbles down her chin.

Eluned takes a deep breath and tries to sound as aloof as she can. Channelling Mabli should do it. 'You need to carry on up this hill and then when you turn right it's on the left-hand side with a blue door. Next door has a baby, so don't knock loud.'

For a short woman, June has a long stride. As she disappears, she whistles a rippling line from the chorus of 'The Lovecats', in a stilted, off-key way. Fuck June for mocking her. No wonder she can whistle, with the gaps between her teeth. She'll never listen to that song again. She wedges the beer bottles in her coat pocket and trudges home.

5

27 October 1984

The men on Lloyd's poster of the Welsh rugby team all look the same, with ruddy cheeks and thick moustaches. She keeps staring at them, because every time she looks down at her hands she sees them digging through the leather to find June's skin. June's spit hitting the pavement rings in her ears.

She only did it because Mabli wound her up about talking to one of them. It's typical Eluned Hughes. So typical of her to get carried away with showing off. She'll let herself be teased about it one day.

'It was good last night, wasn't it, 'Lun?' Lloyd asks, scratching at his belly. It's hard to believe that he has a care in the world. He's enjoying their usual Saturday routine of lying on top of his faded red duvet cover, and listening to Paul Gambaccini run down the American Top 30 Chart. There's not much change; Stevie Wonder will hold on to the top slot for another week, only 'Purple Rain' is likely to catch it. 'Lucky Star' is still hanging on in there, although it never troubled the British charts for long.

'It was tidy,' she says.

'You wouldn't even know they were . . . you know, some of them. It's good to know they care, even though they are all the way up in London. They've even been trying to get the Poles to stop sending coal over.'

'They were rad, yeah.' Lloyd says that the Committee have

asked someone to write an article for the *Valley Star* about it. Hopefully there won't be a gossip section.

'Lloyd!' Jean shouts up the stairs, 'This table is too heavy for me! Come and move it so Eluned can eat with us.'

Lloyd rolls his eyes. 'I don't know why she still makes us eat at the table when you're around.'

'Go and help, Lloyd,' says Eluned.

Eluned fluffs the cushions behind her and listens to the clatter of cutlery on Lloyd's MDF dining table. 'Purple Rain' comes in at number four. This track is simply too *big*; it strains against the walls of Lloyd's box room. His room feels tiny but the space inside her chest feels expansive. She's heard the song before, read the lyrics in one of the magazines in the newsagents, but today Prince's offhand delivery is even more striking, more soulful. Did June ever eat those peaches? Eluned can't stop thinking of her with the tin opened jaggedly between her knees, scooping out soft peaches with her fingertips.

She needs some distraction; she roots around underneath Lloyd's bed for something to entertain her. She pulls out a thin porno magazine, its pages stiff and crinkled. Usually, she'd either shove it back or use it to tease Lloyd until his ears went pink. Slim blonde in a schoolroom. Curvy blonde in a field with sunflowers. Nope. None of these women are doing it for her. It was obviously one person, one moment.

Eluned turns the page and her mouth dries out. This girl leans casually against a motorcycle, hair whipping into her eyes. Her light blue jeans are unbuttoned, showing a sliver of bare flesh beneath. The model's tanned hand rests on her stomach, and the sun casts triangular shadows beneath her pointed breasts.

She's so engrossed that she doesn't hear Lloyd coming up the stairs.

'Mam says tea will be ready in an hour— Fuck! 'Lun, what are you looking at?'

'I love the optimism of you looking at these and thinking you could pull any of them.'

Lloyd laughs. 'Don't be a twat. They might want to shag me, you never know!'

'I don't know if you could handle this one.' Eluned turns the page to show Lloyd the biker girl.

'Could.'

'Go on then, loverboy. Tell me what you'd do to rock her world.'

Lloyd swings a knee over Eluned's body. He scrunches his brow, like he's trying to look stern. It's unnatural on his puppyish face.

'Well, I'd walk up to her and then I'd tell her, "Turn round, bend over the bike."'

Eluned shuffles back down the bed, letting her eyes flutter shut.

'I'd grab her hips from behind . . . and touch her knockers.'

Lloyd leans over Eluned to knock off the radio and pick *Faith* from his bookshelf. That's a good shout, it would be hard to get off with Gambaccini's American accent burbling in the background. Lloyd takes the record from the sleeve and sets it up on the deck. It's not her favourite Cure album, but it could be worse; Lloyd could have picked *Japanese Whispers*. Lloyd turns it up loudly enough to put Jean off the scent.

Eluned turns herself into the biker girl. She conjures the hot sun on her shoulders, the leather seat sticking to her inner thighs. The scene warps and she's in Lloyd's place, the girl's narrow hips in her hands. It doesn't have to mean anything, it's natural to fantasise. *Cosmo* says so.

When Lloyd tries to kiss her, she grabs his jaw and forces his mouth away. 'Keep talking.'

Lloyd grins. He tells Eluned that he wants to kick the girl's legs apart, jeans stretching between her ankles while he fucks her over the bike. They're both sweating now. It smells sour, they're both sweating out last night's beer. Their bellies slide together in the slick they're making. It's messy and uncomfortable. They're both done in well under six minutes.

Eluned uses her foot to push and pull the pram across the pathway in the park off the main road, while Rhiannon smokes with one hand and drinks tea from a Thermos with the other. Eluned's wearing Dad's old sheepskin coat, which she's retrieved from behind the hoover in the cupboard under the stairs. Dan is swaddled in so many blankets that only the little red blob of his nose is visible.

The sky is the colour of a dishcloth that won't come clean any more. Birds hunch on bare branches. Her stomach thinks it's time for lunch, but she's already had a slice of bread and butter and that will have to do until teatime.

For the last few weeks, Eluned has been meeting Rhiannon and Dan. Rhiannon doesn't have Mabli's sharp tongue; Mabli can be like Princess Margaret sometimes. Rhiannon barely smokes or drinks, and she doesn't know who Echo & The Bunnymen are. But without adult company Rhiannon would be half-mad, so Eluned commits herself to these half-hearted trundles around the dismal patch of grass.

'Did you hear about that taxi driver?' Rhiannon asks. 'That block weighed three stone. They can't have meant to hit the car. No one's that stupid, surely.'

Two boys had been up on a bridge, throwing whatever shit they could find to stop scabs going to work. They'd hit a taxi with a concrete block from 30 feet up. The car lost control, hit the embankment, and the driver, David Wilkie, was dead before the ambulance arrived. He was from Cardiff, on the books of some agency that agreed to send scabs to work.

It would have been impossible to miss the story. It's been first up on the news for the past week. Not just the Welsh news, but the UK news too. She's had the same phrase stuck in her head ever since. Grey matter. She isn't wholly sure what *grey matter* is, but it makes her stomach flip.

There have been pictures of David Wilkie in the paper. He could be Dad or Lloyd. Every night since he died she's said a quick prayer for him as she goes to sleep. She asks God to keep everyone on both sides safe, apart from Margaret Thatcher. She prays doubly hard for Lloyd, squeezing her hands together and visualising his deep brown eyes. Kissing someone else was wrong and although she deserves to be punished, Lloyd has never hurt anyone in his life. It seems unlikely that the kind and gentle Jesus from Sunday school would strike down Lloyd to punish her, but that doesn't stop her from jerking awake, sweaty from nightmares of Lloyd's head caved in, grey matter trickling out his ears. Please, God, keep him safe.

'He knew what he was getting into though. You must do, if you take a job like that,' Rhiannon says blandly.

Eluned wrinkles her nose. 'I dunno. The agency might not have said. He might only get an address. Does anyone say goodbye to their children in the morning, and not expect to come home in the evening?'

Rhiannon shrugs. 'Scabs are scabs. Anyway, are you going up London next week?'

Eluned could argue, but she's glad to see the back of that grim topic.

'Yeah, unless Mabli backs out. Lloyd . . .' Eluned falters. It's on the tip of her tongue to say that Lloyd wants to sleep all weekend, but Rhiannon will tell Aled and then it will go three times around the village by teatime. Common sense says that most of the lads must be feeling the same way, but no one will say. Eluned misses her sister. Maybe she could speak to Mabli about the funk he's in, as long as Mabli didn't accuse her of emotional manipulation.

Eluned continues. 'Lloyd's skint, and Mam didn't want me going on my own. Dad called Mabs and asked if she'd go. She tried to play it cool but then she saw an advert in *Melody Maker*, and a free bus trip is a free bus trip. She still won't stay with any gays or lesbians though. Mabli told Graham that we're going to visit Tirion down Ammanford and he's given her money to spend in Llandeilo, so he thinks anyway, but she's booked us a cheap B&B.'

Rhiannon lifts her eyebrows. 'What does she think they're going to do, strap her down and make her listen to Gloria Gaynor? You've got to tell her to keep her gob shut though 'Lun. She can't go telling *him* anything.'

'Don't worry. Graham would go spare if he knew Mabli had lied.'

'What are you going to wear?'

Most of her shifts at Blossoms have been devoted to sketching what she might wear on the inside of flattened, discarded shoeboxes. She's going a little Siouxsie Sioux with her make-up, angular brows and a sharp Cupid's bow.

'You're on your own, you are. I wish I was there to see it. Watch out for Aled farting on the bus.'

6

10 December 1984

By the time they reach the A40, Eluned has eaten her half of Mam's sandwiches. Kevin tries to get a rousing chorus of 'Calon Lân' going, but there's a row about the lyrics of the second verse. Mabli ties a scarf round her face and tries to sleep, leaving Eluned to listen to the mixtape she's made for their Binatone. 'London Calling' is too obvious, so she's started with 'Guns of Brixton', stayed close geographically with 'Electric Avenue', then Siouxsie's first single, 'Hong Kong Garden'. Dad would have killed her if she didn't end with 'Waterloo Sunset'. Eluned had hoped that Mabli might listen along with her, but she's not going to push it. It will be a long weekend if they start rowing now.

Aled sparks a flurry of excitement when he reckons he can see Windsor Castle from the motorway. Eluned stands up in her seat, as far as the seatbelt will let her. If it's a castle, it's a puny one.

London is endless. Eluned rolls up the magazine Mabli bought her and slips it down the side of the duffle bag; surely they will be getting off soon. If they keep going, they'll end up popping out the other side of the city. A bright red bus comes in so close that she holds her breath. It could run them straight off the road; twice as tall as their minibus, posters for a West End show running down the length of it.

Eluned watches out for the red Underground signs. She's never been on the Tube. She's nearly smeared her make-up across the window three times now, jerking herself back from a full-face squish each time. Edgware Road, Baker Street, Regent's Park. If only they had time to get off and explore. No one seems to even look at the people bundled in sodden lumps of fabric around the vents. There's so many of them.

Camden, finally. Her eyes are on stalks. There's a beautiful Black couple with perfectly round Afros and orange sunglasses, and a chiselled punk with a daringly high mohawk. Eluned is officially desperate to get off the bus. Her thighs vibrate enough that Mabli stirs, glaring groggily at her.

Dai cheers from the front of the bus, and it ripples down until Eluned gets a look at what they're shouting at. An angel has painted VICTORY TO THE MINERS in wobbly white letters along the whole of Camden Lock Bridge. Eluned bounces until the plastic tray on the back of the seat in front is clapping, the ashtray threatening to flap open and disgorge all over her lap. It's a shame Lloyd isn't here to see it.

Mabli stirs, lacing her fingers with Eluned's. 'Fair play, that's boss.'

Mabli's hands are warm and still clumsy from sleep. Once more, Eluned thinks of the two of them taking care of Dad after work. Mabli used to put the bowl down with such tenderness, spreading a towel first and then adjusting it so his bony feet could stretch out properly.

They pull up outside the Electric Ballroom for everyone else to meet the member of LGSM that they're staying with. The Committee have got a meeting at the Fallen Angel now, talking tactics with the leaders of LGSM, but hangers-on like Mabli and Eluned are free to do what they want. She's happy to miss the chat about Soviet food parcels and buying a new van, but it's torture to think that June might be there without her, speaking to the Committee. Would that be a good thing? Or would sitting around a table with June and the village's most respected elders make her want to sink through the floor? Eluned has puzzled over the end of their last conversation like a Rubik's Cube, but she can never quite get the colours to align. She's still not sure what set June off, and so she sits poised between anticipation, mortification, and the leaden pain of guilt.

The sign over the door to the Electric Ballroom is dark, the doors locked and covered with scraps of posters for gigs that have already happened. Tonight, the sign will call to them like a lighthouse. Behind the door, there might already be people setting up; dragging sound systems into place, placing buckets along the bar.

Mabli has written out the directions to their B&B on a sheet of paper folded into her Jane Shilton purse. It's galling to accept anything from Graham, but if he's stupid enough to spend his piggy money on letting her and Mabli support the miners' benefit concert, then she won't stop him.

Their B&B is called the Albion and it breathes fussy Englishness, from matching floral valances on the two single beds to the sheet of typewritten rules pinned above the dressing table. Mabli, the family genius, has smuggled a bottle of Chardonnay in her bag. They swig from the bottle, passing it back and forth across the gap between their beds.

Mabli changes into a knee-length dress with a pleated skirt, a shiny black belt and matching patent shoes. So far, so BHS. There's no way that Eluned could have found the money for new patterns or fabrics, but she has tried to create the illusion of having something new. Mam gave Eluned a trunkful of Mamgu's old clothes after she died. They stink of damp and lavender, and mostly Eluned ignores them. But last week desperation drove her into the trunk, and she chose a Welsh wool skirt in a portcullis pattern. It doesn't have the kudos of tartan, but under the lights it'll be close enough. The pencil skirt's waspish waist was far too small for her, so she hacked off a wide strip at the bottom, opened the side seam and tried to match the patterns as neatly as she could. There was no point hemming it; she had tugged a couple of fibres loose to give it a ragged finish. Dad donated to the cause: a black leather glove, confined to the back of the cupboard since he lost its pair. Eluned picked the soft leather apart and cut out as many petal-shaped pieces as she could manage with the scraps of material she had, before sewing them into a loose rose on the shoulder of an old jumper. With the jumper tucked in and the right jewellery, it could look punky.

'Graham used to come up to Scotland Yard all the time, for work,' Mabli says.

Eluned grunts in acknowledgement, dusting her temples with deep pink blusher. Talking about that tosser is a waste of time. This is her chance to enjoy an evening out in London, she's going to make the most of it. Mabli's showing willing, there's no point in starting a fight.

Mabli keeps her own face simple, with a glossy coral lip. She won't let Eluned near her with her blusher brush.

Mabli studies Eluned over the top of Marilynne Robinson's *Housekeeping*. 'You look like you've gone native, if you know what I mean.'

Eluned's hands shake as she dots a beauty spot over her top lip. 'It's just one night, Mabli.'

They leave the B&B in a cloud of Elnett and Anaïs Anaïs. Eluned's face is wine-hot, ankles already wobbly in her kitten heels. Camden High Street is buzzing, people flooding out of the Tube station in coats and scarves. Mabli tugs her past the outdoor market, as Eluned cranes her neck to look at the Levi jeans and thick leather jackets. Blue and yellow signs shimmer in every puddle, turning the street into a dance floor. Large groups cross the road haphazardly, four-packs wedged in their fingers. Eluned holds Mabli's wrist so she can listen to a guitar riff seeping out of one of the clubs. The pavement vibrates.

Here are the venues she's always dreamt of going to: Dingwalls, the Palace, the Roundhouse, the Falcon. Eluned has to stop herself from staring when she sees a boy with a long chain strung round his neck as casually as a scarf, and a pale-faced girl with a fountain of crimped hair and *FUCK THE UK* written along her boots.

An elfin boy sits on a high stool, one leg crossed over the other. He smiles warmly. 'You girls were on the minibus, weren't you? Go on through! Enjoy your night.'

Eluned pauses on the step to look up at the sign before they go in, pressing her fingers hard into her sternum.

The inside of the Electric Ballroom is too much to take in. The wide stage, the spotlights, the balcony around the upper floor. The boys are already at the bar, getting a pint in. They deserve a few drinks after months of being called lazy, selfish and dangerous in the national newspapers. They're the men of the hour tonight. It might be that she's already drunk, but her chest swells with the urge to wrap her arms round every one of them.

Dai kicks off the gig, something she would never have predicted before the last few, strange months. Poor sod. He is brave to do it. He goes on about the common links between their communities, the importance of solidarity. He weaves a story, only half bollocks, about the apparently historic banner stuffed in a cupboard back at the Welfare Hall.

Dai wraps his hand round the mic and leans close, furrowing his brow in the way he does when he's being genuine. Don't put your foot in it now. He promises that when the time comes, their lot will throw their weight behind this lot. What will that mean to Mam's lesbians outside the Swansea Woolworths, to the unmarried men everyone whispers about? Hopefully June was right, and things won't go back to how they were after this. Where is June? She should be here, somewhere. She said she was coming. Eluned might have gone about it the wrong way before, with that thoughtless kiss, but June should know that they're ready to pay the kindness back, when it's needed.

Mabli drifts off to the bar while Eluned feels rooted to the spot; she'll die if she misses any music. Lights streak across the heavy black curtain, lighting dust and cigarette smoke in thick blue curls. The first band is the Moonlighters. Two women, one with a mullet that reminds her of June's, doing bluesy covers with a keyboard.

Eluned dances until her jumper is damp and the balls of her feet ache. The stage is so close she can see beads of sweat rolling down the woman's cheek. Mabli reaches into her Jane Shilton and pulls out two pre-rolled joints.

'Is that weed?' Eluned asks.

'Present from Graham. What's the point of bringing in anyone on a drugs charge if you don't play "finders keepers, losers weepers"?' Mabli says, tapping Eluned on the knuckles with the joint.

'I can't believe you. That's disgusting. And so hypocritical. And after everything you've said about needing to be careful about the strike because of Graham's *position* . . .'

Mabli rolls her eyes. 'Chill out. I'll dance with the lads.'

Eluned flicks her fingers up at Mabli and makes her way to the bar. That snake. She needs a glass of water to cool down. The lads know Mabli's going out with a copper. They'll still dance with her; they can't resist a pretty face or a free puff of grass. In a shaft of cold white light, two men kiss tenderly. She's never seen that before. They cradle each other's skulls, mouths moving slowly. Spit glimmers between them like a string of pearls.

Eluned looks away, and her eyes clap on to June. The white spotlight rolls over June's face, and in its beam her jade eyes are luminous. She probably hasn't come alone. She's probably come with a whole gang of lesbians. Maybe they've laughed at Eluned's provincial stupidity and clumsy kiss. Oh shit, June is making her way over, using her slender frame to slip through the crowd faster than Eluned could manage. Eluned stares, her heartbeat pulsing in her hands.

June and Eluned stand toe to toe. June's wearing the same leather jacket, an X-Ray Spex T-shirt tucked into her jeans. A spirit level couldn't find fault with her flat-top. Her foundation is chalky and behind her black lipstick, a bloody crack oozes.

'How's it going? How is everyone?' June shouts over the music.

'Poor and miserable.'

June cocks her shoulder towards Eluned in the best attempt at a consoling gesture she can manage with a full pint in her hand. 'Thatcher and the rest of those fuckers will get their reckoning one day.'

'This is immense,' Eluned says, gesturing at the large banner behind the bar. It's a punchy image of a chiselled miner in his headlamp against a distressed Union Jack and a huge black triangle. The text, white against strips of black, reminds her a little of the *God Save The Queen* cover. June said she was a printer; maybe it's her work. 'Did you print these?'

June laughs. 'Kev drew the design, and we got them printed professionally. No way I could do something this size in my bathroom. Not without the miner looking like a Picasso.'

'Fair enough,' says Eluned. She wipes off the sweat from her upper lip. June must be roasting in that get-up. 'Look – I'm sorry about what happened. You were away from home, and it wasn't fair to ambush you when you were alone.'

June shakes her head. 'You were fine. Come and dance, Bronski Beat will be on soon.'

* * *

The frontman's voice skids from screech to a low sultry tone, murmuring breathily into the mic. So many legends have played here: Bowie, Blondie, the Sex Pistols. Now she'll always be able to say that she's been in the same place as them. The music is so loud that she can't hear her own screams, but she can feel her throat vibrate.

Eluned wiggles her wool skirt up and bends her knees to dance with June's slotted behind hers, warm as teacups. The air around them is sticky and June's jeans scratch the inside of Eluned's thighs. June is close enough to smell: leather, smoke and something like a freshly watered houseplant. A man's arse rubs against her hip as he dances with abandon.

There are only a couple more hours left, and she's going to wring out every new experience. She's free tonight, dancing with a new friend. She can forget what's waiting at home. A woman dances alone, fists and eyes clenched tight. Pressed against her, two burly men snog, tugging at each other's ears. Eluned watches the back of the darker one, the pink lights catching the sweat running down his muscles, the leather straps criss-crossing its hairy expanse. It's wonderful here. Such a shame they're going home tomorrow. Eluned takes June's narrow hands and draws them up the front of her own thighs. June's fingers spread, and Eluned pushes them down so she can feel the clip where her stockings meet her suspender belt.

June whispers in Eluned's ear, 'One minute you're sorry you kissed me. The next you're making me feel your suspenders.'

A prickly flush creeps up Eluned's chest. She closes her eyes. Leaning her weight back against June is so satisfying. Her spine feels loose and fluid. Her ears buzz with static from the sound system.

June's hands slip from under her own. June's jacket creaks as she pushes herself up on her toes. June can only reach the nape of Eluned's neck.

'I think every woman has a bit of a lesbian inside her,' June says.

'Do you?'

'Yeah. Would you like some?'

Eluned groans. 'That's such a rotten old chat-up line.'

June grins until her eyes disappear into the creases, snaggle-tooth on full display.

'Have you ever had a woman like me? You know, a girly-girl type?' Eluned has to ask.

June's lips close around her teeth again. She huffs. 'I've seen a feminine woman before. We don't sit around waiting for straight girls to deign to talk to us.'

This is hitting the skids fast; there's some lesbian thing that she hasn't got her head around. Words aren't helping. She slips her hand down to June's thick leather belt and pulls. June lets her, bumping her body into Eluned. June's look is inscrutable. It's not enough. She wants June to burn her up like a sparkler.

'God save me from needy straight girls,' June says.

'I'm not needy.'

June gestures at their shared bodies. 'Rutting against me in a room of people raising money for your boyfriend seems needy.'

Spotlights swirl as the room spins. The dance floor tilts violently. Eluned rears back, groping for the bar. June doesn't move. Eluned could push her out of the way, send her tumbling into the crowd. She doesn't.

Instead, she wraps her hand round the back of June's neck. Lloyd has a miner's neck, with a bulky trapezius and hard knots under the skin. But Eluned can draw June in with one hand. The short hair at her nape is damp. Sweat runs down either side of her nose, leaving streaks in her white foundation.

June holds Eluned's eyes like she's wrangling a mustang by will alone. She says, 'I'll do this with you, but I won't do the heavy lifting. You have to know what you want, and you have to name it.'

'I know what I want.'

Eluned will give herself tonight. Tomorrow things will go back to normal. She won't tell her parents about Graham stealing weed and giving it to Mabli. She'll clean away the plates after dinner every night. She'll rub the knots out of Lloyd's neck.

Eluned smashes their lips together but June's remain still. Come on, June. Before someone sees. She presses harder against June's mouth. June's hands press against Eluned's collarbones. The pressure is good, and Eluned moans into June's mouth. June pushes harder, Eluned gapes like a fish pulled from the water.

'Come with me to the loos,' Eluned pants.

June twitches an eyebrow. 'Ah, the natural habitat of my people.'

Eluned shakes her head; it feels like a boulder. She's not drunk, but her lips tingle, the way they do when she's about to heave.

'I don't think this is going to work,' says June. 'I'm going to see my friends.'

'No!' shouts Eluned, grabbing June's shoulder. 'Don't go! I could come with you. I could tell them about what we're doing with the money you've raised.'

'They heard Dai talking earlier. They're dancing now. I'll see you later,' says June. She weaves through one group, then another, and then she is out of sight.

The tealights along the bar are guttering, faint flames flickering in the last dregs of wax. Eluned picks one up, letting the metal casing burn her fingers. She closes her eyes and times her breathing to the throb in her thumb. When her heart is back to normal, she checks her lipstick in her compact mirror and heads across the dance floor to where she left Mabli.

Mabli is dancing between Aled and Kevin, spliff hanging from her fingers.

'I'm having so much fun, 'Lun!' Mabli shouts. 'Graham's such an old fart. He never wants to come dancing. I love dancing. I wish we could dance every weekend.'

Eluned can't take this.

'You know he wants to buy us a house in that estate close to the motorway? Three bedrooms and a garage.' Mabli blows a raspberry.

This is not the time for this conversation. Bronski Beat have already played 'Heatwave' and 'Junk'. It can wait. They don't want to miss 'Smalltown Boy'. Eluned restricts herself to a nod and closes her eyes, pretending she is too far gone in the music to talk.

Eluned watches two women dance as if they were jogging on the spot, pumping their forearms vigorously. One of them has a red bandana on her left wrist. In the space between them, Eluned sees June. It's like an optical illusion; she can either see the women dancing or June's face framed by their bodies.

June pulls out a fag. Propping it between her lips, she lights it without taking her eyes off Eluned. She puffs out the smoke forcefully, nostrils flaring. The weight of June's gaze is as thick as oil paint; it smears across her chest, drips down her legs. 'Smalltown Boy'. Mabli perks up, and by the time the song is over June is gone.

Jimmy Somerville instructs the audience to empty their pockets into the buckets as they leave. Maybe they'll do another encore. He's unstrapped his guitar, but maybe it's a psych-out. A woman in black takes his mic; it's over.

'Do you know the way back to the B&B?' Mabli bellows, then giggles at herself. There's no need to shout any more.

When Eluned gets through the bottleneck the cold air meets the cigarette smoke in the back of her throat, and she hacks forcefully. She's still boiling, her coat dangles off her arm. It's chuck-out time but there's another party outside as people keep singing and cracking open cans. Outside of the club people look less magical, with pockmarks and missing diamantes.

'We need Owain! Where's Owain? He's staying with Marcus and Terry!' Efa, one of the youngest women on the committee, shouts across the crowd.

Everyone else needs to be matched with the gays that have offered to host them, but as soon as they've gathered everyone, someone else wanders off.

'I seen him,' says Mabli. 'He was with Aled.'

And then there's June, standing a little distance away.

'Mabs, hang on a sec,' Eluned says, squeezing Mabli's hand.

Mabli nods and sits herself down on the pavement, putting her face in her hands. One of the LGSM lot sits next to her and rubs over her back.

When Eluned gets to June she glances over her shoulder. The lads dance in the road, kicking their legs like a chorus line. They're drunk, but they've been drunker. Mabs is fine. No one is going to mess with Mabli when they know she's dating a copper; no one wants to be pulled over and roughed up late at night. Eluned is past the point of doing the sensible thing. Mabli has a map and the hotel's business card. She'll be alright.

'Efa!' Eluned calls out. 'Watch Mabli, alright?'

Efa nods, gives a thumbs-up.

'You coming or what?' June asks.

Eluned nods at June, her mouth dry.

June strides away and Eluned scrambles to keep up, only catching up with her as she stops to speak with a group of women in leather jackets. A couple of them nod to Eluned but they walk in silence, moving like a pack of wolves. Right turn, left turn, right again. June is focused, eyes scanning the parked cars, the faces of men on the other side of the street. June points at a house, and Eluned barely has time to take it in before she's ushered down the path and through the front door. Yellow, sandy bricks, a bay window and a messy lawn. Once they're inside, everyone starts talking at once.

A woman shouts to put the kettle and the grill on, unwinding a scarf from round her throat.

Music starts somewhere deep inside the house. Bass shakes the floor, hard enough that a chip of paint drifts past Eluned's face like snow.

'Put some potato waffles under the grill!'

Eluned feels rooted to the doormat. June slides Eluned's coat off her shoulders and places it on top of the heap hanging over the banister. She squeezes Eluned's hand. June's hand is fine and narrow, nothing like Lloyd's big paw. Don't think about Lloyd.

'Straight upstairs?' June asks.

'Huh? Yeah, sure,' Eluned mumbles.

June frowns. 'Are you sure?'

'I think so. I—' Eluned breaks off. She flicks her wrists, shaking the nerves out of her hands.

'Duck to water, mate,' says June.

At the top of the stairs, June kicks open a door to reveal a room with two single beds, a wardrobe and a small green sink. The walls are covered so thickly with photographs, posters and signs that it's hard to see the woodchip underneath. Eluned scans them greedily: June balancing on a woman's shoulders in a park, a large banner reading NF FREE ZONE, and a flyer for a gig at the Roundhouse. She's so engrossed in the walls that she doesn't notice the action in the other bed until a long breathy moan comes from underneath the duvet.

Eluned grabs June's elbow. 'This room is taken.'

'Half of it is my room,' June says, pointing at the other bed. 'The other half is Grit's. Give us some space?'

Grit throws back the duvet with a grumble. She's the double of Iman. Even in the gloom, her cheekbones are radiant. Her lips are ringed with a halo of different shades of lipstick. Underneath Grit is a gangly white girl with dyed red hair, her mouth, neck and earlobe smeared with the same mix of pink and purple.

Grit asks, 'Can't we turn the lights off and keep to our own sides?'

June looks at Eluned expectantly. She can't expect Eluned to . . . No, she can't do that. But, on the other hand, they'd be making noises in the dark, able to smell and hear each other. It's certainly something to think about. Something to consider in the future.

June sits down on the bed and starts pulling off her Docs. The carpet is olive green and thin, peeling up at the corners. You need to name it, Eluned. Name it.

Eluned puts her hands on her hips. 'I don't want to be funny or nothing, but I'm not doing it for the first time in front of an audience.'

'Fine,' Grit says. They gather their bedding and stomp to the hall. Eluned hears the soft thud of the fabric against the carpet outside the room. There's a loud thump, and the door rattles in its frame.

June shakes her head with fond laughter. 'They'll definitely carry on in the hall.'

Eluned perches next to June. She stares down at June's knitted socks. Rib stitch. Her eyes sting. She doesn't know what she's doing. She should go back to Mabli.

June stands in front of Eluned. Her legs are firmly planted on the floor, shoulders parallel to her hipbones. She strips off her leather jacket, lying it gently over a small wooden stool. Next is her T-shirt, flung carelessly to the corner of the room.

Eluned drinks in June's shoulders and arms. June's skin is pasty-white, with dark moles the size of 2p pieces. Her nipples look like kidney beans. She is going to touch that skin. It's going to happen. Someone yelps in the hallway.

'Are you cold?' June asks. 'Are you comfortable?'

Eluned whispers like she's in chapel. 'I'm all good.'

June untucks Eluned's T-shirt, playing with the hem. She whispers back, 'Can I pull this up?'

Eluned nods and June lifts the T-shirt over Eluned's head. She flutters her fingers along the lace trim of Eluned's bra. Eluned arches her back encouragingly, but June sweeps her hands from Eluned's bra to her belly button and back again.

'For heaven's sake,' Eluned blurts, 'I'm not actually a *virgin*.'

She's probably been shagging for longer than June has. June swings herself off the bed and kneels next to it, tummy crumpled over the waistband of her jeans. Eluned draws her toes up along the rough denim inseam, grinding the ball of her foot down into the centre point. June's burning up, and she twitches when Eluned wiggles her toes. She wiggles them again.

June tugs at Eluned's woollen skirt. 'Take this off and come and ride my face.'

'How?'

'I'll help.'

Eluned kicks her skirt off, followed by her suspender belt and cotton knickers.

June noses through Eluned's pubic hair and presses her face firmly to the fat over her mons. She snuffles loudly enough to drown out the moaning coming from other rooms. 'I love the way you smell. Put your feet a bit further apart. Bend your knees. Yes, that's it.'

June spreads Eluned's vulva open with her thumbs and leans between them. Her tongue is scorching. It doesn't take long before Eluned is panting, toes curling on the threadbare carpet. June sucks strongly over her clit, and Eluned's hips jerk forward. She attempts a first tentative thrust. June moans louder, vibrations raising the hairs on the back of her neck. Eluned can discern the bump of June's sharp jaw, the hard bridge of her nose and its softer tip. Eluned tries another, faster thrust, then another, which makes a slick sound across June's face. Eluned stares at the WE RECRUIT banner over Grit's bed. Is that what she is, a recruit? Will she end up on some tally chart somewhere?

June digs into her arse with her stubby nails. 'Look at me.'

Eluned takes a deep breath and meets June's eyes. Her snaggle-tooth scrapes at Eluned as she smiles into her. Right, it's time to go for it. June's hair is short, but she can still clasp it in her fist. With her other hand, she takes hold of June's bedside cabinet. With every thrust, the cabinet bumps the wall.

The house buzzes, thrums with shared pleasure. Eluned can barely hear herself. A headboard bangs next door, and there's slapping in the hall. A woman shrieks in the room above them, and the noises help Eluned along. June bobs on her knees, pushing up into Eluned as hard as she's pushing down.

Eluned holds June in place and grinds against her with short, sharp movements until her thighs burn. She needs consistent pressure in the same place. June kneads at Eluned's stomach, drawing her hands down as if she's trying to pull Eluned's orgasm through her tightly wound body and into June's mouth. It's working. June's going to be left with ten pink crescents on her scalp. The tip of her nose must be squashed sideways.

The thumping from next door pauses. Someone shouts, 'Nice one!' and the noise resumes. June scrambles back onto the bed with a smile splitting her face, teeth gleaming in the lamplight.

As soon as her heart slows down, Eluned pulls June up onto the bed. She licks herself off June's cheeks while unbuckling her belt. She can do this. This is a home from home. But when she reaches down to June's jeans and there's no straining dick, she falters. Surely instinct will kick in.

'Fuck me,' June pants. 'Get inside me.'

June lies beneath her, her legs splayed like a frog's. Her hipbones stand up beneath her freckled skin, and her mons is much flatter than Eluned's, her labia the same rich brown as her nipples. It's easy enough to slip two fingers inside June and use her thumb to rub loose circles around her clit. Inside, June is bumpier than she expected, and the flesh pushes back on Eluned. June's heels drum on the mattress and Eluned fucks her to the beat of them. She's like a horse in a race, pushing for the finish line. Her shoulder aches down to her elbow and into her wrist. She wants to fold herself up inside June like a letter in an envelope.

'Lie over me,' June says.

At first, she braces herself over June, so she doesn't crush her.

'I'm fine. I want to feel you.'

June groans deeply as Eluned transfers her weight. June reaches between them to touch herself; knuckles flexing into Eluned's stomach. June gives as good as she gets, clenching down on Eluned's hand. Whenever Eluned thinks it might be time to bring her fingers out, June's muscles spasm. Eluned pulls her fingers out and examines her wrinkled fingertips. Drums vibrate relentlessly through the ceiling, accompanied by rapid-fire shouting.

'Is that The Clash?' Eluned asks.

'Nah bab, Charged GBH. I only know because they're from up by me.'

Never heard of them. They shuffle about. June rests her head on Eluned's chest and shuts her eyes. Eluned can't sleep like this. Her house is always silent at night. Even when Dad stays up to watch old films, he puts the 888 subtitles on. She looks down at June, eyes still ringed with black liner.

'Are you taking your make-up off?'

June grunts in response.

According to Mabli, every night you sleep with make-up on ages your skin eight days. That seems like a fair price right now. Eluned counts the beats in the song playing upstairs. As soon as she stops concentrating on it, she is seized with a full-body spasm of guilt that brings up goosepimples from her bum to the backs of her thighs. In a way, this feels worse than the fucking. She and Lloyd have never slept together overnight; Jean won't allow it. Eluned has often imagined what it might be like to drift off with Lloyd's arms round her, and now she's experiencing it for the first time with someone else.

7

11 December 1984

Eluned startles awake. Grit and her woman are bundled in their blankets outside the door, and there are others sleeping curled together along the hallway. Eluned picks her way through them, trying to avoid stepping on hair or fingers.

Someone has thoughtfully left the door to the bathroom open, dim shaving light glowing above the mirror. The skin under her eyes is so dark it looks bruised and her eyeshadow has lost its shape. She was expecting to see something different. Something that says, *I just had lesbian sex*. Eluned can't resist having a nosy in the bathroom cabinet. There's not much in there, just a large tub of Sudocrem and a half-full bottle of blue mouthwash.

A quick wee, and then she'll go back to June's room. She won't get back into June's bed, she'll nudge Grit awake so she can go back to bed, and then find somewhere else to sleep. She's not fussy. Eluned taps her feet against the peeling lino floor. Mid-flow, a woman's head pokes around the door. She doesn't excuse herself, just comes in and closes the door behind her.

'Sorry love, I'm bursting.' She sounds like the woman who reads the evening news, with two fat braids of mousy hair and a knee-length nightgown.

Eluned's stream falters. No one has ever watched her piss before. Is this normal here?

'Am I putting you off? We're awful. You can't read in the bath without someone coming in and asking you what you're reading. I'm Lily, by the way.'

Eluned looks at a point above Lily's head. Nothing is coming out.

She gives up and wipes. 'Here, you go.'

Lily darts in behind Eluned, nightie hiked up and pissing before her arse hits the seat. She sighs in relief and gestures for Eluned to sit on the side of the bath.

Eluned asks, 'Did you have a good time at the concert?'

'I wish! I've got a daughter, so I had to stay in,' Lily says.

This doesn't seem like the sort of place where you'd raise a child. She didn't even realise lesbians had children.

'What's her name?'

'Dharma. Are you one of the Welsh lot?'

Someone in this house will know someone from the village, someone from the Committee. What if they've heard the noises coming from June's room? People talk, and Welsh people talk more than most. Her head feels hollow, like she's floating backwards. The lip of the bath is too thin to hold her. She's going to fall back, crack her head on the ceramic tub.

Lily grabs Eluned's thigh. She says, 'Are you alright, my love?'

Eluned stifles a fat sob. Kindness always does it. She can tolerate anything but kindness. It's easier to look at Lily's nightdress, count the forget-me-nots on her knees.

'Who are you staying with?' Lily asks.

'June,' says Eluned. She doesn't even know June's surname. 'Brummie June.'

'Oh, June Carr. June's a doll. Tell her that you're feeling homesick, she'll look after you.'

She would rather eat glass. The last thing she wants is for June to think that Eluned expects her to sort out her mess.

Lily runs a flannel under the cold tap. She gently wipes over Eluned's eyes and scrubs at the mess of her lipstick. It feels soothing. Lily doesn't mention the hot tears soaking into the flannel. She wrings it out and has another go at Eluned's face, until the water is grey. 'I'll see you at breakfast, sweetheart.'

Eluned creeps back to June's room. Grit is flat on her back, snoring. It's cruel to wake her up, she'll kip in Grit's bed. Grit took the quilt and pillows with her, but Eluned will get dressed. And then she looks over to June's bed. June's face is relaxed, lips slack and gold eyelashes fanned over her cheeks. Her legs are splayed open, the sheets underneath her dotted with old bloodstains and cigarette burns. Eluned looks closer at her labia; the gentle gradient from pink to brown is endearing.

Eluned gently shakes June's thigh. 'Can I . . .'

June's eyes are woozy with sleep, but she nods keenly, shuffling her hips so Eluned can fit between them. No difference between the genders there. Eluned brushes the pad of her thumb against June's labia and the delicate skin sticks to her. Eluned darts her tongue over June's hood. When June hisses, Eluned tries a long, flat swipe. She imagines June's clitoris brooch, the funny wishbone shape under the skin. Eluned wedges her hands under June to bring her up to her mouth, drinking from her like a bowl.

June yanks her hair. 'Don't move. But don't stop.' Her body bends upwards, stomach muscles jumping under the skin.

'Did you . . .? Did I make you . . .?'

June nods, pulling Eluned up her body. She reaches down to touch Eluned, but Eluned bats her hand away. It's not that she doesn't want to but the sky is turning indigo, and reality is bearing down.

June asks, 'When does your bus leave? You should rest if you can.'

'Eleven.'

'Try and get an hour or so in. I'll wake you up.'

* * *

Eluned's mouth is parched, her eyes gummy. Above the bed, there's a damp patch in the shape of an old man carrying a bale of hay. June is wedged under her armpit, one arm folded under Eluned's shoulder blades and the other wrapped round her waist. June's eyelids twitch with dreaming, and there's a crop of blocked pores on her chin.

'You alright?' June's voice is hoarse. She must be dying for a cigarette. Eluned wants a bucket of orange squash.

'Fantastic,' Eluned says flatly.

If she could stay here, she might feel better. But there's a hard knot of dread in her stomach. In a few short hours, she'll have to face Mabli, then Lloyd.

June leans over Eluned to root for her cigarettes. She lights two fags, hands Eluned one. June asks, 'Are you going back?'

Eluned is impatient. 'The bus goes at eleven. I said before.'

'Are you going to be on it?' June asks.

What is she going on about? She feels bad enough without June talking in riddles.

'What else am I going to do?'

'There are loads of squats in London. You can always find somewhere. And you could stay with dykes, communists—'

Eluned snaps. 'We're on strike, I'm the only one earning in my house. I can't fuck off to London.'

'Well, LGSM will be coming back and forth to your gaff for as long as the strike is on. I don't know if I'll be with them, but I can always give them the word to take you back with them in the van.'

Grit stumbles through the door, paint-stained T-shirt down to her knees. 'Fucking hell, it smells like one big fanny in here. Open a window! Arrow has been in the shower and I'm going to bath later. Do you want my slot?'

June sniffs her own armpit. 'Yeah, I need a wash. You coming?'

Eluned's hair is stiff and brittle with hairspray, and she's sticky down to her knees.

June grabs two grey towels. It's a bath-shower, a long metal hose with a cracked plastic head roughly tied to a pole on the wall. The water could be hotter, but it's not like she's had a warm shower at home in a while.

June tips shampoo into her palm, slapping the bottom of the bottle to get enough out. It's violently green, and smells of sharp, synthetic apples.

'Let me,' says Eluned. She swipes half of the small pool and lathers it up between her own hands. She works the suds through June's short hair and massages the bony lumps behind the back of June's ears, down the vertebrae of her neck to the top of the spine. They trade places. June's hands are deft and assured, taking Eluned's hair in sections as the shower spurts erratically. Eluned reaches between June's legs.

'I don't think we should,' says June, gently moving Eluned's hand away.

'Why not?'

'Last night was bosting. But you should have a think about what comes next.'

Thank fuck for the cold water pelting her cheeks. She moves her lips, but nothing comes out. Water fills the space between her tongue and teeth. She spits it out over their feet and within seconds it's washed away. Eluned clambers over the side of the bath and wraps herself in June's rough towel. She takes the second one for her hair. It will serve her right, patronising cow. She doesn't even look abashed, sauntering along the hallway nude.

Eluned has got nothing to wear but last night's clothes. If June wasn't such a dwt, she'd ask for a lend. She clips her suspenders into place and pulls on her skirt. It's not her finest sewing, some of the stitches are already starting to pull away. She'll be lucky to get it home in once piece.

June pulls on her jeans and catches Eluned staring at her lean freckled stomach. 'You better get your fill, for when you'll need it,' she says, pulling a white T-shirt and leather waistcoat over the top.

'When's that then?' Eluned asks.

'Tonight. Your wedding night. Every other night until you get boozed up enough to find yourself clawing your nails down the back of some other wife in the alley behind the corner shop.'

What if June's right? She's going to be stuck with this secret for as long as she lives. She's always going to know she is capable of this. What if it happens again? She feels as though she's bobbing along in the pool under Gwladys Falls, only just becoming aware of the depth of the water below her feet.

From a long way away, she hears June speak. 'I'm sorry, I was only joking. I know this must be hard for you. I've been through it myself. It's easy to forget how upset—'

She surfaces. 'It's not hard, it's not upsetting.'

It is both hard and upsetting.

June holds her hands out in surrender. 'Right, fine. Let's get you something greasy for the bus.'

The kitchen sounds rowdy. Cackling, screaming, good-natured bickering. No way she can walk in there. June waits for Eluned at the doorway but when she hovers outside, June shrugs and walks in alone. Eluned peeks around the door-jamb. There are two squashy, mismatched sofas and a coffee table full of dirty glasses and full ashtrays. Women are crushed onto the sofas, tucked underneath layers of crocheted blankets. That must be Grit, wearing sunglasses and a silk scarf tied tight round her head. The blond girl lies underneath her, fag held precariously in her lips. June chatters away somewhere in the room. Eluned should go in. She should thank them for organising Pits and Perverts, for slugging their guts out to raise money for the village. They must think she's a real shit. Everyone else turned out for the miners, and the only thing she was thinking about was getting her end away.

June emerges with two foil parcels. 'Fine fittle for you, sausage and egg. Put brown sauce in, hope that's alright.'

'Brown will do me. Thanks.'

'Stick it in your pocket. You can warm your hands up with it later.'

June's lacing her Docs, leaning against the wall with one knee bent over the other. The foil warms her hip. It would be easy to kiss her, zip up her jacket while their lips meet. She doesn't have the right to do that. This isn't some domestic scene. It's not a Monday morning, June isn't her girlfriend sending her off to work.

Eluned remembers the way back to the Electric Ballroom, but June insists on chaperoning her, rattling on about the neighbourhood; about the posh bastards who want the squat gone, the offie that sells cheap fags under the counter, and the time she saw Steve Strange in Camden Market.

'Do you think it's weird I still live with Mam and Dad?'

'Most of the wenches up Brum have stayed at home until they're married. That's what everyone does, isn't it? What's The Meatsack's worst habit?'

'Bad singing, probably.'

'Toilet seat?'

'Always down. His mam's like Stalin.'

'Sounds like you're sorted then. That's enough for a lifetime.'

At the corner, June's hand wraps round her wrist. 'Hang on. I'll leave you here, but I want to give you these first.'

June hands her two battered business cards. The first is for London Lesbian and Gay Switchboard.

'If you ever need to talk to someone, anonymously.'

That's unlikely to happen. She's not a lesbian. The second is for London Women's Housing Cooperative.

'They can help get you somewhere to stay if you're at a loose end. Whatever the reason. The squat phone number is on the back. We might get cut off, it's happened before, but you might as well have it for now.'

Eluned tucks the cards inside her pocket mirror.

June's hand disappears back into her pocket, and she brings out a Mars bar with a flourish. 'For the journey.'

Eluned swallows thickly as she tucks it into her handbag. It's a ridiculous thing to cry about. They're only 20p. June might not want a hug from her. Not now, not ever. Then June spreads her arms and Eluned steps into them, squeezing her body until her leather jacket squeaks. The smell on the inside of June's collar is more mellow than her shampoo; the smell from between her thighs, under her arms, her bedsheets.

June steps back. 'It's been nice having you stop with us.'

A kiss. One last one. It would be so easy. Instead, she claps June on the shoulder and rounds the corner. Don't look back.

Shit, she must be late. Everyone else is standing near the bus.

'Sorry I'm late!' she shouts brightly, trying to disguise how shagged her voice is.

'Where did you go last night? I thought you were dead,' Mabli shouts, throwing her lit cigarette into the road and storming towards Eluned. Same angry stomp as Mamgu. Mabli swings Eluned's overnight bag off her shoulder and shoves it roughly into Eluned's stomach. That can of Elnett is like a battering ram.

'Mabli! Listen. I was speaking to June from LGSM for a minute. One minute. I came back and you'd left. I didn't know what to do, I didn't know how to get back—'

'That's bollocks! We waited for you for twenty minutes. You're meant to be looking out for me.' Mabli's voice frays at the end.

Mabli's right. She's a liar. Eluned looks down at her shoes. 'I'm so sorry. Please don't tell Mam.'

Mabli sniffs and squares her jaw. Eluned's ignominy seems to fortify her.

'Get on the bus. Don't speak to me until we get home.' Mabli's voice is cold. She briskly unwraps the cord of their headphones from round their Binatone player and places the two speakers over her ears, jabbing at the play button. No sharing today.

Eluned skulks onto the minibus. As he climbs up after her, Aled puts his hand on her shoulder. 'Where did you go?'

'House party in Camden,' Eluned replies shortly, rummaging in her bag for something to pull across her eyes. Mabli's packed Eluned's bag up for her in a deliberately obstructive way, anything useful at the bottom and her knickers right at the top. Eluned's London mixtape is carelessly jammed in a side pocket.

'A house party in Camden. It's like that is it?' Aled teases.

'Leave me alone a minute.'

He slaps her headrest hard enough to make it bounce, rattling her throbbing eye sockets. She gives him the finger and he laughs, making his way down the minibus aisle. Eluned keeps rummaging, eyes on her bag as everyone else files past, taking their seats.

Mabli scoots her skinny arse as far away from Eluned as she can manage, and crosses one leg over the other. Eluned sneaks a look at her; she looks awful, with dark purple shadows under her eyes and dull skin. The speakers hiss. Eluned can just about make out the beat. Mabli can't have slept. Her fear must have been genuine. That sinking, shameful feeling sucks Eluned down again. She reaches across to wrap her fingers round Mabli's, but Mabli shakes her off and shuts her eyes.

Camden recedes into the distance. The Electric Ballroom. VICTORY TO THE MINERS. Their first journey in reverse. God, if she could make it go the other way. If only it could be yesterday again. Eluned ties her jumper across her face. With the sleeves tucked in over her eyes, it blocks out the light. June's butty is still warm. If she eats, she'll puke. Everyone will make a fuss if she pukes, so it's best to close her eyes and pretend she has a cassette player of her own.

Eluned tries to recall Madonna's 'Like a Virgin' video, imagining prancing through Venice in her tulle dress followed by a lion. It's not enough of a distraction. She is an absolute shitbag. What was she thinking? Leaving Mabli alone in London, making a mockery of her relationship with Lloyd. She doesn't deserve her kind, soft boyfriend, or her loving parents. She judges Mabli but she's got no right to; she's betrayed the cause as much as Mabli has. Her jumper soaks up her tears. The bus driver has ramped up the heating, and hot, recycled air is blowing up from the vent by her feet. There are still hours to go. She'll never make it without puking. The window is cold, at least, even though it hurts where it bumps against her face.

Surely a normal girl wouldn't have gone through with it. A snog, fine. A bit of a grope, maybe. Normal girls don't think about Madonna when they fall asleep, and maybe normal girls didn't rip handfuls of forget-me-nots out from between bricks on the way to school to give to their favourite primary school dinner lady.

Eluned prefers to look things directly in the face. When they were children, she and Mabli had found a dying bird in the garden. One wing ripped off, the other blood-streaked and twitching ferociously. She'd wrapped her hands in her jumper and scooped it up, warm blood seeping through the fabric. Mabli covered her eyes, walked ahead of Eluned like a gruesome bridesmaid. Eluned kept her eyes fixed on the lump of gristle where its throat used to be.

She loves Lloyd. She desires him. But it doesn't take a genius to work out what happened this weekend. Eventually someone will piece it together, then the rumour will start, and it won't take five minutes for it to reach Lloyd. When that happens, does she have the strength to lie to his face? If she lies today then there will always be a mine shaft running the length of their relationship, waiting to collapse and take the rest down with it. Can she honestly say it won't happen again? No. June's right. She can't say that. She can't promise that, some years from now, she won't invite friends to their home, pouring too much wine and hoping that the night gets messy.

What if, after all this, Lloyd is still the one that feels like home? If he's moved on before she sorts herself out, will it be worth it?

8

When the minibus pulls up outside the Welfare Hall, Mabli prods the seatbelt fastening and is off the bus before Eluned can pull her overnight bag from underneath the seat in front.

Lloyd is parked up on the gravel. She could pretend to not see him, walk the long way home. He beeps the horn. Deep breath. Before she finishes it, he's jogging over. Her heart speeds up.

'I've missed you! Did you have a good time? Let me take your bag,' he says. He's wearing a freshly ironed polo shirt and smells like Brut.

Eluned twists her shoulder away from him, 'No, Lloyd, I can carry it.'

'Let me put it in the back of the car, cariad. It's heavy.'

Fine. Never mind that she's managed to carry it this far. Fine. Eluned lets the bag slide off her shoulder and land at her feet with a thump.

Lloyd shakes his head as he bends to pick the strap up from the gravel. 'What did you do that for? You like being a dick-head, don't you?'

He pops open the passenger seat, and for a second she's tempted to sit in the back so that she can open the door herself.

'I thought you said you had no petrol,' she says.

'It's only a quarter-tank, so I could pick you up and you could tell me about the concert.'

Lloyd liked 'Smalltown Boy' more than Eluned when it first came out; it wasn't fair that he missed out on it. She wants to go back to his house, lie on his chest and listen to *Seventeen*

Seconds. No, she wants to heave her guts up and stand under a cold shower for as long as it takes for her to feel numb.

'Was it good?' Lloyd asks.

'Brilliant,' she admits. Her throat is raw from screaming, and her voice sounds hoarse. 'They must have raised thousands.'

He pumps his fist. She needs a fag. They'll have to go twos, she's on her last packet for the week. Lloyd can have the first half. He holds it between his teeth as he swings out of the car park towards their usual spot.

He asks, 'Did you see any men dressed as women?'

'A few. They were glam.' She looks out the window, watches the hills roll by.

'Did you ride on the Tube?'

'We didn't do much.'

'Did Margaret Thatcher come?'

'Bitch didn't show.'

Lloyd barks a laugh and strokes her thigh. The road is straight and quiet, he doesn't need both hands to drive. She bucks it off. It's hard to look at him.

Lloyd parks up in their lay-by, beneath the cemetery. He pushes the seat of his chair back and presses play on the tape deck. It's one of the mixtapes she's recorded off the radio; a selection of their favourite singles.

'I missed you.' He lowers his eyes, lashes casting long shadows on his cheek in the weak winter sun.

Eluned presses down the latch on the glove compartment and roots around listlessly, flicking the cassette cases from one side and then the other.

'If you want to put something else on the stereo, you can.'

The dying bird and its throbbing wet neck. That fluttering wing. Time to grab something heavy and do what she glimpsed Dad do through the crack in the door.

'What's wrong?' Lloyd asks, taking off his seatbelt so he can turn and speak to her.

Eluned bashes the door of the glove compartment against the latch. She can't look at him. She does it again. Lloyd puts his hand over the latch. She pauses, holding the compartment drawer.

''Lun, what is it?'

She studies his hand. Those short nails kept fastidiously clean, the square tan lines where his Casio usually sits, the clusters of clear, itchy blisters on the sides of his fingers that spring up after too much handwashing.

'I was unfaithful to you this weekend.'

Lloyd blinks. Come on, say something.

'Tell me you're joking.'

'I'm not joking,' she whispers.

'Was it with one of the boys?'

She can't look up. 'No, it . . .'

'It was a lesbian, wasn't it?'

She nods, twisting the strap of her bag round her wrists.

'You didn't. You can't have. You're having me on. What did you do? Kiss her?'

For the first time, she looks up. His brow is knitted together, eyes ranging around the car.

'More than kissing. I'm sorry. It's like that box. You know, the box. You can't put it back once it's out.'

'Fuck! Bollocks! Fuck!' Lloyd slams his fists into the steering wheel. The car shakes.

Eluned squeezes the door handle. Slowly, slowly – until the door pops open. Thank fuck she hasn't fastened her seatbelt yet. She slides one leg out, transfers her weight to it. Ready. Dad has never laid a hand on Mam and Lloyd is soft as shit, but Mamgu always warned her that men can turn on a sixpence.

Lloyd says, 'Come back inside the car. I won't hurt you. You must know that.'

He moves his hand from the steering wheel to her leg again. She wants to suck the words back in, rewind and tape over them like a cassette. There's still time for her to tell him that it's a lie, that she's having a joke. He'd probably even laugh. He's used to people trying to get the better of him. If she cuffed his head and called him a silly boy, it would go away. Especially if she gave him a blowie afterwards.

'Lloyd, what are you going to do when we win the strike?'

He rubs his eyes. 'I'll go back to work. What else would I do?'

'What if we don't win? Or what if we do, but it shuts down anyway?'

'How am I supposed to know that? Why are you asking me that? For fuck's sake, we were talking about you—'

She won't let up. 'You've learnt so much, you've done well. You could think about doing something different.'

His voice is strained. 'I don't want anything different. I want a normal life, with you. Everything we want is here.'

Lloyd rests his face on the steering wheel. She rubs his back in big circles. This isn't what she wanted.

He shakes her off. 'You won't get any of that if you run off with a woman. I don't blame you for getting swept up. London. The big concert. New friends. We've been together a while and it's good to have fun, but that's not what real life is about. We can forget about it, I won't tell anyone.'

June seemed to be leading a very real life. 'I didn't get swept up. I don't want to forget.'

Lloyd flinches. For the first time, his eyes brim with tears.

'I'm not telling you because I want to hurt you,' she says.

'Well, you are hurting me. Was it the one you was speaking to at the Welfare? The scrawny one with the teeth?'

Eluned folds her arms across her chest, scratches at her elbow.

Lloyd scrubs his hand over his face. 'She wouldn't have been my choice. You know, of the lesbians.'

Eluned snickers, and even Lloyd hiccups out a laugh.

'What now?' he says. 'You going to be a real dyke, shave your head and move to London?'

'I think that's going a bit far. Maybe Cardiff and a trim.'

His lips twitch upwards. Thank God for that. Maybe one day they'll laugh about this.

'Are you sure this is what you want? I've loved you for years.'

'I love you too.' She doesn't need to think about it. It's true. She loves him. She could cry if she let herself, she could work herself up into a right old state. She'd love to be babied and told that it will work out. But it's a mess of her own making and there's nothing she can do but look it square in the face.

'Eluned, can't you at least try?' Lloyd whispers.

'I've been trying, love. I've been trying for years, before I even knew that I was trying.'

Lloyd shuts his eyes. His nostrils flare and a muscle in his jaw twitches.

Eluned asks, 'Could you please drive me home?'

Lloyd twists the key in the ignition and the windscreen wipers shudder into life. The car is sluggish and Lloyd grunts as he heaves the car back on the road. He agrees that they will tell their parents, but keep the reasons between them for now. He assures Eluned that he is in no rush to let the lads know that Eluned has left him after shagging a woman. He won't let her down. As he parks the car, she leans in for a kiss. Muscle memory. In the second before the self-disgust sparks up, it feels pleasurable. This is not right. She pulls back and slips out of the car, weekend bag over her shoulder.

Rain hits the pavement in sheets, pinging off the bonnet. As she scuttles to the house, she hears Lloyd sobbing.

Mam is shouting before Eluned takes her shoes off.

'Thank God you're home. Mabli came tromping in here with a face like thunder. No, "London was great, thank you for lending me your handbag." No, "How was your weekend, Mam? What did you get up to?" She had a cuppa and pissed off back to Graham's house. Can you please offer us some cheerful news?'

'I ended things with Lloyd.'

'No.' Mam sounds winded. 'You haven't. You love that boy.'

'I love him but it's not right.'

Mam blocks her path up the stairs. She needs to get up to her room and have a sleep. Her eyes are the size of golf balls, dry as sand.

'Mam, let me through.'

'You stupid girl,' Mam says, shaking her head. 'Let's face it, you're never going to have the pick of them. Lloyd is not the sharpest, but he's leagues ahead of some of the specimens around here. What are you going to do now?'

Eluned grits her teeth. 'It's not about that, Mam. Let me go up to bed.'

Eluned slides the business cards that June gave her out of her wallet. Her wall is covered with a collage from her favourite magazines. So childish. At the centre she has tacked up a poster of Madonna from *Smash Hits* magazine. Madge looks beautiful: black suede beret, black rubber bracelets up her wrists, red lipstick. That mole over her mouth. It's a good hiding place. She peels back one corner, sticks the cards to the wall, and sticks the poster down over them again.

The Mars bar fits at the back of her bedside cabinet drawer, in between a tin of hair bobbles and a hard white vibrator that Lloyd had managed to buy her from God knows where. It clatters like the shed door in a storm, so she's not done much with it apart from giggling with Mabli, but he was so pleased with himself for finding it. There's an old birthday card from him too, creased and bent around the back of the drawer. Now isn't the time to read it.

She pushes her fond memories back with it. There are six years of the bastards to choose from. In year nine, Claire told Bron to tell Eluned that Lloyd told Morgan he liked her. It was impossible. Her blouse wasn't even from the school shop. Her mother had to take her to Peacocks to get one in a women's size 16. She'd hacked the labels out, thrown them in the fire. She spent every lesson tugging at her collar, always too snug for her fat neck. Lloyd Thomas, fancying her enough to tell people about it! Who would have thought? After advice from Megan, she corralled him after French and asked if he liked Blondie. He did. He asked her if she had *Parallel Lines*, or if she wanted to borrow his copy. She did. There is a funny sort of serendipity in that; he could be listening to 'Heart of Glass' right now.

After he asked her out, she spent every Friday evening in the park with his friends. Cider and chips. His thumbs hooked through her belt loops. There was the time she dressed him up as Robert Smith, snickering behind his locked bedroom door while she ringed his eyes in kohl and applied bright red lipstick. They'd fucked with the make-up on, and afterwards he'd let her take a picture of him. It's still on a roll of film in his room somewhere.

Six years. She's a real piece of work. She fishes dirt out from under her nail with an old earring. Her finger slips, and she jams the post deep into her nail bed. Blood pools. She squashes it with her thumb to see the jammy purple spread out underneath her nail. She should be sadder. She should want to turn herself inside out like an old glove, but now the panic has settled there is something else growing.

Mabli is right about some things. Margaret Thatcher will never be inspirational, but in the village it's hard to do what people don't expect you to do. You float in the same current as everyone else, and tell yourself there's time, still time. She feels like Mam's lavender bush, clipped back to the bare wood to make room for new shoots in spring. She folds her hands over her belly. Her hands rise as her chest fills. She feels the point where she normally exhales and keeps inhaling. She's unstoppable, caverns inside her she's never felt before. Her hands rise higher still. No wedding to plan, no ticking clock. She lets the air go.

9

10 January 1985

Christmas is a bust. 'Do They Know It's Christmas?' does Eluned's head in, especially after Mair changes the label on the miners' fund collection tin to Live Aid. No one's put anything in the tin for weeks, so it's not like it makes a difference. She tolerates the first minute of the Queen's speech, but after the old bat pontificates that 'there is too much concentration on the gloomy side of life' she decisively switches it off. Still, the kiddies get their presents, topped up by donations shipped over from Italy, France and the USSR. LGSM sent over about four grand, but it's a drop in the ocean compared to what they need. Lloyd's Christmas card downgrades her from 'love you forever' to 'best regards', but she gets the *Smash Hits* Yearbook and a set of three Bic pens from her parents.

It's obvious that something is wrong when she walks into Blossoms' stockroom. Mair usually orders new stock about this time, keen to mop up the women buying themselves a treat to tide them over to the spring. Not a hint of a customer. Eluned sweeps up the tiny polystyrene balls of snow from the window. They bounce away into the corners as fast as she can sweep them, which at least gives her something to do. With an hour of her shift to go, Mair calls her to the backroom.

'Bach. I'm not sure how to go about this, but I need a word with you.'

With a sinking feeling, she knows where this is going. The ironmongers never reopened after Christmas, and the pub down by the main road has got a For Sale sign up. It's easier to stare at her knees than to look up into Mair's kind face.

'I'm retiring. All summer I've been using my savings to top us up. But I'm no spring chicken. If I don't retire soon, they're going to be taking me out in a box, never mind the shoes!'

There's no argument Eluned can make. Sales have been dismal; some days she takes more home than she's sold. She tries to earn her keep; the shelves and mirrors are always smear-free. But she can't blame Mair. This is the last part of her old life left, now she's dumped Lloyd and fallen out with Mabli. How can she go home and tell Mam and Dad? How will they manage without her wages? Will the dole office let her sign on?

Mair sounds like she's talking through a kitchen roll tube. 'You look terrible, bach. I'll drive you home.'

The drive passes in a blur. She's not clear how she got up to her room. She's got a hazy memory of the pressure of hands manoeuvring her through the hallway and up the stairs. Muffled voices in the hall. She stares up at Madonna until it gets dark.

Mam opens the door. 'Mair said to give you this,' she says, handing over a shoebox.

Eluned lifts the lid. It smells of the shop; new leather, L'Air du Temps, and their window-cleaning spray. That familiar scent will already be fading, to be replaced by the smell of fat and vinegar, or raw meat, or whatever the shop will be turned into next. Inside the box, one of their bestsellers lies on a bed of white tissue paper. Sensible court shoes in a soft leather. Eluned would rather have her dream shoes, but they'll probably be sent back to the supplier with the rest of the unsold stock. Underneath the tissue paper there are two envelopes. One is cash, the other a reference. Mair is a good egg.

* * *

January trickles past and Eluned spends it staring out of the window for most of the day. Someone comes down from LGSM, but he comes alone. Eluned's head is as blank as the frosted grey sky. Mam and Dad start off inviting her to the Welfare Hall and the picket line, but they soon stop asking. Mam allocates bits of the housework to her, but she's exhausted by the time she's mopped the kitchen floor and dusted the TV. The only thing between her ears is the telly schedule. Some days she turns on *Bullseye*, retreats inside her head, and doesn't resurface until Bully's Star Prize Gamble. On other days she finds herself with the TV and the radio on at once, neither one penetrating the white fuzz in her head. Dad sits with her when he's not at the pickets, his heavy hand pressing on her head, anchoring her to the world. In the afternoons she brings her sketchbook out, shunting her pencil around aimlessly. Her drawings are repetitive, with feathery, fragmented lines.

Eluned sits on Mabli's old bed; the bare walls make it easier to think. Mabli didn't leave much behind. Some bobby pins, a broken stapler and a few naff old records. It's not a surprise that 'Werewolves of London' didn't make the grade, but strange that she didn't take Blondie's *The Hunter*. Eluned stashes it under her armpit. She'll have another listen. There are rumblings that the strike might be ending. Every day there's something different in the papers: the new union in Nottinghamshire, Afghanistan bussing over raisins, Scargill's inflexibility. Too much to make sense of. Mabli would have a take on it, at least. Just when Eluned has talked herself into getting the bus down to Mabli's office and asking to speak to her, she gets a surge of anger at Mabli leaving now, when they're up to their necks in it. Eluned's hanging on by a thread, but at least she's stayed with Dad through all this. If she was like Mabli, she could have called the number on June's business card, got herself somewhere to stay in London. But she's sticking it out to the end.

Lloyd walks past now and again, coming back from the picket or on the way to the Welfare Hall. He's grown his hair and his sideburns out, so he looks like Gerald Davies. Does she imagine it, or does he slow down when he passes by? Does he glance up at her bedroom window? If he does, it's not for long. She listens to Richard Skinner doing the Official Sunday Chart, but shuts it off when he gets down to number three. Foreigner are almost certainly number one with 'I Want to Know What Love Is', and she doesn't feel the need to put herself through that.

Eluned finds a quid stuck in the lining of an old handbag. She should give it to her parents. They could get a packet of fags or some biscuits. Or, she could take it to the phone box down the street. She makes a break for it when her parents are glued to a repeat of *Juliet Bravo*, quid and business card stuffed in her pocket. Squashed into one side of the box, she has a three-way vantage point. The receiver is Baltic. She wraps her hand in her jumper sleeve.

She dials June's number. June said they might be cut off, it's pointless to get excited. The dial tone is jarringly loud inside the small, square booth. A woman answers, and says she'll fetch her, leaving Eluned to listen to the snatches of conversation going on in the squat. The screen displays the money she's got left. It's already ticking down. 95. 90. 85. What if they can't find June in time? What if her precious pound runs down, and all she has to show for it is overhearing the hubbub of someone else's house? Is that worth more than a magazine? A block of cheese? Some tins to put in the food parcels?

'It's me,' June snaps down the receiver. Eluned jumps, fumbling with the handset.

'It's Eluned.'

June's voice softens. 'I was hoping you'd call. How's everything going? We went collecting in The Bell last night. We wouldn't usually, but—'

'Save it for the Committee. I don't want to talk about any of that.'

'What do you want to talk about?'

Eluned wants to scream. How can June be so dense? 'Have you got off with anyone lately?'

'Er – I thought what we had was a one-time thing. You had a boyfriend and I assumed . . .'

'I want to know that someone is living out there. That the world still exists and I can come join it when this is done.'

'Then yeah, I have. Last night.'

June's bed might still be warm. She might not have showered. She'd sell Mamgu's jewellery box to smell the warm spot behind June's ears.

'What was it like?'

More coins drop down into the machine. 75. 70.

'We met at Heaven. I went home with her. She lived in Peckham. She had good tits.'

'Did you eat her out?'

'Mmhmm.'

Eluned's reflection is distorted on the phone's dented metal panel. She leans close enough to see that her pupils are blown, her nostrils flared. She screws her eyes shut. 'I want to do that again. I want to get good at it.'

55. 50.

June's voice is shagged. 'There are other people here.'

If June is flustered, she has the upper hand. She cups her hand round her mouth and the well of filth in her chest bubbles over. She lets the words run out of her until she's down to her last 20p.

'I want to do things to you that I haven't even heard of yet,' she finishes.

The sides of the phone box are fogged up. She writes J+E WOZ ERE with her finger in the condensation.

Her last 10p.

'I've got to go, June. The money's running out.'

'You're a fighter, I swear. You are,' June says.

The line goes dead. June could return the call to the phone box. But that would involve questions about Lloyd and the strike. That's the last thing she needs. Eluned counts to twenty and leaves the box, the frosty air needling her face.

They're about wrapping up the murder by the time Eluned slips into the hallway.

'Eluned, is that you? Come here for a cwtch.'

Mam will only follow her upstairs if she doesn't.

'Duw duw. Your head is boiling but your hands are like ice.'

'I'm fine,' she says, swatting at Mam's hands.

Mam goes back to the telly. They're sitting here, watching some dickhead in a flat cap get nicked. Eluned is floating up near the ceiling, looking down at them. They think they know her, but she's never felt further from them. Her hands are unfamiliar. She fans her fingers, feels queasy at the way the tendons stretch over the knuckles. They're not right, not hers. When she flexes those knuckles, they look like some strange pulsating sea creature. Only the throbbing between her legs feels solid. Dependable. It's the red kite-string keeping her on this sofa, inside this house.

10

11 February 1985

'You need to do something about Eluned,' says Mam from the hall.

Great. This again. Eluned turns *Pebble Mill* up and pulls the crocheted blanket round her shoulders. They're happy to stand in the kitchen and whisper about her, but it hasn't occurred to them to talk to her.

Dad says, 'What can I do? She's fine, she's quiet.'

'Fine? Iesu Grist! She's not fine. Eluned has never, *never* been quiet—'

'Calm down.'

Thank you, Dad. He's washing up, a new development, while Mam does Committee paperwork and harangues him.

'I can't calm down, Emyr. We've got one daughter shacked up with a copper twice her age, and one that's on the verge of the madhouse.'

'Eluned needs time. She went to the Welfare yesterday, didn't she?'

Mam had been brilliant, tallying the food donations and divvying them up into parcels. She'd done the calculations in her head before Eluned had even finished listening to the list of items. Eluned's brain runs so slowly these days, it's easier to stay in bed.

Dad talks her into letting him give her driving lessons. He couldn't teach her how to measure circumference without causing a row, so God knows why he's putting them through this. At least it's something to do. They've had the same car for years. The gearstick is stiff, the ceiling stained yellow with cigarette smoke and the driver's seat black from years of coal dust. It's weird to be in the driving seat. Dad helps her guide the car on to the road and down their steep hill. She squeezes the steering wheel, pulling as if she can control the machine by force.

When the car is on the flat Dad directs her round the corner, to park up outside the shop. He says, 'Your mam is driving herself mental trying to work out why you dumped Lloyd.'

'Don't start with the Jolly Twp Giant stuff,' she says.

'Ah, there's no malice in it. He's good as gold. But what do you think I wanted to do at your age?'

Eluned scrunches her nose. She's never thought about it. 'Something with music?'

Dad mimes throwing a dart. 'Bull's-eye. I would have loved my own record shop.'

She can see it now. The ageing mod, still stuck in his braces, boring pretty women about grain count and sleeve notes.

'Why didn't you?'

'No point thinking of anything else. I'm a miner because my dad was a miner. We had you by the time I was twenty-two. If something good comes out of this, it's that you two can choose for yourselves. I've fucked my back, my lungs. And for what? Prats are writing to the rags to call us lazy traitors.' Dad pokes at the rolled-up newspaper on the dashboard. 'What a waste of time.'

'I think people are afraid of—'

Dad shrugs. 'You and I could drive into that wall and it wouldn't make a difference to anything.'

Iesu. If there's anyone in this family off to the madhouse, it's not her. 'I don't think that's true, Dad. It would make a lot of difference to us.'

Dad puts his hand over hers. 'I know. What I mean to say, is you're down one round, but you've got time to get a few good punches in.'

If only she was small again. Sitting in the back seat, his waxed coat heavy over her knees, raindrops racing across the window.

Dad sells his cufflinks to pay for Eluned's driving test, and her only reward is driving the van for the Welfare Hall. The hills are lethal in this weather. She's taking her life in her hands every time she gets in the van, and it's worse when Rhiannon and Dan the baby are with her. The last thing she wants is to be responsible for them too. Their mission is to collect an oven that's being donated and take it to a family without one.

The van is so cold that Eluned wraps her scarf round her fingers before she is brave enough to touch the steering wheel, and Rhiannon throws a mug of warm water over the windscreen to melt the ice. The two women lash old rope round the cooker, tying it securely to the inside of the van. Eluned shoulders the gearstick and the van creaks up the hill. There are slim pickings when it comes to the music selection. Eluned and Rhiannon settle for *Sgt. Pepper's Lonely Hearts Club Band*, trying to sing 'Lucy in the Sky with Diamonds' loud enough to distract Dan from the banshee-like noise that the frozen branches make as they scrape along the roof.

'Is it true that you pulled a girl when you went to London before Christmas?'

Eluned's hands jump on the wheel. 'Who said that?'

'Aled and Owain said that after the gig you disappeared, and no one saw you until the next day. Then you and Lloyd suddenly break up.'

Eluned shakes her head, trying to look as casual as she can. 'That's not what happened. Owain was late, he didn't even see me. I went back to a party with some of the LGSM lot. I would have invited Mabs but you know how she is.'

Rhiannon nods sagely and slips a mitten back on Dan's hand. Good job they're on strings, he can't manage to keep them on for more than a minute at a time.

'Have you seen Lloyd?'

'Only on the street,' Eluned says.

Rhiannon dangles her housekeys in front of Dan's pudgy face. 'We saw him down the Welfare. He says he's getting back into rugby. Now he's lost his puppy fat he is getting hunky.'

Eluned's throat closes. She tries to swallow but her throat is full of dust from behind the old cooker. 'He was always hunky, I liked him with a bit of meat.'

Rhiannon makes a non-committal noise, letting Dan gnaw on her keyring while she stares out the window at the snow-dusted Fan Gyhirych. 'I've kissed girls before,' Rhiannon says placidly, pulling Dan's woollen hat down over his reddened ears.

'Have you?' That's a turn-up for the books.

'Just random girls, from when we used to go to Swansea. The boys always went wild for it.'

'I'll bet,' says Eluned. 'What was it like?'

'Soft. Delicate. Girls smell better, they don't try and grab you all at once,' Rhiannon says.

Eluned begs to differ. She was desperate to get June's body close to hers. June smelt of beer and fags and sweat and had sharp teeth that nicked Eluned's lips.

Rhiannon lowers her voice. 'One time we kissed in the toilets as well. We'd done it by the bar, but then we wanted another go.'

Eluned could admit it. She could tell Rhiannon that not only has she kissed one, but she's also fucked one. Rhiannon's gaze flits between Eluned's lips and eyes. Oh. She's doing that thing, isn't she? The thing people do. Rhiannon tilts her head towards Eluned. This is a bad idea, a phenomenally stupid idea. Rhiannon is married. Rhiannon is a gossip. But even ten minutes of physical comfort would sort her for at least a month, surely it would. If Rhiannon pulled up her skirt and shuffled about, Eluned's head could fit sideways between Rhiannon's thick thighs.

Dan cries, breaking whatever moment there is. Rhiannon's hands fly under his armpits, dandling him over her knee, and she starts singing 'Dacw 'Nghariad' in her high sweet voice. Eluned joins in, the Welsh coming back to her as she sings. The rolling, repetitive chorus soothes Dan, and he's soon giggling at the pair of them.

Eluned drives them to the house where they're dropping off the oven. They heave it out of the back of the van, working in unison to drag it up the path, over the step and down the narrow hallway.

11

3 March 1985

Dad loves *Dad's Army*. There's nothing worse than watching those boorish old men make mistake after mistake, but at least it raises a chuckle. Someone is bumbling around in a diver's suit when white text appears on the screen. 'National Union of Mineworkers vote to return to work on Tuesday. More at 3.30.'

'Well,' manages Dad.

Eluned puts the kettle on and they wait in tense silence for the familiar jingle of the news programme. Mam hushes the silent room.

The newsreader sits behind his desk with perfect silver hair and a powder-blue suit.

It's the worst result possible. A narrow vote. Capitulation without achieving any of the aims. No amnesty for miners who have been sacked, not even the ones being wound up by the police.

Scargill's tone is conciliatory, measured. After his statement, the camera moves to the crowds outside. NUM executives push through angry miners, barely held back by lines of police. Footage moves to a man in the pub. About Lloyd's age, with sharp blue eyes. He says, 'I feel sold down the river. We've achieved nothing.'

A tear rolls down his ruddy cheek. He swipes it away and takes a long swallow of his pint. Mam stares at the screen, mouth agape. The newsreader announces that they are now going live to the Prime Minister.

Mam's quickest off the mark, seizing the remote and jabbing it at the TV. 'I'm not listening to that witch speak,' she says. 'If I see a smirk on her face, I'll drive to London and smack it off.'

All that strife, all that suffering, for nothing. Pits across the country will close, and others will follow. But until then, Dad will be earning. They won't need her income. LGSM are still fundraising for them, although this time the money is mainly going to men who got the sack while they were on the picket; Mam said they want to capitalise upon the dubious rumour that St Patrick was from here to promote some St Patrick's Day event. The grey slopes of the valley fall away around her like a cardboard film set. It's freedom at a cost, but it's freedom.

The men go back on Tuesday. Mam has written a poem about how proud she is of Dad, and it gets published in the *Valley Star*. He hasn't seen it yet; she's saving it for later. Eluned knocks at Lloyd's house before the formal march. The curtains twitch, and she catches the flash of Jean's eye before the lace is pulled tightly closed. She knocks a second time, then a third. Come on Jean, you fusty old cow. The door swings open, and even though Jean is only five foot and a fart, her glare puts the fear of God into Eluned. At least she won't be dealing with her for the rest of her life.

'I've come to say good luck,' Eluned says. 'Can I come in?'

Jean's mouth squeezes tight like a cat's arse as she opens the door in miserly fashion. She doesn't stand out of the way, and seems to swell with righteousness as Eluned tries to squeeze pass. Eluned turns sideways to shuffle along the wall; if her belt scags the wallpaper, she's not hearing nothing about it.

'He's in the lounge. I'll wait here,' Jean says. The front door stays open.

Lloyd's work jacket is too big. He looks ridiculous, with the shoulder seams halfway down his arms. If he had asked, she would have fixed that for him.

She holds out the blue and white bag. 'I brought you lunch.'

'Mam made me lunch.'

'You've never refused a second lunch before.'

He takes the bag and peeks inside, grinning when he sees the biscuits that she's wrapped in cling film. Bourbons. His favourite.

'Thanks, 'Lun,' he says.

'How are you feeling?' she asks. He's probably excited to head off to work with the lads again.

'It's useless, they'll close the mine anyway. This year, or next. They'll find some excuse and buy in Soviet coal for half the price.'

'When did you get so well read?'

'Everyone knows that.'

'I brought you this as well,' she says. She has a sprig of carnation to pin on his chest. Mam's given one to Dad. The flower is barely open, red petals still folded tightly together. She slips her hand under his lapel to help him pin it on; the last thing he needs is a pin poking in his chest. In the doorway Jean turns her back on them.

'You must be pleased.' Lloyd is so close that she can feel his chest rumble against hers as he speaks. His breath smells of toothpaste and raspberry jam.

'I'm furious that we've lost,' Eluned says.

'No – I mean. You must be pleased you can tell everyone you're a dyke.'

The word lashes her. 'Lloyd . . .'

'Or that you bat both ways.'

'It's got nothing to do with that.'

'You know what I'm going to do next month?' he asks. Lloyd must have sloshed on his dad's aftershave. It's dark and smoky, with something fresh that reminds her of Earl Grey tea. Tiny bristles of black hair break through the pale skin of his neck. 'When I get paid, I'm going to get the bus to Swansea and I'm going to get smashed—'

Eluned interrupts. 'Sensible use of your hard-earned cash there.'

Lloyd ignores her. 'And I'm going to find a bird and I'm going to shag her fucking silly.'

'Shag her silly, eh?'

His gaze is fierce. It transports her to his imaginary night-club. She'd let him shag her silly if she was on that dance floor, if she was that girl. Maybe one more time. But it won't be one more time. Stepping back to Lloyd can only be stepping towards the chapel, to scrubbing his work clothes, to Sundays with Jean.

'I've got to go,' she whispers.

Lloyd seizes her arm. *No*, Lloyd. A tearing pain in her shoulder as she yanks it free. His fingers are too strong. She stamps down hard but misses his foot. Gets a sharp elbow in though. Lloyd grunts with the effort of gripping her wrist. He twists, she winces. His other hand digs into her arse, squeezing roughly. Jean must be able to hear the scuffle, but she'd rather see Eluned get hurt than call her son to heel.

'Get off!' Eluned whispers as forcefully as she can. Finally, he lets her go.

Her wrist is ringed with red. It matches the scram she's left on his neck.

Lloyd fiddles with his cuffs, shuffles his shoes. 'I'm sorry,' he says.

'I've got to go,' she says. 'Good luck.'

Jean grinds her teeth by the door, slamming the front door so forcefully Eluned can feel the gust of air on her back.

Eluned hurries down the main road through the village, nodding at the other women gathering on the street to support the march. They perch on their doorsteps in nighties, housecoats and slippers, kids on their hip. If she'd played her hand different, that could have been her. Her own house, her own curtains, twisting a gold band round her finger.

These men never have any luck, it's already drizzling. The slate roofs are transformed into gleaming black planes. In some of the big pits there have been photographers from the papers, but not here. Mam's leaning on the lamp post outside their house in her best jumper, red carnation vibrant against the admiral-blue wool.

'You missed all the drama,' Mam says.

'What happened?'

'Mabli came round, wanting to say good luck to Dad. He was shaving upstairs. I sent her away with a flea in her ear. He's enough of a wreck as it is, without her upsetting him. She hasn't given him so much as a phone call or a tin of beans, now she's getting sentimental.'

She shouldn't have gone to see Lloyd.

The vibrations shake the ground before the men are visible, pinballing off the walls of the long, narrow terrace. Eluned cups her hands to clap, throwing her elbows into it until the sides of her hands smart.

They round the corner. The emerald cloth banner held high. Behind it, the rest of the men march shoulder to shoulder, five abreast. Eluned keeps clapping. There's Dave, with his lamb chop sideburns, who gave her and Mabli hand-me-downs from his older kids; Ceri, Dad's mate, who bought Eluned her first legal pint when she turned eighteen; Lloyd's shy, stuttering uncle with a grisly orange tiger tattooed on his upper arm; most of the lads in her year at school; and Dad. Dad won't look at them. His eyes are already red-rimmed, even when Mam wolf-whistles in his direction.

Seeing the men dislodges something, like a spade striking water, and then she's the one crying. This might have freed her, but it's brought a way of life to its end. Eluned's hands begin to shake, and the tremor moves up her arms until Mam wraps her arm round her shoulders.

12

4 April 1985

Mair had always gone on about this department store in Cardiff because she knows the manager in some roundabout Welsh way. It's worth a try. Eluned finds the shop in the Yellow Pages and digs out Mam's writing pad. It's got to look tidy, so she uses a guiding sheet and pencil, then traces over it with Dad's black fountain pen. The newsagent is out to rinse her with the price they charge for photocopies, but she makes a copy of Mair's reference and staples it to her letter.

Eluned passes the days driving the last of the food parcels around to people still in need. Howells is at the back of her mind when the letter arrives, inviting Eluned to interview.

The only skirt suit Mam has that fits is mustard, with outdated buttons sewn on to fake pockets. Eluned does her best with a cream chiffon pussy-bow blouse, tied neatly under her chin. Her new shoes are unyielding; she should have broken them in, she's going to be walking like something from the 'Thriller' video.

Cardiff is an hour away. First she's got to cling to the edges of the Beacons and then descend the valley. Eluned smokes in quick puffs as she drives, hands shaking on the wheel, before rooting in the glove compartment for one of Mam's mint humbugs. It's impossible to miss the shop; every door is canopied with carvings of vine leaves laden with abundant fruits. Eluned can't resist stroking her fingers over the brass letters spelling Howells underneath every window. The make-up department is clinically pristine, marble floors shined until they're disorienting to walk on.

Eluned is interviewed in the stockroom, where old posters are propped up against the back wall. She wouldn't mind one of those massive Dior ones, although she might need to chop it down first. Karen has the tightest bun that Eluned has ever seen, the baby hairs flattened with hairspray and combed into pretty loops. As she starts her questions, sweat gathers in the small of Eluned's back. Mair only wanted to know what she got in her maths exam and if Dad was the same Emyr Hughes from Maesmarchog Primary.

Karen sets out two sheets of laminated paper on the desk. One has pictures of different beauty products, the other is full of blurbs about different customers. *Desiree: Out to get a promotion, and her man (oily/mixed),* must surely be hypothetical.

'I'd like you to take your time matching these customers to these products.'

Desiree the maneater gets Lancôme's Dual Finish Foundation; Eluned's read you can use that wet or dry. Rita gets emerald eyeshadow to complement her copper locks. Spotty Claire ends up with the astringent toner that will probably burn. Poor Claire.

'A burgundy? For her?' asks Karen. 'What if she feels a dark lip is a bit beyond her?'

'I'd tell her that if Joan Collins can do it, she can.'

Karen's mouth twitches as she scribbles on her sheet. For all she knows, Karen could be writing 'Absolute chancer'.

Next, Karen gives her a sheet of maths. Karen may be a sadist. When Eluned's sweated herself through that, there are three more questions.

Karen asks, 'Can you clean?'

'Mam would have me on the streets by now if I couldn't.'

Karen continues to scribble. 'Can you talk to everyone?'

'I never shut up,' Eluned says.

'Are you planning to have a baby?'

Eluned swallows her laughter. 'Not part of my plan.'

Karen folds her notes and zips them inside her Filofax. She extends her hand over the table. 'Janet's seven months gone so we're looking for someone to start in about a month. How does that sound?'

The back page of the *Western Mail* has plenty of rooms for rent. Dad insists on reading them with her, convinced he's got a sixth sense for sniffing out weirdos. He circles one ad: a widow looking for a student, or similar, to help her with chores in return for cheap rent.

Eluned lends a quid for the phone box and gives her a call. She is gleeful when she hears Mrs Omar's voice for the first time; she's got a proper 'Arm's Park for half of dark' accent, the sort Dad thinks he can do when he's pissed. She's never heard it in the wild before, sliding from vowel to vowel in a way that sounds closer to Liverpool than to her own much-mocked sing-song voice. Mrs Omar describes her terrace house and its spare room. It's sandwiched between the steelworks and the railway, and only a ten-minute walk into town. She agrees that Eluned won't have to pay her anything upfront, if Eluned starts the housework immediately.

'Don't take that ring Mamgu Fawr gave you. You haven't met this woman; she could be a klepto.'

Mrs Omar doesn't sound like one, but Eluned puts the opal ring back in its box anyway.

'You can't take that skirt with you. It's too short, for a big girl.'

'Chill out, it's knee-length. Put it in.'

Mam packs the skirt with visible disgust. She'd have Eluned in a sack if she could. But what if she's right? Eluned has no idea what women, women like her, wear when they go out these days. She wore that skirt to Swansea over a year ago; fashion has moved on by now, and the lesbian thing complicates things further. Bugger it, it's good fabric. She can always pick it apart.

Mam's sidetracked again. She's flipping through Eluned's sketchbooks. Pages and pages of girls posing like fashion models. June would have a field day with them.

'These are great, you should do something with them.'

'Maybe one day. What about you, Mam? You going to keep on with the Committee?'

Mam squints at Eluned's sketchbook. 'Oh I don't know. It will be quiet around here with you off and Dad back at work. We said we might raise money for the boys dying from that infection. Hey – did you know that it's still illegal for two men to get it on if someone else is in the house? Isn't that nuts? If you live in a shared house, you can't have gay sex if your flatmate is downstairs watching telly.'

Eluned squeals when 'gay sex' comes out of Mam's mouth. She hurls a jumper in Mam's general direction. 'You can't say that!'

'I'm your mother, not a nun! I can say what I want.'

Eluned doesn't think there are any specific laws for girls, but it puts her night at June's in perspective; the whole house was rocking with it.

Mam goes on, 'If the police don't like the look of your face, and you know what they're like, they could bash the front door in, when you're bashing the back ones in!'

'Oh my *God*, Mam! You are so grody.'

Eluned feels like a hostage in an exchange, like those Irish blokes on the telly. Dad drives her down to Splott. She's got to get over thinking that it sounds like a cleaning product. Mrs Omar comes out to greet her: a petite woman with a pink face and a bright scarf wound round her head.

Eluned's new room has dark, bulky furniture and a single bed with a starchy brown blanket. She unpacks her records first, choosing *Like A Virgin* and *The Top* for display on top of her chest of drawers. She tucks the Mars bar from June, and the two business cards she gave her, at the back of the bedside cabinet, along with an old photo of her and Mabli on the swings. She didn't even see Mabli before she left, but it's still her favourite picture from their childhood.

Mrs Omar likes the company and Eluned is happy to listen to her, wedging herself on the sofa next to the woman as she works the story of her life between her fingers like an old handkerchief. She's never met anyone like Mrs Omar before. She says she comes from an Irish family but was raised down the Docks. Mr Omar was a steelworker whose father had been a seafarer from Somalia. They both had seven brothers and married at the Peel Street mosque. Eluned only half-believes it, but Mrs Omar reckons 600 people came to see her draped in her hand-beaded dirac and eating from huge platters of goat and spiced rice. They'd had four boys, now grown up and moved away.

Eluned is free to use the kitchen, lounge and garden as her own. There are rules: no TV after 9 p.m., no outgoing phone calls unless agreed in advance, and towels washed on Tuesdays. Mrs Omar eats like a bird, but she is partial to a tea plate of dates, cheese and walnuts, or porridge made with nutmeg and double cream. Every Friday she gives Eluned money to buy them both a fish supper, though the fish is always too big for Mrs Omar. She flakes the white flesh from the delicate bones with a cake fork, slapping the long strip of batter on Eluned's plate.

Eluned replaces her tatty old *Like a Virgin* poster with a heavenly shot of Madonna with slicked-back hair and a leather jacket. It's dykey to the max. From the market she buys herself a tall, slim houseplant to add a sense of sophistication. The man on the stall tells her it's called Painter's Palette on account of its wide white leaves. Its glossy red flower has a viscerally sexual spike at its centre, which reminds her of June's earrings.

On the weekends she passes the time walking north to the sprawling, ivy-covered graveyard, or south to the Docks, where a white church sits at the edge of the mudflats like it's just been washed up. Last week Eluned saw a long, flat boat unloading timber. It is strange to think of the coal dragged from the ground by her ancestors to be shipped down to Cardiff and then sent out across the world. The Docks, and its lavish Coal Exchange, have been unknown to her until now, although they have undoubtedly affected her life. Now they've been discarded, like the mines themselves.

Eluned's bestseller is cucumber toner, with a pitch that seems to work on everyone:

'We all have a bottle of this at home, it's so refreshing. If you want an extra boost, you can always put it in the fridge overnight. I read that's what Farrah Fawcett does.'

Those tall glass bottles must be nestling between cartons of milk and jars of marmalade all over Cardiff.

Her body knows that she's spent the first part of this year sat on her arse; there's no way she can stand on her feet for a whole day any more. One of the older women gives her a tip: if she puts her elbows on the counter and leans all her weight on them, she can raise one leg and then the other, to get blood flowing the other way.

Despite the way her feet cane, she prefers to walk home. Her favourite route is along the Victorian frontages on the main shopping thoroughfare, across the nest of streets with a celestial theme – Star Street, Orbit Street, Sun Street, Constellation Street – then over the corrugated iron railway bridge. By this point, the last of the day's sun is warming her back and, if she's got time, she stops at the Portuguese bakery for an egg tart. She can't get enough of the soft custard, the flaky, melt-in-your-mouth pastry, or the shavings of fresh nutmeg over the top. Mrs Omar's house is on a terrace that looks like Mam and Dad's, but a street or two in any direction there are grander ones, with tiled porches and bay windows.

Eluned rewards herself with a cold can of Hofmeister on Mrs Omar's patio, underneath the climbing jasmine. She soaks up the heat coming off the drystone walls as seagulls swoop and dip overhead, their bellies painted pink by the sun. Eluned sinks into the deckchair, letting her thighs spread. She has an hour or so before she will need to make dinner for the pair of them, improvising with whatever Mrs Omar has picked up from Splott Market. After that, she'll wash their dishes and then they'll settle in for whichever programme Mrs Omar has circled in her *Radio Times*.

Closing shifts are the best ones, feeling the girth of a fat stack of notes in the till, lining the daily figures inside their columns and faxing them off to Head Office. Before she leaves, she checks the stock in the lipstick drawer. Each name holds a story: 'Tangier', 'Brooklyn Heights', 'Golden Shores'. Once that's done, she unbuttons her white tunic, streaked with foundation and eyeshadow, says nos da to the security guard, and walks home.

The other girls are local, and Eluned is the only one without a man or a baby. She's resigned to the peripheries, browsing through the TV guide while they talk about midnight feeds. Eluned looks down at her belly, outlined by her tight white tunic. Egg white omelettes and a glass of water before dinner aren't going to make a lick of a difference.

Eluned is asked to do demonstrations on customers, and that brings its own perks. One of those perks is Cadi, a paediatric consultant with soft blonde hair like Princess Diana. Eluned drags a cobalt blue pencil under Cadi's eyes. Cadi's skin is dry, sticking to the pencil. If Eluned was at home, she'd stick the pencil in her mouth or down her bra to warm it up a bit. That's the main difference between doing your own make-up and make-up for someone else.

Cadi murmurs, 'You smell lovely. What is that?'

Eluned doesn't bother keeping perfume at home. Every day she has a squirt of something expensive from the perfume counter.

'Poison, by Dior. We're the first store in Wales to stock it, it only came out this month.'

Cadi takes the blue eyeliner and a pot of their bestselling eye cream. After a few months, Eluned is an expert at folding the ends of the tissue paper as she rolls. The last garnish is a gold-edged sticker pressed onto the join. Cadi swipes her card through the machine and signs the receipt.

'Before I go, can I try that perfume?' she asks.

Eluned fetches the bulging purple bottle and Cadi tips her head back, exposing her elegant neck. 'Will you do the honours?'

Eluned squirts until Cadi's clavicles glisten. A drop trickles down her sternum and soaks into the fabric of the bra that is peeking out from her blouse.

'Let it settle for a while and see how the base notes react to your skin,' Eluned says. Low-pressure, pleasingly pseudoscientific.

Eluned hooks the ribbons of Cadi's small paper bag over her fingers and holds the door open for her as Cadi pops the button on her umbrella.

'That's a lot of effort for an eyeliner and some moisturiser,' Elaine says as she wipes the countertop.

Eluned shrugs. 'She was a kiddie doctor.'

In her stuffy box room Eluned has rewound her memories of her night with June so often that if they were a real cassette, the tape would be worn through. She wants to have another go, but she's got no idea where to find women like her.

One evening, leaving work, Eluned is stopped in her tracks. Three women having a pint together outside a grubby pub on St Mary's Street. It's like a mirage. Nearest Eluned there's a fat woman in a sleeveless denim jacket, propping her ruddy arm against the wall. Eluned's mouth waters at the sight of her faded blue tattoos. Next to her there's a woman with a shaved head and a leather jacket covered in patches and pieces of silver chain, holding an amber pint of what looks like Brain's Skull Attack. The third wears a torn-up Clash T-shirt and has a flat-top dyed cherry red. They're all hot; she could take any of them on. All of them together, perhaps, ganging up on her. She's always had eyes bigger than her belly. But the one with her arms out is big enough to hold Eluned down, and the third one looks like she's capable of being mean.

Eluned creeps closer. She lights a fag and leans against a lamp post like she's waiting for a friend. The Clash fan has hooded blue eyes fringed with long lashes; dark circles underneath them. The woman mimes a mishap, jerking her hand so the beer froths over the side of the glass and down over her knuckles. Her friends laugh, shaking their heads. Eluned would happily lick every drop of beer off her hands.

Eluned could approach her. She's always liked The Clash. She speaks to people all day, for heaven's sake. She rehearses in her head. '*What do you think of the rumours that band relations are so frosty that they're using session musicians to record the new album? Did you hear that it won't be released until this winter, if at all?'*

The woman slaps her face with her palm and shakes her head. God, Eluned wishes she was in on the joke. Instead, she finishes her fag, stubs it out, and walks home to her landlady and a family-size bar of Fruit and Nut.

13

27 June 1985

'Your friend is calling,' Mrs Omar shouts out of the kitchen window. Her fine ginger hair is lit up like a halo around her face. Without her headscarf, her face is moonlike, otherworldly. Her forehead is high, heightening the impression of delicate features set in an enormous face.

Eluned struggles out of her deckchair, stuffs her feet back into her sandals and tosses her hat on Mrs Omar's narrow patch of grass.

'I'll be there now,' she shouts.

Rhiannon's voice is warm, her accent rounder than Eluned remembers.

'I wanted to fill you in on our Gay Pride adventure,' she says.

'Your what?'

'The Committee wanted to go up to London for their big parade; see the LGSM lot and that. It was dead fun!'

Rhiannon has got to be bragging. By her telling, half the miners in Wales turned up with their banners intact, and the LGSM lot had even organised T-shirts. Rhiannon's put one aside for Eluned, if she wants it.

'We saw Ian, who stayed with us a few times. Met his new boyfriend, Colin. Adorable.'

Adorable. Like a Labrador.

Rhiannon goes on and on. They started at Hyde Park and ended at Jubilee Gardens, right opposite Big Ben. Rhiannon reckons that London is so dirty that the skin left exposed by her sandals was black with dust after. Oh, and there was a drag queen on a boat on the Thames. Brilliant. Fantastic. Why didn't anyone think to mention it to her? Would it have been too much for June to get in touch with someone at the Committee? Kelly at work had said she'd seen some grubby students walking up Queen Street with banners a few weeks ago. She should have gone.

Rhiannon's voice turns sly. 'I had a good chat with Lloyd on the bus home.'

Oh fuck. Well, their agreement was only until the end of the strike.

'Did you?'

There's a new Cure line-up, and *The Head on the Door* is out soon. He'll have strong opinions, no doubt.

'He told me your hot goss,' Rhiannon whispers. 'We had a long chat. But don't worry. Your secret is safe with me.'

'I don't know what you mean.' Perhaps the only safe route is brazening it out.

The line goes muffly. Rhiannon says, 'Aled, take Dan is it? I'm on the phone to Eluned. Eluned Hughes. I'll be there in a minute now . . . Sorry. Anyway, you're a dark horse; I wish we'd had that snog in the van now.'

Eluned's mouth drops open. 'What about Aled?'

'I told you about what I used to get up to in Barons! It's a laugh.'

There's helping a breeder sort out their shit and helping breeders that don't know they've got shit to sort out.

'I thought you should know, Eluned, because a lot of us felt that it was important for us to go to that march. For you to think about, for the future.'

The sun pours in the small window above the front door, painting a perfect butter-yellow rectangle on Mrs Omar's tiled floor. Somebody other than Lloyd knows, and the sky hasn't fallen in. The ground hasn't cracked. She'd give anything for a pint with Rhiannon and Lloyd down the Welfare. Mabli as well, maybe.

Eluned's on the afternoon shift. On days like this, the wall of windows turns the shop into a greenhouse. By the time she gets in, there's no shade to be had. Her elbows are glued to her sides, to try to avoid scaring off customers with the damp circles under her arms. She's been over to the perfume counter for a squirt over her pulse points seven times today. The only relief is slipping her heels off to rest her soles on the marble floor.

No one is shopping for make-up. Who'd want it on their skin today? Eluned's foundation is making a slow escape down her neck. Mrs Omar is having tea and cake with the other ladies at the mosque this afternoon. Eluned will have to pick her up, it's far too hot for her to be out walking.

Lisa rests her chin in her hands and looks at Eluned. 'That blue eyeshadow pops against your eyes. Why don't you have a man?'

Eluned's glad Lisa noticed. She's been trading in her Outdoor Girl and Boots 17 for something more upmarket, and that pale baby blue is her new favourite. 'I've only just moved,' she says. 'I don't know—'

'My cousin is single! He owns one of the car dealerships on City Road,' Julie says.

Lisa caws, 'Isn't that the cousin that has been in prison for money-laundering?'

Eluned's favourite place to eat lunch is in the small park outside the market, sandwiched between the library and Dead Man's Alley. Her chosen spot is on the bench that runs round the quaint wooden hut, so she can stare at the gravestones they've moved to sit amongst the flowers. Her feet are ballooning out of her court shoes and within a few minutes her parting starts to scorch. The library offers respite. It's a similar sort of building to Howells, the door flanked by statues of snooty Greek women.

In the library, the only lesbo book she can think of to ask for is the one Julie Walters likes in *Educating Rita*. She tucks her work lanyard into her bra, before asking the librarian if they have *Rubyfruit Jungle*. The librarian is off like a bloodhound.

The cover of *Rubyfruit Jungle* is subtle; only a small pink flower gives an indication of its themes. The librarian lines up the date-stamp under the previous ones, stamping firmly on the paper slip stapled to the inside cover. Who took it out? Did they read it for the same reasons as Eluned? The last time the book was taken out was in May. Whoever she was, she's probably still walking around Cardiff with the story fresh in her mind.

Her sweaty fingers slip on the thick plastic cover as she carries it to Howells, pushing it to the bottom of her bag. She'll start it when she's safely in her room. It's so hot that she can only stomach a cold tin of tuna for tea. She excuses herself to read *Rubyfruit Jungle* lying naked on top of her quilt, window directing a breeze at the back of her neck. She pores over coffee stains, dog-ears and the occasional thumbprint, for clues about the previous lenders. The spine is deeply creased on the pages where Molly and Leota fuck. The thought of other women being turned on by the pages in her hand is a turn-on in itself; like a hall of mirrors of women reading, dreaming, wanting. Eluned flicks the pages back and forth until the room darkens around her and she hears Mrs Omar's knees squeaking on the polystyrene mat in the room next door for her last prayer of the day.

* * *

As the months go by, Mrs Omar gets more comfortable with assigning Eluned trifling chores and errands. She renews *Rubyfruit Jungle* twice, but when she comes down to a stack of crime novels on the table with a note asking her to return them on her way to Howells, she takes the opportunity to request some more lesbian books from the librarian. She is eager to take them home and make a start on her reading but, compared to *Rubyfruit Jungle*, they're both disappointing. Neither have been taken out since 1983.

Orlando is a slog. She reads with Mrs Omar's dictionary next to her, looking up words like 'orgulous' and 'hauteur'. The best bit is the skating. Eluned closes her eyes to imagine Orlando soaring across the ice. If Orlando has June's narrow face and pale eyes, that's her prerogative. *The Well of Loneliness* is worse. The pages are so clogged with shame and self-hatred, she can barely turn the pages. By the time she gets to the conclusion, she feels a similar panic to when Graham's horse was bearing down on her. *The Well of Loneliness* feels like a curse on her bedside cabinet, and the next day she goes in to work she gets rid of both of them.

As she hands them back, the librarian points her towards a booklet pinned to the noticeboard in the foyer.

'They are made by some local women,' she says. 'They're not supposed to leave them, but I just cover them with one of the WeightWatchers posters.'

Amongst the posters for baby groups, Bible study and items for sale, there is a booklet with 'Womyn's Liberation Newsletter', handwritten in bubble writing underneath a shakily drawn sun. Every 'O' in the title has been turned into a Venus symbol, and underneath the title it reads, '<u>Women Only. No male readers. Please respect this.</u>' Eluned picks the booklet up and stashes it in the bottom of her handbag until after her shift.

In the safety of her single bed, Eluned reads the chatty foreword where the editor apologises for the delay in printing, as her cat has been poorly. There's a review of a concert in Bristol, and an article about an upcoming meeting of Black lesbians and bisexual women in London. There are adverts for a community-run crèche, a women's disco at the Splott leisure centre, a leathers and motorcycle show and a 'consciousness-raising group' in a house in Adamsdown.

It's a map to a treasure island. Some of the pages are patchy, badly photocopied, but it's worth reading every word. Every page has some reference to some shared understanding or joke. This month's horoscopes are not written by the 'Clairvoyant Mrs Webster', but her sceptic girlfriend. Libras are warned off birds and odd socks, though apparently masturbation could yield spiritual insight. It's worth a try.

The back page is given over to personal ads, illustrated with a sketch of a chubby, girlish Cupid firing an arrow into the chest of a nude, swooning woman.

Eluned skips through the blocky paragraphs, waiting for one to catch her eye.

University professor yearning for intellectual challenge –

Leather daddy searching for eager supplicants –

Earth sign avidly seeking an Air sign to help me realign my –

Young-at-heart Gower lass seeking soft-hearted same for surfing and metal detecting adventures.

If only Eluned had a dog. The beach sounds idyllic; she always enjoyed a long walk over the mountains. This one is worth circling lightly with her pen.

Voluptuous redhead. We'll eat our way around the world and sing our way through the Great American Songbook.

Eluned loves music and she's never been a picky eater. If this woman is describing herself as voluptuous, she shouldn't find fault with Eluned's larger frame. The magazine gives a PO box address. It's not far away, round the corner really. Eluned tucks the magazine away at the bottom of her bedside cabinet drawer and tries to think up an interesting opener for the voluptuous redhead.

She tries every iteration of *'straightforward Valleys girl' and 'feisty music fan'* she can think of, before deciding to stick to the basics.

Walking home in this heat is agony. It's gone on for weeks now. The crotch of Eluned's tights sags, leaving the tops of her thighs to chafe. The waistband rolls down over her stomach until it snaps underneath her gut. On the Black Bridge there are two rats lying dazed with heatstroke, flicking their tails at her but otherwise making no effort to get off the path. By the time she gets to her house she's trotting, holding her tights up with her pinkie fingers. She doesn't spot the note on the telephone pad until she settles in to call Mam.

Lola rang for you. Your ginger friend, she told me to tell you. She said she'll meet you at the Star of Wales at 7 p.m. this Friday.

It's been a fortnight since she replied to the ad; she'd almost given up. But it's got to be her. The Star of Wales. Where *is* that? Lola. *Lola*. A date with a woman. In public.

14

5 July 1985

Eluned borrows a dress from one of Howells' upmarket ranges. Finally, the Cardiff girls have let her in on a secret. They borrow a dress from the shop floor, leave the tags on, and replace it the next day. Everyone else has got away with it.

There's not much in her size, but luckily this dress is a real beaut: velvet lamb-chop sleeves, an asymmetric dropped waist and a satin bow on the hip. Eluned gets volume in her hair with mousse and a diffuser, and an upside-down shake. By the time she's done, her hoops disappear into the mass of curls. Lipstick is the final touch: a scandalous scarlet by Elizabeth Arden, the end of a tester taken out of commission. No harm in slipping it into her bag. Mrs Omar lends Eluned one of her headscarves in the same shade, and Eluned wraps it round her shoulders to disguise how the bodice pulls a bit at the back. She could adjust it, but it's got to be returned intact.

The window of the Star of Wales is fogged up, and it's sweltering inside. Eluned adds her umbrella to the overstuffed rack by the door. Rainwater rises as steam from everyone's coats, mixing with smoke and spices to give the room a diffuse yellow glow. The paisley carpet makes her feel dizzy as she picks her way through tables of dark-suited men.

The waiter leads her to a table opposite the kitchen. She's the first to arrive. She breathes as deeply as her dress will allow. The long wall is decorated with a large mural of

Cardiff's City Hall next to the Taj Mahal, surrounded by a mirrored frame. Eluned salivates at the food paraded past: fried battered balls, dark meat sizzling on cast iron dishes, heaped piles of orange rice. She spies the chef moving up and down a line of enormous frying pans, controlling them like a concert pianist.

The brass bell in the doorway jingles. A woman fights her way through the door, umbrella catching on the frame. She points her umbrella at the ground and Eluned fumbles her lighter. That must be *her.* Lola looks like a grown-up Molly Ringwald, red hair singing against an emerald cocktail dress. The umbrella fights back. The waiter tries to help her press the metal spokes down, but they spring back and scatter water over the diners nearest the door. Lola throws her head back and laughs. She hooks the crook of her umbrella over the waiter's arm and squeezes his elbow with what seems like great enthusiasm, then leaves him to apologise to the other diners.

Lola swivels her hips to pass between the tables. Her pleated skirt brushes a bloke's shoulder and when he looks at her askance, she pats his shoulder and smiles benignly.

'Eluned!' Lola booms. Her skirts are so voluminous that she bounces a little as she sits down. 'Tell me *all* about yourself. I can't wait to hear it!'

Eluned blinks. Where to start?

'Mam's family are from Banwen, and her dad was a butcher. But Dad's family has always been miners . . .'

Eluned's blown it already. Lola covers her mouth with the menu, but her shoulders are trembling with laughter.

'I didn't realise I was getting the whole damn genealogy!'

She's not used to chatting with someone who doesn't know her family, the place she grew up. What else do you start off with? Her sister is studying law, that's kind of impressive. Lola leans into the path of a passing waiter and asks for a bottle of red without even looking at the menu. What if they bring her the most expensive one?

'Tell me about *you*,' Lola says.

Eluned draws stripes in the condensation on her glass with her fingers. 'I love music and drawing. I work on a make-up counter in town.'

Lola leans in, pinching the flame of the tealight between them. 'What would you sell me on your counter?'

Eluned considers. 'A woman can never go wrong with a timeless red lip.' She reaches for Lola's arm and twists it to face the ceiling. The inside of her forearm is pale, with delicate blue veins. 'You've got cool colouring,' she says. 'So, I'd go for a blue-toned red.'

Lola arches her eyebrow. 'And will it smudge when I'm eating you out?'

Who says that? Out loud? The restaurant is packed! Anyone could overhear. She's too sweaty. Borrowing this dress was a mistake. It's too tight, and the label is unbearably itchy against the top of her spine. She's going to have a rash there by the time she gets home.

'I'm joking!' says Lola, knocking back her wine.

Lola orders them two thali, a basket of poppadoms and a tray of chutneys, assuring her that it's the best way to try a bit of everything. She's a bit older than Eluned; the veins on the backs of her hands stand up and the candlelight catches the shallow lines at the corners of her eyes. When she imagined a girlfriend, she imagined them the same age. Someone to share magazines and records with. That's probably because she's used to Lloyd being in her year at school. Now isn't the time to be picky. Lola's pretty, bright, and a professional; Eluned is lucky to be on this date. It's not like there were many women in Cardiff in that magazine.

Lola holds forth, leaving Eluned to try the fried balls of onion, dipping them into first the jammy mango chutney and then the cool mint one. Lola's accent is crisp and English, with long vowels. Eluned can't resist asking her why she came to Wales.

Lola tears off a strip of soft naan bread and swipes it through the thin lentil soup.

'Nursing college. Lot of dykes in nursing, if you ever fancy it. I'm at Whitchurch now, in acute psychiatry.'

'Isn't that dangerous?' Eluned blurts.

Lola hoots. 'What do you think it's like? Women crawling round their rooms talking about faces in the wallpaper?'

Margaret Thatcher is a common enemy. Lola spends a while explaining that Care in the Community is less about their patients, and more about saving money. June would probably agree. Eluned ends up talking about the strike; it already feels like a strange sort of dream. Lola's hand freezes in mid-air when Eluned tells her about Graham and the horse, the wine in her glass trembling slightly.

Lola sets her fork down and strokes over Eluned's wrist. 'A lucky escape. My friend in General said that she saw nasty injuries from the picket line.'

The nurses have been out, too, over pay and conditions. Lola reckons they'll be out again before long. They compare battle scars and rallying cries, and Eluned forgets she's with a stranger until she chokes on something in her curry. It feels like wood and tastes like liquorice, and she spits the green lump and its black seeds into her cloth napkin.

'Did you eat a cardamom?' Lola crows. 'Oh bless you! Here, put them on this tea plate.'

Lola starts on her second bottle of wine, Eluned on her fourth pint of lager. Good job she booked the day off tomorrow. The curl is falling out of her hair and she's dribbled some of the bright orange sauce down the front of her borrowed dress. That will need sponging off before bed, or she'll have to pay for it. As the restaurant empties around them, the conversation turns. Lola asks about June and Eluned tells her.

Lola sighs extravagantly. 'Oh, I'm jealous. I've never had a punky-butchy one.'

As if Eluned's the expert. 'She was hot. Bovver boots and leather jacket, all of that.'

'Delish! And you liked it?'

Eluned's got to laugh. She sloshes back the end of her fourth pint. 'I liked it, yeah. Liked it so much I jacked in a six-year relationship and shacked up with an overbearing landlady.'

Lola cackles. 'Women will do that to you.'

Lola seizes the bill when it comes, handing over her Barclay-card and tossing Eluned one of the chocolate mints.

As she signs her receipt Lola asks the waiter, 'Could you be a brick and call my friend a taxicab? She needs to get back to Splott.'

The restaurant foyer is dark. Cowbridge Road East is quiet-ening down. The staff are back in the dining room, industri-ously clearing the last of the day's plates. Lola grabs Eluned's elbow.

'Would you like a kiss, or shall I keep my garlic breath to myself?'

She would, very much, like a kiss. Her mouth does taste of garlic, but her own must too. As she deepens the kiss their breasts squash together. Never had this problem before. Lola's neck smells of sandalwood. Is that Obsession? It's certainly familiar. Lola kisses like a woman who doesn't step out of the way of men on the pavement.

Outside the foyer, the driver beeps. One short toot, then two long ones. Footsteps on the other side of the door. The staff must be coming to see what all the beeping is about.

Eluned pulls back. 'Do you want to share my taxi?'

The kiss has heated her slowly, like one of those summer days when you don't notice that you're burnt until the sun goes down.

'No, darling. I'm only round the corner. Suggested this place in case I got so pissed the cabs wouldn't take me. Crawling distance.' Lola taps her head with her first two fingers. 'Nurse's tip for you.'

The fourth pint was a mistake. Eluned wakes to Mrs Omar pounding her bedroom door. She's afflicted with a dry mouth, hair stiff and crunchy with Elnett. She grapples her way to sitting, trying to ignore the sudden onset of nausea.

'Hang on,' she tries to shout. Her voice is creaky, barely louder than a whisper.

Mrs Omar thumps the door again. 'Come and see! There's a treat for you in the kitchen.'

Lola has sent flowers. They take up half the work surface, towering over the kettle and the novelty spaghetti jar from Italy. Two spectacular birds of paradise sit in the middle, framed by waxy cheese-plant leaves. Three white calla lilies are set in a diagonal line at the front. The whole arrangement sits against a background of pampas grass, dyed bright pink. It's obscene. The most opulent thing she's ever seen. Where can she even put them in her tiny box room? They'll block the telly in the lounge. For all their brashness, the note is coy. No fussy message, just '*To Eluned*', in copperplate handwriting.

15

21 October 1985

Eluned wants to go where the other gays go. Lola's wangled a brass key for the gentleman's club with the light-up floor. There's no queue, just a steep flight of stairs leading to a fluorescent oasis. Next, the Showbiz, which won't serve Eluned beer in a pint glass; the Terminus, inexplicably nick-named the Gayhound; and, finally, a rough pub that has been 'colonised by lesbians,' as Lola puts it. Eluned is knocking back soupy ale when a glass soars above her head. It bounces off a bar stool and explodes into fine shards, beer foaming over the wood. Two women stand screeching in the middle of the mess. The pub's colossal bouncer steams in, bald head sweating, hauling them off and out into the street.

The Tunnel feels illicit, down an alleyway a street over from Howells. Lola grips her hand tight as they are ushered down a flight of stairs and into the club, which smells damp, like the backroom of a chapel. Like the name suggests, it's long and narrow, with arched alcoves leading off the main room.

Eluned loves watching the DJ work; she's only seen mixing on the telly before. Mabli would love it. She allows herself a couple of seconds of worry about Mabli before she distracts herself with watching the DJ. His hands hover over the deck; scratching, looping, extending and distorting so that Eluned takes a few seconds to recognise the tracks. Lola tells her she could go on *Name That Tune;* as if you can think of anything other than 'Master and Servant' when you hear that intro.

The DJ plays around with it, mashing the synthetic beat machine noise into the plodding keyboard at the beginning of 'Babooshka'.

Lola looks like she's come straight from work, in her colour-block shirt-dress and sensible heels. Her lipstick is beautiful, could be Honey Bee Mine, or Cherries a la Mode. Eluned shrugs her jacket off, and they kiss against the dank basement walls, stones scraping her shoulder blades. Bodies writhe together in every smoky alcove. Finally the drag queens come strutting out, posturing across the stage with plastic nails like daggers and piles of brassy hair.

The queens bend over the crowd, choosing who to single out.

'Oh, Annie's fallen on hard times!' Bara Bitch calls out, pointing straight at Lola's curly red hair. The spotlight moves sluggishly over the crowd to highlight Lola's face. Lola grins, twirls for the crowd.

Bara Bitch fires words like a machine gun. 'You're a fag hag right? Here with your best friend? Oh – no, you're holding hands.' She moves her finger to Eluned's face, 'Duw duw, you're pretty! Big girls always have cute faces. Have you noticed that? You can smell the Valleys coming off her though. Watch out for this one, you know what Valley girls are like. Anyway, why do dykes always hold hands everywhere? I'm serious. They do!'

'Because otherwise people ask us if we're sisters!' Lola yells up to the stage.

'Sisters?' Bara Bitch crows. 'Flattering yourself. More like mam and daughter. You'll take care of your wee old mam, won't you?'

Eluned is weak with laughter, turning her face in to Lola's shoulder to mask how her cheeks are flaming. When she pulls back, Eluned sees that Lola's face is thunderous.

'You shouldn't encourage him,' Lola says.

Eluned rolls her eyes. 'Come on, it's part of the act.'

At the bar, the queens clap Eluned on the shoulder for taking it well, their hair almost scraping the basement ceiling. It's overwhelming, like having a brush with a real celeb. The Tunnel closes with the whole club shouting 'I Will Survive', shoulder to shoulder with strangers.

By the time they leave, Cardiff is quiet, aside from the stream of revellers trickling through the streets. The further they get from the Tunnel, the more diluted the queers become. Lola's hand slips out of Eluned's like a conker from its shell. At the crossroads, she smiles at the George Michael lookalike she saw in the club. Inside, he'd been glistening with sweat, muscles rippling under tight leather straps, but now he's got a sensible blue shirt buttoned up to his throat. He nods in recognition, then disappears northwards towards Cathays.

Lola's house is on a sun-bathed crescent of red-brick houses, curving around a small park. They are nearly identical; each has a bay window, a tiled porch and a wooden front door with an etched glass panel. Lola's house is differentiated by the lilac wisteria climbing around her porch. The delicate, tapering flowers trail low over the entrance, tickling the top of Eluned's ponytail. She could swipe them away, but a few stray petals might look cute.

Eluned juggles her bottle of Black Tower while she watches Lola's copper hair bob down the hall through the pattern cut in the glass. She slips her heels off at the door, as Mam insists upon, and lets the terracotta tiles cool her feet.

Eluned blinks as her eyes adjust to Lola's gloomy living room; the windows are crowded with a spindly cheese plant. Three walls are covered with groaning bookshelves, and the last is dominated by a majestic wooden fireplace. Above the fireplace there's a framed photo of Lola and another woman, both in long floral dresses, in a small rowing boat. The coffee table is polka-dotted with wine glasses, purple dregs swimming at the bottom. Mam could never stand this mess, she'd be mortified. Lola doesn't seem mortified; she lights two sticks of incense and stuffs them in a holder hidden behind a large chunk of amethyst. Eluned is left to sink into the knackered chesterfield while Lola bustles off to the kitchen. There's a jumper bundled up down the side of the sofa, and Eluned pulls it out and folds it like they do in Howells. Face-down, crosses the sleeves at the back, and then folds over the shoulders at the back.

'What are you doing with that?' Lola snaps from the doorway, eyes hard and mouth twitching towards a sneer.

Eluned jumps like a child being shushed in a library, letting the jumper tumble off her knee and down to the floor.

'Sorry,' she says. 'I sat on it by accident.'

Lola's face clears and she moves across to Eluned, picking up the jumper and holding it to her chest. 'I'm terrible, I hate myself. But you're perfect! Seeing your face has been the best part of my day; my shift was a killer.'

Eluned's chest flushes with embarrassment at the compliments. 'No, no,' she says. 'I should have asked before I started poking around.'

Lola kisses her forehead. 'I'll go finish up in the kitchen. It's just some stroganoff and dumplings I've had in the slow cooker, I'm afraid.'

Lola has a new hi-fi entertainment system with a turntable, a cassette player and slots for compact discs. That's at least two months' wages. She prods at it, until GOOD DAY scrolls across the screen in blocky green text. There are enough slots for six CDs, and it looks like you can shuffle songs across all six of them.

'I'll put something on the stereo,' says Lola, handing Eluned a crystal glass of wine that is certainly not Eluned's Black Tower.

The record crackles at first, but then the call of a solo trumpet fills the room. Those speakers are fantastic. The singer delivers each phrase slowly, like she's having a direct conversation with Eluned.

Lola's stroganoff is heavy with red wine and paprika, beef so soft you could eat it with a spoon, and the cheesy dumplings are tangy and rich. After they've eaten, Lola twists her feet up on to the sofa between them, groaning deeply.

'Come here. Give me your feet,' Eluned offers.

'My feet are ghastly.'

No feet can be as disgusting as Dad's, and she gave him a massage every Sunday night for most of her childhood. Lola lays her feet across Eluned's lap. Her big toe is crushed to one side like a boxer's nose. No wonder when she's on the ward in heels all day. Underneath the rose-scented talcum powder they smell like fresh sweat. The backs of Lola's calves are threaded with blue varicose veins, and Eluned traces her fingers over their tracks.

'Oi! Don't judge those. You stay in your profession and they'll come for you, sooner than you think.'

She's right. The backs of Karen's legs are like Stilton. Eluned pulls each of Lola's toes until they pop and grinds her knuckles into Lola's arch. Lola's mouth drops open a little. Her overbite stops Eluned from seeing her bottom set of teeth most of the time, but now she can see the neat, stubby row, and her wet tongue above them.

The music stops, but the table continues to spin. The room is quiet, save for the crackle as the needle moves over the record and Lola's soft noises. Just as her eyelids start to droop, Lola bounces up. 'You're a healer, I'm a new woman. Dance with me.'

Lola flips the record to the B-side and gathers Eluned close. She takes one of Eluned's hands in hers and puts the other on the small of her back. The snare keeps a soft, slow rhythm.

Lola's delicate fingers burn in her palm. The singer's voice is mournful. The trombone slithers down Eluned's spine. Lola moves one of her thighs in between Eluned's thighs.

'Did you know Billie was bisexual?' says Lola.

'No, I didn't.'

Lola leads Eluned in a basic waltz, whispering about Billie Holiday all the while. She covers disputes with her label, racial segregation, drugs and financial mismanagement. Lola is so knowledgeable. Light lands on the rug like beads of amber. This close, Eluned can smell that she was right, Lola does wear Obsession. The sandalwood and musk undertones are heady tonight. Lola tops up her wine every time she gets near to draining a glass. Eluned steps back from Lola. The spell breaks. The needle skips, looping on the singer's plaintive cry.

'I should go home,' she says. 'I need to go home.'

Lola kisses over her knuckles, with a hint of teeth. 'You'd be welcome to stay the night.'

Eluned has never cock-teased anyone before. She'd fucked Lloyd within weeks. The allure of being one of the anointed band of girls who'd done *it* was too great. It was a relief to get it under her belt, ticked off the list. With June, she felt desperation like nothing else. She still remembers taking off her knickers for the first time, watching the film of wetness stretch between her labia and the cotton. This time, she wants to make Lola wait.

Eluned creeps into Mrs Omar's living room. Mrs Omar has a whole shelf of records behind her wedding photos, and Eluned drags them out. She kneels on the carpet and sorts through them until she finds *The Best of Butetown Carnival*. That'll do. The cardboard sleeve is so caked with dust that blowing at it is useless. Mrs Omar won't notice Eluned sneaking it upstairs. Eluned fits the record on her record player, dropping the needle as gently as possible. Age has made it sputtery. She moves the volume dial carefully; quiet enough to be unobtrusive but loud enough to mask any other noises she makes. She clicks her bedside lamp off. There, she shouldn't disturb Mrs Omar. The vocal has the same languid richness as Billie Holiday. She forces her eyes closed, lets herself imagine what might have happened if she'd stayed the night.

16

16 November 1985

Lola invites Eluned to her 'literary salon', which is a posh way of saying book club. The library has a copy of *The Colour Purple*, and Eluned chips away at it during her lunchbreaks, touching up her mascara and concealer afterwards. That red dress, and the song! When Celie had packed them off to Tennessee she could have cheered. Eluned wraps Mrs Omar's wooden chopping board in tin foil and covers it with cubes of Cheddar and tinned pineapple speared on cocktail sticks, like Mam used to do for parties.

'This is adorable!' Lola says, lifting the chopping board from her hands and heading to the kitchen.

Eluned follows along and leans herself against the warm radiator in the kitchen. The work surfaces are covered in vibrant ceramic dishes filled with olives, stuffed peppers and, on the grandest plate, devilled eggs topped with fresh chives.

Lola's friends arrive in dribs and drabs. They're serious-looking women with short, puffy hair, clothed in natural colour palettes. Lola seats them at her dining table and shuts off the main lights until they're lit by candlelight. No sign of the cheese and pineapple sticks amongst the dishes. Fuck it. Eluned stuffs one in her mouth every time she goes to the kitchen, tossing the cocktail sticks into the sink.

Lola introduces Eluned as her 'paramour', clasping Eluned's hand to her own breast. 'Can you believe that she was hiding from me up the Valleys?' Lola asks the group, to indulgent noises.

Eluned tugs her hand away from Lola; she doesn't need them thinking she's a fool. Lola starts the salon by asking Eluned what she thought of the book. She's happy to tell them. Nettie's a bit like Mabli, young but clever, and when she was little Eluned would have done whatever it took to protect her, too. Alice Walker's done a good job there.

Lola chuckles and rubs her hand over Eluned's knee. 'That's a naturalistic interpretation. What do you think, Gloria?'

Gloria pontificates about the symbolism of the 'text'. She picks out things Eluned had forgotten and connects them like she's at Bletchley Park. Lola nods fervently, circling words in her copy.

When they've exhausted themselves, Lola ushers them into the lounge and follows them with her cafetière, clear espresso cups with fiddly triangular handles and a saucer of joints. There aren't enough seats, so Eluned pulls a magenta cushion off Lola's favourite armchair and flings it on the floor to perch on. Lola crosses one leg over the other and rubs her stockinged feet through Eluned's hair, working Eluned's scrunchie out with her toes. With effort, Eluned keeps her head still. After a few puffs of the joint it's less irritating, and she pushes her head back into Lola's foot like a cat. Eluned has only smoked cannabis a handful of times and the earthy smoke gets stuck in her throat.

'Having trouble with the green, green grass of home, are we, Eluned?' Diane says. Diane arrived in a cream trouser suit like something out of *Brideshead Revisited* but, after they retired to the lounge, she undid the first few buttons of her blouse. Now every time Diane leans forward, Eluned gets a good look at her dark brown nipples, surprisingly perky for a woman who must be knocking forty.

Lola hoots, dancing her toes over Eluned's shoulder. 'We're

helping Eluned find out how green her valley is . . . or something like that.'

Between the cannabis, normal fags and the incense sticks, there's not enough air in the room. It's like someone's sat on her chest. She needs to get out in the garden for a moment. Eluned is halfway to her feet when Diane starts reading her poetry aloud to the room. Unsure of the protocol, she sits back down. Lola closes her eyes while Diane reads, moving her head in time with the beat. She certainly looks like she's enjoying it, but it's not for Eluned.

'What did you think of Diane's poetry?' Lola asks, shutting the door behind the last guest.

'It was interesting,' Eluned says, popping a cheese and pineapple stick in her mouth.

'Load of cobblers, wasn't it? Ethereal rhyming with delirium, please!'

'It was "grace" and "unlaced" that made me lose it.' Mabli would have eaten her for breakfast.

Lola holds the kettle under the tap. 'She was always writing when we lived together.'

'In nursing college?'

Lola smirks. 'No, darling, we *lived* together.'

Lola surely can't mean as partners. She would have told Eluned first.

'She's your ex?' Eluned asks. She feels ridiculous, standing with a dirty ashtray in her hand while Lola stares like she's got five heads.

'We experienced life together as lovers,' says Lola.

Eluned slams the ashtray down on the work surface with enough force to make the dishes clatter.

'"*We experienced life together*,"' Eluned repeats. 'Why didn't you tell me?'

'Why does it matter?'

Isn't that obvious? Lola's long-stemmed wine glasses are sat in the drying rack. Eluned could strike her hand through the lot of them like dandelions.

'I wanted your friends to like me, but you were in on a joke without me!' Eluned deflates. She strips the scrunchie from her hair and winds it round her wrist instead.

'I don't want to row about this. I don't want any unpleasantness to come between us,' Lola says. She takes Eluned's cheeks in her hands and kisses the frown between her eyes. 'Please don't let there be any unpleasantness.'

'I'm sorry,' Eluned says. Apologising feels wrong. She doesn't feel sorry. But still, it's stupid to get annoyed. Women are bound to be more sensitive, more emotionally intense. If Eluned was more mature, then she'd be able to handle it without feeling so insecure. She should work on being more relaxed and open-minded. Lola invited Eluned to her book club when she didn't have to. She can't look a gift horse in the mouth.

'Don't worry about it, it's all forgotten,' says Lola. 'Have a seat in the lounge. Maybe you shouldn't smoke weed again, it doesn't agree with some people.'

Eluned nods, both chastened and relieved to have been excused from the argument. She opens the windows in the lounge to release the last of the cannabis smoke. Eluned roots through Lola's box of records for something to put on. Sondheim. Ellington. Porter. Judy Garland.

Lola clears her throat in the doorway. Jesus. She's a screen siren in a sheer black dressing gown. Nothing underneath, just a pair of lace-top hold-ups. Eluned can't take it all in at once. The sweet crease in her soft, full stomach. Her shell pink areola. The red curls on her shoulders. It's the feeling of a surprise birthday cake covered in candles, or a brand new twenty-pound note from the hole in the wall.

'I won't be given a runaround by a girl in her early twenties,' Lola purrs.

Eluned's tongue clacks uselessly inside her mouth.

Lola toys with the tie of her dressing gown, and Eluned kneels up on the carpet. She'll crawl, do whatever it takes. Her cunning and ambivalence have vanished like a cheap magician's trick.

'Darling, are you going to come to the bedroom? Or are we going to sit around and play *Juke Box Jury*?'

Eluned mashes her lit cigarette into the side of the ashtray. Go out, you bastard. Lola sweeps out of the room and up the wooden staircase. Eluned presses hard on her thighs to push herself up, hauling herself to her feet using the arm of the sofa. Why is she always so graceless?

Lola's bed is grand, with a heavy wooden headboard and velvet curtains. The whole room smells like the lining of Lola's mac: incense, Obsession, and something more astringent. Eluned's dress and tights are on the floor as quickly as she can shuck them off. Luckily, her underwear is tidy enough. Black M&S, with ivory butterflies.

Lola reclines against the mountain of velvet pillows, beckoning Eluned after her. 'What a pair we make. It's enough to make me want a mirror on the ceiling,' says Lola.

It's certainly a thought.

Lola stands at the end of her bed, twisting her hair into an elegant chignon. Her blue nurse's dress is neatly pressed, watch dangling from her pocket. It shouldn't be sexy. She's a professional, not a costume, Eluned reminds herself as Lola straightens the back seam on her nylons. Lola had told her about nurses protesting outside a restaurant called Bedside Manner in London. She wouldn't want to be contributing to that sort of objectification.

'Will you pin my hat in for me?' Lola asks. 'I'm leaving in ten, but I can give you a lift if you get your things together. I wasted time, and now doth Sister Powell waste me.'

Eluned scrabbles for her clothes, scraping her hair back in her scrunchie.

'Where to are my shoes?' she asks.

'"*Where to are my shoe-uhs?*"' Lola parrots back.

'What?' Lola can't have just made fun of her accent.

Lola laughs. 'Just teasing. They're here,' she says, kicking Eluned's daps with the toe of her polished black brogues.

Lola's breakfast is black coffee and a cigarette. Eluned passes; she'll have something when she gets home. The inside of Lola's car is ankle-deep in crisp packets. Last night she had imagined spending the morning in Lola's bed, listening to Billie Holiday. Lola hadn't mentioned that she was working. It's probably her own fault for not making sure Lola had time to hang about the next day.

Lola drives with the window open, while Eluned rubs her hands over her knees to warm them up. She feels lopsided, like when she puts the rest of her face on but forgets mascara. Lola drops her off in Splott without so much as a peck on the cheek, the red Cortina accelerating down the street before Eluned has even fished her keys out. She sprints up the stairs and into the shower. Working the Salon Selectives through her sweaty, matted hair, she picks over the evening. She did well at the sex, there's incontrovertible proof of that. But she's woken with the strange-fuzzy anxiety that she used to have after nights out in Swansea; when she was certain that she said something stupid, but she's not sure what or to whom. It's hard to pinpoint when the coldness crept in.

17

1 December 1985

Eluned's feet have blown up like footballs; it's these long Advent shifts, and Mrs Omar turning up the heating system way too high. She lies with her feet on the quilted headboard, trying to get her blood to run the other way. As she gets comfortable, the phone starts ringing. It's probably not even for Eluned. Lola's on a night shift, and it's unlikely to be anyone else. Unless it's Mrs Omar herself. She's staying with Abdi, her youngest son, this weekend. Eluned's taking advantage of the opportunity to bleach her work tunics; Mrs Omar complains about the smell if Eluned does it when she's around. She plonks herself on the bottom step, cord stretched straight across the hallway.

'Hi 'Lun, I'm calling to give you a bit of news,' Mam says. Something's up. What is it that can't wait for Eluned's next visit home? She said she'd come back on her next free weekend.

'What is it? Is Dad—?'

'No love, it's good news. Graham and Mabli are expecting a baby, and they've decided to get married.' Mam's tone flicks up at the end, like she is trying hard to sound excited.

Eluned's heart sinks, but Mam obviously wants her to sound pleased. 'That's lovely news. Graham will be a great dad. He dotes on Mabli.'

Mam's voice turns icy. 'He dotes on Mabli because she's young and pretty and doesn't realise what she's capable of.

She will, one day. I don't know how doting she'll find him then.'

That's the thought that puts chills up Eluned.

Mam clears her throat. 'I didn't mean that. It'll be lovely to have a baby around.'

Eluned leans her head on the banister. If she closes her eyes, it could be Mam's shoulder.

'Don't be sad, cariad. Maybe if you're working next weekend, I could get the train in from Neath, and you can doll me up like a posh old lady. And it's only a few weeks until Christmas.'

Eluned squashes up to the banister. A sudden urgency grips her. 'Mam, something's happened.'

'What is it?'

'Since I've been working down here, I've met a woman.'

'Met a woman?'

'*Met*, Mam. Not like "met in Tesco's". Don't be dense.'

'Duw duw. One lesbian, and one marrying a copper,' says Mam, trying to sound serious.

'You don't mind, do you?'

Mam sighs. 'I might have, this time last year. We know better now.'

Mam's even written an article about people poorly with AIDS for the *Valley Star*. The Committee are trying to do a bit of fundraising. Things really have changed. Eluned's hands unclench, knuckles sore from her death grip on the receiver.

'I better go, bach. Can I tell Dad?'

'Yes. Especially if it softens the blow of ending up with a pig in the family.'

By Christmas, Eluned has squirrelled away enough for a second-hand car, mostly due to Mrs Omar's half-hearted approach to rent collection. She's not fussed on make or model, but when a man two streets over tells Mrs Omar that he's selling his Austin Metro with only a few miles on the clock, Eluned snaps her up. She's got square lights and a long snout, and Eluned nicknames her Madge.

Karen is kind enough to let Eluned leave after cashing up, leaving the other girls to deal with the carnage generated by straight men panic-buying. Abdi has already picked Mrs Omar up and driven her back to his house in Penarth. Eluned floors it up the A470, then snakes around the bottom of the Beacons. A freezing fog is descending, and the higher the road climbs, the thicker it becomes. The bushy conifers disappear on both sides of the road, and Madge's headlights turn from a full beam to a diffuse glow. 'Do They Know It's Christmas?' has been phased out this year, although Janice Long has played 'Merry Christmas Everyone' twice already. That retro style is a bit naff, but Mrs Omar says he's a Cardiff boy and a communist to boot.

By the time she pulls up outside Mam and Dad's, the sky is pelting something between rain and snow, spattering on her windscreen in fat streaks. Eluned grabs her suitcase and her sack of presents and runs. Somehow, those streaks of slush manage to find their way down the back of her neck in the three yards between the car and the house.

Mam's in full Welsh mam mode, tucking a blanket round Eluned's legs and fetching her a hot toddy that's half rum, and a microwaved mince pie with bubbling filling. She takes it slow, trying not to burn her tongue.

'Rhiannon called in earlier to ask if you're going down the Welfare. We're stopping by for one,' Mam says.

Dad changes his grubby Small Faces T-shirt for a clean buttoned shirt, and Eluned pulls on the black lurex dress she's borrowed from work. Her hair is a scraggly mess, so she gathers it up to the side in a high pony.

The hall has had the same Christmas decorations for as long as she can remember, thin strips of red tinsel taped the whole length of the bar and around every ashtray, gold foil garlands unfolded and stretched across the ceiling tiles, and foil concertinas that hang down low enough to bounce into Eluned's eyes.

''Lun! You're back!' Rhiannon shouts, waving them over. She's sat with Lloyd and the boys. With his grown-out hair, he looks like Rob Lowe. Carly's joined them, squashed in between Aled and Lloyd. Maybe she's noticed his hair, too. Dan's sat on Rhiannon's lap, industriously scribbling on a Christmas-themed colouring-in sheet.

Aaron nudges Eluned with his elbow. 'How's Cardiff? I've heard there's been a lot of fishy smells around.'

Mark sniggers. 'Have you been down the lido? Cardiff is supposed to have loads of opportunities for diving.'

Doesn't take a genius to know what they're getting at, but she can't be arsed to dignify it with a response. Instead, she strokes Dan's head. He looks like a proper little boy now, but his head is still baby-soft.

'Da iawn Dan, your drawing is coming on,' Eluned says. 'Have you left your carrot out for the reindeer?'

Dan nods shyly, and Eluned digs around for the presents she's bought for them both. Rhi's got a three-pan eyeshadow palette: shimmery violet, deep burgundy and a metallic bronze. For Dan, she couldn't resist a sweet-faced teddy with 1986 embroidered on one foot.

'You're too lush!' Rhiannon says. 'I haven't got you nothing.'

'They're only gestures. I didn't get anything for Aled. I'll get him a pint later.'

Rhiannon waves her off. 'He doesn't need any more of those. I'll tell him you bought one when he wakes up tomorrow. I doubt he'll remember.'

'Do You Really Want to Hurt Me?' starts. They played it when June first came down, didn't they? God, that feels so long ago.

'I haven't heard this in ages,' Eluned says.

Mark makes a face. 'I'm sorry if the music is so much better in Cardiff.'

Carly raises her head slowly and skewers Eluned with cool blue eyes. 'Where do you go out in Cardiff? My cousin lives there.'

Eluned could lie. She could give the name of some bland breeder club like Barons in Swansea. But fuck it. It's not like they don't know. She tells them her favourites; the Casablanca is not strictly a gay pub, but it's certainly not judgemental. Throw a stone in there, and it will bounce off people speaking six or seven languages. It's a seedy sort of bar in an old church. The sign pokes out of the arched brick doorway, a white light-up box with a picture of a camel and a palm tree. Lola loves the live jazz, performed on a small stage where the altar used to be, and Eluned lives in hope that one day she'll see Steve Strange pop in. The Tunnel is Eluned's ultimate favourite. She likes that it gets so sweaty that the ice in your drink melts as soon as the barman hands the glass over. The toilets are full of women moaning, MDF cubicles rattling. She's seen at least four scraps by the sinks, one ending in teeth knocked out on the taps.

Carly ashes her fag. 'I've never heard of them.'

Eluned tries to explain where they are in relation to Caroline Street, which seems to be Carly's only reference point. She's such a Joanie. Even if she did know where the Tunnel and the Casablanca are, she wouldn't get it.

Mid-sentence, Carly cuts her off. 'Someone's at the bar. Sorry. Got to go.' She extricates herself from the bench, squeezing out as only skinny girls can.

Lloyd follows Carly to the bar, and Eluned tags along behind him. She runs her fingers over the wood, following the trail of white circles and burn marks. This is just about where she met June for the first time.

'How have you been doing?' Eluned asks.

'Pretty good,' Lloyd says. 'I've been doing more stuff with the NUM. They're still not happy with Thatcher, and I've been going to the meetings. They're alright. You look glamorous,' he says with a shy half-smile. Carly's eyes drift over to them as she pours another pint.

Good for him. There's no mistaking the warmth in her chest, the urge to give him a short, sharp punch in the arm.

'So, everybody knows about me now,' says Eluned.

Lloyd startles. 'I only told Rhiannon. I swear. We went up London last summer for the march. I wanted to do it because I believe in rights for gays. But I kept on seeing girls like *her*. And I thought, "I could be settled down with a wife at home and a baby on the way if it wasn't for the likes of you."'

Selective memory. Even before June, she would have never wanted to be at home raising babies.

'Don't worry. Mam is a big gossip. She's probably the one who told everyone. She could gossip for Wales.'

'I did get a wink off a gay though,' Lloyd offers.

'A wink! I thought you said something else then,' says Eluned, laughing. 'Go on then, show me your best gay wink.'

Lloyd wiggles his eyebrows and scrunches one eye, tilting his head to the side in an impression of campery. In other times they would have laughed each other into bed; she would have made him do his funny wink with him resting inside her.

'I've got a present for you,' Eluned says. Finding a gift for Lloyd had been a ball-ache. Everything in the men's department is designed for yuppies. It's all leather business card holders, Filofaxes and novelty ties. Then she remembered the itchy blisters that he always used to get down the sides of his fingers and bought him a moisturiser that's meant to be a wonder balm for eczema. He slips it, unopened, into his back pocket. He's always so good with presents, never opens them early. She's never had the self-control for that.

* * *

Eluned sits by Rhiannon, pushing her pint across the table. Dan's asleep over her lap, wrapped up in her coat like a china doll. Nights at the Welfare always seemed endless when she was a kid, listening to the adults go on and on. Sneaking illicit sips of beer was about the only fun to be had, but Dan's a bit too little for that.

Mark raps the table. 'Girls, we're going to have a party at Aaron's house. You coming?'

It's surprising, but she's up for it. She's had a couple, and she fancies a dance.

'Will you do me up proper?' Rhiannon asks.

Eluned's got her make-up bag with her. It feels natural, she spends all day with it now. Rhiannon's complexion is paler than hers, but she can still share eye make-up, lippy and blush. She takes Rhiannon to the toilet and props her make-up bag on the loo roll holder. The cubicle is barely big enough for them to squeeze themselves into, and the grubby white walls and harsh fluorescent lights do nothing for Rhiannon's skin.

Christmas is an excuse to use rich berry colours. They look good on everyone, and she's got a beautiful raspberry blush in her bag. She holds one brush in her teeth and works with the other. Eluned bends into Rhiannon's space to blend a shimmery gold shadow into the corners of Rhiannon's eyes. Yes, that opens them right up. A dusting of the same eyeshadow on her cheekbones. Oh, that's gorgeous.

Rhiannon stares up at Eluned. 'Eluned, you're so pretty.'

'Thanks,' Eluned says. 'I think we're almost done.'

Rhiannon parts her lips and leans forward, pressing her lips against Eluned's. It's gentle, tentative, Rhiannon's tongue sneaking between her barely parted lips like an eel from a rock. Maybe she should grab Rhiannon by the hair and give her something to remember. Then Lola's face swims into her mind and Eluned jumps back, bumping her hip against the loo roll holder. She'll get a bruise there. Her make-up bag clatters to the floor, cosmetic tubes rolling across the dirty tiles.

'Rhiannon, what . . .'

Rhiannon crosses her arms. 'Oh come on!'

'I told you about Lola. Would you kiss a woman if you hadn't been drinking?'

'No! It's just messing about. I've got Aled and Dan . . .'

Eluned retreats as far as she can in the cubicle. 'It was a mistake coming back here, thinking that everything would be the same.'

'Don't go. I've missed you and I haven't been out in ages.'

'I'm going home, but I'll finish your face first. You need a bit of lippy. Here, have mine.'

She's pushing the boat out tonight with a Chanel lipstick. She was hoping she'd be able to show it off. Eluned fills in Rhiannon's Cupid's bow and tidies up the corners. She's done a good job; Rhiannon looks beautiful.

'Thanks,' Rhiannon mumbles.

'Have a good time. I'll help Mam with Dan.'

Eluned pushes open the door to the lounge.

'That was quick,' Mam says, holding her finger to her lips. Eluned can see Dan splayed out over Mam's stomach. She's not going to start shouting her head off.

'I didn't feel like going to the party in the end,' Eluned whispers back. She lays her coat over the back of the sofa. 'Is Mabli coming back tomorrow?'

Dad sets down his dainty sherry glass and picks up the bottle, uncorking it with a pop.

'No,' says Mam. 'She said she wanted to have a romantic first Christmas in their new house, before the baby comes. It's a special time, I'll give her that.'

Dad snorts. 'Would have been nice if she'd told you before you did the shopping. And you haven't told Eluned what happened earlier.'

'What happened earlier?' Eluned asks.

'I called Mabli, to make sure that she wasn't reconsidering, and she told me that Graham has invited his whole family round for Christmas.'

'No!' Eluned says.

'She was in a right flap! Asking me how I make my stuffing, whether I brine my turkey.'

Mabli's never been a confident cook as it is, let alone doing a Christmas dinner for a group of people she doesn't know well.

'Surely she can't be lifting a massive turkey when she's pregnant,' says Eluned.

'I told her to tell him that if he wants his family around, he can cook! If he starts creating fuss, she can always come back here.'

Mabli's stubborn, though, she'd never do that. Eluned should have brought some of Lola's rose and fennel teabags with her; they're good for settling the stomach.

'She won't do that,' says Dad.

Mam nods. 'Earlier she said she couldn't expect him to do any cooking, he's been working too hard.'

Dad knocks his sherry back in one gulp. 'What's he been doing? Sitting around in lay-bys and playing with his walkie-talkie.'

'It's a cheek because we've barely seen this new house. Every time we suggest visiting, Graham seems to be on nights . . . Anyway, I'm off to bed.' Mam slithers out from underneath Dan and settles him onto the sofa cushions. She hands the rest of her sherry over to Dad.

Mam's told her about Graham and Mabli's new house down in Neath, with its wood-panelled kitchen and stone-effect fireplace. Boot-licking must pay well these days.

When Mam heads up the stairs, Dad lets out a long, deep sigh and scrubs over his face with his hand.

'You alright?' Eluned asks, inching the box of Quality Street towards him.

He takes a toffee penny. 'Yeah, I'm alright.'

That's about as much as she was expecting to get out of him. On screen, a blond actress unbuttons her blouse. Her red lips shine like an apple as she licks them lasciviously.

'What do you think of her then?' Dad asks.

'What?' Eluned blusters.

'If that's what I'm supposed to talk to you about now,' Dad continues, lighting a fag.

The actress is down to her last button. Oh, now they're out. Jesus, she didn't think they could show stuff like this on normal telly. She can't deny that they're decent boobs. She's probably stared at them for too long now, she better answer him. 'She looks pretty good to me.'

Dad gives her a lopsided grin. 'I wouldn't mind trading your mother in for one like that.'

Hah! The cheek of it. As if he could do better than Mam. He is a funny one.

'Get to bed, bach. She'll want you up and peeling sprouts by seven.'

'Alright, Dad. Love you,' she says, dropping a kiss on the top of his head.

Before the sun comes up, Mam and Eluned are shelling peas and peeling potatoes to a soundtrack of Welsh carols. Mam listens to the same battered old vinyl every year. Eluned busks through the alto part, while Mam sings the soprano part with the brightness of the sun glancing off a teaspoon.

Mam and Dad get Eluned smart new mats for Madge's footwells, and a cassette called *Psychocandy*, which Dad promises will blow her mind. Mam hands over a long, slim envelope with something stuffed inside it, 'This is for her. Your friend. It's only a book token. You said she was a big reader. But I don't know what she likes, see. It's only a fiver, but that should get her a paperback.'

It's more than Lola will get from her own family. She'll be on the ward, working right through to Boxing Day. Lola had described Christmas at the hospital as the 'same dinner, same shit on the telly, but with less simmering resentment and thinly disguised hatred'. It's a depressing way to look at it, but at least she doesn't feel left out.

Maybe next year Eluned could bring Lola here for Christmas. She doesn't want to let on about the age gap, not after the hassle she's given Mabli, but Lola's feminine looks and easy charm would be palatable, unthreatening, next to someone like June. Mam could almost pretend to herself that Eluned isn't a total dyke.

Mam calls Mabli while Eluned coaxes Dad into Scrabble. He lays 'MUFF' with a triumphant clack. She adds 'INGER' to his F and they giggle like kids while Mam shushes them, pressing the receiver tight to her ear. After his second victory, she leaves him reading through *Britain's Greatest Beers*.

18

2 May 1986

On their regular, Mrs Omar-sanctioned, Thursday-night phone call, Mam lets Eluned know that Mabli has sent her a letter. She makes Eluned swear that, whatever it says, Eluned will give it a fair hearing. Ominous. When the letter comes it's brief; Mabli writes that she's planning to make a shopping trip to Cardiff and that she understands that Eluned is working in one of Cardiff's grandest department stores, so would she like to go for tea with her? Eluned ignores the flattery, but can't ignore the printed review of *Tinderbox*, Siouxsie's new album, cut out from some magazine and stuck at the bottom of the letter. Mabli's drawn an elegant, sharp-pointed arrow next to it: *Have you got this yet?*

Eluned hasn't, but the DJ at the Tunnel played the Extended Eruption remix of 'Cities in Dust' the other night, and the club almost brought those damp basement walls down with the force of their dancing. It's enough to tempt Eluned into replying, and so she writes back with a date and a time. They've got a café on the top floor of Howells. On a rainy day you can watch the umbrellas float down St Mary's Street like lily pads. Tea and scones are outrageously dear, but with her hefty staff discount she can afford to treat her sister.

When the day comes, Eluned shares her lunchtime plans with her colleagues, for the first time. She's been thinking over all the things Mabli might say, and the most likely by far is that she wants to ask Eluned to be her bridesmaid. She and the other girls pass the morning swapping stories about serving as bridesmaids, and Eluned tells them about the time she was a flower girl for her second cousin in 1973, when the videographer caught her spitting salmon en croute into her hand at the top table. When Karen taps her out for lunch, Eluned takes off her tunic, folds it under the counter and checks her lipstick before she walks up to the top floor.

Eluned buys a pot of tea for two and two fruit scones with clotted cream and jam. The tea comes in a utilitarian steel teapot, handle hot enough to burn her fingers, beside another matching pot filled with hot water. She fiddles with the tea set for a bit, mashing the teabags against the sides of the pot, then settles to watch the cream curdle under the hot cafeteria lights.

In her trench coat, Mabli is barely showing. Only the belt hitched up higher on her waist gives it away. It's vaguely disgusting to think of a tiny human sloshing around in there. Mabli has that mythical glow; her hair shines like a satin ribbon on a birthday gift. When Eluned leans forward to kiss her cheek she can't help breathing in deeply. Mabli's always worn Anaïs Anaïs, but today the bergamot and orange blossom are popping, the scent of a young Aphrodite in the sun. Compared to Mabli's fresh face, Eluned's make-up feels heavy and cartoonish.

Eluned spreads the jam and cream over her scone in one go, scraping a spoon around the edges to make sure she uses it all. Mabli cuts each half into three strips and dabs on her cream.

'This place is spectacular. I've got to come back here with the baby. God, it makes you think, Blossoms was so pokey.'

'You should come and stay, Mrs Omar won't mind. I'll take you to the Casablanca. You'll love it, they get jazz musicians in from America!'

Mabli cuts one of her slices in half and half again, until it's the size of a postage stamp. 'I don't know about that. I'm pregnant and . . .'

'I wouldn't drink without you. It's about the music, no one's going to ram into you.'

Mabli sucks her lip into the corner of her mouth. 'I don't think Graham would be comfortable with it. I'm sorry.'

On the table opposite them two suited-up men sit with a stack of loose paper between them. One combs through the stack sheet by sheet with a fountain pen as thick as a cigar, circling passages as the other one talks.

'They must be solicitors,' whispers Mabli. 'They keep on talking about ancillary relief.' Mabli continues to eavesdrop as Eluned smokes, mouthing what she can glean across to Eluned behind her hand. '*She's going to rinse him.*' For the first time, Eluned notices her engagement ring: a large pink ruby, surrounded by smaller teardrop diamonds.

'So, tell me what's going on with this wedding.' Eluned tries to erase Graham in her mind, replacing him with a plastic figurine from the top of a wedding cake. This isn't about him, this is about making her sister happy.

Mabli nods, taking a folder out of her handbag. 'We're going to do both the wedding and the christening at St Margaret's.'

Creunant! By Christ. It's certainly not the family chapel.

'Is that where Graham's family goes?' Eluned tries to keep her voice light and breezy.

'No, but it's got a lovely green space for the pictures. And the stained-glass windows are exceptional,' Mabli says, fetching out a swatch of turquoise fabric.

'Our bridesmaids' dresses are going to be this colour, with Diana sleeves and a lace trim.'

Eluned will look sallow in turquoise, and her shoulders will look massive. She schools her face into a pleasant smile. If Mabli is happy, Eluned will make sure she seems happy.

Mabli picks up her last piece of scone. With her eyes on her scone she says, 'I've asked Tirion and Hannah to be my bridesmaids.'

'What?' Eluned splutters. 'We never see Tirion. We've barely seen any of those cousins since we were fifteen. Hannah-from-work? From *work*?'

Mabli sets her scone down again. 'Graham didn't think it was appropriate to ask you. We are getting married in a church.'

Eluned can hear the words she's leaving out loud and clear. 'Pull the other one, Mabli. You're knocked up. There's no point getting pious now.'

Mabli's cheeks flood bright red. 'I haven't seen you in months and then Mam tells me you're suddenly a "lesbian".' Mabli accessorises the word with air quotes and a whisper that might as well be her normal speaking volume. 'You might turn up with a shaved head and a suit.'

If Mabli doesn't understand that Eluned is the same person she's always been, then she's got no hope. 'What have Mam and Dad said?'

'I haven't told them much about the wedding. They're not being supportive.'

Eluned asks, 'Am I even invited?'

'Of course you're invited, you silly mare!'

'But I have to sit there and let everyone look at me and wonder why you've not picked me.'

Mabli pinches the bridge of her nose. 'Why didn't you tell me how you were feeling? This started when you disappeared in London, didn't it? We sat next to each other on that bus for hours, you could have told me something.'

Eluned folds her arms. 'Well, you could have called after Mam told you about me and Lloyd.'

'I was tamping. You've got no idea how scared I was without you. It was the first time I'd ever stayed away from home. I didn't want to leave the Electric Ballroom in case you came back. Everyone else went off with their gays. The roadies packed up and left, turned the lights off and locked the Ballroom up. Some twat walked past and asked me how much

I was charging. At the B&B I woke up every half-hour to see if you'd made it back. You can't begin to picture what I thought had happened. I wrote down what you were wearing in case I needed it for the missing person report. I rehearsed what I'd say to Mam and Dad. Then the next day you come skulking back like "Hia, sorry I'm late!"' Mabli stops and takes a sip of her tea, smoothing her napkin over her lap. 'Graham would rather you didn't come. He doesn't want you glaring daggers at him, and he doesn't agree with your lifestyle. He's been called to that bar, the Talk of the Abbey, five times this month. One time, there was a glassing. It's a rough lifestyle, and he doesn't want to be associated with it. This is the compromise option.'

'You built up your case flawlessly, Mabli. You're fully exonerated. You must be good at your job.'

Eluned scrapes her chair back and grabs her handbag. She jams the chair back into the table, causing the cups to rattle and overflow onto their saucers.

'Eluned!' Mabli calls. 'Wait!'

Eluned's not looking back. She needs to clean up her make-up before she resumes her shift. What if Mabli goes down to the make-up counter? She wouldn't tell Karen, surely. They could give Eluned the sack, dress it up to make her look like some sort of a pervert. The customers probably wouldn't want her to touch their faces if they knew she was a dyke. She'd like to think that Mabli wouldn't snitch, but she is dating a copper.

19

3 June 1986

Lola teaches Eluned how to make paella in her cast-iron pan: throwing sherry over hot metal, dropping in strands of saffron to paint the stock yellow. Thick discs of sausage leach their orange oil into the starchy rice. Eluned shreds parsley and pokes in a circle of dark blue mussels. They eat at the kitchen counter, straight from the heavy pan. After the paella, Eluned rubs her thumbs into Lola's arches while she reads the *NME* album reviews, weighing up *Tinderbox* against the new Eurythmics release. Lola has the Womyn's Liberation Newsletter open over her knees. She has already performed the theatre reviews, and now she puts on her best Scouse accent for her and Eluned to play their silly 'Blind Date' game.

Lola reads out three personal ads, and Eluned chooses a date with a soulful Scorpio with her own allotment. Not bad. Lola goes for a student from West Germany.

'I'm imagining a Heidi type, with long braids and strong milking hands,' Lola says. 'Anyway, there's a bit here about the Gay Pride March in London. Apparently, this lot are running a minibus. Of course, we'll drive up.'

'Why don't we go on the minibus? It could be a laugh, we might meet some new people.'

Lola sniffs. 'I don't think we need to worry about getting to know any of that lot.'

* * *

As a surprise, Lola books them a night in a hotel near Leicester Square, and it's difficult to argue with that. Lola's Diane tells them that she is booked into an all-women hostel, with bunk-beds and a shared shower block. Apparently, that's where everyone else from outside London stays, and after dark it quickly becomes bacchanalian. It's a shame to miss out, but Lola has promised that their hotel room has a free-standing bath big enough for two.

The sun is a sliver of pink on the horizon when they leave Cardiff. Eluned packs them a Thermos of tea and two rounds of sausage sandwiches, with enough brown sauce to squeeze over the crusts. Lola says she won't mind if Eluned dozes off, but there's no way she'll be able to sleep. Lola navigates them through central London without consulting a map. They come into the city through Hammersmith and Kensington, the rising sun illuminating the Natural History Museum so it glimmers like a cathedral. Next, they pass Harrods, burgundy flags fluttering over racing-green awnings. It's the gold standard of window displays. If they've got time, Eluned'll pop back and see if she can pick up any tips.

Their hotel is tall and thin, with potted lemon trees either side of a glossy black door, and boxes of pink geraniums hanging from the windows. A world away from the pokey B&B she shared with Mabli. Lola parks her car and hands the keys to a red-hatted valet. The receptionist balks at handing over the keys for a double room, but Lola wields her posh voice like a knife slipped underneath the ribs, and they're soon handed a thick leather fob.

Lola changes into a flared pink dress that clashes extravagantly with her red hair. Eluned has made herself a sleeveless shirt-dress in a cotton that's breathable enough for a day when she'll sweat conkers, but heavy enough that it won't crease. It's a shameless copy of one from work. She draws two interlocking Venus symbols on the fat of her cheek with eyeliner and uses her Visa to create a sharp, pink cheekbone.

Lola pulls their placards out of her duffle bag. Between the NUM and the RCN, they're both well practised at making placards. Lola has written 'Lesbianism is Beautiful' on hers, and Eluned has painted a wreath of peonies to frame the words. Eluned had deliberated before writing 'WALES REMEMBERS' in blocky letters. No. Not specific enough. Eventually, she'd chosen 'Don't Die Wondering.'

'Can we carry them in the bag for now?' Eluned asks. 'I don't want mine to get bent.' It's a bit much, walking with it to the march. It will be alright when they're together. She won't feel so vulnerable then.

Lola raises her eyebrow. 'You're going to be walking through the middle of London. You better get some practice in.'

Eluned tests the weight of her placard in her hand. The wood is still rough. She's bound to be sucking splinters out of her fingers for days. Lola suncreams their arms and chests, and Eluned refills their water bottles. Lola strides through the lobby with her placard thrown casually over one shoulder, beaming at the receptionist. Eluned keeps her head down and the placard turned to face her legs.

The meeting point is near their hotel and a small crowd is already forming, placards and banners flying like the sails of a great armada. The police are circling, keen to keep the queers in line. Next to the Met Police, Graham and his band of thugs look like softies. Eluned's hand convulses within Lola's grip, and she pulls hard on Lola's arm to steer her in a wide circle around them. They find themselves a shady spot under a tree, where Eluned can lay down her placard and light up a fag. Lola trots over to the Gay Nurses Society, and Eluned scans the crowd for anyone she knows. It's good to smile at someone and know they're smiling back for the same reason.

The leaders blow their whistles; the crowd is big enough that it takes a while for Eluned and Lola to have enough space to move forward. Lola strides out like an actor on the stage, balancing her placard on her shoulder while she waves at the passers-by. Eluned can barely look up from her shoes.

'*One. Two. Three. Four. Open up the closet door!*
Five. Six. Seven. Eight. How'd you know your kids are straight?
We're here! We're Queer! Get used to it!'

If there's anything that Eluned's childhood equipped her for, it's a spontaneous political sing-song. She breathes the same rhythm as those in front, bodies working together as one machine. Lola improvises with her, subbing in both 'Stop the violence, stop the hate' and 'Pussy tastes really great'.

Policemen flank the march, staring impassively in the same way they did at the pickets, but the crowds behind them look mostly curious or bemused. A handful of men with shaved heads and denim jackets scream 'faggots' and 'pillow-biters'. They don't look like the sort of people that want to be won over. Eluned averts her eyes and smiles at a young woman watching from a doorway, hands folded up inside her sleeves.

By the time they reach Kennington Park, Eluned's arms are numb from holding her placard, and her face is prickly-hot. The first marchers have laid down their banners and are lying about with guitars and bottles of cold beer. Eluned gropes in her bag for cigarettes and water. As she slips a cigarette between her lips, she sees June, only a metre or so away. There's no shortage of short-haired women wearing leather at the march, and Eluned has done a double-take at many of them, but she's certain that this is June. Mind you, Eluned had been convinced the last one was June, until she noticed that her jacket was brand new and impeccably tailored.

'June! June, it's me!' Eluned shouts. Her heart is thumping. She can feel it in her throat, in her temples, in the pads of her fingers. It must be the heat, bringing the blood to the surface.

June's not looking. Come on June, just turn round.

'I'll get her,' says Lola, before she sticks two fingers in her mouth and blows to make a sound so shrill that Eluned jumps and several people turn round.

June stops. Her stance is defensive, shoulders hunched as she scans the crowd. When their eyes lock June grins, and jogs over in her creased Doc Martens, Tippex smeared up the sides.

'Happy dyke Christmas,' June says. The end of her nose has caught the sun, and her pale scalp looks pink and sore. She's wearing jeans, a leather waistcoat, and not much underneath it. A large metal rectangle with DYKE stamped unevenly onto it hangs from her ear. Eluned presumes that, like her clit brooch, June must have made it herself. Her other earlobe is bare, with flecks of crusted-on blood around the hole.

Lola grins, sweeping her red curls out of her face. 'Happy dyke Christmas to you, too. Peace be with you!'

'And also with you,' June returns.

'Lola, this is June. June was part of the Lesbians and Gays Support the Miners branch that supported us. They literally kept us from starving. June, this is Lola. My girlfriend.'

June's eyes flicker over Lola, lingering over muscular, ward-honed calves. 'Do you live up here now then? Eluned, you should have said! What about—'

'No, we both live in Cardiff. I'm lodging, and Lola has her own place.'

June nods enthusiastically. 'You did it! That's rad. We're having a party later. You'd both be welcome.'

'Oh no. We've made dinner plans with Lola's old Oxford college friends,' Eluned says.

There's a flash of sly humour in June's eyes. *Dating a posh bird, are you?*

'Where's the party?' she asks.

Lola answers for her. 'Shepherd's Bush. Our hotel is near Leicester Square.'

Eluned only has a limited understanding of how London fits together like a giant jigsaw.

June hums. 'Ah, out west. We're in Camden. You can get the Central line across to Tottenham Court Road and then up on the Northern line. We party late, so join us after your dinner if you want.'

Lola claps. 'Sounds perfect, I'll swipe some good plonk off Bernie.' She leans forward to feather a kiss on June's cheek. 'How special to meet you, June. Thank you for the invitation to your soiree.'

Eluned doesn't dare do the same. June's shoulders are red, and that leather looks roasting. Her skin is probably deliciously salty by now.

'Thank *you*,' June says smoothly. 'Gotta love a pair of girlie dykes.'

Eluned claps June hard on her upper arm. 'See you later, mate.'

Bernie lives in a smart townhouse with a bronze lobster-shaped knocker. The lobster is so enormous that Lola can't fit her hand round its body. Instead, she knocks with one of its claws.

Bernie rips the door open, shouting, 'Lola, you ghastly old goat! Get in here!'

Lola squeals and bustles into the house, leaving Eluned stumbling after her. Bernie's hallway is nothing like Lola's, with champagne-coloured walls and gleaming white tiles.

'Follow through, girls! We're in the dining room.'

The dining room is decorated in the same style, with a grand oval table and carved chairs. The women are birds of a feather, full of esoteric knowledge and not shy of speaking over each other. Reminiscing about their old-fashioned dons and rowing along the Cherwell takes a whole hour. Bernie hasn't brought out any food yet, and Eluned could happily eat her cloth napkin. She passes time thinking about how things might be going in Camden.

'Eluned, Bernie was asking if you had joined my salon . . .' Lola says pointedly.

'I know that she usually insists that her acolytes do.'

Bernie smirks while Lola giggles. There's something going on.

'When I look that word up in the dictionary, I know I'm going to need to punish you for letting her get away with that,' Eluned says to Lola, trying to keep her tone upbeat.

'At least it wasn't catamite. Anyway, Bernie's just jealous,' crows Lola.

Lola's migraine hits like a storm rolling in across the sea. First she knuckles her temples but, as it worsens, she slurs a little, like her tongue is too big for her mouth.

'Do you need to go back to the hotel?' Eluned asks.

'I can get the . . . you know. The train back by myself. Or I'll call a whatsit?'

'Are you sure you should go on the Tube by yourself?'

Lola grimaces. 'You shouldn't let your friend down.'

She is grey in the face. A good girlfriend wouldn't let Lola travel home alone while feeling unwell. Eluned wants to be good.

'Eluned, don't patronise me.'

Fine then. She tried. She can hang on to that. She helps Lola to the Tube station.

'It was all that sun earlier,' Lola mutters. 'All I can see is stripes.'

They both get the Central line back to Tottenham Court Road, and then change to the Northern line. Eluned is going north, while Lola heads south. Eluned waves as Lola shuffles off down the platform, one hand clasped over her eye like a pirate's eyepatch.

The squat's front garden is strewn with abandoned banners and placards, pavement vibrating slightly with bass. Eluned knocks as hard as she can. What if the offer has been rescinded? June might have only wanted Eluned-and-Lola as a package deal.

The door swings open and there's June grinning, hands wrapped round a stubby beer bottle.

Her outfit looks more like something you would find in a stable than in a clothes shop. The leather straps do nothing to cover her up; she's naked from the waist up. Her nipples are circled by O-shaped rings, holding the leather straps in place. They run in parallel lines down her stomach, throwing the gentle curve of her waist into sharp relief. Another strap runs horizontally across her chest, over her sternum, and Eluned wonders if June would fall into her if she tugged it. When they slept together, June was ghostly pale, blotted with dark freckles. But her skin is warmer now, and more substantial. Her right nipple is pierced with a silver hoop like the one through her nose, and her thin neck is ringed by a short length of chain, a rusty padlock hanging down into the dip of her clavicle.

'So you dance in Depeche Mode videos now?' Eluned says.

June hollers. She wobbles, then whispers, 'I've been on the beers since about two!'

Jesus. She must be hammered, there's nothing to her! 'Well, it is dyke Christmas after all.'

'Where's Lola?' says June.

'Migraine. She gets them terrible.'

There's another woman behind June, leaning on the banister so she can toe off her trainers. She gives Eluned a slow, appraising look before grabbing a six-pack of Breaker from her rucksack and heading off through a door.

June leads Eluned past the mountain of discarded boots and the odd high heel sticking out from between them. Eluned tugs a neon-green shoe out by the heel to look at the label. Only Topshop. The kitchen looks like the Tunnel, full of bodies pressed together tightly. 'You Spin Me Round (Like A Record)' blasts so loudly that the glasses in the cupboard chatter.

'Here's where your best stuff is,' says June. 'Booze. Jaffa Cakes. Booze. Party Rings. Maybe a bit of something stronger, depending on who you ask. Twiglets. Wagon Wheels.' She points through the door to the lounge. 'That's where your proper lesbian food is: hummus, olives, mung bean salad, stuff with nutritional content.' She rolls her eyes back in her head, letting her tongue loll out of her mouth, then pours rum in a glass and tops it up with lemonade. Eluned stacks four Jaffa Cakes in her hand.

Outside, the music is loud enough but stops short of rattling your skull. The day's warmth is still bouncing off the paving slabs, but people are starting to drift towards the bonfire.

June grabs two deckchairs and drags them over to two women curled over each other in one chair. Esther is squashed on the bottom, hair wrapped up in an apple-green scarf that sings against her rich brown skin tone. On her lap is Joy: aptly named, with a wide, round face and full cheeks that push her glasses up when she smiles. They're childhood sweethearts from Trinidad, now both nurses at St Barts.

'Give us a Jaffa Cake,' June says, holding out her hand. Eluned frowns but tosses one to her. June nibbles around the edges and picks off the chocolate, before dangling the jelly disc over her mouth. Eluned tells Esther and Joy about Lola, and they end up talking about Care in the Community, their new uniforms, and the stagnant wages. It's like her dad swapping stories with the miners that came to visit from Yorkshire. Same shit goes on everywhere.

'June!' A woman shouts from a window above them. 'June, come up here!'

June gets up from her stool. 'I thought that the benefit of communal living was that other people would share the work.'

Esther reaches under the deckchair and pulls out a four-pack. She cracks one open for herself, then Joy, and passes a third to Eluned.

'Alright comrades, what's happening?' shouts Grit.

Eluned snickers. The only person she's heard using 'comrade' in a social setting is Dad's trainspotter mate who sells the *Socialist Worker* door to door. She says as much.

Grit picks up the fourth beer and makes a chucking gesture at Eluned, before grinning and pulling the ring open.

'June said you came up for the march with your missus. Where were you standing?' Grit asks.

'Behind that drag queen in the purple dress, and the gay Christian lot.'

'Ah,' says Grit. 'Did you see a group of about ten skinheads with those stupid fucking braces?'

'I saw a couple of skinheads shouting, but not ten.'

'Good,' says Grit decisively. 'We must have seen them off then. They were waiting near the park and of course June wanted to have a go. Rather her than me. I thought she was going to lose an earlobe at one point. That stupid earring.'

Small girls are always like Jack Russells when they scrap. She can't blame Grit for staying out of the way. The fash are full of hate for everyone, but they cut their teeth on anyone who isn't white. Grit's well out of it.

'Well done on the strike,' says Grit, stretching her legs out next to the fire. An air pocket bursts inside one of the logs, showering them with fine embers that burn out before they land.

'We lost. The Tories broke us.'

Grit shrugs. 'In revolution you fail until you win.'

Maybe she'll try that on Dad, the next time he's moping about.

'What are you working on?' Eluned asks.

Grit tells her they've been making money for a women's shelter, and for the new HIV testing centre in London. 'June's designed some new posters that are *bad*. They're up in her room. Ask her to bring them down later.'

As if Grit has summoned her, June springs out of the house and across the garden, leaping over piles of blankets and spare wood. 'They're practising for when they do a scene at the next Chain Reaction,' she pants. 'Arrow's going on in a minute, Eileen is finishing. She's topping Aida, but I made her do one on me!'

June points to a thin red welt across the surface of her nipple. That must have stung.

'You coming?' June asks Eluned.

Eluned gets to her feet, asking for an explanation as they make their way around the bonfire. People have already sat in their deckchairs, and more guests are drawing up wooden pallets and kitchen chairs.

June answers. 'It's a night in a gay bar in Vauxhall. Whips, chains and performance art. Absolute heaven, obviously. If you come up again, we'll have to go.'

And she'd thought the go-go dancers at the Tunnel were racy. Maybe she'll ask Lola if there's something like that in Cardiff.

Back in the lounge, someone has made a stage from two low tables, with a fluorescent tube light propped up beside them. The room is packed tight, even with the sofa pushed into the corner. Grit, June and Eluned squeeze through the crowd. Eileen is poured into a PVC corset, dark hair pulled back from her face. In front of her, a fat girl who must be Aida leans over a kitchen chair, arse like a tiger.

Eileen prowls around Aida, crop held loosely in her hand. She waits before striking. Eluned holds her breath. She must be calculating where to do it, how hard to do it. It looks like Eileen barely flicks her wrist, but the leather whistles when she brings it down. Aida flinches as her flesh ripples; her teeth are gritted tight, and Eluned can't help wincing in sympathy. June is on her tiptoes, cheering.

Some of Aida's tiger stripes have raised up into blisters, and Eileen kindly works around those, sticking to the skin that is carnation pink. Eileen is clever. She's watching, always watching, Aida. Eileen moves down to fresh skin at the crease of the thighs and Aida bucks, crossing one foot over the other until her knees buckle.

'Bend properly,' Eileen instructs, and Aida's legs unpeel themselves. Eileen gives a brisk swat between them, and Aida howls.

Eileen whispers in Aida's ear and she nods back, curls bouncing. Eileen helps her up, folding a flannel dressing gown around her. Someone runs over with a pint of orange squash and a curly straw, handing it over to Aida. The women rise together, bowing and waving to the room. Eluned shoves her fingers between her teeth and tries to whistle like Lola.

Grit changes over a cassette tape in the corner of the room and people drift away from the stage. Some women dance with their tops off. It's certainly warm enough; the windows are steamy, and the lights are hazy with a fog of cigarette smoke.

June leans up to shout in Eluned's ear, 'Arrow's coming on next. No one knows what's going on most of the time. It's a bit conceptual, but someone usually gets naked.'

Arrow's mouth flaps gormlessly as she mouths along to Poly Styrene before she starts careening in circles, in time with the crashing guitar. This is a good one; Lloyd taped her 'Germ Free Adolescents' off the radio a lifetime ago. When the sax kicks in, Arrow brings her hands up to her mouth, miming playing. Arrow is a whirlwind. She seems to move without fear or thought. Her knees hit the wood. She skids across the stage, and then appears to be dragged up by an invisible rope round her waist.

Arrow turns around and draws her top off, exposing the sweaty curve of her back. She runs her hands over her buzzed head, writhing so that the muscles along her sides shimmer like waves. *Whoosh,* and her skirt lands somewhere across the room, exposing a merkin made of artificial flowers, the sort you see laid on graves. It's on the knife-edge between sexy and hilarious. Eluned is rooted to the spot.

Arrow squats at the edge of the table and plucks off a petal, throwing it out into the crowd.

Another petal is ripped off, this time bringing a couple of others with it.

Arrow reaches out and hovers her hand above the women until someone jumps up to seize it. Arrow's in control. She leads the woman's hand to the merkin and lets her choose between the petals. Lilac. Ruby. Coral. Magenta. The woman rips off a violet one and cheers, showing her friends her plastic prize. After that, they yank rose petals off Arrow in handfuls, showering themselves with joyful abandon, until everyone can see the tiny mesh thong where she's poked the flowers in. Maybe it says something about women giving and giving until there's not much left. The crowd's greediness is surprising. They seem happy to reach out and strip the petals from her, some even ripping out a whole flower and its plastic stem in one go.

By the time Arrow makes her way to Eluned and June, her petals are practically gone. She squats, so that almost all her vulva is on display. One of her inner labia has fallen out to the side, where it hangs like a rose petal itself.

'Pick a flower, *flower*!' Arrow purrs.

June plucks a petal the colour of egg yolk and throws it behind her. Eluned picks its twin, and Arrow plays to the mob, making an agonised face as if Eluned has ripped it straight from her skin.

'You can touch me, if you want.'

June moves her hand down, brushing her fingers though Arrow's pubic hair. Arrow stretches her mouth wide, more like a gargoyle than a coquette. Eluned can feel the press of the crowd at her back, restless and wanting. Poly Styrene yells over the speakers. June keeps going, feathering her fingers over the point where Arrow's labia meet. June's eyes move to Eluned's face, holding her gaze. Eluned gingerly places her fingers on Arrow's mons, like it's dough she doesn't want to knock the air out of. June's narrow fingers pass over Eluned's and dip between Arrow's labia. They come out glistening. The women move closer, jostling to get a look. Eluned can smell Arrow, clean and salty, so June must be able to, too. The voyeurs will have to imagine that part. Eluned watches June's rhythm closely, copying it in a mirror image. Arrow shudders, her knees shaking on the tables in front of them. Their fingers move together.

'God, I wish this was you,' June whispers.

Eluned's fingers falter. 'Do you?'

'Yes,' says June, and before the sound fades, Eluned is on her. June tastes of synthetic orange and bonfire smoke, and Eluned hooks her finger round her leather collar to pull it tight round her neck. The harder she tugs, the more urgent June's groans become. June's breath hitches as it cuts off her air. Eluned makes rumbling noises from the pit of her stomach that feel as strong as the bass from the speakers.

'I don't want to kiss you—' says Eluned.

June jerks back. Her hand folds across her chest, rubbing at her clavicle. Eluned tries to peel her forearm away, but it's like an iron bar. June's nostrils flare.

'No, no,' Eluned pleads, 'I don't want to kiss you and feel guilty.'

June's jaw flutters. Her teeth must be working under there.

'I think it's time we have a chat,' June says.

She's right. It's way overdue. They slip out of the crowd, leaving Arrow to twist and tantalise on the makeshift stage. June picks up a green jumper from the back of one of the sofas, pulling it roughly over her harness.

Joy and Esther are still squashed in their deckchair, hands and feet drawn in tight underneath a tartan blanket. The bonfire has grown, sending flickering shadows around the garden as women chat and sing in its glow. June leads Eluned to the back of the garden, where it's darker. They walk behind a raised bed full of something tall and leafy. From what she can see it's home-made, old bits of wood hammered together roughly. Eluned wedges herself up to sit on the edge of it. Orange embers drift past like fireflies.

'Get this in your donnies,' says June, placing a beer in Eluned's hand. 'Let me see you do that trick again,' she says.

Eluned puts the neck of the first bottle at an angle to a wooden pallet and thumps down hard on it.

June lights a fag and pops it directly between Eluned's lips before leaning in with a cigarette dangling between her teeth, lighting it from the end of Eluned's. *In France, that means we fuck*. The red glow illuminates June's face. Even down here, you can still hear the music.

June sits with her thighs spread, hands dangling between them. 'Why is Grit playing this shit? Is this The Bangles?' June asks.

'It's Madonna. "Crazy For You". Listen, the flute bit will be coming up.'

'I'll bow down to your superior Madonna knowledge.'

'Bow to me, I like the sound of that,' Eluned says. Oh dear. It wouldn't have been so bad if she'd been able to keep her tone light, mate-to-mate, laddish. But it came out low and direct.

June blows a narrow plume of smoke up to the sky. 'What would Lola have made of that display we put on in there?'

'Funny you can remember Lola's name but never got your head around Lloyd.'

June shrugs. 'I try not to remember men's names unless I need to.'

Nothing about June suggests she's sorry. 'I think Lola would have enjoyed it.'

There's no way that Lola wouldn't have joined in. She'd have ripped those petals off Arrow's merkin faster than anyone else, mugging for the crowd all the way.

'Is it an open relationship?' June asks.

Eluned thought not. She isn't seeing anyone else, and Lola is prone to grand statements, like how she's never met anyone like Eluned. Nevertheless, a few things have rattled her. The casual way Lola introduced her ex. Bernie's careless mention of 'acolytes'. She gets a strange feeling in her gut sometimes.

'Bollocks,' says June. 'I don't want to break one of my Cardinal Dyke Rules. It's not sisterly.'

'What are the other Cardinal Dyke Rules?'

'Well, "Don't fuck with anyone with a boyfriend" and "Don't get attached to anyone outside London." I'm not doing well.'

Well, fuck. That's not something Eluned would have predicted. If she had, she'd have gone about some things differently. She'd always assumed that the last thing June would want was Eluned, a foetus in lesbian years, trailing after her. June seems to sink into herself, chin on her sternum, shoulders knitting around her ears.

Eluned keeps her tone light. 'Is there a rule against thinking about your ex-boyfriend when you wank sometimes?'

Pining after June is a given, but it's Lloyd that makes her feel like a fraud.

June laughs. 'Well, you had a whole six minutes or more each time. That's a lot of reminiscing material. What about with Lola?'

'Oh, we're talking *Gone with the Wind* length. Including the intermission. I always look hungover if I'm on an early the next day.'

'Lucky cow.' June takes another drag of her cigarette.

How would this have gone if Lola wasn't poorly? Less late-night introspection, more heading upstairs to see if they could fit three adults into June's narrow bed. Or would they have taken her back to their hard-won double bed at the hotel, trailing the unapologetically dykey, leather-clad June through the marble reception?

June must be waiting for her to say something incriminating. They sit through 'Slave to the Rhythm', a long remix that sends only the bassline and occasional French horn to the bottom of the garden. The back of her brain is always ticking over, working out what's playing. She can't help it. After Grace, there's the new Hüsker Dü track, 'Don't Want to Know If You Are Lonely'. That's her guess, anyway. Punk mostly sounds the same when you can only hear the bass and the drums.

June scratches the end of her nose. 'How many lesbians are there in Cardiff?'

'Dunno. It's nothing like London.'

'But still a lot, yeah? It's a decent city.'

'I guess.' There's enough to sustain the events advertised in the back of the Womyn's Liberation Newsletter. She's always fancied the roller disco at Splott Leisure Centre, but Lola says skating makes her feel sick. Mostly there are the same faces at every event, and half of those are couples. Happy, monogamous couples should stay at home.

'How many women did you meet, before Lola?' June asks.

Smoke makes her eyes itch and water. Her hair will smell of fire tomorrow. She closes her eyes, tries to invite in the excitement that she had sitting across from Lola at the Star of Wales back into her body. Lola's scarlet nails and her garlic breath, her warm breasts against Eluned's.

'None. Just Lola.'

June raises her eyebrows at Eluned. 'And you weren't tempted to shop around?'

'I wanted to get it under my belt,' says Eluned. 'I wanted to be able to say that I'd made the right decision.' Eluned has always been so impatient. To the heterosexual palate, Lola is as challenging as Babybel. She's the first Oxford graduate Eluned has ever met, financially solvent and with a wisteria-draped Victorian home. Eluned has done well for herself.

June gets out another cigarette and lights it with shaking fingers. This time she forgets to pass one to Eluned. The skin on the sides of June's fingers is red and bitten. If June was hers, she'd apply soft creams to them, pumice off the spots where the skin has grown back thick and hard.

Gravel crunches as people stomp down the path. There's a bang, and a thump, and then giggling. A woman's voice. 'Who is that? June and . . . someone?'

Grit answers. 'Let's turn round and go back. I think they'll be a while.'

Eluned bounces her leg as June smokes and stares at the fence. She guesses the next song by the drums alone. 'Absolute Beginners'. They must be taking the piss. Down here, the twinkling piano is lost. She never bothered to see this in the cinema, in the end. By the time Bowie gets to the soaring chorus, her pulse throbs through her palms. Absolute beginners, indeed.

The moon silvers the clouds, and the leaves tremble in time with the percussion. It's sacrilegious to talk over this saxophone. Instead, she counts the beats while she watches June swig her beer. June pitches the bottle up and over the fence so it crashes into next door's shed, spraying shards of glass into the night.

Eluned might as well be honest. If it gets uncomfortable, she'll give June a fake address and never come to Camden again. Easy. 'If you felt attached, then why didn't you ring me last March?'

June starts, 'Mark wrote to—'

'Your branch of LGSM wrote, the Lesbians Against Pit Closures, too. They had a fun day! I wanted to hear from you, June Carr of Camden Town.'

'I thought about it a lot. I made a couple of things, wondered if you'd like them. Sometimes I'd put a tune on and think, "What would that saft Welsh cow make of this?" After that mad phone call, I didn't know where I stood.'

Eluned is going to scream. 'I'm sorry, it was after I got laid off. I was going mad watching telly all day. I needed someone to *see* me.'

June rubs the back of her neck. 'That'll send you yampy. Why didn't you call us to help you move your shit to Cardiff? Dykes love any excuse to get stroppy in a van.'

'I didn't need you to help me move. My parents drove me.'

'After the strike ended, I went back home for the first time since I left. I think you made me want to,' June says.

This is a turn-up for the books. 'How did it go?' Eluned asks.

June aims a half-hearted kick at the fence in front of them. 'It went. The strike was different there, not as solid, but Dad stuck it out. We're both Tauruses.'

June kicks the fence again, sending a chunk of wood towards their feet. Figures that she's a stubborn old bull.

'He's back at work now. But he's not the same. He don't talk,' June says.

'Mine's quiet too. Mam says he needs time. What have you got on?'

'A bit of cash-in-hand. I've done some cartoons for me and Dharma to read together. And there's these.' June draws her hand along the surface of the soil. 'We're doing a veg swap with two other squats in North London.' She smiles wryly. 'It's all go here.'

Eluned doesn't need to be thinking of June patiently drawing cartoons for the little girl or pulling up vegetables and washing off the soil to see what they've grown. The wood is cutting into Eluned's arse, giving her pins and needles down her thighs. June stretches, jumper riding up to show her soft white stomach and the leather straps across it. She still wants to know what happens if she tugs those straps. It's time to go back. She says as much, and June tells her to get the N2 night bus, tracing her fingers over Eluned's crumpled map to show her where she needs to go. Eluned walks through the garden, waving to Grit, Joy and Esther.

June stands on the lip of the front door. It makes her taller. Still a dwt though. She strips her jumper off her head and passes it over. The wool is still warm. June's nipples pebble in the cool night air. It's soft against Eluned's sunburnt shoulders, smells of June. Baggy on June, it pulls underneath Eluned's armpits and barely stretches over her stomach.

'Thanks. I'll give it back to you when I see you,' Eluned says.

June reaches out and tugs at the seams of her jumper, evening them out. 'There you are. Keep in touch, Eluned,' she murmurs.

Eluned doesn't want to go. She wants to chat around the fire with June until the sun comes up, a blanket over them so no one can see their entwined limbs.

The music fades into silence as she reaches the main road. Maybe she'll treat herself to a Walkman. It would be less creepy if she could walk with music. She tells herself it's no different from walking back from Casablanca to Mrs Omar's.

It stinks of baked piss. There's only one other person at the stop, a boozed-up bloke with a tray of chips, staggering between the bin and the edge of the pavement. She lets him clamber on before choosing a seat a few behind him. Best to keep him in eyesight.

When Eluned gets in, their hotel room reeks of vomit.

'Lola? Lola, are you okay?' she shouts.

Her handbag spills out over the carpet as Eluned runs through their suite. Lola lies huddled on the far side of the bed. Please don't be dead. Lola's sick-stained face hangs over the side of the bed. She's breathing. The peach valance is streaked with sick, but Lola has caught the rest with the bin. Breathing through her mouth barely helps with the smell.

Eluned washes out the bin in the peach shell-shaped bath and runs one of the hotel's monogrammed flannels under the cold tap before taking it through to wipe Lola's face.

'Here you go,' she soothes, 'You'll be more comfortable now. Do you need anything?'

Lola shakes her head feebly, gazing up at Eluned. 'Thank you,' she breathes.

Eluned spoons against Lola's sweaty back, kissing her hair. She feels terrible. Lola's been here sicking her guts up while Eluned has been getting cosy with another woman.

'I love you,' Lola whispers.

Eluned ralphs. She stumbles from the bed, pressing her hand to her mouth, fingers clamped together to stop the flow. It's the acrid smell that's setting her off. That's all it is. Too much sun, too much booze, and the smell of vomit.

Lola's Cortina's seats compress Eluned's broad shoulders, and her legs are too long for the footwell. She turns on one hip, and then the other, to give her knees a rest.

She made a mixtape for the drive, but Lola says she doesn't

want to be distracted by anything new until they're on the motorway. After Junction 8 Eluned gives up waiting. Lola hasn't listened to any of the records she's loaned her. Eluned holds June's jumper on her lap and smooths it like a cat, letting the bonfire smell take her back to last night. If she closes her eyes, she can hear the crackle of the logs and the women laughing.

Maybe she's being too harsh. Lola is probably knackered; migraines always exhaust her. There are some rowdy songs on Eluned's mix.

'Two of June's friends are nurses from Trinidad. They were telling me about it,' Eluned offers.

Lola jumps in, 'One of my first practical tutors came over on the *Windrush*. She trained at the Tavistock—'

Eluned's patience is short today. Maybe it's the hangover. But she's nodded through whole evenings while Lola shares tales from her nursing training. Lola is not getting away with taking over this conversation.

'Joy explained this new system where nurses rate patients based on dependency . . .'

Lola inhales, but Eluned won't let her interrupt. Lola's eyes widen and her hands tighten on the steering wheel when she describes Eileen and Aida's performance. When Eluned gets to Arrow's petal merkin, she trails off. Dangerous ground.

Eventually, they hit the Severn Bridge. When she was little, Eluned used to pretend it was the Brooklyn Bridge. 'I love crossing the border,' she says. 'It's so funny to think you've been to a whole new country.'

'Principality,' Lola says. 'Wales isn't a country, it's a principality.'

'Of course it's a country. How is it not a country?'

Lola gives a tinkly laugh that seems to insinuate that she doesn't think anyone could be so stupid as to believe that Wales is a country.

'Do you need a passport to get over the border? No. Do you have your own currency? No. You don't have a head of state, and you didn't want a baby parliament.'

Eluned splutters with indignation, struggling to sit up properly in her seat. The seatbelt cuts into her sunburn. 'We've got our own language, our own flag. It's not our fault that we were colonised. We had our own laws way before *you lot*. And I wasn't old enough to vote in that referendum. I would have voted yes.'

'It always bores me when Welsh people say, "The English this, the English that". Wales was conquered by Henry VIII and hasn't been its own country since. You're undermining your own argument, darling,' Lola says.

'Conquered,' Eluned spits. 'But still a nation.'

'If you want to say Wales is a nation, you can. I'm helping you think critically and refine your arguments.'

White noise buzzes in Eluned's ears. Smug, condescending bitch. It's tempting to make her pull over and hitchhike the rest of the way to Cardiff. Eluned is sweating cobs, and she fishes for a Chinese takeaway menu to fan her face with.

'Are you staying in Splott tonight?'

'I told Mrs Omar that I'd be back after work on Monday, so she'll be startled if I turn up tonight.'

'You do pay her rent, darling, she's not your grandma. You can stay there whenever you want.'

'Do you want me to go back? Is that what you want?'

'I thought you might have changed your mind,' Lola says, gliding her car smoothly between two lorries.

'Have you changed *your* mind? Is that it? You're trying to get me to say I've changed mine.'

'Why would I do that? You're so suspicious.'

They sit in silence for the last hour, while Eluned stares at green slabs of nothing. Finally, Lola pulls off the motorway and starts driving through Cardiff. Maybe it would be better if she just went home. Mrs Omar will be settling in with *Coronation Street* and a box of Black Magic by now, and Eluned wants nothing more than to join her.

'I'm knackered. Drop me off in Splott then, if that's what you want.'

Lola parks up and gives Eluned a brief peck over the gear stick. She's got déjà vu. The door handle in her hand. The bag at her feet. Feeling sick to her stomach. It's like when she broke up with Lloyd. Now she's messed it up again. Her throat constricts, her eyes prickle. No. She won't cry. Not now.

'I'll give you a call in the week,' says Eluned. Lola's car disappears round the corner before Eluned has even got her key in the lock.

20

6 July 1986

Lola's choice for the next salon book is bizarre. Eluned doesn't bother to finish it; the protagonist is a cold heiress fucking two married women. She spends most of the book shuttling between different parties, avoiding her lovers like they're painted figures inside a cuckoo clock.

They've barely seen each other since London. Lola says it's her shift pattern. Eluned has had a long week too. Thanks to the summer sale, none of the girls get a break in their shifts, and the heatwave is making her feet swell enough to make her feel like she's smuggling grapefruits in her socks. Madonna releases *True Blue* and Eluned buys both the vinyl for her room and cassette for Madge. She lies in the breeze underneath her open window, listening to 'La Isla Bonita', dreaming of white sand and rolling waves. The only time she moves quickly is when she hauls herself to the hi-fi to skip over 'Papa Don't Preach'. Mabli's wedding is this Saturday, and Eluned is grateful for the distraction of staying at Lola's for the weekend. Mam and Dad have both tried to persuade her to come, but there's no way she's sitting in the congregation like it's normal to get married and not have your only sister as the bridesmaid.

Lola leaves her front door on the latch. The humidity hits Eluned as she enters the hallway. The heavy fabrics and general clutter trap the heat in; no wonder that Swiss cheese plant is doing so well. Eluned takes one last deep breath before she crosses the threshold. Lola shuffles her tarot cards, silky vest tucked into a forest-green devoré skirt. Lola waves her hand at the wine on the coffee table.

'I've brought beer.' Eluned settles herself on the sofa arm. She rubs Lola's freckly bare shoulder. 'I missed you. I've barely seen you.'

'I've been working. The hospital has been bedlam recently. Not literally, but you know what I mean.'

'That's okay,' says Eluned. She gently pulls a chunk of Lola's hair away from the rest and starts plaiting. When they were small, she loved to plait Mabli's hair. Lola keeps shuffling, eyes on the fireplace. You can usually never shut her up. Is she angry? Was someone else from Cardiff at the party, did they see June and Eluned together? Lola deals three cards, setting them down with a decisive snap.

The first card is upside down, some woman sitting on a throne. The second two are upright. They're not famous; one has a man face-down with a long row of swords in his back, and the other is a heart with three swords driven through it.

'What do they mean?'

Lola gives Eluned a baleful look. 'Nothing good.' She flicks one across the coffee table. It spins until it bumps into the overflowing ashtray. 'Loss, betrayal, ignored instincts.'

Lola knows about Mabli's wedding. She should know Eluned is feeling fragile. It's a shame Lola can't put her theatrics off until after the weekend; Eluned really doesn't have the hwyl for it. If she's got suspicions about what Eluned did at the party, she needs to spit them out now.

'Maybe the cards are telling you what they thought of the book?'

Lola gives a hollow laugh, 'Maybe.' She continues to shuffle and deal, shuffle and deal, exuding a sense of frostiness so distinct it overpowers the humidity of the room. Eluned's half-finished plait hangs near Lola's ear, gradually working itself out.

When the doorbell goes Lola springs up, face lighting up as she strides to the door. She's transformed into someone altogether more effusive and magnetic, pouring out wine and slotting dishes of griddled artichokes into the fridge.

'How was the march?' Diane asks. 'I'm gutted that I didn't manage to make it up to London.'

'It was fantastic, wasn't it?' Lola doesn't wait for Eluned's response. 'I popped in on Bernie. Always a delight!'

Once again, Eluned might as well be an inert object. 'I went to a party at my friend's house, too. She lives in a squat and—'

Lola cuts in smoothly, 'There was a bigger turnout this year, and fewer religious nuts telling us to go to hell.'

'Claudia said they had a laugh in the hostel too. Soho is so pricey these days, so they bought some voddy and took it back to the dorm. They were sharing with some girls from Newcastle. Four in the bed, by all accounts!' says Diane.

Next time, Eluned will stay with everyone else.

Lola draws her thumb and index finger across her mouth. *Smile*. Eluned didn't realise she wasn't. She smooths her forehead, twitches the corners of her mouth up.

'Where does your friend live, Eluned?' Diane asks.

'Camden.'

'Eluned got around on the night bus by herself! I was so impressed. Do you remember the night we fell asleep after New Year, Di? We woke up in Tottenham Court Road station, didn't we?'

When the other women arrive, Lola calls everyone to attention by tapping the side of her glass with a cake fork. 'So, what do we think of *The Passion of Miss Ella*?'

Eluned thumbs through the pages of her library copy. She doesn't have a lot to say.

'I could practically taste those desserts.' Deidre lowers her voice to a conspiratorial whisper. 'And the sex scenes weren't bad either, were they?'

Deidre mentions a scene where Ella has her maid get her off underneath her massive skirts. It's bullshit, not arousing at all.

'I don't get how a feminist publisher thought this was alright,' Eluned blurts. 'Ella never asks, she tells her to do it. The maid would get the sack if she said no.'

'I think it's subversive to let Ella have that power,' Lola starts. 'The house is a liminal place.'

Eluned protests. 'The maid doesn't work there because she likes it.'

Deidre smirks. 'She's been reading her Marxist literary criticism!'

Diane chimes in with something characteristically tiresome and meandering. Eluned promised she'd call Mam tomorrow, but she will just want to talk about the wedding. Considering Mam doesn't even like Graham, she certainly has a lot to say about their nuptials. She's even been drying out rose petals to scatter on their tables. It's not that Eluned wanted her parents to boycott the wedding because of Mabli's ridiculous homophobia, but Graham is still Graham. What happened to 'All Coppers Are Bastards'?

'Are you quite with us?' Lola says, cutting through Eluned's thoughts.

This is the part where Lola goads her into saying something stupid and repeats it back to her in a sing-song accent.

'If you're not going to join in, maybe you could put some coffee on.'

Eluned blinks.

Lola turns to Deidre and adds, 'I think Eluned had hoped to catch up with her reading on our trip, but I think she ended up following her own passions.'

'I don't know what you mean.'

Come on then, spit it out. Why couldn't she have said it earlier?

Lola raps her fingers against the base of her glass. 'It's a good job I'm not a suspicious woman.'

Diane loses her grip on her book; it bounces off the table and lands on the floor. The other women are silent, eyes as big as dinner plates. Eluned burns from her toes to her scalp. It's a set-up, Lola's a minotaur. How many other young women has she gobbled up like this? Have these women watched each one? They're old enough to know better. Eluned floats somewhere over her body.

'I'm going to take the cheeseboard out of the fridge,' she says. It sounds like another voice.

Eluned rises gracefully, like a string is tied from her head to the ceiling. Her own hands look unfamiliar. She runs them under the hot tap until she can feel the stinging heat in them. She's got to think it through properly. She's got to add the figs and walnuts to the cheeseboard. No rash decisions this time. She can't afford to burn bridges in Cardiff.

Lola closes the kitchen door with a soft click. 'Why are you embarrassing me?' she demands.

'Me? Embarrassing you?'

'Storming off, making it look like I've upset you.'

'I don't know what you think you're accusing me of—'

'Yes, you do. Coming back at 3 a.m. after stranding me on the Tube. I know you've got form.'

Bringing up Mabli is a low blow. 'That was entirely different!'

Lola lowers her voice. 'I told you I loved you and you vomited and went to sleep.'

'I hurled because all I could smell was your spew, which was at least ninety per cent red wine, by the way.'

'What happened at the party?'

'Can't we do this later?' Eluned pleads.

'Something happened,' says Lola, eyes corvine. 'I know it.'

Fine. She'll apologise now to shut Lola up. A movement catches her eye. Diane's gleeful face peeking through the glass panels in the door.

'Fuck this, I'm off,' says Eluned.

She rips the kitchen door open and Diane freezes, like a child tiptoeing away from the biscuit tin. She's a clueless middle-class cow that's not woman enough to face Eluned. Eluned is exhilarated, drunk on power.

She could give the tablecloth a firm tug. Make a monstrous spectacle of herself, like they so clearly want. Send plates and glasses flying before their eyes. Instead, she swipes her handbag, leaving her copy of that awful novel open on the table. In the hallway, she stuffs her feet in her shoes. She braces herself with her whole hand on the mirror, leaving a print. It has needed a clean for a long time; maybe Lola will finally do it now.

Lola rounds the corner, hair like a flaming halo. 'Why are you showing me up like this?'

'Me showing *you* up? You orchestrated this evening around calling me back to heel.'

The coat stand is laden with jackets, bags and scarves. Eluned gives one sleeve a hard pull. The stand topples diagonally across the hall, with a crash so loud that some of the other women scream. Lola's nostrils flare, and a muscle at the side of her mouth twitches. She lifts her long skirt, and steps neatly over the fallen stand. Her look is so cold that it puts the fear of God into Eluned, and she scrabbles at the door, fingers fumbling with the latch, the handle. Lola is right behind her. Eluned charges into the street, bag swinging wildly.

'Eluned, come back inside,' Lola instructs. Her voice is low, slow, like she's talking to a non-compliant patient.

'No,' Eluned spits. Now they're outside, the panic ebbs away. Madge bolsters her. Beautiful Madge. There to take her wherever she needs to go. 'I don't have to answer to you. You're a fraud! I can't believe they let you look after sick people!'

There's so much scurf in her handbag. Eluned roots through it, waiting to close her hand round her keys.

Lola catches up with her. 'You should think carefully. It's not going to be easy to find someone to guide you like I've been doing.'

'I don't need you to guide me.'

'It must be difficult when you feel the urge to sabotage your relationships because you're not happy . . .'

What does that psycho-bullshit even mean? She sees herself reflected in Lola's window, mouth distorted with rage and jacket hanging off her shoulder. Beyond the reflection she sees the salon watching like they're out for a night at the opera. She'll give them something to watch. Eluned picks up one of Lola's plant pots and hurls it into the window. The smash is satisfying. Shards of pottery and lumps of dirt scatter across the front garden. The faces behind the window disappear.

Lola grabs Eluned's wrist. 'Being in a same-sex relationship is more emotionally complex, and not everyone has the necessary maturity.'

It's nothing to do with maturity. She doesn't love Lola because she's a psychopath. She loved Lloyd, and she could love June if they ever spent more than a day together. She needs to pull free. She needs to get in Madge and start driving. She's not going to end up like Mabli.

Lola tightens her fingers round Eluned's wrist but Eluned jerks her arm, shaking herself free. Lola stumbles on the uneven concrete, yelping as her ankle rolls underneath her. Her eyes are wide and watery, lip caught between her teeth. It was an accident. Eluned could stay for a few more minutes, let

Lola lean on her arm until she can walk again. No. She turns her back on Lola and rips Madge's door open.

She throws her handbag into the passenger's seat. Lola is reflected in the wing mirror, limping along the pavement.

'You'll hurt her, too.' Lola hooks her fingers over the top of Madge's door, so Eluned can't pull it shut.

'Are you attached to those fingers?' Eluned asks.

Lola moves her hand back, lets it flop at her side.

Finally. Eluned's off. She works a fag between her lips and stabs at the cassette player. The tape is left on 'Open Your Heart'. She cranks it up and winds down the windows, fag in her teeth, to let the sound ring through Canton. She sings with her whole chest. The sun is still out, Madonna is a goddess, and the road is unspooling in front of her.

She pulls off the motorway when she can, following the yellow glow of Wimpy. She orders two cheeseburgers and a Coke, and then finds a payphone. She calls Mrs Omar and tells her not to expect her home. If she's gone longer than the weekend, she'll have to call in and pull her first sickie. That's a long way away. She shouldn't count on a warm welcome.

By the time Eluned gets to Camden, her arms are numb. She leaves her handbag in the footwell. Taking it with her is tempting fate; she's only popping in for a chat. But it is London, so she kicks it under her seat.

The front room curtains are pulled tight. Eluned hammers at the door for long enough to start considering whether she should drive back to the guest house she spotted on the high street. Then a chain jangles, and June's green eye appears in the crack before June opens the door properly.

'Eluned! How come you're back so quick?'

Eluned's face crumples, tears welling up. June scratches her ear. This isn't the impression she wanted to make. It's better to stare at June's left hand; it's silver with pencil lead, only the shallow creases left white like wintery tree branches. Focus on them instead.

'Did you . . .?' June starts. 'Isn't this the weekend your sister . . .' She trails off.

Eluned nods tearfully.

'Jesus. I'll make you a tea.'

June's face is so earnest that it sets Eluned off laughing, a wild sort of cackling.

'Come on, neither of us are shocked. I think the bigger shock was that I managed to drive through London without crashing the car.'

June's mouth twitches. 'Everyone else is down the pub. I've been stuck looking after Dharma, you'll have to come up with me.'

June makes two cups of dark tea in mismatched mugs.

'You could trot a horse across that,' Eluned says.

June bumps her hip against hers and wedges a half-empty packet of digestives in her back pocket.

Lily and Dharma's room is up in the attic. Eluned wraps her hand round her mug to stop from spilling her tea up the steep, narrow stairs. June leaves a trail of drips up the carpet. It's eerie to be in the house when it's silent. Eluned has only known it full of noise.

Dharma is asleep on her back, clutching the tail of a stuffed shark, its head squashed and misshapen. She has a proper crib, but Lily sleeps on a mattress on the floor. June flops down onto it, clearing a space for Eluned amongst her debris.

June shuffles on the mattress so she can sit on folded legs. 'Tell me what happened.'

Eluned cops to the fight in the street. June's lips twitch, hand moving restlessly over her notepad as Eluned speaks. Shapes emerge out of the nest of scribbles: a curly-footed coat stand, a flowerpot, an open book.

'I got in the car and followed my instincts,' Eluned concludes.

June thumbs rhythmically at the corners of her sketch-pad. There's a mural above the bed: two pink, frilly jellyfish linking tentacles. A small red crab with a bowler hat. A stingray with a kindly smile. The longer she looks, the more she notices what's underneath the paint. Freckles of black mould swamp the body of a blue whale. Paint bubbles underneath the skin of a long yellow fish. Elsewhere, strips of paint have peeled away altogether, exposing beige striped wallpaper.

Eluned looks over at the bed. 'Isn't the damp bad for Dharma?'

'Probably. But Lily wants to live here, she's got her reasons.'

'Can't you fix it?' asks Eluned.

'We pay a nominal rent, and the council tolerate us because we do the garden. We've no idea when we might have to move on.'

'You said there are a lot of houses?'

'All over London. Some people have been given full-on mansions, they're like villages.'

'Do you think I could stay for the weekend? I know the timing isn't good. It's never been good. But I want to get to know you better.'

It's tempting to rip that notebook out of her hands and fling it across the room. June loops her arm round Eluned's back. Their conversation meanders through music, places they've eaten, people they know, and back again. As they talk their bodies slide into each other, until Eluned is lying with her head resting on June's chest, June's socked feet rubbing along her calves. Eluned's Swatch is somewhere underneath June's back. She has no idea how much time passes before there is a hammering on the door.

June springs to her feet. 'You watch Dharma, I'll talk to Grit.'

June returns upstairs with Lily, who hiccups as she shrugs off her jacket, letting it pool on the floor as she leans over to kiss Dharma's cheek.

'Grit doesn't mind sleeping on the sofa,' June says.

Lily drops down to the mattress, kicking her heeled boots off as she drags the duvet over herself. 'Go and get on with it then girls.'

On June's bed, Eluned stares at the damp on the ceiling, finds the old man carrying a bale of hay. June's T-shirt is rucked up. Eluned plays a game, touching each of her fingers to one of the brown moles on June's stomach. It's awkward; she's got to stretch out her little finger and curl her thumb underneath her hand. June pinches firmly at the back of Eluned's neck, rolling Eluned's flesh between her fingers. June must be hitting some sort of voodoo point there; the tension in her shoulders evaporates.

'Are we ever going to . . .?' Eluned asks.

'I wasn't sure how long your mourning period was. It seemed like the body was still warm, so to speak.'

'Oh. It's cold. The coffin is in the ground.'

'Is the wake done?' June asks.

Eluned digs into the metaphor. 'Definitely. We've had the dried-out egg sandwiches. Next, there'll be the national anthem, except most people can't speak Welsh and will be making random noises.'

'I bet that sounds beautiful. My family just fight and mainline whisky.'

'I wouldn't say no to a whisky.'

'I've got a bottle under the bed, help yourself.'

Eluned leans over the side of the bed, pulling out a large plastic box. She roots around, looking under the sketchbooks and wallets of photographs. At the side of the box there's a plastic shaft with a ring round it, connected to a tangle of leather straps. Underneath, she finds a bottle of whisky and two small glass tumblers. The label has a stag looking off into the distance against a purple tartan background. She's never heard of it.

'What it lacks in depth of flavour, it makes up for by being forty-eight per cent,' June declares as Eluned pours two fingers into each glass.

Eluned strips the pins from her hair, letting them pile up on June's dresser. The gel is thick enough to keep her hair standing up by itself. Hard to believe she only did it this morning. There's an old party trick she used to do to make Lloyd laugh.

'Watch this,' she says, wedging her stubby whisky tumbler into her cleavage. She twists the glass until it feels stable and bends forward, so the whisky sloshes up the side of the glass. The bed is soft underneath her knees, so it's hard to keep steady.

June lets Eluned pour it over her lips and down her throat. Her swallow is audible, even against the music coming from the room next door. June smacks her lips, letting her pink tongue trace the rim.

'Do it again.'

Eluned tops up the glass and leans forward. She kneels on a knackered part of the mattress, and falls forward. The whisky fills June's mouth until she coughs, dribbling down her chin and neck.

'That burns!'

June's neck tastes of whisky and salt. The slower Eluned drags her tongue along June's sinewy neck, the faster her pulse jumps.

'You do it,' demands Eluned.

June's not wearing a bra, and her nipple ring gleams in the lamplight. She slaps her tiny tits. 'How can I hold a glass with these?'

'Push them together! Come on.'

June presses the glass against her sternum and does her best. Eluned lies back, and June shoves her chest forward. Whisky splashes over Eluned's face and hair, freckling the bedsheets. It stinks. Her hair is going to be a wreck tomorrow. One giggle turns to hysteria. June catches it, and the bed trembles with their laughter.

'June!' A voice comes from the other side of the wall. 'Shut the fuck up, man!'

'I'm sorry,' June wheezes, 'I'll clear it up for you.'

June laves her tongue across Eluned's chest and sucks at her lace bra. June's lips are as red and glossy as strawberries doused in sugar and left in the sun.

'Hang on – I need a piss.' June struggles to her feet.

Away from June's bed, Eluned feels unmoored. June holds her hand, squeezing to warn her of the creaking floorboards.

The bathroom mirror is a horrible shock. Under the fluorescent lighting, she has a sallow tinge. The front of her hair is limp and stringy, while the back is tangled and matted. 'Ych-a-fi.'

June scrubs at her face with a bobbled old flannel. 'You what?'

Eluned picks at a blackhead. 'I look grody. You can probably pull any night of the week in any pub in London.'

'I kicked Raquel Welsh out of bed last week.'

'Will you laugh at me in the morning?'

June prods at Eluned with the end of her toothbrush. 'I'm not entertaining you. Do you want to borrow this? We ain't got no spares, so it's the best I can offer until morning.'

Eluned takes the offered toothbrush. The bristles are all bent and splayed, but it will do for now. June sits on the edge of the bath and rests her head on Eluned's hip, humming as Eluned works her spare hand through June's hair as she brushes.

21

7 July 1986

Eluned is woken by the crunch and thwack of June biting off her fingernails and spitting them into the ashtray on her bedside cabinet. They better be going in the ashtray, anyway. June's single bed is too small for two adults; Eluned has slept with her arm twisted up like a shark fin and now she's got a dead hand and a sharp pain in her neck. She wiggles her fingers until the feeling comes back, and cracks open an eye.

June has a crossword book on her knee, one pencil between her fingers and another tucked behind her ear. 'Yellow spice used as a dye,' says June.

'Turmeric?' Eluned suggests.

'Perfect. Book of the Bible. Four letters?'

'John? Mark? Luke?'

'I know *those*!' June protests. 'I'm not a degenerate. I went to Catholic school. Oh! Acts.'

Catholic school. Huh. June kneads Eluned's breast as she pencils in another answer. Eluned closes her eyes, lets herself drift, tethered only by the scratching of June's pencil. The next time she wakes, June is clambering back into bed with a stack of toast and marmalade.

'Do you want to stay the weekend?' she asks, settling the plate on the duvet between them.

'Are you sure?'

'I wouldn't have asked if I wasn't. I've got stuff that I need to do, but it would be less boring with you around.'

Having a weekend off is a rare treat. She was planning to stay with Lola over the weekend; walk some of the Taff Trail and pop into the Leccy Club for the women's disco. She hasn't got a clue what June's 'stuff' is, but maybe she'll be selling T-shirts outside the Palace or going out to see a band. She wouldn't even mind a brawl outside an embassy if that's what June has got planned. It's a beautiful morning. Mabli has probably been awake for hours, having her hair teased and curled and sprayed. Hannah and Tirion will be pinning her veil in with pearl pins and helping her step into white satin heels.

There was no way that Eluned was going to be relegated to the second row, crammed in with Graham's piggy mates. She can't watch her sister marry someone who wants to shrink her, year on year. No thank you. If Mabli had really wanted her there, she could have found a way to give Eluned the message by now.

Maybe it's the adrenaline, or the sex, or the whisky sweats, but Eluned is honking. She can't even bear to touch her T-shirt. June drags out a battered cardboard box from underneath Grit's bed.

'They're all ours,' she says. 'There's some knock-off shit and some London bands: Cock Sparrer, Killing Joke, the Slits, that sort of thing.'

Eluned roots through the tangle for some XLs. She picks out *WITHOUT LESBIANS, THERE'D BE NO MELODRAMA*. There's a more outrageous one underneath, a silhouette of two women in leathers, one standing in pointed boots and the other kneeling at her feet. It's a clever design, the way June uses negative space to suggest a sheen on the leather, and the shape of their hair.

'Please let this one be an XL,' Eluned says, holding it up against her.

'I dunno,' teases June. 'You lot are a dirty bunch, the rude ones go quicker in the biggest sizes.'

Sadly, she might be right, as this one is a medium, and she can't see any others. Eventually, she chooses a mustard T-shirt with 'Rubyfruit' printed in round, raspberry letters. She did love the book.

June and Eluned take the Northern line and Victoria line to St Pancras. She emerges from the Tube sweaty and squinting, but June doesn't let her rest. She hoofs them full lesbian speed through squares of smart houses, black iron railings and neat green grass. There it is, Gay's The Word. She's heard so much about it, but she's never been. June explains that today they are shaking buckets for Body Positive, a meeting group for people with HIV.

Eluned is determined to be vigorous, downright relentless. She wants her shoulders and back to ache from the weight of her bucket. June hits the street first. Eluned pauses. The awning hides her in shadow, and she eyes up the shoppers. For heaven's sake, she's a saleswoman. She does this day in, day out. All she needs to do is step out and ask if they're interested in donating to charity. A smart-looking man in chinos strides past.

'Sorry to stop you, cariad. Could I talk to you about something called Body Positive?'

He looks startled by her accent, staring at her mouth like he's having trouble working out the words. His eyes flit between her bucket and the name of the bookshop.

'I'm in a rush,' he bites off.

June withdraws money from people quickly. She's nimble, fearless, moving around people like a dancer. She walks backwards as they manoeuvre around her, bounces and skips to keep up with them. June doesn't bother to explain Body Positive, just leaps around people until they throw coppers at her in exasperation. She does particularly well with the women, coaxing a smile out of most of them.

'Checking out the options?' Eluned teases. Half-teases.

'It's the easiest way.' June grins. 'Find the ones who look at you as if you're resting right on the line between what they want and what they fear. Let them know you see them.'

Cadi the paediatric consultant from Howells is the first thing that comes to mind. The Electric Ballroom, staring at June through the frame of the two women dancing, is the second.

A woman with a glossy blond Dusty Springfield fringe bobs towards them, tote bag swinging from her elbow.

Eluned moves into her space. 'Is that Rive Gauche you're wearing?' She'd know that bergamot and rosemary anywhere. Half of Cardiff are wearing it, and she sold it to most of them.

The woman hoists her tote bag further up her arm. 'Yes.'

Eluned wastes no time, touching her forefingers lightly to the woman's wrist. 'Have you heard that Princess Diana has been doing a lot of charity work with AIDS sufferers?'

The woman tries to tug her arm back, but Eluned meets her eyes. Her wrist slackens under Eluned's hand, and she doesn't look away. Eluned rhapsodises about Body Positive in the way she talks about her creams and powders at work, until she squeezes two fat pound coins out of the woman and into her bucket. June smirks over the woman's shoulder.

It's 1 p.m. by her Swatch. Mabli will be getting ready to glide down the aisle of St Margaret's Church in her high-necked puffy-sleeved nightmare of a gown. Maybe Graham's already at the top of the aisle, chatting with the vicar. Hopefully Mam will remind Mabli that it's never too late, there's still a way out.

Two blokes come to relieve Eluned and June, and they head back inside. June sits on the cash desk and devours a packet of prawn cocktail crisps, then lets the shop's giant white dog lick the neon orange dust off her fingers.

Eluned's never been in a gay bookshop before. It's overwhelming to see shelves full of gay lives, gay stories. She picks up a novel with two women in evening dresses on the cover. One of them is a redhead wearing a tight green pencil skirt. She looks a lot like Lola. On a sunny day in London, Eluned is surprised to feel that her anger has already cooled, giving way to something like nostalgia.

Eluned pays for the novel. When she gets home, she's going to write 'Sorry about the plant. Best, Eluned,' on the inside cover, and pop it in the post. It will make Lola laugh. Maybe she'll even get it framed, the mad old bitch. Something to show to her next 'acolyte'.

After lunch, the air prickles. The sun dips behind the tall red townhouses, casting long grey shadows across the street. Sirens wail faintly in the distance. A well-dressed man calls June a 'dirty dyke', and his teenage son laughs. Eluned's hand clenches round the handle of her bucket so hard the coins inside rattle. She's tempted to pull the prick forward by both ends of his red scarf and give him a smack.

June's face is carefully blank. 'Enjoy the game, mate.' She swings herself away from him and mutters, with feeling, '*Tosser.*'

'You alright?' Eluned allows herself to slip her fingers into the back of June's waistband.

'Don't worry about it. We've made a few quid today.'

They head into Gay's The Word's backroom and tip the coins out onto a large table. Eluned is used to cashing up. She stacks the coins, calling out the totals for one of the other women to write down in a ledger. It's over £200, and June seems happy. It's not a bad start. She's already itching to come back tomorrow and have a go at beating it.

They cross Euston Road and walk the long way home through Camden. While June gets fags, Eluned finds herself staring at a faded rack of postcards outside the newsagent. Mabli would like the one of the sun setting behind St Paul's Cathedral. Maybe she could buy it and write something heartfelt? The moment is broken when June barrels out of the shop, ripping out the gold paper from her fag packet.

Next, June stops them beneath an apple tree, incongruously planted on the grass verge alongside the road. She pulls out a tightly knotted Tesco bag from the inner pocket of her jacket, and hands it to Eluned. The trunk is dark, bark blackened with ash. June scours the grass, kicking aside cans and fag packets. Eluned is the first to find an apple. It's pinched and gnarly, a melancholic shade of green. Mamgu would say they weren't fit to give to horses.

June isn't deterred, shimmying up the trunk to seize fruit direct from the branches and pelting them down at Eluned until they're bulging out the bag. Back at the squat, they have the run of the kitchen. June pulls up two mismatched dining chairs, a stool between them. She rinses the apples under the tap and takes the washing-up bowl out to the garden to dump out the water. She hands Eluned a short, sharp knife with a worn wooden handle, and a plastic bag for the peel. Eluned can barely bring herself to touch the apples. The first one she tries sinks into brown sludge between her fingers. June is braver, hacking off chunks of wrinkled skin and bad flesh, flicking white grubs off her fingers and into the bag.

They talk as they work, filling the bowl with the best of the apples. June rubs flour, butter and sugar between her fingers to make a rough crumble. Eluned heats the apple on the stove with two spoons of dusty brown cinnamon. She hasn't done this for years. Mabli always used to like a crumble, the tarter the better. Every summer they'd have baskets of rhubarb from Dewi's allotment, all methodically stewed down for pies and tarts. They'll be at the reception now, tucking into the wedding breakfast.

'How are you doing, bab?' June says, kicking Eluned's chair leg with her socked foot. 'You look miles away.'

Eluned shrugs. 'Tired.' June probably wouldn't get it. She ran away to London after all, and she's hardly the type to want to be a bridesmaid.

After tea, June gets the crumble out of the oven, doing a twirl for everyone hooting at the sight of her in a floral apron and oven gloves. Eluned spoons while June switches out bowls underneath the lip of the oven dish. When the bowls run out, they fill up saucers and plates and, finally, mugs.

Eluned eats hers squashed between June and Grit. *University Challenge* plays on the telly in the corner of the room. Her family don't watch it, but she's happy to play along. Abusing the contestants is a sport for June's housemates. Grit calls a watery-eyed boy from Durham an 'inbred, bow-tied cunt', before he even says his name.

A lad from Corpus Christi blinks erratically when Gascoigne asks him an easy music question. It's Jim Morrison, obviously. Eluned mutters 'Tweedy weirdo,' when he answers Jimi Hendrix. Hendrix! Grit grins and slaps Eluned's arm, while June shifts so her cold knees press into the side of Eluned's thighs.

Eluned is full of secret glee when she gets two questions right. The first one is primary school. What does *Llan* mean in a Welsh place name? Gascoigne says it means church, but it's closer to parish.

The next one takes her by surprise. She has no idea where the answer comes from. She spent most of science staring out of the window at the rugby pitch. Yet she finds herself blurting 'pancreatic duct' out from wherever it's been hiding since her O levels.

June whistles. 'You could be up there.'

That's ridiculous. 'Wouldn't catch me with those wankers!'

After the jaunty theme tune finishes, they slope off to June's room. They make love under the sheets with the lights off. Eluned slithers down into the dank heat of the duvet. June smells strong and sour, like crab apples. They've spent the whole day together, and she can taste it on June's skin. As she licks, she massages the backs of June's wiry thighs. Maybe she's feeling the strain of the day here, too.

Monday comes round quickly. June's got to sign on for her dole and she's got some cash-in-hand work in the afternoon, repainting the toilets of a local pub. Grit says she's happy to sleep on the sofa if Eluned wants to stay longer, but it's time to go home. She's working an open-to-close tomorrow, and they're getting a Japanese brand, Shiseido, in for the first time. There'll be free samples, and she's not missing out.

June leans through Madge's window, handing over a cassette and a sandwich with a thin slice of orange cheese between two slices of white bread.

'Here you are,' she says. Eluned pops them on the passenger seat and looks up at June. June worries the tiny white ulcer on the edge of her lip, wedging her fingers under her armpits. Eluned fetches her mirrored aviators from the dashboard and puts them on, swallowing hard around the lump in her throat. She can't bring herself to start the engine.

'Oi, what do you call the West Midlands' only cheese and communism society?'

'What?' says Eluned, checking her fuel and angling her wing mirrors at the same time.

'Red Leicester.'

'That's horrendous.'

June grins. 'Absolute shite. I just made it up now.' She shuffles from foot to foot, shoving her hands deep in her pockets.

What seemed simple now seems complex. If they had a bit more time. Just a day or two. The sky is a deep cobalt blue. They could be entangled on June's bed, soaking up the sunbeam that falls upon the covers at this time of day before it creeps across the room and on to Grit's. She can always come back. It's a quick run down the M4. She pushes her key into the ignition, and watches June wave in the wing mirror until she turns the corner.

'Eluned!' Mrs Omar shouts from the front room. 'Is that you?'

'I'm putting the kettle on; I'll be there now.'

Eluned makes two strong teas and brings them through, pinching two chocolate digestives from the plate on the coffee table. She's timed her drive well, arriving right at the start of *Coronation Street*. The camera moves over the familiar rows of red-brick houses and the ginger cat settling itself on the roof. It starts with the Cabin, Rita and Mavis refilling enormous glass jars of sweets in their corner shop.

'Spontaneous weekend in London?' Mrs Omar asks. Eluned indulges herself in a fantasy of Mam phoning Mrs Omar in a flap to insist Eluned comes back for the wedding. It gets lurid quickly, Mabli crying down the phone, begging for her big sister.

Eluned tucks her toes into the blanket. 'Just to see an old friend.'

'And you didn't stay with your friend after the book club?'

'Nah.'

Mrs Omar fixes Eluned with canny eyes. 'I take it that you'll be staying in with me on Monday nights from now on?'

Eluned nods, dunks her biscuit until it sags. Comfort is a mushy digestive.

'It's best that you work this out now, my love. I had a boy in Newtown when I was your age. A sweet lad, but he always put his mother first. Never a good sign. Anyways, I met Yusef the next year.'

Eluned grabs another biscuit. Mrs Omar always likes to natter on when she's been home alone a while. Yusef Omar was certainly handsome; there's a studio photograph of the pair of them on the lounge bookshelf. Eluned has often stopped dusting to admire his oval face, the light bouncing off his cheekbones, and pork pie hat slightly askew on his head.

Mrs Omar continues, 'The Somalis are poets, see. They're born with a natural affinity for language, like the Welsh.'

She's heard this bit before as well, but it makes her smile every time Mrs Omar says 'Som-ahhh-li', with that hard, slanted pronunciation.

'They've been in Cardiff since Queen Victoria, did you know that?'

Eluned didn't. That's about when her own ancestors came from west Wales to the Valleys.

'Doesn't mean it was easy to court a Somali man though. Not even down the Docks. Allah? I wouldn't have minded if he'd worshipped Cliff Richard! I thought he was *gorgeous*!'

In the hallway, the phone goes. Eluned unwinds herself from the blanket and pads to the hall. 'Cardiff four, six, four, seven, seven, eight,' she answers, stretching the phone line taut so she can sit on the stairs.

'This is London nine six one, seven six two, three one three, four hundred and six. June speaking. Do you read me? Over.'

'Shut up,' Eluned hisses. 'That's how Mrs Omar likes me to answer.'

'How was the drive home?'

'I timed it well. Stopped for a Wimpy and back in time for *Corrie*.'

'We were watching that as well, Rita looks like a drag queen tonight. I've phreaked the payphone, so we can chat. Did you have fun this weekend, bab?'

'Did you?' It's obvious that Eluned did. It was beyond her expectations.

'You know I did. Why are you making me go first? Is it because I've got *short* hair? Do you want me to be the *boy*?'

'Don't be stupid,' Eluned splutters. 'I thought it would go without saying that I'm keen.'

Saying it out loud feels like opening a window on a warm day. She can't get too carried away, but it felt good to stay the weekend. There's something worth growing. Eluned scrunches her eyes shut. It's easier to imagine that June is there. She curls the telephone cable tight round her finger.

Mrs Omar appears in the doorframe, blanket folded over her arm. She says, 'I need to go up to bed, bach. I keep nodding off. I've put the rest of *Corrie* on to tape. Can I get by you?'

Eluned shuffles across the stair so there's room for Mrs Omar's swollen ankles and fluffy slippers to pass.

'Is that the legendary Mrs Omar?' June whispers.

Mrs Omar strokes Eluned's hair with the tips of her papery fingers as she passes, 'I'm glad God brought you to me, Eluned Hughes.'

'Me too. Nos da, sleep well,' Eluned says. Mrs Omar grabs the banister, heaving herself up the top step.

They lapse into silence, June's breathing loud and crackly through the receiver. Eluned is knackered. The drive has done her in. She turns so she's sitting on her hip with one cheek pressed against the stair carpet. Her breathing lengthens until she hears June shout, 'You're falling asleep! Go to bed, I'll give you a ring tomorrow.'

Upstairs, she opens her bedside cabinet and roots around until her fingers find the Mars bar that June gave her after her first trip to London. In the dark, she peels back the plastic wrapper and digs her teeth into the soft nougat.

June's first letter arrives in a creased envelope, one addressee already crossed out. The stamp is wrinkled, as if it's been soaked off one envelope and glued back on to another. The first part of the letter is a small card, with a job advert for an electrical engineer on the other side, stapled on to some larger pages of writing paper.

'LEEN,' June writes, with a jagged, jackknifed L that the other letters fit inside. It takes her a second to work out that it's an English approximation of 'Lun. June's writing slopes down the page and creeps back up the margins.

Thought I'd write. I'm waiting for my giro. They probably think I'm busy writing in for a job, thick bastards. Sorry for smudges, I'm caggy-handed. Getting the DLR to meet Grit after – handy the office is by the station. Got some CIH at a house clearance. They said we can car-boot anything we think 2 good 4 skip. Staff here are on shit money. I've seen one woman working down caff. Had my eye on her in case she was there to rat us out, but just skint. Bosting night at RVT yesterday. Grit said now I've got a woman I need to stay in to look after the babby. Fuck that! Lily didn't want to come anyway. We had a great dance. New queen on the block – big fake tits like bowling balls. Grit ditched me – went up to Abney Park to see who's at it in the cemmo.

June illustrates her letters when spelling seems to stump her. Her drawings are not elaborate, just loose lines and a bit of cross-hatching. She draws herself with a lumpy, jacket potato-shaped head, a few swipes of the pen for hair. Her mouth is one single line, bent into an 'o' or an upwards slope or the tentative curve of a smile.

Eluned is stooped over her ledger, tallying up her sales for the week, when a slight gentleman in a cream Burberry coat sidles up to the counter.

Eluned asks, 'Can I help you?'

'I'm looking for a lipstick for my wife,' he says.

'What sort of colours does she like?' Eluned asks. She doesn't have high hopes; husbands usually can't distinguish between taupe and scarlet. She has no qualms about selling them the top-range choices, along with a liner, a gloss and a bottle of Lipcote for good measure.

'She has remarkably similar colouring to me. She's called Rhona, my wife.' Then he winks.

Who knows what that wink is about, customers can be a funny bunch. She rolls up two of their best-sellers, Black Honey and Misty Cinnamon, and draws them across her forearm in two thick lines.

'Do you think Rhona would like these?' she asks.

He leans in to Eluned and speaks under his breath. 'I've seen you around. You're always drinking in the Showbiz and the Quebec.'

Eluned falters. 'Oh really?'

It's not like she's done anything wrong; people can drink anywhere they like. Her pulse quickens. No one at Howells has any idea what she does outside of work, but if they overhear, they might have some questions.

'You may have seen me, or Rhona, there before, too.' He winks again, slowly.

Oh. Her pulse slows. Not a threat, after all. Comradery.

'Misty Cinnamon is pretty. I think Rhona's a little old to be wearing full-on slutty red these days, though she might like to,' he says.

Eluned holds her hand up beside his face. 'Are we ever truly too old? But Misty Cinnamon is warmer, complements green eyes.'

He buys the lipstick. Eluned packs it up and throws in a handful of perfume samples and sachets of moisturiser. She says, 'I've put something in there for Rhona. Next time you see me out, you must say hello.'

He leans in to give Eluned a kiss on the cheek. 'Darling, I'll buy you a drink.'

The next week, a willowy woman makes her way over to Eluned. She says, 'Rhona sent me in, I'm looking for new foundation.'

Eluned sits her down on a stool and tilts her chin towards the windows. Her foundation is too light. It looks like Sudocrem.

'I bought it from a catalogue. I couldn't try any on, I went with the lightest.'

Eluned finds her a better shade and wraps the glass bottle up with a handful of free samples they've been given. A travel lipstick. A concealer. Blue mascara.

When she's gone, Toyah sidles over. She says, 'You shouldn't serve them, you know. It puts other customers off.'

Eluned slaps the notes into the till, clacking the lever down on them. 'You don't like me making more sales than you?'

Toyah stalks to the other side of the concession, making a right meal of tidying up the boxes. It's a shame that Rhona and her friends even need to come in and look at these old trouts. Maybe Eluned should start buying it with her staff discount instead, splitting the difference between her and the customers. With the samples and free gifts she gets, plus the odd missing lid or damaged box. Could be a good side-earner.

Eluned has been saving up stories to write June. She's already written down the story of getting blanked by Lola at the Tunnel, and dancing with a girl with long swinging braids and cool, dry palms at the Casablanca.

June replies on a messy note shoved inside the front cover of a back copy of *On Our Backs* magazine.

> *Well done Leen! You're our woman on the inside. Bonus of blending in, I guess, like Ben.*

Ben's their civil servant, a principal at the Treasury. He's an anaemic sort of bloke, with a pinstripe shirt and a widow's peak. She suspects they keep him around for his access to the government printers. Eluned's infiltration isn't on the same scale, but at least Rhona and her friends have somewhere to get their slap. Eluned's found a rhythm of taking orders from them when they're out at the bar, bashing in the corners of the packaging and buying the products up for cheap.

June can't get on a bus without someone shouting at her, or worse, but Eluned still dreads being called a contemptible 'straight gay'. She confesses as much in her letter and is shamefully gratified when June sends back her doodles of Eluned's body: her arm striking the cap off a beer bottle, the backs of her calves, a dainty chain strung round her thick neck. The lines are strong but fluid, the proportions well observed. June writes, 'Nah mate. You reek of lesbianism, but the make-up fools the breeders.'

22

18 August 1986

The kettle shakes like a dog having a nightmare. Eluned loops the stubby half-pint bottle of milk over her little finger. They're out of milk, again, but Mrs Omar would rather send Eluned to the corner shop three times a week than risk an ounce going to waste. Eluned has only just taken her shoes off; she's not going out again. She dribbles a teaspoon of milk into her tea, trying to leave enough for Mrs Omar to have another before bed. Her tea is still transparent, the same colour of bricks. Oh well, it's warm and it's wet. It's only when she slots it back in the fridge door that she sees a six-pack of Babycham plonked in the middle of the big shelf. Mrs Omar doesn't drink.

There's a shard of scrap paper stuffed into the cardboard finger-hole. It says, in Mrs Omar's shaky hand, that Mabli's baby has arrived. Kelly Claire Jones. Seven pounds, four ounces. Eluned should drive up to the hospital. Screw pride, she should buy Mabli some flowers and drive over there. Then, Graham's smirking face, swinging a truncheon. Mabli's slim fingers, worrying that awful turquoise fabric. Eluned leaves the tea and takes a bottle to the hall and punches June's phone number into Mrs Omar's phone from memory.

'Mabli's baby is here.'

'Oh wow. How much does it weigh? Why do I always ask that? I've no idea how much a baby is supposed to weigh.'

Eluned picks the foil off with her finger and snaps off the lid on the side of the banister. What is Babycham anyway? Fizzy pear juice?

'I don't even know if she wants me to come and see it. If she'll let me, even,' she says. She couldn't take being turned away at the ward.

'You're the queer sheep of the family now. Get used to it.'

Eluned frowns at the leaping fawn on the bottle. Sounds trite enough to go on a T-shirt. Is it one June's already made, or has Eluned given her the idea? 'You're talking to me, not writing for *Spare Rib*,' she says.

'This is a rite of passage. Not everyone is going to value you enough to pull their head out of their arse.'

'She's my sister.' Her voice is claggy with tears. She clears it with a slurp from the bottle. No dainty glass here. This fizz goes down easy.

June snorts, the sound turned into a white fuzz of noise through the cheap receiver. She asks, 'So what are you dreaming of, in your alternative timeline? Bringing your kid to the hospital to see their new cousin? Lloyd and the pig having a wee dram in the waiting room?'

'No,' Eluned snaps. 'Of course not. But can't you be nice?'

June is more perceptive than Eluned will admit. It's worth it, but there is a part of her still grieving for what she gave up. If only June was there. Eluned wants to wrap her hands round her back, breathe in the warm scent of her neck.

'You'll never guess what happened earlier,' June says.

'What?'

'Grit said she saw that bloke from Depeche Mode and his missus in Chinatown. I said, "Where are they?" and she said, "Oh no, Dave Gahan."'

'June, what are you—'

'Dave Gahan! They've gone!'

Oh Jesus, but she can't help laughing.

June's voice softens. 'Look, why don't I book myself a train ticket to Wales?'

Eluned wraps her hands round the receiver like it's a hand saving her from drowning. She'd need to work out her shifts, ask Mrs Omar, think of somewhere to take her. But she would love June to come and visit.

That weekend, Eluned takes June for Welsh cakes straight from the bakestone, a walk around the Docks for June to photograph the mudflats and the cranes, and a night out at the Tunnel. Sunday evening, after June leaves for the train station, Eluned turns to the space to the right of her and asks, 'Get the sugar out the cupboard, will you Ju'?'

It's a beat before she even realises her mistake. Her fingers feel strange, disconnected as they grip her mug.

'Sit down,' says Mrs Omar from the doorway.

Eluned plonks herself down on an old kitchen chair. The peeling plastic coating crackles under her thighs. Sat down, Eluned is short enough that Mrs Omar has no trouble wrapping her arms round her. Eluned holds herself stiff for a moment but as she breathes in the smell of rosewater and talc from Mrs Omar's clothes, she relaxes. Not Mam, but still comforting.

'It's horrible to say goodbye to someone we love,' she whispers into Eluned's hair.

Oh no. They'd been careful. She has no idea how Mrs Omar would feel about June, and the last thing she needs is to be sleeping out of Madge until she finds somewhere else. Mrs Omar would be well within her rights to ask Eluned to leave if she wanted to. Maybe it would have been better if she hadn't lied. They're not big lies. But she never corrected Mrs Omar, and she did invite June in under false pretences.

Eluned scrambles. 'It's not—'

Mrs Omar squeezes her shoulders harder. She says, 'You think I've never seen a woman like you before? I'm old, not thick.'

Eluned wriggles, but Mrs Omar keeps talking. 'There was one on this street twenty years ago. A working girl, if you can believe. She kept another flat on Bute Street. Mr Omar said he didn't know how her customers went for it. He said it would be like trusting a vegetarian butcher. Anyway, she lived with a Valleys girl for years. Delyth, a tiny mousy thing. Sylvie went first and Delyth wore Sylvie's long mink coat until she followed her. It looked ridiculous on her.' Mrs Omar looks up thoughtfully. She pauses, then says, 'But then I've kept a drawer of Yusef's old shirts.'

Eluned's stomach lurches as she imagines June shuffling around in Eluned's jumpers, the fabric falling off her shoulders.

'I'm not as naive as you think. I don't think any less of you, either. Now, there's Quality Street to be eaten and *Coronation Street* to watch.'

She takes Eluned's arm, holding it tight to her side as she manoeuvres her through to the lounge. Eluned picks out the strawberry creams, levering the chocolate base off with her teeth and scooping out the fondant with her tongue before collapsing the empty shell against the roof of her mouth. She keeps her legs folded to her chest. Eyes on the screen, mind somewhere else.

Mrs Omar knows that she's queer and doesn't seem to care. She could talk about June when she pleases, share stories, tell Mrs Omar where she's off to. Maybe next time she and June could stay in the same room, save June from the ancient sleeping bag and the rusty zed-bed. Her insides feel like an elastic band that has been twisted up too many times and is now starting to uncurl.

Eluned is starting on the toffee pennies when the phone in the hall starts. She sprints to it.

'June?'

'I'm in a phone box. We got cut off again. But I got back alright. Anything happening in *Corrie*?'

'Emily is being a right old bitch to Rita.'

'Emily Bishop? I can't believe that.' June's breath rattles. 'It feels weird to be back without you. I love you.'

Her voice is like strawberry creams. 'I love you too. I'll write you tomorrow. Nos da.'

'North star,' June says, and the line clicks off.

Walking under the Brain's bridge, Eluned stops to admire a row of posters for New Order's new album, *Brotherhood*. It's not out yet, but she's heard the limited editions have real metal covers, the way that notorious Durutti Column one had sandpaper. The poster is simple: a photo of brushed metal with faded grey text, the Factory Records logo set underneath it on a white border. When June came to Cardiff, she told Eluned that some Manc guy had started talking to her and Grit when they'd been selling T-shirts round the back of the Palace. They'd legged it, Grit darting off down the cut, but he'd caught up with June. June thought she was going to cop it, but he wanted to say he liked the designs. He reckoned he owned a small design studio and had some vague connection to Factory Records. June had been sure that he was talking bollocks; apparently everyone in Camden makes out they are best mates with Paul Simonon. Nevertheless, Eluned allows herself a moment to consider what June could do on a canvas like this.

23

8 February 1987

Eluned keeps flicking back to the same advert in the back of the Womyn's Liberation Newsletter. It's a quarter-page stuck underneath the personal ads, with a grainy pencil drawing of a farm on a cliff. Some farmer in Pembrokeshire is letting dykes stay in his outhouse. He only wants a tenner for the weekend, although you do have to feed yourself with a camping stove and bring your own thermals.

Ringing him in Mrs Omar's house feels like being spotted coming out of Love Story on St Mary's Street with a bag under her arm. Booking a dirty weekend away, Eluned? Duw duw.

June meets Eluned at the train station, as far west as you can get without a car. On this route the train sticks so closely to the coastline that for a while it feels like you're flying on water. The lights on the carriage have a blue hue, like a butcher's shop at night. June's the only passenger, her skin cast a sickly grey. Eluned's hands tighten on the steering wheel. June roughly lumps her rucksack on her back and leaps with both feet from the side of the train. Eluned flashes her headlights and June jogs over the gravel, cradling her leather camera case as it bumps against her chest.

June swings into the passenger seat, rubbing her hands in front of the dashboard heater. Her camera strap is already wearing red marks in her neck. Her nose is ruddy with cold, and there are bloody cracks in her lips. She props her boots up on the dashboard and lights a fag. The heater sucks in the smell of manure and woodsmoke and spits it back out at them.

The hedges are so tall that they might as well be driving in a tunnel. Good job Madge is a supermini. Eluned puts her foot down. Not long now until they're free in their bed on their first holiday. Madge's whine gets louder in the cold and Eluned pats the plastic dashboard, ignoring June's gentle ribbing. A rabbit leaps into the path of the car and off into the thickets, transformed into a silver crescent by her headlamps.

'Where's the sea from here? I think I saw a castle from the train, can we go?'

Eluned nods. She's not thinking of castles, just June's tight body underneath her own. Birds scatter outwards, dipping into the headlights' beam before streaking off into the dark. Eluned speeds up, clipping a thicket of brambles as she takes a tight corner. *Island Life* is in the deck. June leaves it on, nodding her head to 'Love Is the Drug' and tapping the drum beat onto her handrest. The night is so quiet, the people in the farmhouses must be able to hear snatches of Grace's deep voice as they speed past.

The farmer's outhouse clings to the end of the land. On the phone, he had promised Eluned a sea view. It's too dark to see, but the rhythmic roar of the waves sounds fearsomely close. She certainly won't be striding off without looking.

The farmer lends them a small torch and Eluned takes charge of it, watching the round toes of their Dr Martens peek in and out of the light. As the waves grow louder, Eluned takes smaller steps. The grass under their feet is speckled with sand, and she can already smell the glorious saltiness that evokes spending the two rainiest weeks of August in a caravan in Porthcawl.

Eluned sweeps the torch's beam right into the eyes of a sheep. The light bounces straight back at them, giving them an extraterrestrial green glow. The sheep bleats belligerently. June's fingers dig into Eluned's forearms. For heaven's sake. Eluned tugs June around the sheep to where she can see the building where they are staying. They're so close now.

Eluned flashes the torch around their cottage. Dry-stone walls. Rusty, twisted sheets of corrugated iron. Perfect. Eluned scrabbles through the tissues and lipsticks in her coat pockets, plucking out the small steel key and handing the torch to June as she unlocks the peeling door. June trails the circle of cold white light around the room while Eluned hunts out candles and matches. It's incredibly basic: a low double bed and coffee table made from the same wood, blanket, a threadbare armchair and a gas stove. She's been told there's a cold-water tap on the outside of the hut, and he's left out a white enamelled jug, bowl and two cups for them to use. Eluned lights the candles, setting them into the small alcoves in the brick where there are already white cascades of hardened wax.

June twists off the torch, leaving the candle flames to dance around the whitewashed walls. The shadows become strange and monumental, in a way that makes Eluned feel like she's hurtled back a few hundred years. The fine bones of June's face are illuminated by the gold light. The candles are too small to offer much warmth, the air stings as it hits the back of her nose. Eluned perches on the end of the bed. Apart from Mam and Dad's, it's the first double bed she's slept in. Earlier, she'd been so sure that she was going to throw June down over the bed, her skin had burned with it, but now she's bashful. She plays with the tassels at the end of the blanket. It's lovely. Traditional Welsh wool, thick and rough, with a portcullis pattern in orange and olive on the top, the inverse showing where it's been folded down.

'I'm looking forward to this weekend,' June says.

She unzips her own jacket and untucks her T-shirt from her jeans, laying them out over a chair while Eluned watches the hairs on her arms rise with goosepimples. 'It's Baltic, are we going to get in this bed or what?'

Thunderous waves wake Eluned. They must be breaking right against the side of the cottage. Wind whistles through the tiny gaps in the stone and one half of her face is numb with cold. Usually when they sleep together, they wake up entwined, peeling apart sweaty skin and shaking out pins and needles. June's huddled at the far side of the bed, mouth open and one icy shoulder poking out of the blankets. Eluned rearranges the sheets to cover her. It must be dramatic out there. She's got to have a look; but it would be unfair to wake June after her long journey. Instead, she tries to lie quietly and count her blessings. She doesn't need to paint on a face and adopt her work persona. Mrs Omar isn't going to be knocking the door to offer them a tea. Grit isn't going to insist that they get up for some protest.

The window frames rattle in the wind. That's it, she's got to see what's going on out there. Eluned kneels up and pushes the unhemmed, unlined curtains aside. The glass is covered in feathers of white frost and she vigorously elbows it clear. It's worth the frozen elbow. The sea is right there, the distance between the cottage and the cliff short enough to feel like they're on the water. It's not a postcard scene; fog hangs so low that you can barely differentiate water from sky, and in some places the churning waves are a velvety shade of grey.

There's no toilet in the cottage, just an old lean-to round the back of the farmhouse. It's a long walk at this hour. Instead, she pulls on her double-breasted coat and sneaks out round the cottage.

She's grateful for the outhouse behind her, for fear of being blown away. Even the seagulls are struggling to fly against the gusts, spinning and squawking as they are buffeted away from land. Eluned squats and pisses with her back to the outhouse, scooping her coat up in her arms. Her jet steams as it hits the frost-tipped grass and snakes over the side of the cliff to join the swirling water.

Sneaking back into bed, Eluned spoons against June's back. Her back and buttocks scald Eluned's thighs.

'Why are you so cold?'

'I've been outside, lazybones. The sea is incredible, it looks furious. We should take your camera out.'

The possibility of getting some good frames usually rouses June. She stretches out alongside Eluned, straightening her legs like a corpse until her knees pop.

June coddles a kettle of water on the old gas camping stove. When she's done, Eluned makes scrambled egg in a milk pan. She adds milk but they still end up the texture of the rubber at the end of a pencil. Eluned uses the left-over water to fill a Thermos with more tea, and browses through *The Pleasures of Vegetarian Cooking* by Tarla Dalal while she finishes her coffee. Someone has left a postcard of Frida Kahlo tucked inside the book, between the recipes for aloo gobi and red lentil dal.

'This is the most lesbian place I've ever been,' June says, propping Kahlo up against the lamp. 'How many women do you think have come on that bed? I'm surprised there isn't a squirt stain on the mattress.'

'There might be, I haven't checked yet.'

It's a soothing thought. Eluned likes to imagine that they are part of a long lineage of women coming to stay in the outhouse.

The cookbook is a marvel, full of golden pastries and mounds of yellow rice. The ingredients are photographed in leaf-shaped bowls: chickpeas and herbs and lumps of a pale white cheese that she's never heard of before. Some pages have sunny turmeric thumbprints and Eluned lays her own thumbs over them, imagining a woman making food for herself and her lover, busily moving from the stove to the cookbook and back again. Fry the onions, add the garlic. Toast the spices separately and add them. She could do this.

She points at a dish of buttery potatoes and lush green spinach. 'Do you fancy this when you come to Cardiff next?'

'That looks bostin'!' says June, layering a jumper and jacket over a home-made pair of fingerless gloves that go halfway up her forearm.

Eluned's coat is long and will probably flap in the wind, but at least she can flick up her wide lapels to protect her cheeks and the back of her neck. To climb down to the sea is to take your life in your hands. The metal rail is roughly bolted into the stone, and Eluned grips it with both shaking hands as she takes one tentative step, and then another. June squeezes Eluned's wide calves, guiding them down to each step. Her hair whips her face, until it's easier to screw her eyes shut for as long as it takes to get to solid ground.

When they do, the sand is grey and tightly compacted, undisturbed by footprints. A faded baseball cap lies half submerged in a rockpool. June can't have walked on a beach in years; she puts her weight forward, leaving deep gouges in the sand with the toes of her boots. She'll have sore calves later, but Eluned will happily rub the heels of her hands along the narrow bands of muscle until June yelps with pain.

The farmer has issued them a handwritten timetable of the tides, and a map so worn that holes are forming in the creases.

June kicks a rotted wooden post. 'Do you think these are old ships, 'Lun? Pirates or smugglers or something like that?' She pushes her hand into her pocket. She adds, 'I always wanted to be a pirate.'

Her boots are planted hip-width apart on the wet sand and it's the perfect picture: June the Pirate. It's no stretch to imagine her standing like that on the bow of a ship or scrambling up the rigging.

They walk until Eluned's cheeks are chapped by the wind. June stops to photograph their long winter shadows and the bleached remains of a long-dead crab. Eluned should have brought her watercolours. They aim to walk as far as a jut of red sandstone in the distance but, by the time they reach it, another bay has opened out and they find themselves walking across that one too. The gorse is already flowering, yolky yellow flowers bursting out of the spiny bushes.

'We could be the only people in the world,' says June, looking gleeful. Eluned can't help herself stealing a salty-lipped kiss, holding her hair out of the way so it doesn't wrap round June's head. June's cheeks are as cold as the kitchen floor first thing in the morning, but her tongue is piping hot. June's hands slither into Eluned's pockets, tangling their fingers together.

June unscrews the Thermos, pouring out tepid metal-tainted tea into two cups barely bigger than thimbles. She knocks it back and says decisively, 'We should move out here.'

'What on Earth would we do?'

'Live!' June exclaims. 'It wouldn't just be us. We'd run it like a cooperative. There must be old farm buildings for sale. We could do it up together. Grow our own crops, keep chickens. Equal labour. No hierarchy, just cooperation.'

June is delusional. She can't even drive, and Eluned has never seen evidence that she's done more than hammer in a nail. It's hard to imagine her in a pair of wellies or washing shit off fresh eggs. And, judging by what June has said before, creating something dynamic nearly always seems to involve endless meetings where the terms of reference are ripped up and defined anew.

'Grit hates the idea of moving to the countryside,' says June. 'She says she feels doubly marked out, as a Black dyke. But out here you don't have the old English Tory foxhunting brigade, do you?'

Eluned snorts. In June's mind Wales is still the land of unspoilt, rolling hills and happy radicals. 'We might surprise you; we have our own racists. And you're telling me that you'd move from London, where you can walk out of a club at 4 a.m. and get food from any country in the world, and move to a ruin in Pembrokeshire?'

June shrugs. 'I've always wanted to get into carpentry.'

She says it as simply as if she was talking about getting into jazz or crime novels. How could she want to leave the city? Eluned won't flatter herself with thinking that it's got much to do with her.

'What's brought this on?' she asks softly.

June takes off down towards the sea, arms held out straight from her sides like a crow. Eluned stamps after her, hands balled up in her pockets, watching the halo spread outwards from her feet as she displaces the water in the sand. The wind bites at her eyes until they stream. June's eyes are the same pale grey as the waves. The tide laps at her boots, the laces darkening as they suck up water. June works her jaw, then picks a flat pink stone from the sand and hurls it at the waves.

'You know that bloke who reckons he drinks with Saville?' June says.

'Factory Records Saville?'

'I saw him again last week when me and Grit was flogging T-shirts, and he was talking to me about his studio. He asked me if I wanted a job as an apprentice.'

'June! That's tremendous!'

June gets what she needs, with her dole and her T-shirts and the extra bits of cash-in-hand. It's not like Eluned would ever want her to go corporate, but it would be nice to think that she had a plan somewhere up her sleeve. To work for a designer, even as an apprentice, even if he doesn't know anyone in Factory Records, would be a coup.

June goes on, 'It's up in Manchester. He wants someone fresh, which I hope is yuppie speak for someone they don't have to pay properly, and not because he's another Nilsen.'

'Could you go up there for a bit, to see if you like it?' Eluned coaxes.

'My woman from the dole office would be doing laps around the place. I don't know if it's for me. What if I had to sell – I don't want to compromise . . .'

Eluned can't help laughing. 'Compromise your beliefs?' she says. 'You haven't even accepted yet. Getting paid to draw? I'd be biting their hand off.'

Eluned takes June's hand, but it lies like a dead fish in her grip.

'What are you scared of?' Eluned asks.

'I can't leave. We've built something together, in that house.'

Eluned gives her hand a squeeze. 'You can go back if you want to, if it doesn't work out.'

'Until the police or the council chuck us out. What if they do that while I'm gone?'

'You could squat another empty building, if you wanted to stay together.'

'I don't know about that,' June says. 'Grit's getting serious with her girl. Lily and Dharma have gone up the council list. I want to enjoy it while it lasts.'

Eluned tries to gather June in under her arm, but she shrugs her off. She bends over, eyes scanning the sand for more rocks.

Eluned talks to the back of June's jacket. 'All the more reason to give it a go. Everything changes, you've said it yourself. What are you scared of?'

June kicks at the sand until she turns up a stone the size of a fist with a thick seam of white quartz running through it. She brushes the sand off it on her jumper.

'I left home when I was sixteen. July twelfth. My confirmation name is Veronica, the patron saint of photographers. I chose her because Dad got me an Instamatic as a confirmation present.' June strokes her fingers softly over the barrel of her lens. She continues, 'I waited until Veronica's feast day to do it. I cut my ponytail off, left the house, got the bus into Birmingham, and then got the train to Euston Road.'

June's never told her this before, but it's got that intrinsic camp flair that she tries to disavow. Eluned knows exactly how June would sketch it out in one of her letters: the ponytail curled up on her bed like a sleeping mouse, and a curtain fluttering in the breeze of an open window.

'I slept round by the taxi rank for a bit. There was a bit of a camp going, mainly punks and rockers. One of them gave me my first pair of decent leather boots.'

1980 had been a crap summer. Cold and wet. She'd spent most of it either fucking to *Boys Don't Cry* or rowing with Mam and Dad about staying on for sixth form after her underwhelming O levels. June is freezing; Eluned can feel her goosepimples through her jeans. Eluned cwtches her up as much as she can.

'Some business type tried to pick me up. He'd been cruising round the back of the British Library but he'd had no luck. When he saw I wasn't a lad he walked me down to Soho, never put a hand on me, and introduced me to some older dykes. One of them let me stay with her for a few nights. There was a price attached; I was thrilled to have a warm bed. After a couple of days she gave me the number for Switchboard and sent me on my way. There were a surprising number of women seeking bed-share arrangements in return for accommodation, but I didn't think it was for me. I told them I wanted to get involved in politics and they gave me the number for a squat.'

June takes the stone from her pocket, shines it like an apple on her jeans, and hurls it towards the sea where it lands with a satisfying *doosh*. Eluned isn't naive, she's watched *Cathy Come Home*. What must June's parents have subjected her to, to make dodging serial killers and sleeping on cardboard a more attractive option? Eluned gets a sharp recollection of June handing her those dog-eared business cards. She'd been so dismissive, writing her help off instantly. June was still vulnerable herself, trying not to pull up the drawbridge after her. Eluned fishes for her Bensons. June probably wants a smoke. She hides her face in her lapels to protect the flame from the wind. And if it also hides her face from June, all the better.

June takes the fag from Eluned. She says, 'I wasn't at number 46 then. I was in Chelsea, in a proper old mansion. I had bedbug bites everywhere you can imagine.' June absently scratches at her neck. 'Grit moved in after the riots in '81. She lived in a big house in Peckham for a bit, but she moved out because she couldn't stand the menagerie. In six months or so, those council fuckers chucked us out of the mansion, and we bounced around a few places before we squatted number 46. The best of everything I've ever had is in that house.'

June sniffs loudly and wipes her nose with her jumper sleeve. It's understandable. But she's got to go. Opportunities like this don't fall out of the air often. Eluned lets June recover herself while she hunts for a suitable stone, settling on one with an edge like a hand axe.

Eluned hands it to June. She says, 'It's not thousands of miles away. They'll visit, I swear.'

June runs her finger along the stone's sharp edge before giving it a freewheeling throw. It goes farther than the last.

'Have you asked Grit what she thinks?' Eluned asks.

June's mouth twists. 'I wanted to speak to you about it first. As my girlfriend.'

Every word sounds like it's been dragged out from her, like a car being winched from a river. It's flattering, considering that June's already expounded to her about disrupting the bias towards nuclear family units.

'What are your reasons for not doing it?' Eluned asks. Even she is getting cold now. She tucks her fingers under her armpits to bring back the feeling in their tips. June could have started this discussion indoors.

'I don't know anything about Manchester.'

'It always looks interesting on the telly,' wagers Eluned.

Even sharing a double bed last night hasn't changed her feelings about moving to London. But she knows what will happen if she moves. She'll be stuck as June's naive little Valleys piece for ever. She won't swap her room for being squashed in a single bed, with Grit fucking some girl opposite them.

June had told her that a friend of a friend lived in a squat where the whole back wall had come away in one sheet, pulling water pipes with it. Eluned's had a few sleepless nights thinking about it since. Splott is practically subaquatic but there's no damp, whereas June's room is being gradually reclaimed by the River Fleet. Her damp patch in the shape of an old man has been morphing; he now has a bigger hump, a longer beard and a lumpier knapsack.

It's not like she knows much about Manchester either, but moving there would be different. A blank slate. Not June's other half, but a person in her own right. She loves the sound of a nightclub in an old warehouse run by Factory Records, with rooms named after Soviet spies. Cardiff Library would probably be able to find her a list of department stores in Manchester, and then it's a case of getting her CV copied and sending it off. There's that huge shopping centre too, the Arndale. Somewhere will want her.

Eluned takes a breath. 'What if I came with you? We could get a place together.'

June's brow furrows and Eluned's heart sinks. June asks, 'What about Mrs Omar?'

God bless June. At least it's that, and not something to do with Eluned. Lola always seemed to assume that Eluned would be happy to cast Mrs Omar off like a coat she had grown out of.

'She only wants a lodger for company in the evenings. Abdi doesn't live too far away. I'd finish off her odd jobs and help her put a notice in the paper for someone else. I can always pop in when I come back to see Mam and Dad.'

'You shouldn't feel like you have to.'

'Cardiff is great, but it is expedient. I had a lead on a job and my parents could help drive me down in one afternoon,' Eluned says. She digs the sand with her foot until water rushes into the hole she's made. Cold seawater seeps in either side of the leather tongue, soaking into her socks.

June sucks at her lip. 'We could get somewhere with a bath, and I could stay in as long as I liked.'

It's a surprisingly decadent idea for June, whose few Earthly indulgences seem to be fags, crosswords and scraps of leather.

Eluned lights up another fag. June lets her have a few drags, then pinches it off her. 'I can't believe you'd move to Manchester with me,' she says.

'We can always move back. How did you leave it with that bloke?'

'He told me to think it over. He said he'll be back in London in a couple of weeks to see a band at the Bull and Gate. He knocks about with Fat Beast.'

'You should go. Ask some questions, find out how much you can squeeze him for. You're an up-and-coming artist in the capital, remember?'

June bumps Eluned with her hip. 'Shall I put you down as my agent?'

24

10 February 1987

June and Eluned play cards sprawled out on the bed like teenagers. June keeps score on the back page of her crossword book. Eluned takes two games of cribbage before June teaches her a simple game called old maid, and an Irish one called twenty-five.

'I've brought something with me,' June starts, flicking through her cards. 'If it's not something that you're into, we don't have to use it. But if you are interested, I thought it might be fun.'

'What is it?'

June leans over the edge of the bed and grabs her bag, rummaging at the bottom until she withdraws the same tangle of straps that Eluned once saw under her bed at home. June fetches a hunk of blue plastic, shaped approximately like a penis, and pokes it through a circular ring until it hangs in the tangle of straps. She holds the web up like she's doing a trick with a yo-yo. Eluned should count herself lucky that it's at least penis-shaped; June has told her about sex toys shaped like dolphins and ballet shoes to avoid seizure by customs.

'Do you want me to wear it?' Eluned asks incredulously. She can't imagine herself wearing anything like that. She'd feel ridiculous, waddling about with a lump of plastic hanging down between her legs.

June blushes. 'No, I was thinking I might. If that was alright with you.'

The image of June thrusting on top of her is much more appealing. She nods, and June strips off her jumper, her T-shirt and her vest. She's already covered in goosepimples. June kicks off her jeans and pulls on the strap, bending and twisting until the cock lies over her mons. Her skin looks even paler against the royal-blue plastic, her veins standing out beneath her skin.

Eluned shuffles forward so she lies at the end of the bed. She reaches out and pulls June to her, using the toy as a handle. She tenderly takes it in her mouth. It's cold, smells of nothing, and squeaks against her teeth. June's socked feet turn in when Eluned draws back and flicks her tongue over the tip. Eluned's going to need to play-act a bit, but it will be worth it.

June pushes her hips shallowly forward. The toy barely tickles the back of Eluned's mouth, but June looks mesmerised, eyes tracking the toy as it appears and disappears. June is paralysed, seemingly hovering above the bed while Eluned bobs her head.

Eluned pulls back, a long string of spit hanging between the toy and her lips. 'I want you to fuck me.'

June walks round the bed and the dildo bobs in front of her; she grabs it like an unruly wind chime. Eluned rolls on to her back and draws her knees up as far as she can manage, June leaning her weight on the front of Eluned's calves. June is clumsy at first, fumbling with her fingers to get the toy in the right place. She keeps her strokes shallow, rolling her hips in time with the waves outside, whispering fiercely into the shell of Eluned's ear.

Eluned is used to stifling her moans, swallowing them down or hiding them behind her hand or a pillow. But here at the edge of the cliff she's free to make as much noise as she wants. When June hooks her hand in the sweaty bend of her knee, using the leverage to twist Eluned's body and rock in deeper, she gives over to rumbling groans. Eluned wedges her hand between them, straining upwards to kiss at June's neck. She comes with her fingernails dug firmly into June's upper arms. Afterwards, they strip the straps from June and June kicks the dildo from her body. Eluned's skin is pebbled with sweat. For the first time, she's not desperate to get under the blankets. The webbing has left angry red marks on June's skin, and Eluned kisses along them before moving down June's body.

They wake nose to nose, sunlight pooling on the blankets like butter melting on hot porridge. Eluned wriggles a foot out of the bed but jerks it back when she feels the frigid air. June nuzzles her face in the curve of her shoulder, gently kneading the side of Eluned's stomach. The sea sounds less angry today, one steady rush rather than the roars and clashes of yesterday.

June combs the beach for driftwood, picking up the long, gnarly pieces that have been bleached bone-white by the sea. Apparently, she knows exactly what she'll make with them. Eluned chooses a dog cockle shell that sits neatly in her palm, fragile edge perfectly intact. Inside, it's as smooth as nail polish, shades of cream, orange and brown in a jagged pattern that gives it a similar iridescent effect to tiger's eye.

When the candles burn down, Eluned pokes a fresh one into the pool of hot wax. Over the weekend, it's made a sculpture on its own and June kneels to take a picture of it in its twisted, lumpen glory. For the last photo of their holiday, June stands on the top of the mattress and captures the deep wrinkles and abstract water marks that they've made on the bedsheets. When she's done, Eluned strips the sheets from the bed and balls them in a pile by the door.

Eluned drops the keys back into the farmhouse and buys a dozen fresh eggs to take back for Mrs Omar. How many other couples think of the outhouse as their second home, as a refuge from the rest of their lives? How many women have gone back to their homes and dreamt of looking out to the sea, and of dinner for two on a gas stove?

Eluned drives June to Cardiff Central station. June is dozing before they reach the M4. She sleeps with her feet bent up on the dashboard, woollen socks in front of the heaters, stinking up the car. It's hard to resent her when she looks so sweet cradling her camera in her lap, mouth lolling open against the window.

A fat envelope comes in the post. June's handwriting. Inside, a canary-yellow Truprint wallet with gurning heteros on the flap. Eluned washes her hands and pulls the wad of photos out by the edges. Eluned posing in the doorway of the pub. Melted candle wax running over the wooden stool next to the bed. A field of malevolent cows. A close-up shot of the frothing waves that has come out badly, water speckled over the lens. The empty bed. There's a sweet one that Eluned took of June from behind a hand of cards, eyes promising mischief.

The last photo is a careful portrait of Eluned. They'd been walking across the fields and June could barely get over the stone stiles, hampered by short legs and tight jeans. Eluned had needed to shove her up the arse to launch her over. Once June had stopped laughing, she'd got her camera out and turned it on Eluned as she was about to start clambering over herself. The stile itself is beautiful, a huge piece of limestone with a groove worn smooth and shiny from generations of hands. In the picture, Eluned is still half laughing, double chin resting on the turtleneck of her jumper. Her hair is wild, stiffened by the salt water. Her eyes are crinkled, dark as the stone itself. When she's done scrutinising her own face, she notices the photo is slightly bumpy and puckered. June must have written something on the back.

Leen, had a pint with Mike at the Black Cap yesterday. Told him I'd take the job. Haven't told anyone here yet. Fancy an adventure?

The photo flutters to the kitchen table. Eluned stands up. She opens the cupboard and shuts it again. Iesu. She rushes to the hall, fumbling over the buttons on the receiver.

'Hello!' she blazes into the receiver. 'It's Eluned. Is June there?'

'Ah – no, she's out. I can write something down and stick it on her door?'

'Yes! Tell her, "yes"!'

25

5 May 1987

June tells Eluned she'll speak to her mate who volunteers at Switchboard. Her mate directs June to Manchester's Lesbian Link, and they recommend a hostel popular with gay tourists. June stays in a mixed dorm, where she is kept up until the early hours by backpackers bringing men back for a fuck, then awakened by travelling labourers getting up for their shifts at five. She leaves index cards in the windows of corner shops. There's always a queue for the phone box at the hostel, so June reverts to letters. They come scrawled on dot matrix paper, folded like an accordion. June bends the perforated edges over, scribbling vigorously over the holes so the letters are dotted with tacky blue circles that still smell of ink.

Apparently, June took it on herself to start on some nutjobs handing out leaflets against abortion, to feel more at home. She's been living off polystyrene trays of egg-fried rice and Marathon bars, and now her stomach will never be the same again.

June's job seems to involve cutting around images given to her by senior staff with a scalpel, using Cow Gum to stick them together. Reprographics sounds like something to do with childbirth, but June seems to go there an awful lot. From her writing, Cow Gum seems to be as much of a hindrance as a help. She writes about scraping it from the finished product and rolling it into bouncy balls. She doodles her colleagues bent over their tilted drawing desks and towers of dirty mugs.

Eluned's favourite drawings are the ones where June draws herself, squiffy-eyed and bandy-legged, emerging from the spray-mount booth after inhaling the aerosol fumes.

June works hard trying to find them somewhere to live. It's not easy on a budget as tight as theirs, and her hair and clothes seem to scare off landlords offering anything they could afford. Eluned could get the train and attend the viewings herself, playing the unthreatening Valleys girly-girl, but she can't spare the shifts. While she's waiting, she calls every department store in Manchester. In the meantime, she hoards what she can from Howells: make-up with battered boxes, left-over free gifts, company samples, and bits and pieces that no one will miss. She stacks them up in her wardrobe, a nest egg for her to sell while she's waiting for someone to take her on.

Eluned tells Mrs Omar over fish and chips, while they manoeuvre a long strip of golden batter from her plate to Eluned's. Mrs Omar listens, all the while stripping white flesh away from needle-thin bones, until Eluned's finished. Then she takes another mouthful of lemonade and tells Eluned it will work out.

When she phones Mam, she gets bemused resignation. Mam's more preoccupied with a set of curtains that she's sewing for Mabli. Eluned sits on the last stair, winding the telephone cord round her index finger, getting it as tight and even as she can before letting it spring back into a loose spiral.

'Can you do us some curtains for our flat?' Eluned asks. 'I don't think we'll have much.'

June's measured the windows and Eluned's jotted down the numbers in her notebook. She isn't fussy about material or pattern; something heavy for the bedroom and something bright in the kitchen.

'Will you need them?'

'Will we need curtains?' It's a ridiculous question. They're on the first floor, so they won't have to worry about peeping Toms, but it makes a big difference to the heating bills.

'Will you want anything as formal as curtains?'

Eluned laughs. '"Formal?" What do you mean, "formal"? Everyone needs curtains.'

'I don't know where you'll be living. I don't know the sort of place you'll find yourself in, or who you'll be associating with.' Mam sounds nervous.

Eluned surges up. The phone table wobbles, and she reaches down to check the phone is still plugged in to the socket. Her hand sweats round the receiver. 'Well, you gave Mabli all of Mamgu Fawr's blanket box.'

It's not like she wants to get married, but it's the principle of the thing. She and June are taking an important step, and Mamgu Fawr loved Eluned just as much.

'You're moving into a bedsit with someone you've known five minutes.'

'I've known her two years,' Eluned argues, twisting the cord round her hand. No. Fuck it. 'Don't worry, Mam. I'll sort it.'

Eventually, June calls to say that she's found a flat above a shop in a place called Rusholme. It's a fair way out of the city, but June promises a whole street of Indian restaurants. She draws Eluned a floor-map, with illustrations of themselves hanging out in the living room. Eluned had begun to worry that she'd pressurised June into moving, but why would June have drawn them as grinning dollies, wearing nothing but intricately drawn underpants, if she wasn't excited? Their own place, in a brand-new city. It's happening. She zips the letter firmly in the inner pocket of her handbag. None of the girls at Howells seem to care, beyond the fact that Eluned was usually willing to cover a shift at short notice. Her explanations are brief, but the last thing she needs is for Karen to write her a poor reference because she's a dyke. On her last day, Karen presents Eluned with a lidded casserole dish in the Eternal Beau pattern and reassures her that it's oven, freezer and microwave safe. The girls drag her out for a surprisingly enjoyable few rounds of cocktails, until everyone with husbands and children heads home and Eluned stumbles blearily towards the Kings Cross to find Rhona. Rhona knows Eluned's moving, but they should have one last drink together. Eluned's got her Filofax, she'll be able to give Rhona their Rusholme address and phone number. Eluned prowls through the dance floor and the loos of the Kings, before walking down to the Terminus. No sign there either, so she has a vodka soda alone, hiding her casserole dish under her jacket.

Eluned only feels a little hungover when she turns her key in Madge's ignition the next morning. Shades on. Madonna in the deck. *A–Z* on the passenger seat. An old Tesco bag of cheese sandwiches and salt and vinegar crisps from Mrs Omar. It feels like she left at dawn, but she still doesn't arrive until the afternoon. June is waving wildly on the pavement when Eluned finally pulls up. Their front door is narrow, squashed between a newsagent and an Indian fabric shop. The window of the latter is full of dress forms draped with scarlet material and gold chains. She's seen Indian brides in red, but there must be a whole rainbow of silk behind that glass. She can't wait to see them change with the season.

'Welcome home. It's so good to see you.'

June's on the pavement in bare feet. She hugs Eluned tightly, hair as fluffy as down, smelling of orange and jasmine. She hands Eluned a bunch of keys and stands aside to let her open their front door for the first time. June's fingers inch into the top of Eluned's jeans and press firmly on the sore spot at the base of her spine, where the tension gathers when she's driven for too long.

Eluned tries not to let her shoulders slump when the door swings inward to reveal a steep set of stairs. It smells like mildew, and the striped carpets are almost worn away. The stairway is so narrow that Eluned needs to pass her houseplant and handbag to June before she can get up them.

June's fingers return to the sore spot as Eluned fiddles with the lock on the second door. 'It's better inside. I promise.'

Thankfully, June is right. The living room has a high ceiling and windows running its length. Eluned doubted June's measuring skills when she cut out the fabric for their curtains, but they are certainly wide. Eluned squints at the vertical blinds fitted on the windows. They're yellow with nicotine, and a couple of the slats are missing. Even the bobbly plastic trim has come away, with one strip hanging down off the windowsill like a tail. They look like they've come from a loan shark's office. Good job she made the curtains. The windowsill itself is deep and thick, white plastic, currently only inhabited by June's ashtray and a fuzzy bluebottle lying on its back. Eluned plonks her Painter's Palette down in the middle of the long windowsill. She'll come back to the fly after a cuppa.

June has improvised a bookshelf against one of the walls, using whitewashed bricks and long planks. Her books have slid down on their sides; they need some of Eluned's to prop them up. Later, she'll sit down and have a good look at what June's brought with her. Thankfully, the room already has a sofa, a fat three-seater with scagged fabric in a pattern that looks like marbled paper. That will have to go. On one side of the sofa is a hardbacked book that looks much newer than any of the books on the makeshift shelf, the *Letraset Graphic Design Handbook*. June said she'd salvaged them a coffee table, but she didn't say that it was so comedically tall that if you were sitting on the sofa, you'd need to pitch things up onto it.

June hands her a bunch of salmon-pink carnations, still in their crinkly wrap. 'These are for you, from me. And this came for you yesterday,' she says, handing Eluned an envelope.

Dad's writing. He's sent her a naff card with a cartoon leprechaun on the front. One from the corner shop. The sort of card you buy in desperation when you've forgotten a birthday. Inside, there's a cheque for £20. 'To Eluned and June, good luck in your new home. Love Mam and Dad.'

June whistles. 'Not bad.'

'It's tidy,' Eluned agrees. June already has a kettle, and they've got two record players, but fuck all else. Dad's twenty can go in the pot for appliances. A toasted sandwich maker would be immense.

June offers to unload the car without asking how many boxes she's got. Mug. Eluned could barely look out of the rear-view mirror on the way up. There's a burning band of pain round her back from driving, so she's not going to volunteer if June is happy enough to do it herself. Eluned tucks the *Letraset Graphic Design Handbook* under her armpit and wanders through the rest of the flat.

The bedroom is sparse. The carpet certainly needs a bit of Shake 'n' Vac. The duvet is cheerful enough, mustard daisies and ferns on a beige background. One side is rumpled, the other still perfectly smooth. Eluned presses down on both sides of the bed, testing if she'll let June keep the side she's bagged, or whether she'll turf her out. June's been using a wooden school chair as a bedside cabinet, with photos of Eluned and various friends propped up against her plastic alarm clock. They'll have to find a frame for them. Sat in front of the pictures are three of the seashells June found in Pembrokeshire, arranged in a neat triad.

Eluned inspects the kitchen next. It's pokey, with a dip in the floor. They've got tiled splashbacks flecked with grease and a gas cooker that protrudes awkwardly into the room. She's going to get so many bruises from that. In the fridge, there's nothing that can be described as fresh. A half-eaten tin of baked beans, a shoebox-sized slab of pale Cheddar, and a jar of neon-yellow lemon curd.

There are two mugs: a brown one with a Smarties logo, and the other made for the opening of a refuge in Hackney. Eluned bags the Smarties one. June's bought decent teabags, but whole milk. At least there's some nutrition in that, more than in that neon curd. She settles herself down on the sofa to leaf through June's design book. There are whole chapters on fonts. There's a dizzying variety, from straightforward Folio to outlandish Candice. June has marked pages with slivers of ripped-up takeaway menu.

June's hands claw round the doorframe as she hauls herself into the room. When she's caught her breath, she kicks Eluned's suitcase forcefully across the carpet.

'Careful with that!' Eluned says. 'My records are in there.'

'You could have told me the car was fit to bursting. Where do you think we're moving, Aston Hall?'

'I've driven across the country; I deserve a rest.'

'Fine,' says June, plonking herself down next to Eluned. She picks up her mug like a pint glass and chugs. 'I bought some candles to make it romantic. Go to the kitchen for five and I'll light them.'

'You bought candles but no biscuits?' All she's eaten today is Mrs Omar's cheese sandwiches, and she could murder a Wagon Wheel.

'There's a corner shop downstairs, go and get some yourself,' June says, flinging her legs over Eluned's. Eluned pokes her finger through a hole in her sock and tickles her sensitive arches. 'What's for tea?'

'Fuck all. Thought we could celebrate with a takeaway and some tinnies?' June suggests. She swings her feet off the sofa and retrieves a stack of menus, fanning her face with them like a Georgian lady.

June tosses them into Eluned's lap and folds herself onto the sofa again. 'I've already been to the New Taj Mahal, Sanam and Shere Khan. You pick somewhere new.'

Eluned's stomach grumbles as she looks at the pictures of pillowy bread, creamy yellow sauce and platters of rice studded with cinnamon sticks and star anise, like jewels amongst gold coins. She picks a menu at random, circles a couple of dishes with familiar names and then a few things she's never heard of, and hands it to June to do the same.

June picks the food up while Eluned sweeps the dead fly into the bin and lights the candles. Not enough time to put her curtains up, but the candles soften the bare white walls. June's left her own record collection on the side, and Eluned can't resist having a rummage. Mabli always used to sort her records by alphabet, but Eluned preferred genres. It was tricky sometimes, with records that blurred the edges, but she could find what she wanted easier that way. She's curious to see how June does it. As she expected, they've got a few doublers. *The Sound of Music* is a surprise. There must be a story there. So many bands she hasn't heard of. June's probably been to see them live, back when they were starting out. She's intrigued by a cover with a sort of optical illusion, either an ambiguous portrait peering out or a massive fingerprint. She slides it on the player, and soon finds herself nodding her head to the fast piano, driving guitars and snappy vocals.

While June's still out, Eluned unzips the leather-look vanity case that houses her most personal effects. Mam had sent her a soft-cover album of pictures of Mabli and Kelly. She hasn't been brave enough to sit down and look at it until now. Graham's only in one, and thankfully Mam has folded the picture over so that you can only see his arm holding Kelly. Kelly is substantial, with a full head of hair, a squashed-raspberry nose and the dark, Snowdonian eyes they get from Mam. Eluned has missed so much already. Mabli and Kelly behind the Sgwd-Yr-Eira waterfall brings on a deluge of hiraeth. She remembers holding Mabli's hand as they picked their way up the gleaming stone steps, trying not to slip. The roar of the water. The humid smell of the ferns. Then, from the top of the ledge, reaching out to catch the spray from the falls.

'Gloria Mundi!' June shouts up the stairs. 'Good choice!'

As June kicks the door shut, Eluned slides the album back into the elasticated pouch and zips the case shut, kicking the vanity under the sofa. Even through the foil containers, the smell is tremendous, garlic and spices covering up the musty carpet smell.

Eluned takes June's two plates and levers off the cardboard lids with a fork, steam rising into her face. The smell gets more tantalising as she lifts plump pieces of lamb and golden ribbons of onions out of the carton. Orange grease runs along her thumb and down her wrist. She licks it off.

June fiddles with the record player. 'They used to mentor Bauhaus. You can hear it on this one,' she says as she moves the needle back to an earlier track. It had sounded familiar to Eluned's ear, but she hadn't been able to place it.

Eluned tears the naan apart, stuffing a piece in her mouth before June's even sat down. She shuts her eyes, attempting to block out everything but the music, but she's got to have another bit of that bread. June rests a carton on her knee, picking out green chillies and flicking them on to Eluned's plate.

'I can't believe we've got our own place,' says June, moving sag aloo directly from the carton to her mouth. 'It's mint.'

'Tomorrow I want to walk down to the high street and see the shops. Maybe I could get the bus into the centre and meet you after work?'

'I could take you down to the Village.' June hands Eluned a bottle of beer. 'Do your old trick again? Use the corner of the coffee table if you like. I fished it out of a skip.'

26

2 June 1987

They were celebrating down the pub. June had stayed late on Friday to word-process and photocopy Eluned's CV, and Eluned shopped them around until she was offered some hours at a department store in the Arndale. The Arndale seems bigger than the village she comes from, with its own radio station and an ornamental pond next to a hexagonal aviary full of disorientated birds. When her boss asks Eluned what's brought her to Manchester, she contemplates telling them about June, but they won't make their rent if the job goes tits-up. Even if June does have the knack of fiddling the meter. Instead, she visualised the hi-fi system she wants and told her that she wanted to move somewhere bigger than Cardiff but can't stand southerners. It did the job.

June had called the Lesbian Link for a list of events and dutifully copied them onto the calendar hanging on a nail in the kitchen. They tried the teetotal discos and the Women's Café in the day, but mostly they like going out for a few pints and a dance. Now, at least, they have a group of women to do that with. On Fridays, the huge old boozer, the Rembrandt, hosts a bar for women upstairs, Sappho's. It's the closest that any of the women's venues get to cool, even though the bamboo furniture and straggly cheese plants make her think of some demented conservatory. Later on they're heading to the Number One Club, with its bodacious lit-up dance floor, and then the Archway, if Eluned can keep her eyes open until 4 a.m.

June's joined a printing cooperative down Moss Side, reappropriating half-knackered Magic Markers from the office every Wednesday night. As if she doesn't get enough of printing at work. But it allows Eluned to spend her Wednesday evenings with a magazine in the bath, until June comes singing up the stairs with her forearms smeared with oily black ink. Eluned needs to find something of her own, something to stop her and June from rolling into each other like old plasticine. They can't always be the Welsh one and the English one, the fat one and the thin one, the dark one and the fair one. Eventually they'll end up one of those lesbian couples who use the same shampoo and before they know it, they won't have had sex in ten years.

Morgan cartwheels one of the spindle-backed chairs above her head, swinging it down into place next to Eluned, while the old queens crane out of their seats to tut. Morgan is the first Welsh woman they've met up here, a broad, tattooed hospital porter from Pwllheli. The job suits her. Her hands are like tiger paws; she could wheel you around like you weighed nothing. She's promised to take Eluned and June walking up the Pennines. Cardiff and Manchester are flat, and the muscles at the backs of her calves are slackening. She's looking forward to stretching them out. Last weekend a barman asked if they were sisters. Everyone got a good laugh out of it at the time, but Eluned found herself bringing it up again to other people, '*Can you believe he thought we were sisters?*'

'Anderton's off his head,' Kez says. 'I mean, did you hear him on Radio 4? He reckons he heard God's voice. People have been locked away for less.' Kez is a social worker, originally from Bolton, with a gleaming fountain of jheri curls. They first met at a Gaye Bykers on Acid gig at the Hacienda, when June managed to dance herself into Kez's full pint. Shortly after, Eluned spotted her fingering the last copy of the new Frankie Knuckles release at Eastern Bloc, Eluned's favourite record store. Kez kindly invited them both back to her flat in Whalley Range to listen.

June stabs her fag out violently into the ashtray. There's practically a thundercloud over her head. It's a sticky subject. James Anderton, head of Manchester's rozzers, gave a speech that said that gays are 'swirling in a cesspit of their own making', then decided to disgorge his conviction to any radio station or newspaper that would have him. In the same month, June's been back to London on the train for funerals four times. There's another one coming up soon, and, under that pressure, June's hatred has become as hard and sharp as any diamond. Eluned gives June's leg a squeeze under the table, then asks, 'Do we reckon Anderton's a closet case then? Hairy daddies do well for themselves in certain quarters.'

Kez laughs. 'His voice is fruity. I've always thought that.'

Morgan swaggers over to the table, holding in her stomach to wedge herself in between the table and their booth seats. She tears open a bag of Burton's Fish 'n' Chips, ripping the foil so everyone can take some, and nudges Eluned with her meaty elbow. She says, 'Beth sy'n bod ar June?'

What's wrong with June? 'Mae June yn . . . pissed off . . . gyda James Anderton,' Eluned offers.

Mamgu would be proud of her for using a little Welsh, even if Eluned can only talk like a five-year-old.

'Siwr,' Morgan says, 'If we can give Thatcher the sack, he won't be far behind.'

'That won't happen,' says Eluned. 'Kinnock's getting a real kicking in the rags.'

'They're going hard on Labour being the party of militant gays and nonces,' June breaks in. 'The Halsbury Bill will get through before the election. Did you see the *Labour's idea of an education?* poster?'

The bill, with its amendment to stop local authorities 'promoting homosexuality', has already passed the Lords. Kinnock is a wet fart, but Benn's doing his best. They're no match for Thatcher though; the bitch is like a dog with a bone. It might get voted down in the Commons on some weaselly lawyer grounds, but they'll bring it back in another guise. The Tories won't stop until they've stripped away any gains the queers have made. If Eluned had read these books that they're frothing at the mouth about, *Young, Gay and Proud* and *The Playbook for Kids About Sex*, then what might have been different? Could she have understood her feelings better, bypassing the pain she caused Lloyd? Might she have had a vocabulary to talk about her attraction to June, other than understanding it as a warped form of class solidarity?

Eluned jumps as if she has been scalded when a woman coughs significantly right next to their booth.

'Excuse me,' she says. 'Are you the woman who sells make-up?'

Eluned nods, reaching between June's feet for her swag-bag. She hauls it up and scatters some out on the table while June keeps a look-out.

'I've got Clinique, Shiseido, Estée Lauder, Clarins,' Eluned says as she delves in.

She keeps the best stuff back for women like Rhona who might not get served in store, but sells to girly dykes, camp queens, drag queens, cross-dressers, and anyone else who wants it.

'How much do you want for these?' she asks, holding up an Estée Lauder mascara and cheaper nail varnish.

They strike a deal, and Eluned throws in a few sachets of eye cream.

'We should do something,' suggests Kez. 'A protest.'

'What would our focus be?' asks Morgan.

'Ongoing harassment,' suggests Eluned. 'I've heard they've got boats down the canals again to look for boys cruising.'

The Sun's just published another load of shit about AIDS. The usual. Irresponsible behaviour. Should know better. Debauched, and depraved. Those smug journalists have probably never yearned for human interaction after years of loneliness, never found it at 2 a.m. on a crowded dance floor. It gives her the same helpless anger as the shit they spewed about Dad and Lloyd. Well, she's not helpless today.

'And stigma,' adds June. 'That's what's stopping people going to the clinics. We could do a "Fags and Dykes Together" sort of angle.'

27

7 June 1987

Eluned finishes her placard while she's on the phone to Mam. They've only got the thin, blue-tinged fax paper June scavenges from work, but Chief Constable Anderton doesn't deserve anything better. Eluned butterflies a cornflakes box and glues the paper down over it, before shading in Anderton's hooter. Working on the gradient between the full-on Santa red on the bulb of his nose to the peach blush at the bridge is pleasingly hypnotic, and she puts aside a charcoal-grey for his beard. The telephone table is only light, made of bamboo, and it rocks as she colours in.

When she's wrapped up her call she goes back to the lounge, chucking a spare pair of socks into June's shabby rucksack. It's already almost full. Toffees. An extra roll of film. Their large tub of Vaseline from the bathroom, whatever that's for. A Stanley knife? Oh for fuck's sake, June.

'You're not going with that in your bag.'

'Always feel better with it on me. It's from the office, so they can't prove intent. Don't trust the local fash. Here, look, I'll put this in as well,' June says, flinging in a small tin of Cow Gum after the rest.

As if that's going to placate her. 'So they can say you're a huffer and a slasher?'

June sourly removes both the knife and the tin. 'Fine.'

'I'm not being unreasonable,' Eluned says. 'We said we'd make our point and leave.'

'What did your mum have to say?' June asks.

'Don't distract me. I'll tell you on the way.'

It's not that she doesn't understand why June, clockable as she is, wouldn't need the protection. It seems best not to give the coppers an excuse. The word on the pickets was that the Met Police were the harshest, but Greater Manchester Police weren't far behind.

June dresses to be seen, complete with a self-printed T-shirt of Thatcher with red eyes and gnarled horns, and a red paisley handkerchief rolled like a pancake and knotted round her neck. She wears her old clit brooch, although one of the clitoral bulbs has got knocked off. Eluned picks out a striped jumper from BHS and a pleated skirt. Next to June, she looks like a mam on the school run. Maybe she's a coward, but she doesn't fancy painting a target on her back.

'What shall I write?' Eluned asks. ' "The only cesspit is police corruption" or, "Gays pay taxes too"?'

'I'm doing "Real Lives Over Church Lies".'

'That's good.'

'I should have started last night. I could have done a Celtic-style border, like the *Book of Kells*,' June says. She reaches over to Eluned's coloured pencils, picking up an emerald green and a bright yellow like a cat's eye.

June's got so confident lately. She used to keep her ideas entangled in a thicket of sarcasm and defensiveness. These days she's expansive, bounding ahead like a spaniel.

They head in to Deansgate on the long Oxford Road, along the grey railway bridges and narrow canal. As they pass by the Palace Theatre, Eluned spots two dykes in matching Levi's. They're so close to Southmill Street, they could be making their way to the protest as well. Morgan has all sorts of friends to invite. Eluned and June walk behind the denim dykes for a few blocks, before losing them around the Midland. Shame.

Eluned will never tire of walking near Manchester Central Library. She doesn't know many round buildings; it looks like it could have been beamed in from New York. Columns sprout up like oaks, beckoning passers-by to search, to look, to aim higher. Not a handout, but a way for working people to get knowledge. It's like those magnificent old Miners' Institutes built like mansions, with newspapers on mahogany sticks and stained-glass windows turning light into the sort of glossy golden oil that she sells in bottles with long droppers.

'What's the craic, then?' June asks, as she presses the button at the pedestrian crossing.

'Mam was saying she's got Kelly all this week. Mabli's going back to the office part-time, one of the partners is making noises about retiring. She wants him to mentor her before he goes.'

June's eyebrows rise. 'Every day? What's Fuckhead doing then?'

Eluned rolls her eyes. 'He's on nights. He told Mabli that she can't control Kelly well enough while he's resting, so Kelly's got to stay at Mam's during the day when Graham's asleep.'

The cars aren't stopping, and June pummels the button with the side of her fist. 'Bollocks to that.'

'I know. Mabli milks herself every morning, so Mam has enough to feed Kelly. Then she does it again at work, so she doesn't leak everywhere. She went straight through a blouse the other day.'

June keeps her thumb jammed on the button. She always does that. It never works. The cars aren't stopping, and a fine drizzle starts to mist their faces. Water beads on June's fine eyelashes.

June asks, 'Can't she feed Kelly powder?'

'That's what I said, but Graham has convinced Mabli that only shit mums use formula, and if she doesn't breastfeed, the baby will be thick.'

'Jesus,' says June. 'That's not healthy.'

'I know. That's what Mam says.'

'If she won't listen to her mother, do you think she'd listen to you?'

Eluned barely notices the green man flashing, or the red Toyota Corolla braking for them. 'There's no point. I've been banging that drum for years.'

June stares at her. 'What's he got to do so you'll intervene? She didn't listen to you before? So what? She was a kid!'

The driver of the Corolla flashes their lights at them. Yes, yes, we're going. Eluned brushes her damp baby hairs off her forehead and strides into the road.

'I'm just saying,' says June, 'That you keep saying how stubborn she is. And maybe she is stubborn, God knows you are, but you're not leaving her much space to admit she was wrong about him.'

'Alright!' Eluned shouts at the car, 'We're moving!' She grabs June's wrist and tries to tug her along. June resists her, feet planted firmly on the road. Her left hand moves up to fiddle with the strap adjuster on her rucksack.

'I'll go without you,' Eluned warns. She's got her placard. She doesn't need June to chaperone her.

June's wrist goes floppy, allowing Eluned to pull her to the other side. 'We could send her something in the post. I don't know, an Eccles cake or something? Might give her a bit of a lift.'

Eluned just wants to get to the protest. All morning she's been planning what she'd say to Anderton. She's supposed to be defending homosexuality, not proving that they're a bunch of dysfunctional screw-ups. June keeps picking at this hardened scab. But what's underneath is not smooth, healed skin, but a gush of anger at her sister for abandoning their family when they needed her most. Still, the Eccles cake isn't a bad idea.

* * *

Manchester Central Police Station is as flat as a palm. Four storeys. That's a lot of rozzers. The grey-streaked Portland stone blends seamlessly into the sky. On Bootle Street you can see into the police station courtyard, but all you can see from this side is a barred gate.

Their protest group are already loafing around at the corner with their placards in bin bags. Morgan, and Julia, and a few faces Eluned recognises from the pub and the dry meetings at the Broad Street community centre.

Morgan nods at Eluned, clapping June on the shoulder. 'Bore da. We're only waiting on you two.' Morgan's casual Wenglish gives her a sensation that's the opposite of hiraeth; that homeliness is nebulous and can be tapped into as required.

'How many are we?' says June, stretching up on the balls of her feet for a head-count.

'Ten,' Morgan answers. A red-headed femme slaps a maroon Reni hat into Morgan's hand. Morgan unfolds it and jams it on her head, rain already beading on the fabric.

'Chwarae teg,' says Eluned.

'You've done a boss job,' June agrees.

The redhead unzips her rucksack and pulls out a small megaphone, hefting it in her hand like a gun. With her thick fringe, already curling up in the damp air, she looks like Sarah Ferguson. Similar wide, blue eyes and forthright chin.

'You want to speak first?' June asks.

There's barely any footfall here, just an elderly couple with plastic rain hoods gathered under their chins. One of them hugs a large Boots bag closer to herself as she scuttles along the pavement.

Dyke-Fergie shrugs, and grips the megaphone. It's a protest veteran, with a dented horn and smooth, shiny finger-grips. Most of the women they know, from the pubs and the community centre on Bloom Street, skew to June's aesthetic, and Eluned appreciates Dyke-Fergie's softer style. Even her earrings are classy: rose, yellow and white gold twisted up into neat hoops.

'We're here to protest the comments made by James Anderton,' Dyke-Fergie starts, and takes a breath. 'We demand an end to the harassment of our brothers in gay bars, and an end to stigma.'

June whoops. 'Yes! Faggots and dykes together!'

Eluned claps until her palms sting. There's a grey, bearded face at one of the windows above. Is that Anderton? The window slams shut with a bang that echoes down to the street, followed by the scrape of the lock. The face fades back into the gloom.

Dyke-Fergie drops the speaker of the megaphone. It swings and bounces on its coil like a bungee jumper, reverb screeching up to the window like a retort.

'Someone take this,' she says, pushing her wet curls out of her eyes.

Eluned takes the megaphone. They're happy to judge us and slag us off on the radio, and yet they don't have the decency to listen. They think they can do what they like because they'll always back each other up. Eluned wraps her hand round the speaker. The button won't go down tidy, must have been jammed down many times. She squeezes until the speaker clicks in her fist. It buzzes on.

'Hello,' she says. It's unnerving, how it bounces off the wall across the street and comes back at them. 'Gay is natural. It's beautiful. It's not dirty.'

June pushes her thumb into the dimples in the small of Eluned's back. June always finds the spots where the muscles draw themselves into tough lumps under the skin. One of the perks of spending all day on her feet. Eluned doesn't notice them forming until June attacks them when she's at the sink or in the shower. The pain isn't unpleasant; it seems to help her focus more on what she's trying to say, and less on how Welshy she sounds.

A woman pushes her stroller round the corner, then circles back on herself. June lifts her sign as high as she can, waggling Anderton's cartoon face in the air. The ink has started to run, trailing grey tears down the paper. Another woman rounds the corner, umbrella angled sharply towards the protestors. Fine drizzle cools Eluned's red cheeks.

Eluned takes a deep breath. 'You don't have to struggle. You don't have to fight. You can start your life today.'

The woman with the umbrella moves it from her left shoulder to her right so she can peer over at them.

'Ready for a Happening?' June shouts to the group.

'Barod!' Morgan shouts back. June's picked that one up from Eluned by now. They're ready.

The street could be busier. It's high-footfall time, surely. Usually in the shop they'll be taking a few hundred quid an hour at this time of day. Where are they? Everywhere but sodding Deansgate.

The women pair up. Eluned flickers her eyes around the group. Some of the other pairings are obvious. Morgan and Kez. Elaine and Sammo. That will give her and June something to goss about when she's getting their tea on, that's for sure.

June gives Eluned a soft look under her lashes.

'Let's go,' says Eluned, returning June's look with a tentative smile.

Eluned's mouth is claggy as hell, thanks to shouting on the megaphone, and June's lips are perpetually dry, so for the first few seconds their lips rasp ineffectively against each other. Tension tightens Eluned's shoulders like the lid of a jar. She's braced for a stick to the back of the knees, a thump to her head hard enough to make her teeth clamp down tight over June's tongue. Eluned rolls the bones of June's hand between her fingers until they crunch.

'Why is it never the ones you want to see kissing?' The shout cuts across the street, followed up by a long mocking whistle and the noise of men jostling.

June keeps her lips glued on to Eluned's. The movements are mindless, like workers on a production line.

'Ladies. We don't have time for this,' says a low voice a few feet away. 'If you persist in these actions you could be looking at a breach of the peace.'

June pulls off Eluned's lips with a pop. 'I don't think so. For a breach you need to have a threat of harm. Kissing ain't threatening. There's nothing illegal in what we're doing. Not yet anyway. Though I'm sure Maggie and your boss are working on it.'

The copper tugs at the side of his helmet. There's a line of white sebum bumps where his hat must aggravate his skin. He could do with a good exfoliant.

'Look, girls, I don't know if you've seen the new Public Order Act, but you should have given us written notice of this. I'd be willing to overlook it if you move on peacefully now.'

'We've got a right to have a say! How come you've got this prick' – Eluned gestures at the runny caricature of Anderton – 'on the radio spouting off like he's a politician. Why can't you stick to burglaries, rather than acting like the paramilitary wing of the Conservative Party?'

June thrusts her placard into the air. Another navy-clad prick comes down the steps and claps PC Whiteheads on the shoulder.

'PC Armstrong. Chief says to leave these. They'll be off for some chickpea soup soon enough.'

With that, he strides past Eluned, bringing his gaze over her like she's no more than a postbox. No. She's not having that. She sidesteps into his way, hefting her sign up to her chin. The rain makes two tracks either side of her nose. It's not a dignified look.

'Excuse me, ma'am. We've been tolerant today, and we've

given you a fair opportunity to protest,' he says, eyes focused somewhere above her head.

The same reckless urge comes over her as it did on the pickets. She's floating outside herself, looking down on the scene.

Her jaw burns, teeth gritted so hard that the bone feels like it's about to pop straight through the skin. His truncheon hangs at his waist. Regular issue, the same polished black handle that almost knocked her out.

June's hand wraps round Eluned's wrist. 'Come on 'Lun,' she whispers. June must be able to feel her pulse through her skin.

She turns back to PC Armstrong. Other than his whiteheads, he could be good-looking. Strands of blond hair peek out beneath his helmet. His lips are dusty red, and his Cupid's bow is two distinct mounds with a valley between them.

'You're a pretty boy,' Eluned taunts. 'Do you try and catch them at it then? Is that what they have you doing? Do you like hiding out in pissy toilets?'

His blue eyes widen, and he takes a step back.

'Do you ever wish you could stay?' Eluned skewers him, leans forward into his space. His breath smells of black coffee.

'Shwsh!' hisses Morgan. 'Cau dy geg, Eluned.'

Fine, she'll shut her mouth. Armstrong coughs, pulls his helmet further down over his spots and follows his colleague to their van.

The women regroup. June is all for finding a way through the white archway gate and down into the courtyard.

'I don't think trespassing is going to get us anywhere,' says Eluned.

Dyke-Fergie suggests doing another Happening near the town hall, where there might be more people around. The fight has gone out of Eluned now. She looks up. A shadow shifts behind the glass.

'They're watching us.'

'Good,' says June decisively. 'We've made an impact. Well done everyone.'

While they talk over what to do next, a woman emerges from the station. The noise her heels make on the stone steps is quicker, sharper, than the coppers and their heavy boots. She's petite, in a double-breasted dress with buttons shaped like naval knots, and shoulder pads that make her head look like the top of a pin.

June raises an eyebrow at Eluned in the way that usually means, 'She's class, isn't she?' The woman lingers on the top step, looking between their gang until she seems to decide that Eluned looks the least intimidating.

She says, 'The Chief Constable wants you to move on.'

Kez yells, 'Go back inside and tell him to piss off.'

'If you don't move on, he's going to get you in the cells,' she says, gesticulating to the grilled windows peeking out over the pavement.

June's probably bang-on with her knowledge of the law, knowing her, but it's not like they can't do what they like.

The woman grabs the metal bobbles at the top of her framed handbag and twists until they open with a click. The satin lining of her bag is pristine. She's carrying a mini-Filofax, a travel bottle of Chanel No. 5 and a packet of Silk Cut, which she fishes out and brandishes at Eluned. The gold paper on the inside has been stripped out to leave the cardboard clear. Obviously. Tucked inside the packet is a business card.

'Why don't you have a cigarette?' she asks, tilting her head significantly.

Eluned takes a fag and slides the card up the sleeve of her jacket. The woman lights both Eluned's cigarette and her own.

'You've got nothing on us!' interjects June.

The woman snorts. 'They'll find something. James is on the phone right now to close personal friends in London.'

There are rumours, of course, about how Thatcher stepped in to protect him after his most bonkers outbursts.

'That's my brother's card. He's a freelance reporter, he's had bylines at the *Guardian* and *Gay Life*.'

'What good is that?' asks Morgan. 'It's been in *Gay Life* for years. We know! It's these lot who need to know.' She throws open her big arms, pointing at a middle-aged woman with a banana-yellow coat. Her eyes widen at the sight of Morgan's fist thrust in her direction.

Anderton's PA, or whoever the hell she thinks she is, rolls her eyes. 'Believe me, he's desperate to prove some risk to the rule of law. Bands of marauding lesbians will be like Christmas to him.'

'Okay,' says Eluned. 'We'll go.'

June squawks behind her.

'No, she's right. We've made our point. Thanks for the tip.' Eluned touches the stiff business card beneath her jumper. 'Good luck.'

The woman smiles faintly, hitches her bag up into the crook of her elbow and crosses the street.

The rest of the women crowd around Eluned.

'Who is it? Who is her brother?' Dyke-Fergie asks. 'Show me! My ex, Michelle, writes for them occasionally.'

'June,' says Kez, 'Eluned's right. It's not a fair fight. He'll make out like we're unhinged perverts. Let's give this woman's brother a go and try and get more coverage next time.'

Morgan claps Eluned on the shoulder. 'Pub?'

Election night is traumatic. At 10 p.m. they dutifully turn on the BBC just in time to watch the ridiculous animation of Big Ben. June complains that the graphics alone probably cost as much as commissioning a series written by a Black woman, but they'd never do that. Eluned unpacks June's Peking duck and pancakes while June cracks open a bottle of cheap whisky. Duck pancakes are a rare treat for June. Eluned encouraged June to order them when the pundits started suggesting that there might be a 'penetration' into the Tory's swing seats; someone even mentioned a hung parliament. They are left hanging for the first hour, picking their way through the mountains of foil cartons they've ordered to sustain them until dawn. The first seat goes to Thatcher. Torbay, that's to be expected. Eluned and June both cast their votes for Gerald Kaufman in Manchester Gorton, and he comes through with a decent majority. Neath, Mam and Dad's seat, is a Labour hold, as it will be until the mountains crumble into the sea. In Mrs Omar's constituency of Cardiff South and Penarth, James Callaghan seamlessly confers his seat to a younger Labour man. Grit and co. see the Tories off in Holborn and St Pancras, even though June says her old house had been torn between Labour and a more radical group. Only June's childhood seat lets the side down.

June cheers in Diane Abbott and Bernie Grant, topping up their glasses so they can take a shot when Bernie talks about the divisiveness of Thatcherism. They toast the people shouting 'shame' and 'fascist' when Maggie herself is voted in in Finchley. The night takes a dark turn after that, as the map gets progressively bluer. The anchors cut to Piccadilly Circus, where Thatcher's pixelated face looms out from the illuminated hoardings. Two a.m. is truly the twilight zone, as June admits through giggles that Neil Kinnock's voice makes her feel 'warm inside', leaving Eluned to conclude that June must have some sort of Welsh fetish. The only explanation.

The euphoria of sleeplessness wears off around four when the BBC starts broadcasting from a victorious Conservative Party HQ, blue and gold balloons floating off into the sky. June viciously thwacks their picked-out mushrooms into the bin while Eluned holds her knees and sobs. How can a majority of people in this shithole country want another four years of Tory sadism? The Halsbury Bill might have failed, but the Tories certainly won't give up on the principle of the thing.

28

14 August 1987

Eluned ambles along the canals after her shift; if June can wangle the afternoon off, she'll know to meet her here. The canals are grubby but they're a novelty, with their black and white locks and low bridges. She perches on a wall, trying not to inhale the stink of fetid water, and rubs the backs of her hands over her knees to get rid of the vestiges of swatched lipstick.

Eluned likes to tease June that the canals must sing a siren song to her, the same way the hills do to Eluned. As she's got some time to herself, she could pick one of the pubs she's not been in and have a quick pint. On a day like this a Carling and lime would be lush. Maybe even have a quick game of pool by herself; it's less intimidating without the dykes pecking each other like pigeons.

They'll probably end up having a heavy weekend, so maybe she should pop in the Bloom Street Café for a tea. Or she could browse in Gaze, the gay bookshop, first.

At Gaze, Eluned admires the strapping strawberry blonde behind the counter and finds Lesbian Romance. Nothing new. Instead, she thumbs a woman's poetry collection imported from the States. Too many mangoes and pomegranates. Next, Eluned picks up an anthology of young London writers. June will most likely have personal beef with one of the contributors. Throw a 2p piece in London and you'll hit some dyke that has a problem with June. It's worse than the People's Front of Judea.

In the shop Eluned spots a familiar face: a woman she's sold foundation to in the pub. She looks good. She's guided her eyebrows into a high arch so that they frame her hooded hazel eyes, and dusted a deep, coppery bronzer underneath her jaw and above her temples. The woman holds a slim novel, *Beatrice The Sixteenth*, and a magazine called *Fanfare*. *Fanfare* looks home-made, with a blocky fashion illustration of a woman printed in black on magenta paper.

Connie introduces herself, climbing her fingers up her auburn ponytail. She's from the West Country and as soon as she names it, Eluned hears the slightly comic roll on the R. Eluned tells Connie about the new stock at the shop, and what she thinks she can get at a discount. She roots around for her Filofax and flicks to the notes at the back to make note of the products Connie wants. Eluned doesn't have business cards, but she writes down her home phone number and rips the strip out as close to the pale blue lines as she can manage.

Connie gestures to the book and magazine under her arm. 'I'll give you a ring in a week or so and see if you've got any stock in.'

Eluned mooches over to the spinning rack of greetings cards. A lot of the cards are erotic photographs of clichéd gay fantasies. Coach and rugby player. Priest and confessor. Policeman and yobbo. There's one she *must* buy Lloyd. Two topless men in what is probably supposed to be the pithead baths. Both have tanned skin and rippling muscles artfully dusted with black smudges. Their fingernails are pristine. One leans over the bench, picking up his T-shirt, while the other looks at his arse. It's kitschy and borderline disrespectful, but it will make him laugh. Lloyd knows she's living in Manchester, but they haven't written in ages. Rhi's told Eluned that, after spraying his spunk all over Swansea, a girl has caught and they're making a go of it. They've bought a place down in the Sandfields, close enough to walk to the beach. Good for him.

Eluned picks up another card, a black and white image of a woman sitting at her dressing table, to send to Rhona and invite her to stay. Eluned pays for her cards and the book, then lingers around the corner of Bloom Street. Muriel Gray's still covering for John Peel, a Friday treat for when she gets in. Eluned and June both fancy Gray, with her thick Glaswegian accent and dykey hair. June said she went to art school as well. It won't be long before Eluned is joining her.

June's beaten her home. Eluned almost trips over her when she gets in. She's on the telephone, cardboard poster tubes scattered all over the hallway.

June crosses herself. 'Thank God you're home,' she mouths. 'It's your sister.'

June thrusts the receiver into Eluned's hand with a grimace.

'Mabli, what's wrong?'

Mabli lets loose a long, rattling sniff that hisses through the speaker. 'Graham . . . Graham . . .' Her voice skitters upwards to where she's barely understandable.

June pokes an envelope under her nose: *Big row. Books?!*

As Eluned takes the receiver, June edges out of the hall and eases the door closed behind her.

Eluned pinches the bridge of her nose. 'What's the dick-head done?'

'My folders! My study books! They're gone!'

'What do you mean? Where have they gone?' Eluned asks.

Another sniff. Eluned holds the phone away from her ear.

'I don't know!' Mabli shrieks. 'Somewhere – he said I didn't need them.'

Eluned manages to get out of Mabli that since she's been back at work, Graham hasn't stopped suggesting that it's having a detrimental effect on Kelly's development. His favourite game is to put his revolting head behind Kelly's tiny body, jiggle her arms and sing-song, 'Mammy, why are you leaving me again?'

According to Graham, his dinner is always cold, and his shirts are always wrinkled. Mabli made the mistake of asking him what he thought of upping her hours, so she could finally get her FILEX under her belt. If she gets through this next set of exams, she'll be well on her way to being a legal executive. It's not the same pay as a solicitor, but she'd be able to take on much of the same work. She's come so far from when she was taken on as a typist. That had set Graham off, and now Eluned's left holding the phone while Mabli sobs her heart out.

'I've been working on it for years!' Mabli shouts into the phone. 'My essays, the research I'd photocopied from the library, my references from clients. It was in order and now it's *gone*. I'll never be able to do all that again. He told me to stop being so stupid and . . .' Mabli dissolves into tears. Eluned hasn't heard her this distraught in years. In the background Kelly joins in.

'Shwsh, cariad. It's alright. Mammy's alright,' Mabli whispers.

'Where are you? Have you been to Mam's?' Eluned leans her back against the anaglypta wallpaper.

'I'm in a phone box. Graham is on a shift, but he always checks the phone bill. If I go to Mam and Dad's he'll follow, and I don't want him causing trouble there. That's why I called you, he won't guess that I've called you. You remember when he had the boys follow Dad?'

It's the first time she's admitted it. Previously, she's always maintained that it was coincidence that Dad was suddenly finding himself trailed by a police car everywhere he went, just after he spoke to Graham about Mabli's age.

'What are you going to do then, Mabli?'

That was the wrong approach. The tears resume. It's

terrible, but the world and his dog have told Mabli what Graham's about. There's not a lot Eluned can do. Manchester is hours away, and they've only got one bedroom. The stairs to the flat are steep and narrow, not suitable for a pram.

'I can't be here any more,' Mabli sniffles. 'I don't know what to do. I'm trapped. If I try and leave, he'll make me go back.'

You read things in the paper. Slashed tyres. Smashed windows. No point going to the police, it's all sniggering and winks down at the station. Then come the counter-allegations. Mabli's a step ahead, with her job, but it's an uphill struggle. Eluned reaches into her bag for her fags and her Filofax. She's got addresses at the back, and somewhere amongst them is Lola's social worker friend who was involved in the Lesbian Line. There's a house in Cardiff somewhere, not just for lesbians but all sorts of women.

'Why don't you call this number? They might be able to help?'

Mabli squeaks. 'I can't talk about this with a stranger.'

'If you stay in Cardiff, you'll be able to get to work easily, and you can see if your colleagues can help get you another copy of your study books. The trains run late.'

'Okay,' Mabli says, subdued. 'Thanks Eluned. Nice to talk to you. Say goodbye to Auntie Eluned, Kelly.' Kelly gurgles in the background. 'Bye then.'

Then Mabli's gone. Eluned replaces the handset and pokes a cigarette between her lips. It had to come one day. At least Kelly's too young to know what's going on. She takes slow, long pulls on her cigarette, turning the problem over in her mind.

June pokes her head round the door. 'Are you off the phone? What do we need to do? I packed a bag for us. Jim-jams, toiletries, chequebook, first-aid kit. And I made some sandwiches for the drive.'

'What?'

'For your sister. For us, in the car.' June hops from foot to foot.

'I gave her the number for someone to call in Cardiff.' Mabli can't come here. It's madness. Kelly is used to seeing her grandparents regularly, and Mabli's been at her firm for years. This is their flat, hers and June's. They're free to do what they want; play Sisters of Mercy at the threshold of pain, fuck on the bathroom floor, order takeaway three nights in a row.

'Will she ring them?' June demands. 'Will they be able to help?'

'Dunno.' Eluned shrugs. 'But we can't go down there tonight, we've said to Kez that we're going to Sappho's.'

'Fuck Sappho's! How can you want to drink when your sister is stuck with that monster?'

'It's not like she hasn't had warning,' Eluned says. 'Even when he tried to bash my head in, she told me it was my own fault! Mam and Dad tried everything to stop him coming round the house. First, they—'

June cuts her off. 'You've said that before. It doesn't matter now. That child might be at risk. Stop being a prat.'

Mabli has always been the same; she's happy to make Eluned feel like the thick one, but as soon as she needs something it's big sister to the rescue.

'Mabli's having a tantrum. He'll buy her a new handbag and she'll be all over him, then she'll make you feel like you're the irrational one for being worried. You don't know her, but she won't thank you for this.' Eluned holds her cigarette box out to June. 'I haven't even sat down yet! Let's have a beer, and then we'll talk about what we're doing this evening.'

Eluned turns the radio on while they drink a Boddingtons. Her make-up will need a spruce-up if they're going out later. Muriel Gray introduces the new Beastie Boys song, 'No Sleep till Brooklyn'. She's never liked attention-seeking guitar riffs, but the rapping is joyful. She'd love to go to New York, watch the b-boys dancing on the pier and the old men stooped over mah-jong. Mabli was fixated on New York once; she had an old print of Audrey Hepburn over her desk for years. Eluned had almost forgotten. June plays with her bottle-cap, using its metal ridges to shift gunk out from underneath her nails, wiping them on yesterday's *Guardian*.

'Hey – do you remember that interview Muriel did with Pete Burns on *The Tube*? He was wearing elbow-length latex gloves and was a complete cunt about Boy George.'

'Maybe.'

Eluned tries to stretch her legs out over June's, but June pushes them off. She can be a moody cow sometimes. 'Dad said to us, "Who's that woman then? She's alright. Lovely lips!" and we all fell apart laughing. He genuinely thought Pete was a woman!'

The corner of June's mouth twitches. 'Your dad's decent.'

June fetches a cotton tote bag and a tub of pungent leather polish. She sits cross-legged and pulls a bundle of leather straps from the bag. She works through them patiently, smoothing the paste on and briskly buffing it off.

'What are you polishing?' Eluned asks, and June holds it up for her to see. It's a harness, thin strips of leather held together with silver rings. When it's on it will form some sort of H-shape. It's not one Eluned's seen before.

'Where's it from?' Eluned asks, cracking open a beer and putting another next to June.

'It's Grit's,' says June. 'When I left, she said I could have my inheritance early.'

It looks supple, warm to the touch, like it's only just left Grit's skin.

Eluned plants her boot on the armrest.

'Do mine,' she instructs.

June's throat bobs. Obediently, she swirls her rag into the

pot and smears it into the round toe. June's brow creases as she works the viscous, honey-yellow polish in. June presses hard enough that Eluned's toes are pushed down into the sole, the heat travelling through the leather and into her skin. June might have a cob on about Mabli, but she knows what side her bread is buttered. They'll go out, have a bit of a dance, come home for a shag, and forget about Eluned's errant sister. June's silent, tilting Eluned's foot back and forth so she can follow the creases of the leather as it curves round her ankles. Beeswax and lemon rises between them, stronger than her own perfume. June bends forward to work between the yellow stitches, using her nail to scratch dirt away from the tightly woven threads of Eluned's laces.

Now her boots are looking tidy, Eluned changes into her best jeans and a lace bustier. June shrugs on her jacket and stands by the door like a dog waiting for their daily walk.

Canal Street is a walkable distance. These terraces have a different flavour from the Welsh homes built from uneven blue-grey stones, with whitewashed brick placed round the windows. These are all planes of smooth red brick, delicate Gothic details tucked under the lips of the roofs.

Two lads on bikes watch them. They're like a couple of vultures, with their elbows splayed and backs bowed over their handlebars.

'Lesbos!' the bigger one yells.

'No flies on you, are there?' June says.

He stands a little taller and puffs his chest. 'Give us a fag?'

Eluned exhales grey smoke out of her nose. 'On your bike, son. You're only nine.'

'I'm eleven, and you're dykes!' he shouts. They push off, sailing down the street.

June takes a puff. 'I don't know why breeders bother.'

Sappho's is already busy. Heather and Kez are in a throng

of women on the dance floor. The DJ's warming up, playing 'Boogie Oogie Oogie' with lots of bass. Kez is working into it, flexing her knees and reaching her arms straight up so the whole bar can see her armpit hair. It's hard to worry when they're playing tracks like this. June gets in another pint of Boddingtons. On a whim, Eluned orders a vodka cranberry. If she's going to hit the floor, she can't be doing that with a full pint.

June's hand grazes the small of her back. 'You dance, I'm going to prop up the bar.'

Eluned's learnt the hard way that unless June has a yen for dancing, there's no point cajoling her. She leaves her beneath the glossy cheese plant and moves through the crowd until she finds Kez. The DJ spins old disco hits, and the crowd bob and sway at once. Cranberry juice is sour and sweet on her tongue. Two women kiss next to Eluned, their hips bumping against hers as they dance. Energy flows through Eluned, down into the floor below. This is her life, this is where she belongs. It's probably all blown over between Mabli and Graham tonight, he's probably taken her to that tacky Italian she used to love.

When she's finished her drink, down to the thin shards of melting ice and the last pale-pink dregs of juice, Eluned fights her way back to the bar. June is where she left her, resting on her elbow and talking to Morgan.

Eluned slips her arm round June's waist and reaches for her beer. June is quicker, moving it to her own mouth. When June puts it down, she slaps her own hand over it.

Eluned laughs. 'Why are you being tight? Morgan, you'll let me, won't you?'

Morgan smiles indulgently and Eluned grabs her can of Breaker, taking a long slurp before smacking her lips next to June's ear. June shivers, and Eluned takes it further, sucking June's earlobe into her mouth.

June lightly shoves Eluned away. 'Stop being a nawse. Look, Morgan was telling me about Bala Lake.'

June usually likes Eluned doing that, why is she being funny for? Eluned scans the crowd for anyone that might have taken June's fancy. There's another broad girl with a curly mullet at the bar, wearing coral lipstick that does nothing for her ruddy skin. Perhaps Eluned has more to fear from the muscular butch with the Celtic knot tattoo right over the knobble at the top of her spine. Neither this girl, nor Grit or any of June's London crew, would have a problem with swooping down the motorway to rescue Mabli. She remembers June saying that she didn't need any encouragement to get stroppy with a van. A thought hits her, and her stomach twists.

'I've been saying we should go to North Wales,' says Eluned. 'You never listen to me.'

June rolls her eyes. 'You said yourself you've not been up north since you were a kid!'

Morgan looks from June to Eluned and back again, curiosity written on her face. Eluned kisses them both on the cheek and heads back to the dance floor. Another DJ has taken over for the second set, a tall woman with skinny dreads swishing over the decks as she bends over to mix. She's pushing the tempo up, looping the same riffs. Eluned keeps her hips moving to the beat, but she can't stop her mind from drifting back to Mabli. What did Mabli say to Eluned once? 'No one's going to save you from your shitty life.' That was it.

Curry Mile has gone to bed, every restaurant has its shutters pulled down, but there's still a faint waft of grilled meat and roasted spices hanging in the air. Heat rises from the tarmac. June walks at full lesbian speed, silently. Eluned scuttles after her in her cone-heel pumps. Every so often she misses a step, her plastic heel-tip scagging on the pavement. Her face and chest are flushed, but her arms are freezing. Eluned zhuzhes them with her palms, then manages to sweep her hand full-tilt into a wheelie bin, sending it clattering into the wall. The noise seems to set June off.

'The thing I can't get my head around is that I thought we were on the same page,' says June.

Eluned scrunches her face. 'Wha' you on about?'

'Lesbianism and individualism don't mix. I don't believe in settling down and then drawing a little line around us.' June chops her hands in a circle like she's building a picket fence. 'We're part of a wider society. I don't want to pull the drawbridge up.'

June's phrasing calls to mind something Thatcher said. Eluned pulls on her earring. 'It's funny you're practically calling me a Thatcherite, when Mabli's the one who's voted for the bitch.'

'Mabli is a young mum living with a control freak. It's an urgent situation. You never know, this could clue her in a bit.' June takes a step back from Eluned. She scrubs her hand over her face. 'Were you always so selfish?' she asks, staring through Eluned with her pale, clear eyes.

Eluned's chest tightens. She feels the same as when she first offended June on the hill outside the Welfare all those years ago. Eluned's vision swims, and she sinks down onto her haunches.

'Get away from her, you bastard!' Two men, about their age and dressed in football casuals, jog over to Eluned and June. As they get a look at June from the front, they stop, looking from Eluned to her and back again.

The bigger man turns to Eluned. He says, 'Is this dyke bothering you?'

Eluned strains, pushing herself to her feet. She rolls her shoulders back so she's as wide as she can be. 'Leave us alone,' she says.

'Hey – we're only trying to help!' the other guy chips in. He rubs Eluned's arm. 'You're freezing.'

'Get off me.' She's losing patience. It's been a long evening, and if these twats think they can push her around, they've got another think coming. She has a brief, bloody fantasy about tussling one of them to the ground and smacking his head into the pavement until the gravel is embedded in his face like nuts on an ice-cream.

'Eluned, you need to cool it.' June speaks slowly, deliberately. 'We're on our way home,' she says in the same tone, but directing it at the men.

They eyeball June, shifting from one foot to the other. If they lay a finger on June, Eluned will flatten them both. They seem to decide that it's not worth it and amble off towards the amber light of the off-licence.

June lets out a deep breath and shakes out the sleeves of her leather jacket. 'Let's just get home.'

June takes off down Wilmslow Road, before making an abrupt turn down Platt Lane. Eluned straggles after. Her oesophagus burns and before she can stop herself, she ralphs twice against the shutters of the fabric shop below the flat. Sorry, Mr and Mrs Khan. They're a nice couple, always keen to talk cricket with June. The last thing she wants is this incident jeopardising their tenancy.

'I'll get some water now. I'll clean it up,' Eluned sputters.

'Don't worry, I'll do it. You go to bed.'

Eluned hooks her nails into the anaglypta wallpaper as she hauls herself up the stairs. She feels her way through their flat and drops into bed, wrapping their duvet around her head to mask the sound of June clattering in the kitchen, water drumming on the bottom of their plastic mop bucket.

29

15 August 1987

Eluned dreams of sour milk and she wakes alone to find their cotton sheets crusted with vomit; it must have rubbed off from her hair in the night. She strips the bed as fast as she can, trying to ignore the headache squeezing her skull. Bundling the sheets under her arm, she wanders to the kitchen. June's mug has been washed and stacked on the drying rack; there's a single teabag on the saucer next to the kettle. The smell of toast and cigarettes hangs in the air, but June is nowhere to be seen. Kind of her to let Eluned sleep in before work. Eluned has a late start and finish today, sorting out deliveries.

June's not there when Eluned finally gets home, feet burning and head pulsing. She picks up prawn pathia, onion bhajis and roti for two, leaving June's half covered on the side. June will be back soon, no doubt moaning that Eluned's had more than her fair share of prawns. The telly's showing a repeat of the second series of *Prisoner: Cell Block H*. Aussie accents are grating, but it's good to see dykes on the telly.

Eluned tries to pay attention to the TV, but she has a nagging worry that June has sloped off to London. Or, even worse, there's the possibility that she's been bashed and dumped in the canal. Eluned didn't like those blokes last night. She could call Grit. One call, and she'd be out of her misery. But if June's in London and doesn't want to speak to Eluned, she'll look desperate. Ringing round the hospitals in Manchester would at least mean that she can rule out the worst. How could she describe June to them? Would they just chalk it up to dyke drama? The night is close and airless. Eluned opens the windows to the street. Cars and conversations outside are reassuring. Time is moving onwards.

June never comes home. For a second night, Eluned wakes up alone. Her clock radio is blaring Mike Smith's *Breakfast Show*. He plays 'I Just Can't Stop Loving You'. There's a peaceful moment in the space between sleep and wakefulness before Eluned realises that June never came home. She smacks the radio off. She's awake, she doesn't need it next to her head. His vocal tics are irritating, the lyrics unbearably twee. Mabli never liked Michael Jackson much either. Iesu, Mabli used to be so funny when they'd listen to the Official Sunday Chart; commentary sharper than raspberry sorbet. It's unthinkable that she's ended up with someone who wants to shrink her, hide her brilliance under drab cardigans. June is right, they've got to do something about it.

June sneaks in while Eluned is getting ready for work. Eluned is buffing at her foundation, but it keeps settling into her dry patches. The bruised hollows under her eyes are unsalvageable, but she presses on some shimmery blusher to try to bring a bit of life to her cheeks.

'Where have you been?' Eluned demands, gripping her blusher brush tightly in her hands.

'I went for drinks with the team. I couldn't afford a taxi, so Susan put me up.'

'Phone lines down, were they?' Eluned asks. She can't look directly at June. She keeps her eyes fixed on her compact mirror, layering up her mascara until her eyes look even more like piss-holes in the snow.

Eluned can see the lower half of June's face reflected behind her in the mirror. June's jaw works, chewing the inside of her cheek.

Earlier this morning Eluned had plaited her unwashed hair and thought of Mabli twisting her hair into those elaborate French braids she used to do. Eluned's fingers aren't nimble enough for those. Earlier, the radio played 'Total Eclipse of the Heart'. Mabli used to love singing along to that, lingering over the last line before the instrumental, letting the syllables hang as delicately as dew on a leaf.

June doesn't understand that Eluned has been trying to blank out these risks for years. They all have. Mabli was always so certain that she had all the answers. Eluned sat up so many nights, hoping to see Mabli get home safe. She's listened to poison drip from Mabli's lips, knowing that it's him that's put it there. All this time, it has been too painful to think about, easier to write it off as a defect in Mabli's character. If she goes back to Graham, he will frame Eluned as a deranged dyke, stealing Mabli away from family life. It could even prevent Mabli from keeping Kelly. But Eluned can't hold on to those fears any longer. She's got to act. Mabli can't be relying on a helpline, when she and June could provide what she needs right here. If Mabli has come this far, then surely there's got to be a chance Eluned can help her unpick the rest. And then maybe Eluned could have her sister back.

'Look – I was thinking that I could give Mabli a call and see if she wants to come and stay.'

June sucks at her bottom lip. 'Would you like me to stick around, or will it be too crowded?'

Eluned grabs her wrist. 'Please stay. I don't know what I'm doing.'

June surges forward and gives Eluned a swift, ungentle kiss. Her snaggle-tooth catches on Eluned's lip, leaving a sharp pain behind.

When June pulls back her face has sharpened; she looks like a fox out in the moonlight. 'I'm really glad you're doing this. Don't call her at home. We don't need him seeing our area code.'

'I've got her work phone number in my old Filofax, I'll dig that out and pretend to be a client.'

'Pickett and Watkins, Siwan speaking. How may I direct your call?' After the flat Mancunian accents around her, the receptionist's Welsh accent is obscenely fruity.

'I'm Eluned Hughes, Mabli's sister. I need to speak to her, it's urgent.'

'I'll patch you through.'

There's a moment of silence, and then Mabli's voice. 'I'm meant to be taking my lunch in a bit, I can take the company phone out with me.'

'I'll call back in twenty,' Eluned says.

Time crawls. Eluned stretches out her legs on the sofa. She uses the Manchester Poly prospectus that June brought home from work as a coaster. They've both been looking at the Art and Design section. Eluned fancies studying fashion at the Toast Rack, not far from their flat. Apparently, C&A and Topshop poach students directly from the course. Eluned is finishing off the crossword they gave up last night. The answer for 'oily' is on the tip of her tongue. She can see the shape of the word, but it won't come into focus. Finally, it's time to call Mabli.

Mabli answers after half a ring.

'What you having for your lunch?' Eluned asks.

'Coronation chicken baguette from the bakery,' says Mabli. 'It's too crusty, so I've broken off the ends. And there's too much mayo, so I've scraped that out. And the tomatoes are so pale, there's no taste to them.'

'Basically, you've got a bit of chicken and a couple of raisins?' Eluned suggests.

'And lettuce.'

'You should try to eat. You don't have much padding to lose, and you've got to keep your strength up.'

'I know.' Mabli sighs.

'Things still tough?'

Mabli makes an agonised noise. 'He thinks we're back to normal. I'm doing everything by the book. This morning he took my bank card off me and said I was irresponsible. This baguette has come out of the office petty cash! Michael said he didn't mind as long as I got cakes for the office on my way back.'

'Have you told people at work?'

'Yeah. They've been tidy. Colin, one of the partners, has offered me to stay at his. His kids have flown the nest, and he said he'd be excited to do it again.'

'What are his expectations?' The last thing Mabli needs is another older man seeking to dominate her.

For the first time, some warmth creeps into Mabli's voice. 'I don't know if I'd mind that. He's a gentleman. Lovely hands. But I need some time for me and Kelly.'

'Maybe you could do your own divorce and save yourself a few quid,' Eluned suggests.

'Colin said that I "shouldn't see it as a failure of marriage, but an opportunity to succeed at divorce." It's what he tells all our clients.' Mabli laughs until it turns into a choked-off sob. 'Oh God, I can't cry. I'm right out in the open here. I've already seen two bloody jam butties. I'm already drawing attention to myself with this brick phone.'

Eluned fills with fury. Her sister acting like a fugitive when she's the one who hasn't done anything wrong! 'I'm sorry that I wasn't more sympathetic. It was a shock. The last couple of years, it's like you didn't want anything to do with me.'

Mabli swallows thickly. 'I should have listened to you after what he did at the pickets. I had nightmares about it. And I should have put my foot down when he said he didn't want you to be bridesmaid—'

'Stop. You're not supposed to be crying, remember? It doesn't matter. You can come up to Manchester for as long as it takes for you to sort everything out.'

Mabli's breath hitches on the line. 'Thank you, Eluned. I want to. But he could say that I've kidnapped his daughter and claim reckless endangerment.'

Eluned thinks of Lily and Dharma. June had obliquely implied that there's a backstory there. She'll talk to June, find out what they can do. 'None of us have done anything wrong. You're not on trial. There's nothing wrong with visiting your sister.'

'I've got a diary where I've written down everything that's happened,' says Mabli.

'Bring that with you. June said you should buy a return and pay in cash.'

Mabli sniffles again. 'I'm so embarrassed.'

Eluned can't help but laugh. Her mind jumps to almost slamming Lola's fingers in the car door. 'Don't be. I've got a lot to catch you up on.'

30

Eluned watches from the window until Mabli's taxi pulls up. June goes downstairs to let her in while Eluned puts the kettle on. It's a relief. Graham is on a night shift, but she's been terrified of him finding out and tipping off Greater Manchester Police in advance. What if they intercept Mabli and take her to the station on some bullshit charge? There was a drama on the telly where a WPC was standing up for battered women, and at least that gives her hope that there would be at least one good egg in the GMP.

Part of Eluned wants to see Mabli contrite, but she sweeps up their narrow stairs in a resplendent cobalt-blue coat, complete with shoulder pads that brush against the walls. The hallway fills with powdery Anaïs Anaïs. Mabli carries Kelly in her arms, while June clatters after her with the rest of their bags.

Mabli jiggles Kelly and her nose wrinkles, umber eyes opening blearily. 'Say hello to Auntie Eluned,' Mabli urges.

'Don't wake her, she's fasto. Just pop her on the sofa.'

Mabli is so confident with her, cupping Kelly's head all the way down until it's resting on their grubby throw cushions. Mabli slips her hand out from between Kelly's head and cushion, keeping her eyes fixed on Kelly's face. Kelly doesn't stir.

Mabli shrugs off her heavy wool coat and hands it to Eluned. Underneath she wears a belted wiggle dress in a lighter shade of blue.

'I'm glad your journey went alright,' says June. 'You look well.'

'I was thinking of shaving my head to go undercover, but I wasn't sure it would suit.'

June snorts, putting a large spoon of sugar into her own tea. Their Hackney Refuge mug has been retired, and Eluned has invested in four identical, octagonal cherry-red mugs from the homeware department at work. They cost more than she wanted to spend on mugs, but they do look classy together on the coffee table.

June slouches in their armchair, legs spread wide and fingers tap-tapping against her thighs. Eluned takes a seat next to Kelly, still sparked out on her back. Her hands clench and release like starfish. Eluned can't resist poking the tip of her little finger into Kelly's palm. Kelly's fingers close round it, and Eluned leans closer to look at her chubby knuckles, her conch-pink nails.

Mabli is restless. She paces the room, squinting up at their pictures.

'Bet you're glad you don't have to bother with this aggro, aren't you?' Mabli asks the room.

June snorts. 'I don't know about that. Ask your sister about it some time. All I'm saying is stay away from coatstands if you value your life!'

Mabli gives Eluned a look of *Eluned, what did you do?* and takes a sip from her tea, screwing up her face. 'Iesu. Do you have shares in a dairy farm these days?'

'You need to keep your strength up. Talking of, I'll warm you up some faggots, peas and chips.'

Mabli used to love faggots when she was little. Eluned had bought some at the market earlier and left Mabli's on a tray in the oven. Up here they're called savoury ducks, and Mabli will be pleased that there's less liver in them than the ones Mam used to buy. These are as big as tennis balls, spiced with something sweet like mace or nutmeg, yellow mustard seeds scattered through the dense meat and onion. Good for Mabli's iron levels.

While the fan oven whirs, Mabli rummages in their record boxes like she's at a car-boot sale. Eluned could happily grab June's wrists to stop that tapping. It's June's nervous reflex, faced with potential hostile bodies in her personal space. If it wouldn't freak Mabli out, she'd sit on the padded arm of the chair and curl into June. Instead, she throws the crossword book over into her lap to distract her.

June turns to the puzzle they'd given up on. 'Mabli, you got a long word for "oily"?'

Mabli pauses with *Glorious Results of a Misspent Youth* in her hand. 'Obsequious?'

'Legend,' June says. 'That sounds about right.'

Mabli lifts one of David Bowie's singles, 'Can't Help Thinking About Me', out of its crate. It's an old one, from when he was still singing with the Lower Third, doing the mod thing. 'You stole this off Dad! He blamed me, but you had it.'

Eluned laughs. 'I don't want it! I hate that tambourine-y crap. You take it with you when you go.'

'Nah, you're alright.' Mabli fingers June's copy of *Touch*. 'Gosh. This takes me back. I haven't listened to this in years.'

'It's a good album,' says June mildly. 'Put it on if you like.'

Mabli pulls *Hounds of Love* out of the box. 'This one. I want to lie down and listen to "The Big Sky" and pretend that I don't exist in corporeal form.'

She slides the record from its cardboard sheath and slips it onto the hi-fi deck. 'This is a tidy piece of kit.'

June grins. 'Your sister bought it, probably cost more than her car.'

'Just a bit,' says Eluned, sliding a hot plate of food for Mabli onto the table with her oven gloves.

'You're doing well then,' Mabli says. 'I'm glad.'

Mabli finally sits down. She's tentative with her food, picking up a chip with her fingers and dipping it in the large pool of gravy underneath the faggots. They are big old things. When Mabli carves into them the knife handle disappears into the spongy brown ball before it touches the other side of the plate. Mabli gets up a surprising pace when she really tucks in. It's satisfying to watch.

'You know that Kate wrote the whole album on a Fairlight, not a regular piano?' June asks.

Mabli nods. 'Yeah, and the helicopter sound effect is the same one in Floyd's *The Wall*.'

June widens her eyes. 'Get out of here! That's a bosting fact.'

Mabli's halfway through her food. She's just about given in to the urge to mash her chips into her gravy like she used to do as a kid when Kelly stirs. She grumbles tentatively, as if waiting to see whether it's worth expending energy on a proper wail.

'Eluned, can you sort her out? She just wants a cwtch.'

Eluned's shoulders bunch. She feels an adolescent urge to protest, like she's been asked to iron clothes that aren't hers, but it's such a relief to see Mabli stuff a whole forkful of peas into her mouth, gravy gathering at the corner of her mouth.

Eluned looks down at her niece. 'Come on then, Trouble,' she says, tentatively sliding her hands under Kelly's armpits. Kelly's too small to help Eluned at all, so she gracelessly humps the baby's body onto her lap. When she's there she seems happy enough, chubby legs splayed either side of Eluned's thigh. Then, without warning, she lets herself fall backwards, and Eluned jerks her chin out of the way before it smacks the back of her delicate head. Just in case Kelly makes any more sudden movements, Eluned laces her fingers together across her belly like a fleshy seatbelt. For the moment, it seems like Kelly is content to let her weight rest against Eluned and gurgle quietly, prodding at the face of Eluned's Swatch. Mabli and June are talking about the Irish percussion on 'Jig of

Life', so Eluned quietly puckers her lips against the swell of her niece's head. Her hair smells of sick and Mabli's Anaïs Anaïs, feels softer than a rabbit's paw.

With her toes, Mabli pushes her popsocks down her legs, and leaves them lying on the carpet like two used condoms. Eluned should put them in the wash; she will when she doesn't have Kelly lying on her. Mabli closes her eyes, lets her head rest heavily on Eluned's shoulder as 'The Big Sky' reaches its rolling, frenetic climax.

AUTHOR'S NOTE

During my writing process I used a variety of primary and secondary sources, before combining research with my own experiences and imagination. If you were around for the 1980s, please forgive my inevitable errors.

In *Neon Roses* I have relegated towering figures like Dai Donovan, Hefina Headon, Mark Ashton and Mike Jackson to supporting roles in Eluned's story. It is not my intention to minimise their actions, but to give fictional characters more space to breathe. I hope that the respect I have for them is evident in the text. Many readers will already know that the London LGSM group fundraised for people in the Dulais Valley, but I have chosen to be vague about where, precisely, Eluned and her family live.

Although I have lived here all my life, writing about the Dulais Valley has given me a greater appreciation for this incredible, yet overlooked, part of south Wales. As well as being the land of St Patrick's birth, it also boasts Roman roads and forts, Celtic stones, and waterfalls.

We should all be grateful to those who supported the miners and their families during the strike, and those who have steadfastly stood with the LGBTQ+ community. I certainly am, you are my heroes. As I have been writing and editing, it has been disturbing to feel that the progress we have made since the 1980s is tenuous. Parallels can be drawn between Section 28 and the current surge of transphobia and moral panic aimed at LGBTQ+ people, as well as concerns about policing, the erosion of workers' rights and the right to protest. Please direct your support to organisations such as the Orgreave Truth and Justice Committee, Lesbians and Gays Support the Migrants and any local mutual aid funds near you. Let's all join a union!

ACKNOWLEDGEMENTS

Thank you to my agent, Imogen Morrell, at Greene & Heaton. I am so grateful for your sharp insight, and your tenacious and positive approach. It has also been brilliant to work with editors at John Murray Press, Abigail Scruby and Becky Walsh. It is overwhelmingly flattering and exciting to have your expert eyes on my work, and to be able to talk about writing with you.

Thank you to all at Literature Wales: special thanks must go to Petra Bennett for her support in early 2020, Katherine Stansfield for her excellent teaching, and Rebecca F. John for her mentorship and friendship. I'm also very grateful for the friends I've made through Literature Wales, particularly Efa Lois. *Diolch i Efa am y crempogau a'r sgyrsiau.*

Thank you so much to Lisa Power MBE, Kevin Franklin, Joyce Timperley, Grace Timperley, Sue Bundy, Mam, and everyone else who has answered a range of questions about life in the 1980s. Mam, you deserve a medal for answering my questions about your favourite 1980s 'pulling moves'.

Many thanks to Stefan Dickers at the Bishopsgate Archives. It was so helpful to see your material about Wales, and even better to have a look through some 1980s copies of *On Our Backs*! It was also thrilling to visit the People's History Museum and to be given the privilege of handling the original LGSM documents. Thank you so much for letting me see those.

Thank you to Siobhan Fahey for setting up the online Rebel Dykes Film Club, and for being so warm and encouraging. Similarly, thank you to the Out On The Page team and the

Writers With Faces group for keeping me going during lockdown. Thank you to the researchers at the Coalfield Women Project for your informative events.

It is brilliant that so much information is freely available online. Thank you to the Manchester Dance Music Archive, Colin Clews from 'Gay in the 80s', the team behind the Log Books podcast, Museum Wales/Amgueddfa Cymru, People's Collection Wales, and everyone else who runs a blog or online archive. There is a wealth of information on YouTube, from the *Dancing in Dulais* film made by LGSM to recordings of BBC radio jingles, and full coverage of the 1986 election. Thank you to the photographers who were there to bear witness to what was happening in pickets across the country. In particular, Martin Shakeshaft's photograph of women in Maerdy and John Harris's photograph of Lesley Boulton at the Battle of Orgreave had a formative impact on my understanding.

I started my reading with Tim Tate's *Pride: The Unlikely Story of the Unsung Heroes of the Miner's Strike*, *Red in the Rainbow* by Hannah Dee, *The South Wales Miners 1964–1985* by Ben Curtis, and *The Fed* by Hywel Francis. I am sure you could start your research with any number of excellent books, but I got a lot out of these.

Bethan, thank you for everything. From driving me round the Dulais Valley to all of your dramaturgical guidance, and the things I won't say here. I'm so grateful to have such inspiring and wonderful friends. I would like to offer heartfelt thanks to our community here in Cardiff: Aimee, Amo, Catriona, Chrixtobel, Claire, Crash, Fionnuala, Frances, Jaz, Kat, Kate, Nazmia, Nia, Rob, Sam, Sara, Tove, Zara.

Thank you to my parents for your support and love. Mam, you're a legend and I love you. Uncle Len, thank you for passing on your obsessive love for music, but I'm sorry that I can't agree that the 1960s were the best decade for records. Sue and

Jude, thank you for gifting me a line for this novel in our wedding guestbook. Dawsons, please don't make me change my name back.

Thank you to Lisa and Georgia next door for keeping me sane in 2020. Georgia, pop it back on the shelf for a bit!

Thank you to Christina Thatcher for establishing Roath Writers, and for your encouragement and friendship over the years.

A massive thank you to Angela Eshun, Candy Ikwuwunna, Edward Whelan, Emily Butler, Helen Dring and Izzy Rabey for reading early chapters of this and giving me your feedback.

A Literature Wales New Writer's Bursary supported by the National Lottery through the Arts Council of Wales was received to develop this novel.